P9-CCP-580
Danger bound
them together.
Desire will
set them free.

DON'T MISS THE MAIDEN LANE SERIES

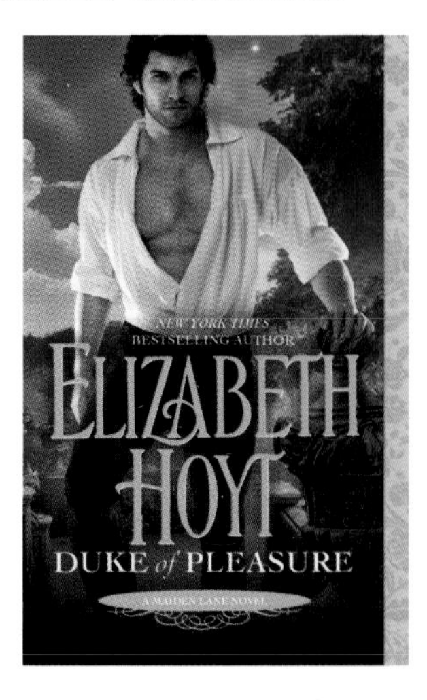

Please turn to the back of this book for an excerpt.

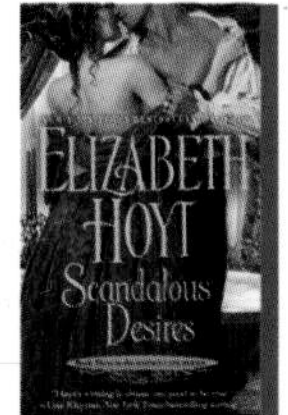

Love shouldn't be this hard.

But Raphael was nearing the bottom of the stairs now and if she didn't move he would be out of sight.

And she might lose him.

She couldn't let that happen, no matter how hard or how stubborn he might be.

"Wait," she called. "Wait!"

He turned. Rain was running down his face. "Go back."

She shook her head, raindrops splattering off her nose and chin. "No. Where you go, I go too."

"I forced you to marry me. I was selfish. Now just let me go."

"I can't," she said, exasperated. "You're my husband. I'm your wife. I *married* you."

"I can't stay here with you," he said starkly. "You are too much temptation. You've proven it already."

She held out her hand, the palm filling with rain. "Then give in to temptation."

PRAISE FOR ELIZABETH HOYT'S MAIDEN LANE SERIES

"Hoyt's writing is almost too good to be true."

—Lisa Kleypas, *New York Times* bestselling author

"There's an enchantment to Hoyt's stories that makes you believe in the magic of love."

—RT Book Reviews

Duke of Pleasure

"4½ stars! Top Pick! Hoyt...[is] a powerful storyteller whose novels have a depth of emotion and originality that lifts the genre to new heights. Always unique, wonderfully romantic and highly sensual, Hoyt's stories take readers' breath away." ***—RT Book Reviews***

"Hoyt once again successfully deploys her irresistible literary triumvirate of marvelously engaging characters, boldly sensual love scenes, and elegant writing brightened with just the right dash of dry wit."

—Booklist

"So many ingredients make this story phenomenal. First and foremost, the chemistry between our hero and heroine. It drives the narrative and we can't get enough of their interactions."

—HeroesandHeartbreakers.com

Duke of Sin

"4½ stars! Top Pick! Hoyt delivers a unique read on many levels: a love story, a tale of redemption, and a plot teeming with emotional depth that takes readers' breaths away. Kudos to a master storyteller!"

—***RT Book Reviews***

"A darkly humorous and lushly sensual historical romance.... Hoyt truly outdoes herself in *Duke of Sin*."

—HeroesandHeartbreakers.com

"Hoyt has created two dynamic characters.... [The book] includes a delicious collection of hot and steamy scenes. A wonderful balance of comedy and pathos, Hoyt's latest is a deeply satisfying read." —***BookPage***

Sweetest Scoundrel

"While I've long been a fan of the Maiden Lane series, I think this is my favorite."

—FictionVixen.com

"4½ stars! Maiden Lane and its inhabitants have long captivated readers, and the latest series installment is just as enchanting as fans could desire.... It is a story that takes your breath away and leaves you uplifted. Hoyt does it again!" —***RT Book Reviews***

Dearest Rogue

"[This] superbly executed historical romance is proof positive that this RITA Award–nominated author continues to write with undiminished force and flair. When it comes to incorporating a generous measure of dangerous intrigue and lush sensuality into a truly swoonworthy love story, Hoyt is unrivaled."

—*Booklist* (starred review)

"4½ stars! Hoyt takes an unlikely pair of characters and, through the magic of her storytelling, turns them into the perfect couple.... A read to remember."

—RT Book Reviews

"Sexy, sweet, and emotionally satisfying.... *Dearest Rogue* is everything the reader of a Regency historical wants; it's funny, fast-paced and has plenty of historical flavor and a romance that develops as naturally as a flower opening in the sun. Fans of the Maiden Lane series will cheer for this couple."

—BookPage

Darling Beast

"Hoyt's exquisitely nuanced characters, vividly detailed setting, and seemingly effortless and elegant writing provide the splendid material from which she fashions yet another ravishingly romantic love story."

—*Booklist* (starred review)

"4½ stars! Top Pick! *Darling Beast* is wondrous, magical, and joyous—a read to remember."

—RT Book Reviews

"A lovely book that I very much enjoyed reading. I love the Maiden Lane series and can't wait until the next book comes out!"

—BookBinge.com

Duke of Midnight

"Top Pick! A sensual tale of forbidden love.... Plenty of action and intriguing mystery make this a page-turner."

—*BookPage*

"Richly drawn characters fill the pages of this emotionally charged mix of mystery and romance."

—*Publishers Weekly*

"4½ stars! Top Pick! There is enchantment in the Maiden Lane series, not just the fairy tales Hoyt infuses into the memorable romances, but the wonder of love combined with passion, unique plotlines, and unforgettable characters."

—*RT Book Reviews*

"I *loved* it. I loved Artemis. I loved Max, and I loved their story. I have enjoyed every Elizabeth Hoyt book I have read (and I have read most of them)."

—All About Romance (LikesBooks.com)

Lord of Darkness

"*Lord of Darkness* illuminates Hoyt's boundless imagination.... Readers will adore this story."

—*RT Book Reviews*

"Hoyt's writing is imbued with great depth of emotion.... Heartbreaking.... An edgy tension-filled plot."

—*Publishers Weekly*

"*Lord of Darkness* is classic Elizabeth Hoyt, meaning it's unique, engaging, and leaves readers on the edge of their seats.... An incredible addition to the fantastic Maiden

Lane series. I Joyfully Recommend Godric and Megs's tale, for it's an amazing, well-crafted story with an intriguing plot and a lovely, touching romance.... Simply enchanting!"

—JoyfullyReviewed.com

"I adore the Maiden Lane series, and this fifth book is a very welcome addition to the series.... [It's] sexy and sweet all at the same time... This can be read as a stand-alone, but I adore each book in this series and encourage you to start from the beginning."

—*USA Today*'s *Happy Ever After* blog

"Beautifully written.... A truly fine piece of storytelling and a novel that deserves to be read and enjoyed."

—TheBookBinge.com

Thief of Shadows

"An expert blend of scintillating romance and mystery.... The romance between the beautiful and quick-witted Isabel and the masked champion of the downtrodden propels this novel to the top of its genre."

—*Publishers Weekly* (starred review)

"Amazing sex scenes.... A very intriguing hero.... This one did not disappoint."

—*USA Today*

"Innovative, emotional, sensual.... Hoyt's beautiful blending of the essential elements of a fairy tale into a stunning love story enhances this delicious 'keeper.'"

—*RT Book Reviews*

"All of Hoyt's signature literary ingredients—wickedly clever dialogue, superbly nuanced characters, danger, and scorching sexual chemistry—click neatly into place to create a breathtakingly romantic love story."

—Booklist

"When [they] finally come together, desire and long-denied sensuality explode upon the page."

—Library Journal

"With heart and heat rolled into one, *Thief of Shadows* is a definite must-read for historical romance fans! Hoyt really has outdone herself... yet again."

—UndertheCoversBookblog.blogspot.com

"A balanced mixture of action, adventure, and mystery and a beautifully crafted romance.... The perfect historical romance." **—HeroesandHeartbreakers.com**

Scandalous Desires

"Historical romance at its best.... Series fans will be enthralled, while new readers will find this emotionally charged installment stands very well alone."

***—Publishers Weekly* (starred review)**

"4½ stars! This is the Maiden Lane story readers have been waiting for. Hoyt delivers her hallmark fairy tale within a romance and takes readers into the depths of the heart and soul of her characters. Pure magic flows from her pen, lifting readers' spirits with joy."

—RT Book Reviews

"With its lush sensuality, lusciously wrought prose, and luxuriously dark plot, *Scandalous Desires*, the latest exquisitely crafted addition to Hoyt's Georgian-set Maiden Lane series, is a romance to treasure."

—*Booklist* (starred review)

"Ms. Hoyt writes some of the best love scenes out there. They are passionate, sexy, and blazing hot.... I simply adore Ms. Hoyt's books for her sensuous prose, multifaceted characters, and intense, well-developed story lines. And she delivers every single time. It's no wonder all of her books are on my keeper shelves. Do yourself a favor and pick up *Scandalous Desires*."

—TheRomanceDish.com

"*Scandalous Desires* is the best book Elizabeth Hoyt has written so far, with endearing characters and an all-encompassing romance you'll want to hold close and never let go. If there's one must-read book, especially for historical romance fans, it's *Scandalous Desires*."

—FallenAngelReviews.com

Notorious Pleasures

"Emotionally stunning.... The sinfully sensual chemistry Hoyt creates between her shrewd, acid-tongued heroine and her scandalous, sexy hero is pure romance."

—*Booklist*

Wicked Intentions

"4½ stars! Top Pick! A magnificently rendered story that not only enchants but enthralls."

—*RT Book Reviews*

Other titles by Elizabeth Hoyt

The Raven Prince

The Leopard Prince

The Serpent Prince

The Ice Princess (novella)

To Taste Temptation

To Seduce a Sinner

To Beguile a Beast

To Desire a Devil

Wicked Intentions

Notorious Pleasures

Scandalous Desires

Thief of Shadows

Lord of Darkness

Duke of Midnight

Darling Beast

Dearest Rogue

Sweetest Scoundrel

Duke of Sin

Once Upon a Moonlit Night (novella)

Duke of Pleasure

ELIZABETH HOYT

DUKE *of* DESIRE

GRAND CENTRAL
PUBLISHING

NEW YORK BOSTON

This book is a work of fiction. Names, characters, places, and incidents are the product of the author's imagination or are used fictitiously. Any resemblance to actual events, locales, or persons, living or dead, is coincidental.

Cover design by Elizabeth Turner
Cover illustration by Alan Ayers

Grand Central Publishing
Hachette Book Group
1290 Avenue of the Americas
New York, NY 10104
grandcentralpublishing.com
twitter.com/grandcentralpub

First Edition: October 2017

Grand Central Publishing is a division of Hachette Book Group, Inc.
The Grand Central Publishing name and logo is a trademark of Hachette Book Group, Inc.

The publisher is not responsible for websites (or their content) that are not owned by the publisher.

The Hachette Speakers Bureau provides a wide range of authors for speaking events. To find out more, go to www.hachettespeakersbureau.com or call (866) 376-6591.

ISBN: 978-1-4555-3914-7 (mass market); 978-1-4555-3915-4 (ebook)

Printed in the United States of America

OPM

10 9 8 7 6 5 4 3

This book is for you.

If you have read the eleven other books in the Maiden Lane series: Thank you for your faithfulness and for accompanying me on this odyssey through Georgian London. I hope you enjoyed the people, the sights and sounds, and above all, the passion.

If you have never read one of my books:

Oh, my dear. Sit back, have a cup of tea, and let me tell you a story....

Acknowledgments

Publishing a book is a group project. It's true that the ideas, the characters, and the first draft are all mine, but after that I have a *lot* of help. Thank you, then, to my editor Amy Pierpont, who has never flinched at one of my proposals—not even the one about the psychotic duke—and has been patient, kind, and perceptive all at the right times. Thank you to my beta reader, Susannah Taylor, who has both cheered me on and, perhaps more important, told me what really bugged her in the first draft. Thank you to my agent, Robin Rue, who sends me little emails when she hasn't heard from me in a while just to see how I'm doing. Thank you to my assistant, Mel Jolly, who keeps me from going insane, OMG. Thank you to my copy editor S. B. Kleinman, for keeping me from embarrassment. Thank you to the art department team, who work hard on the covers of my books (particularly this one): Alan Ayers and Elizabeth Turner. Thank you to the editorial department and the sales department and all the people who work at Grand Central Publishing who I never see except at rushed cocktail parties in New York.

You've all made this book not only *readable* but also far, far better than I could make it by myself.

And a very special thanks to my Facebook friend Galia B., who helped me name Tansy!

Chapter One

Once upon a time there lived a poor stonecutter....

—From *The Rock King*

April 1742

Considering how extremely dull her life had been up until this point, Iris Daniels, Lady Jordan had discovered a quite colorful way to die.

Torches flamed on tall stakes driven into the ground. Their flickering light in the moonless night made shadows jump and waver over the masked men grouped in a circle around her.

The *naked* masked men.

Their masks weren't staid black half masks, either. No. They wore bizarre animal or bird shapes. She saw a crow, a badger, a mouse, and a bear with a hairy belly and a crooked red manhood.

She knelt next to a great stone slab, a primitive fallen monolith brought here centuries ago by people long forgotten. Her trembling hands were bound in front of her, her hair was coming down about her face, her dress was in a shocking state, and she very much suspected that she might *smell*—a result of having been kidnapped over four days before.

In front of her stood three men, the masters of this horrific farce.

The first wore a fox mask. He was slim, pale, and, judging by his body hair, a redhead. His inner forearm was tattooed with a small dolphin.

The second wore a mask in the likeness of a young man's face with grapes in its hair—the god Dionysus if she wasn't mistaken—which, oddly, was far more terrifying than any of the animal masks. He bore a dolphin tattoo on his upper right arm.

The last wore a wolf mask and was taller by a head then the other two. His body hair was black, he stood with a calm air of power, and he, too, bore a dolphin tattoo—directly on the jut of his left hip bone. The placement rather drew the eye to the man's...erm...*masculine attributes.*

The man in the wolf mask had nothing to be ashamed of.

Iris shuddered in disgust and glanced away, accidentally meeting the Wolf's mocking gaze.

She lifted her chin in defiance. She knew what this group of men was. This was the Lords of Chaos, an odious secret society composed of aristocrats who enjoyed two things: power and the rape and destruction of women and children.

Iris swallowed hard and reminded herself that she was a *lady*—her family could trace its line nearly to the time of the Conqueror—and as such she had her name and honor to uphold.

These...*creatures* might kill her—and worse—but they would not take her dignity.

"My Lords!" the Dionysus called, raising his arms above

his head in a theatrical gesture that showed very little taste—but then he *was* addressing an audience of nude, masked men. "My Lords, I welcome you to our spring revels. Tonight we make a special sacrifice—the new Duchess of Kyle!"

The crowd roared like slavering beasts.

Iris blinked. The Duchess of…

She glanced quickly around.

As far as she could see in the macabre flickering torchlight, *she* was the only sacrifice in evidence, and she was most certainly *not* the Duchess of Kyle.

The commotion began to die down.

Iris cleared her throat. "No, I'm not."

"Silence," the Fox hissed.

She narrowed her eyes at him. In the last four days she'd been kidnapped on her way home from the wedding of the *true* Duchess of Kyle, she'd been bound, hooded, and thrown on the floor of a carriage, where she'd *remained* as the carriage bumped over road after rutted road, and then, on arrival at this place, she'd been shoved into a tiny stone hut without any sort of fire. She had been starved and had only a few cups of water to drink. Last, but most definitely *not* least, she'd been forced to relieve herself in a *bucket*.

All of which had given her far too much time to contemplate her own death and what torture would precede it.

She might be terrified and alone, but she wasn't about to surrender to the Lords' plans without a fight. As far as she could see she had nothing to lose and quite possibly her life to gain.

So she raised her voice and said clearly and loudly, "You have made a mistake. I am *not* the Duchess of Kyle."

The Wolf turned to the Dionysus and spoke for the first

time. His voice was deep and smoky. "Your men kidnapped the wrong woman."

"Don't be a fool," the Dionysus snapped at him. "We captured her three days after her wedding to Kyle."

"Yes, returning *home* to London from the wedding," Iris said. "The Duke of Kyle married a young woman named Alf, not me. Why would I leave the duke if I'd just married him?"

The Dionysus rounded on the Fox, making the other man cringe. "You told me that you *saw* her marry Kyle."

The Wolf chuckled darkly.

"She lies!" cried the Fox, and he leaped toward her, his arm raised.

The Wolf lunged, seized the Fox's right arm, twisted it up behind his back, and slammed the other man to his knees.

Iris stared and felt a tremble shake her body. She'd never seen a man move so swiftly.

Nor so brutally.

The Wolf bent over his prey, both men panting, their naked bodies sweating. The snout of the Wolf mask pressed against the Fox's vulnerable bent neck. "Don't. Touch. What. Is. *Mine.*"

"Let him go," the Dionysus barked.

The Wolf didn't move.

The Dionysus's hands curled into fists. "*Obey* me."

The Wolf finally turned his mask from the Fox's neck to look at the Dionysus. "You have the wrong woman—a corrupt sacrifice, one not worthy of the revel. I want her."

"Take care," murmured the Dionysus. "You are new to our society."

The Wolf tilted his head. "Not so new as all that."

"Perhaps newly *rejoined*, then," the Dionysus replied. "You still do not know our ways."

"I know that as the host, I have the right to claim her," growled the Wolf. "She is forfeit to me."

The Dionysus tilted his head as if considering. "Only by my leave."

The Wolf abruptly threw wide his arms, releasing the Fox and gracefully standing again. "Then by your *leave*," he said, his words holding an edge of mockery.

The firelight gleamed off his muscled chest and strong arms. He stood with an easy air of command.

What would make a man with such natural power join this gruesome society?

The other members of the Lords of Chaos didn't seem happy at the thought of having their principal entertainment for the evening snatched out from under their noses. The masked men around her muttered and shifted, a restless miasma of danger hovering in the night air.

Any spark could set them off, Iris suddenly realized.

"Well?" the Wolf asked the Dionysus.

"You can't let her go," the Fox said to his leader, getting to his feet. There were red marks beginning to bruise on his pale skin. "Why the bloody hell are you listening to him? She's *ours*. Let us take our fill of her and—"

The Wolf struck him on the side of the head—a terrible blow that made the Fox fly backward.

"*Mine*," growled the Wolf. He looked at the Dionysus again. "Do you lead the Lords or not?"

"I think it more than evident that I lead the Lords," the Dionysus drawled, even as the muttering of the crowd grew louder. "And I think I need not prove my mettle by giving you this woman."

Iris swallowed. They were fighting over her like feral dogs over a scrap of meat. Was it better if the Wolf claimed her? She didn't know.

The Wolf stood between Iris and the Dionysus, and she saw the muscles in his legs and buttocks tense. She wondered if the Dionysus noticed that the other man was readying for battle.

"However," the Dionysus continued, "I can grant her to you as an act of…*charity*. Enjoy her in whatever way you see fit, but take care that her heart no longer beats when next the sun rises."

Iris sucked in a breath at the sudden death sentence. The Dionysus had ordered her murder as casually as he would step on a beetle.

"My word," the Wolf bit out, and Iris's fearful glance flew to him.

Dear God, these men were monsters.

The Dionysus tilted his head. "Your word—heard by all."

A low growl came from behind the wolf mask. He bent and gripped Iris's bound wrists and hauled her to her feet. She stumbled after him as he strode through the mass of angry masked men. The crowd jostled against her, shoving her from all sides with bare arms and elbows until the Wolf finally pulled her free.

She had been brought to this place hooded, and for the first time she saw that it was a ruined church or cathedral. Stones and broken arches loomed in the dark, and she tripped more than once over weed-covered rubble. The spring night was chilly away from the fires, but the man in the wolf mask, striding naked in the gloom, seemed unaffected by the elements. He continued his pace until they reached a dirt road and several waiting carriages.

He walked up to one and without preamble opened the door and shoved her inside. "Wait here. Don't scream or try to escape. You won't like my response."

And with that ominous statement the door closed. Iris was left panting in terror in the dark, empty carriage.

Immediately she tried the carriage door, but he'd locked or jammed it somehow. It wouldn't open.

She could hear men's voices in the distance. Shouts and cries. *Dear God.* They sounded like a pack of rabid dogs. What would the Wolf do to her?

She needed a weapon. Something—*anything*—with which to defend herself.

Hurriedly she felt the door—a handle, but she couldn't wrench it off—a small window, no curtains—the walls of the carriage—*nothing*. The seats were plush velvet. Expensive. Sometimes in better-made carriages the seats…

She yanked at one.

It lifted up.

Inside was a small space.

She reached in and felt a fur blanket. Nothing else.

Damn.

She could hear the Wolf's growling voice just outside the carriage.

Desperately she flung herself at the opposite seat and tugged it up. Thrust her hand in.

A pistol.

She cocked it, praying that it was loaded.

She turned and aimed it at the door to the carriage just as the door swung open.

The Wolf loomed in the doorway—still nude—a lantern in one hand. She saw the eyes behind the mask flick to the pistol she held between her bound hands. He turned his head and said something in an incomprehensible language to someone outside.

Iris felt her breath sawing in and out of her chest.

He climbed into the carriage and closed the door,

completely ignoring her and the pistol pointed at him. The Wolf hung the lantern on a hook and sat on the seat across from her.

Finally he glanced at her. "Put that down."

His voice was calm. Quiet.

With just a hint of menace.

She backed into the opposite corner, as far away from him as possible, holding the pistol up. Level with his chest. Her heart was pounding so hard it nearly deafened her. "No."

The carriage jolted into motion, making her stumble before she caught herself.

"T-tell them to stop the carriage," she said, stuttering with terror despite her resolve. "Let me go now."

"So that they can rape you to death out there?" He tilted his head to indicate the Lords. "No."

"At the next village, then."

"I think not."

He reached for her and she knew she had no choice.

She shot him.

The blast blew him into the seat and threw her hands up and back, the pistol narrowly missing her nose.

Iris scrambled to her feet. The bullet was gone, but she could still use the pistol as a bludgeon.

The Wolf was sprawled across the seat, blood streaming from a gaping hole in his right shoulder. His mask had been knocked askew on his face.

She reached forward and snatched it off.

And then gasped.

The face that was revealed had once been as beautiful as an angel's but was now horribly mutilated. A livid red scar ran from just below his hairline on the right side of his face, bisecting the eyebrow, somehow skipping the eye itself but gouging a furrow into the lean cheek and catching the edge of his upper lip, making it twist. The scar ended in a missing divot of flesh in the line of the man's severe jaw. He had inky black hair and, though they were closed now, Iris knew he had emotionless crystal-gray eyes.

She knew because she recognized him.

He was Raphael de Chartres, the Duke of Dyemore, and when she'd danced with him—once—three months ago at a ball, she'd thought he'd looked like Hades.

God of the underworld.

God of the dead.

She had no reason to change her opinion now.

Then he gasped, those frozen crystal eyes opened, and he glared at her. "You idiot woman. I'm trying to *save* you."

Raphael grimaced in pain, feeling the scar tissue on the right side of his face pull his upper lip. No doubt the movement turned his mouth into a grotesque sneer.

The woman who'd shot him had eyes the color of the sky above the moors just after a storm: blue-gray sky after black clouds. That particular shade of blue had been one of the few things his mother had found beautiful in England.

Raphael agreed.

Despite the fear that shone in them, Lady Jordan's blue-gray eyes were beautiful.

"What do you mean you're trying to save me?" She still held the pistol as if ready to club him over the head should he move, the bloodthirsty little thing.

"I mean that I don't intend to ravish and kill you." *Years* of anguish and dreams of revenge followed by months of planning to infiltrate the Lords of Chaos, only to have the whole thing collapse because of *blue-gray eyes*. He was a bloody fool. "I merely wished to spirit you away from the

Lords of Chaos's debauchery. Oddly enough, I believed you would be grateful."

Her lovely brows drew together suspiciously over those eyes. "You promised the Dionysus that you'd *kill* me."

"I *lied*," he drawled. "If I'd meant you harm, I assure you, I'd have trussed you up like a Christmas goose. You'll note I didn't."

"Oh, dear Lord." She looked stricken as she flung down the pistol, staring at his gory shoulder. "This is a mess."

"Quite," he said through gritted teeth.

Raphael glanced down at his shoulder. The wound was a mass of mangled flesh, the blood pumping from within at a steady pace. This was not good. He'd meant to have her securely on the road back to London tonight, guarded by his men. If the Dionysus heard that she'd shot him, that he was *weakened*—

He grunted and tried to sit up against the swaying of the carriage, eyeing her, this woman he'd only truly met once before.

He'd first seen her in a ballroom where he'd gone to meet members of the Lords of Chaos. In that den of corruption, swarming with his enemies, she'd stood out, pure and innocent. He'd warned her to leave that dangerous place. Then, when she'd walked alone back to her carriage, he'd shadowed her to make sure she made it safely there.

And that would've been that—had he not discovered that she was all but engaged to the Duke of Kyle—a man tasked, on orders of the King, with the risky job of bringing down the Lords of Chaos. Raphael knew that as long as Kyle pursued the Lords, Lady Jordan would be in danger. Because of this, Raphael had spent no little time worried about her. Had even gone so far as to trail her into the country to Kyle's estate.

There he'd seen her marry Kyle—or so he'd thought.

At that point Raphael had been forced to consider the matter at an end. Lady Jordan's protection was no longer his concern, but her husband's. Raphael might be loath to admit it, but Kyle was more than equal to the task of protecting his wife. If Raphael had felt some small twinge of longing... well, he'd made sure to bury it deep inside, where it would die a natural death from lack of light.

Yet now...

It was as if his previously stopped heart jolted and started beating again. "Are you truly not the Duchess of Kyle?"

"No." She reached for him, and he was astonished at how gentle her hands were. She had no cause to be gentle with him—not after what she'd been through tonight. Yet she placed both small palms about his left arm—the unharmed side—and helped him stand. He lurched across the moving carriage and half fell into the opposite seat.

"I, too, saw you married to Kyle," Raphael said evenly.

She glared. "*How?* Alf and Hugh were married inside their country manor. The King was there, and I assure you there were guards everywhere."

"I saw Kyle kiss you in the garden at the celebration afterwards," he said. "There might have been guards, but I assure *you* they neglected to search the woods overlooking the garden."

"It rather serves you right that you confused the matter since you were *spying*," she said tartly. "I don't remember Hugh kissing me, but if he did it was in a brotherly manner. We're *friends*. It doesn't matter anyway. Whatever you *imagined* you saw, I'm not married to Hugh."

He closed his eyes for a moment, wondering *why* she'd bothered moving him, when he felt the bulk of a fur rug bunched over his nude body. He hadn't even realized that he was shivering.

Ah, of course. The rug that had been stored in the bench he'd been sitting on. "Yet it was well known in London that you were to marry the Duke of Kyle."

"We let the gossips think I was the bride at the wedding because his real wife is without family or name." She shook her head. "'Twill be a scandal when the news comes out. Is that why you saved me? Because you thought I was the duchess?"

"No." Raphael opened his eyes and watched as she unwrapped the fichu from about her neck, exposing a deep décolletage. Her breasts were sweetly vulnerable. He glanced aside. Such things were not for one as tainted as he. "I would have rescued you in any case—duchess or not."

"But why?" She flipped the fur away from his shoulder and pressed the flimsy fichu hard against the wound.

He inhaled, not bothering to answer her nonsensical question. Did she think him a demon?

But then she *had* just seen him attending what was at base a demonic rite.

"You have to stop the carriage," she was saying. "I can't halt the bleeding. You need a doctor. I should—"

"We're near my home," he said, cutting her off. "We'll be there soon enough. Just keep pressing. You're doing fine, Lady Jordan. You tend a wound nearly as well as you dance."

Her blue-gray gaze flicked up to his, wide with surprise. "I wasn't sure if you recognized me from the ball."

This was intimate, her face so close to his. He naked and she with the upper slopes of her breasts uncovered. He felt hazy with desperate temptation. He could *smell* her, above the scent of his own blood—a faint flower scent.

Not cedarwood, thank God.

"You're hard to forget," he murmured.

She frowned as if uncertain whether he complimented or insulted her. "Is that why you rescued me? Because you knew me from that one dance?"

"No." *Not at all.* He hadn't known whom the Dionysus meant to sacrifice tonight. Hadn't known there was to *be* a sacrifice—though of course that was a possibility. Would he have rescued any woman?

Perhaps.

But the moment he'd seen *her*, he'd known he had to act. "You seem oddly competent at handling a gunshot wound."

"My late husband James was an officer in His Majesty's army," she said. "I followed him on campaign on the Continent. There were times when tending a wound became very helpful."

He swallowed, watching her from beneath half-lowered lids, trying to *think*. He couldn't afford to show weakness in these parts—it was why he'd brought his own servants from Corsica. The Lords of Chaos were powerful in this area. If the Dionysus discovered that he was wounded, he—and she—would be in peril. The Dionysus already wanted her dead and expected Raphael to kill her.

A wicked idea crept into his mind.

She was a temptation—a temptation aimed at his one weakness. He'd walked alone for so long. For his entire life, really. He'd never thought to seek another. To permit any light into his darkness.

But she was right here, within his grasp. To let her go again was beyond his control right now. He was weakened, dizzy, lost. Dear God, he wanted to keep her for himself.

And the means to convince her to stay with him had just dropped into his lap.

"The blood has soaked my fichu." She sounded upset, but not hysterical. She was a strong woman—stronger than he'd first realized when he'd pulled her from the revelry.

He made his decision. "You need to marry me."

Her beautiful eyes widened in what looked like alarm. "What? No! I'm not going to—"

He reached up and grasped her wrist with his left hand. Both her hands were pressed firmly on his wound. Her skin was warm and soft. "The Dionysus ordered me to kill you. If—"

She tried to recoil. "You're not going to—"

He squeezed her fragile wrist, feeling the beating of her heart. Feeling this moment in time.

Seizing it.

"*Listen.* I meant to have you safely on the road to London tonight. That isn't possible now that I'm wounded. The only way I can protect you is to marry you. If you're my duchess, you'll have my name and my money to shield you when they come, and believe me, Lady Jordan, the Dionysus's men *will* come for you. They need to silence you, for you know far too much about the Lords of Chaos now."

She snorted. "They thought I was the Duchess of Kyle before. *That* certainly didn't protect me."

"*I* am an entirely different duke than Kyle," he replied with flat certainty. He brought his other hand up and untied the rope around her wrists. "And I also have my servants."

She frowned down at her freed wrists and then at him. "How will they keep me from being murdered?"

"They are Corsicans—brave and loyal to a fault—and I have over two dozen." He'd spent his life filled with rage, grief, and a drive for revenge. He'd never even thought of marriage. This was a flight of fancy. An aberration. A diversion from the strict path he'd set for his life. Yet he could not find it within himself to resist. "My men answer only to me. If you're my wife—my family and my duchess—they will protect you with their lives. If I die due to your gunshot wound and you do *not* marry me, they may look upon you far less favorably."

Her plump mouth dropped open in outrage. "You'd *blackmail* me into marriage? Are you deranged?"

Oh, indeed. Probably on both counts. "I'm *wounded.*" He arched an eyebrow. "And attempting to save your life. You might try thanking me."

"*Thank* you? I—"

Fortunately the carriage halted before she could articulate what she thought of that idea.

Raphael kept a firm hold of the lady's wrist as the door was opened, revealing Ubertino, one of his most trusted men. Ubertino was nearly forty, a short man with a barrel chest and graying hair clubbed back in a tight braid. The Corsican's bright-blue eyes widened in his tanned face at the sight of his master's blood.

"I've been shot," Raphael told him. "Get Valente and Bardo and tell Nicoletta to come."

Ubertino turned to shout the orders in Corsican to the other men behind him and then stepped into the carriage.

Lady Jordan backed away warily.

"Tell Ivo to take the lady into the abbey," Raphael ordered. He wouldn't put it past her to run once she was out of the carriage.

"Did she do this, Your Excellency?" Ubertino muttered in Corsican as he put his shoulder against Raphael's bad side.

Raphael grunted and stood, clenching his jaw. He would not pass out. "A misunderstanding merely. You will forget this."

"I think it will be hard to forget," Ubertino said.

Carefully they negotiated the two steps down from the carriage.

He was cold. So cold.

"Nevertheless, I order it so." Raphael stopped and stared at the servant. In another life he might've counted this man his oldest friend. "You will protect her no matter what happens."

The Corsican inclined his head. "As you wish, Your Excellency."

Valente and Bardo came running into the driveway.

Valente, the younger of the two, began asking questions in Corsican, but Ubertino cut him off. "Listen to *lu duca*."

Raphael's hands were in fists. He would not fall down here before his men. "Go to the vicar in town. You know his house, by the English church?"

Both men nodded.

"Wake him up and bring him here." He could feel the blood trickling down his side, oddly hot against the chill of his body. "Do not let anything he says or does keep you from your task. Hurry."

Valente and Bardo ran to the stables.

They knew only a few words of English. The vicar might very well think he was being robbed or worse. Raphael ought to write a letter explaining the matter.

But there was no time.

Behind them Lady Jordan exclaimed, "Take your hands from me, sir!"

Raphael raised his voice. "Ivo is merely helping you into my home, my lady."

"I don't wish to be helped!"

He turned to see her glaring at him, her blond hair a halo about her head in the carriage's lantern light, and felt his lips quirk. She really was rather extraordinary.

A pity he could not make her his wife in reality.

Her gaze swept past him and to the facade of the building behind him, then widened in what looked very much like horror. "*This* is your home?"

He turned to look as well. The abbey was ancient. The original structure had been a fortified keep, which had been added to and modified over centuries, first by monks and then, after the dissolution of the monasteries, by generations of his ancestors. This was where he'd spent most of his childhood. Where his mother had breathed her last breath. The place he'd hoped never to see again.

His mouth twisted. "*Home* might be a bit of an exaggeration."

Chapter Two

The stonecutter lived with his two daughters in a tiny hut at the edge of a great barren plain of rock. It was a desolate place and few godly things dwelled there, but the stonecutter found plenty of stones and, since he'd never learned another trade, there he stayed....

—From *The Rock King*

The edifice that rose before Iris loomed like a decaying giant in the flickering lantern light, somehow both gloomy and forbidding.

"What is this place?" she whispered.

"Dyemore Abbey," the duke replied.

Even now his voice was a sensuous rasp against her nerve endings. His skin was pale and sweaty, his horrid scar standing out like a red snake writhing down the right side of his face.

"Come," he said and turned toward the entry.

She didn't want to enter this ghastly mansion with him. She didn't entirely trust him, wounded or not. He might've saved her from immediate rape and murder, but he'd been participating at that revelry tonight. He was obviously a member of the Lords of Chaos.

And the Dionysus had ordered him to make sure she kept their secrets. To *kill* her.

The scowling manservant to her right—Ivo—gave her no

choice, however. His firm grip on her elbow compelled her forward and across a graveled drive.

Only one window held a light—a dim glow from within, as if it struggled not to be extinguished beneath the tons of dark-brown stones that made up Dyemore Abbey. The mansion must be four or five stories high, with rectangular windows set deep in the facade. Behind the monolithic central tower loomed craggy shapes, as if a mountain range of other wings or ruins was beyond.

The duke mounted the front steps with the help of his manservant. The door was arched, but over it was the overlarge face of a demon or gargoyle, holding up the lintel of the window above. The gargoyle glared down at them, its mouth stretched wide in a grimace.

Iris shuddered.

Obviously the dukes of Dyemore weren't concerned with welcoming guests to their ducal seat.

The door opened, and a plump woman immediately began chattering in Corsican.

This must be Nicoletta. She was older—perhaps in her fifth decade—and her black hair was scraped back from her scowling face and hidden under a plain white cap. The woman held a candle in one hand and seemed to be scolding the manservant who was helping the duke. The servant who had assisted the duke from the carriage said something, and the Corsicans all looked at Iris.

He'd told them who had shot their master—she just knew it. Nicoletta's black eyes narrowed.

Her gaze was not benign.

Iris shivered, remembering the duke's words. His servants would rightfully blame her for his wound. Was there any way she could explain herself? But most of them weren't speaking English, and she didn't know Corsican.

Besides, Dyemore's wound *was* her fault. Whatever the duke might be, he *had* saved her from the Lords of Chaos, and she'd repaid him by shooting him.

Lord. She blinked back sudden tears. Her nerves were stretched taut from days of uncertainty and fear, and now to know she'd done this to another, even in defense of her own person...

Iris swallowed and straightened her back. She mustn't break now. Mustn't show weakness when she didn't know who these people were or if they meant to do her harm.

Dyemore snapped something in Corsican at that moment, and the servants looked away from her, moving again.

They led her into the house. Iris tried to swallow her apprehension as the Corsicans talked in their own language and Ivo's grip on her arm remained firm. The hall was grand—marble floors, carved wood paneling, and high ceilings that might be painted—but it was cold and dim. The only light the maidservant's candle.

Dyemore Abbey felt... *dead.*

Iris shook away the morbid thought as she followed the procession deeper into the entry hall. At the back they mounted wide stairs leading to a landing with another staircase branching out from each end. Portraits peered down from the walls in the gloom as they took the steps to the right. On the upper level Nicoletta led the way to a large sitting room and warmth at last.

Near the fire—the only point of light in the cavernous room—Dyemore sank heavily into a huge wing-backed chair.

One of the men poured him a glass of wine from a crystal carafe.

"I apologize for my lack of hospitality," Dyemore said after taking a sip of the wine. "Most of my Corsicans are guarding the house outside. It's imperative that you not wander in the abbey. Some of the rooms are locked for a reason. Stay out of them."

His words were arrogant and he lounged in the chair as if it were a throne, but his face was positively gray.

She glanced away. She couldn't look at him. At what she'd done to him. "You must lie down."

"No," she heard him say, his deep voice even, as if they were discussing the price of ribbons on Bond Street. "The vicar will arrive soon. I will remain upright. We must keep the truth of my injury from the Lords as long as possible."

Her head jerked up at that. "You're *naked* under that fur and *bleeding*. How are you going to hide your injury from the vicar? This is ridiculous!"

She made an impatient movement toward him, but Ivo held her back.

"Let go of me!"

The Corsican looked at her stonily.

She held out her free hand to Dyemore. "*Tell* him."

He stared at her a moment, his gray eyes glassy, and she wondered if he was beginning to lose his senses. Lord, if he fainted now it would be a disaster. His servants would turn against her.

Dyemore said something in Corsican to Ivo, and the servant released her.

Immediately she was across the room and bending over the duke.

Nicoletta hissed her displeasure.

Iris ignored her. "Ask your maidservant if she has any bandages to stop the bleeding. And tell your men to fetch a doctor from the village at once."

Out of the corner of her eye she saw Nicoletta slip from the room. Did she understand English?

"No." Dyemore's eyes were on her, calm, cold, and

emotionless, though he must be in pain. "No doctor. I don't trust anyone in the village. You may bind it yourself, if you must."

"Oh, I think I *must*," she replied tartly. "The ball is still in your shoulder and has to be taken out."

He blinked slowly. "We haven't time for you to remove the ball. My men will be back with the vicar soon. Bandage the wound so that it doesn't bleed. Ubertino will help me into some clothes."

"This is insane," Iris muttered, but she moved to do as he bid. Perhaps she had fallen under some spell. Perhaps she'd gone mad from her internment in that horrid little hut the Lords of Chaos had kept her in.

Perhaps this was all some dream and she would soon awaken in her boring room, safe in her brother's London town house.

Except she was a practical woman, a woman not given to vapors or delusions, and she knew well enough that this was no dream. This was a real man bleeding under her hands, his skin solid and much too cold.

She hadn't touched a man like this since James had died five years before.

She blinked and looked at her fingers, smeared with Dyemore's scarlet blood. The wound was in the duke's right shoulder, a jagged, oozing hole below his collarbone. It hadn't seemed to have broken the bone there. That was lucky, at least.

Nicoletta returned with two more male servants following her, their arms filled with clothing, bandages, and water pitchers.

Iris reached for one of the bandages, but the maidservant snatched it first.

"Let the lady have it," Dyemore barked. "She has experience tending the wounds of soldiers."

The Corsican woman pursed her lips, but gave the bandage to Iris.

"Thank you," Iris murmured as she accepted it.

Really she supposed she couldn't blame Nicoletta. She was obviously very loyal to the duke and didn't trust the same woman who had shot him to nurse him now.

Iris took the bandage, wet it in the water one of the men held, and began wiping the worst of the blood away. Dyemore's skin was darker than her own, noticeably so, cool and smooth. She set aside the dirty bandage and folded a clean one until she had a thick pad. This she placed against the wound.

"Hold this, please," she said to the plump maidservant.

Nicoletta pursed her lips again, but moved to do as she asked.

Iris wound longer strips tightly around Dyemore's chest and over his shoulder.

When Iris was done she stepped back.

Dyemore sat upright in his chair, his jaw clenched, his forehead beaded with sweat.

He met her gaze and said gently, "Wash your hands, please, my lady. Nicoletta will help you with your coiffure."

Iris blinked. She wasn't sure she wanted the other woman near her hair, but she followed the maidservant to a corner of the sitting room. Two of the manservants came with them, obviously to keep her from bolting out the door. This was insane—she was being prepared to *marry* Dyemore, a man she neither knew nor completely trusted.

Belatedly Iris realized she wasn't even sure what part of England they were in. She'd been kidnapped from Nottinghamshire, but it had taken several days' journey for the Lords of Chaos to bring her to her hut prison. Even if she were to dash from Dyemore Abbey, she wouldn't know in which direction to run.

Or to whom.

Perhaps she could enlist the vicar's aid when he arrived? Signal to him that she was being married under duress? But he would be one man against two dozen of Dyemore's Corsicans. Even were the vicar the most valiant of men, she didn't see how he could prevail.

And Dyemore was right: the Lords of Chaos would be after her when they discovered that she still lived. They'd track her down. Bring her back to their ghastly revels. Or simply murder her outright.

He was her only safety.

Her only hope.

Nicoletta deftly combed out her tangled hair and pulled it into a simple knot. She was quick and competent. More importantly, she didn't vent her anger by pulling Iris's hair.

"Thank you," Iris murmured to the woman.

Nicoletta met her eyes and nodded. Her soft mouth was still pursed in disapproval or irritation, but her eyes had gentled a bit.

Or at least Iris hoped so.

One of the manservants came running into the room. He said something in Corsican.

Dyemore replied, "Send the vicar up, then." He turned to Iris. "Come here, my lady."

She swallowed. Was she really going to do this mad, mad thing? Unlike some widows, she'd not discreetly taken a lover. She'd waited—perhaps naively—for a gentleman who esteemed her enough to make her his wife. More than that, she wanted to be *cherished* when next she lay with a man.

When next she married.

She'd not wanted another cold, loveless marriage.

This was not at all what she'd planned.

Dyemore watched her hesitate. He'd dressed in a black

silk banyan while Nicoletta had tended her hair. It was buttoned all the way to his neck, making him look severe and dour. He might just pass at a glance for a gentleman lounging at home, perhaps a little the worse for drink.

He held out his good arm to her, his hand commanding. "Come now. The vicar is here. We haven't much time."

He should look weak, sitting there in front of the fire, his face pale and sickly, his black, shoulder-length hair sticking to the sweat at his temples. He seemed a stark figure of death, here at the center of this house of gloom.

But his eyes were icy gray and in control.

She wished desperately that she knew what he was thinking.

He'd already saved her once. What other choice did she have?

Iris crossed the room and placed her hand in Hades's palm.

Raphael gripped Lady Jordan's hand with the hazy notion that if he let her go she'd flee his rotting abbey. Leave him here all alone in his house of death and despair.

Take her light away from him.

He blinked, straightening. His shoulder was throbbing, as if some animal had burrowed within his flesh and were steadily gnawing, attempting to reach his heart.

But that was fantasy.

He needed to focus his mind. Keep and protect her, this woman with the blue-gray eyes and sweet pink lips.

Valente entered the sitting room. Behind him was a small spare man, his bobbed wig askew on his shaved head. The man gripped a black book in both hands. He looked both completely bewildered and completely terrified.

Bardo brought up the rear, towering over the vicar. "He thinks we will murder him, Your Excellency."

Raphael nodded. "Vicar, what is your name?"

The man, who had been staring at Raphael's scar in horror, started. "I...Er, Jonathon Webberly, sir, but I must protest. Who are you and what—"

"I am Raphael de Chartres, the Duke of Dyemore." He hadn't time for histrionics. "And I sent for you so that you might wed me to my fiancée."

He drew Lady Jordan closer to him, ignoring how she stiffened.

The vicar's gaze shot to her. "Your Grace...That is... This is very unusual. I—"

"Can you marry us legally or not?" Raphael rasped.

"I...Yes, of course the marriage would be legal, Your Grace. I'm ordained in the Church of England and need only register a marriage. But this is highly irregular, especially for a gentleman of your importance." The vicar licked his lips nervously, glancing at Lady Jordan. "Surely you must wish to call the banns and celebrate your nuptials in the village church?"

Lady Jordan made an aborted movement.

Raphael tightened his hand around hers, keeping her still. "Do I need to call the banns or be married in a church for this marriage to be valid?"

"No, Your Grace," the man said, looking distressed. "The Church naturally frowns upon such hasty weddings, but *legally* there is no requirement to call the banns. That is—"

"Then I have no desire for delay. I wish you to marry us at once." He stared at the man coldly, well aware of the impact of his visage.

Mr. Webberly nodded jerkily and opened his book.

Raphael concentrated on staying alert. He let the vicar's words wash over him, aware of her fingers in his hand all the while.

She was...different from other women in some way he

still was unable to understand. She was more pure, more bright, more *golden*. She called to him on an animal level. Her song had seeped into his veins, his lungs, and his liver until he could no longer divide her from his marrow.

He *needed* her.

And now he was marrying her, Iris Daniels, Lady Jordan.

The notion was as wrong as that of a spring robin tied to a carrion raven.

Yet he would not stop this monstrosity. More, he'd kill any man who tried to gainsay him.

He wanted her.

Past reason. Past honor and good taste. Past his own vows and the things he must see done in this life. Perhaps this was madness.

Or the evil of his father.

If so, he'd succumbed.

The vicar droned on until it was time for them to make their vows. Raphael turned to see if she would protest at this late stage. Perhaps weep and say that she was being forced to do this. Beg Mr. Webberly to help her from this dreadful place and her hideously scarred presumptive husband.

But how could he forget that this was the woman who had faced him down with a pistol? Who had *shot* him only an hour or so before?

She was nothing if not courageous.

Lady Jordan made her vows in a cool, clear voice.

He responded in turn, his voice as ever emotionless and firm.

The vicar pronounced them man and wife and closed his black book, looking up. His eyes strayed to Raphael's injured shoulder and widened.

Raphael realized that his wound had bled through the cloth.

He nodded to Ubertino. "Pay him well."

The Corsican bowed, took a heavy purse from his pocket, and handed it to the vicar.

The Englishman's eyes widened. "Your Grace, this is much more than I am accustomed to receiving for a simple wedding."

"My duchess and I are most appreciative of your inconvenience," Raphael replied silkily. "And, of course, I will expect the utmost discretion from you on this matter, Mr. Webberly."

Any fear that he'd been too subtle was laid to rest when the vicar paled. "I... I... Yes, naturally, Your Grace."

"Good. I do so value my privacy. I would not *enjoy* being the subject of gossip."

The man gulped and backed a step, clutching his book and purse to his chest.

Raphael nodded to him. "My men will see you safely home."

"Thank you, Your Grace." The vicar hurried from the room with Valente and Bardo close behind.

Raphael sighed and let his head fall against the chair back.

Beside him his new duchess tsked. "You scared him half to death. Was that truly necessary?"

"If word reaches the Lords of Chaos that I am weakened, both our lives will be in danger. Therefore, yes, it most definitely was necessary." With an effort he opened his eyes and glanced at her. There were shadows beneath her eyes, and her pale pink lips drooped. A smudge of dirt highlighted her left cheekbone, and he had the ridiculous urge to wipe it away. "I think now I will retire if you do not mind, madam."

She knit delicate brows. "Not before the ball is removed from your shoulder."

His eyelids were so very heavy. "I cannot think such argumentativeness is attractive in a wife."

"Perhaps you should've thought of that earlier," she retorted, but her tone was gentle.

"Humph."

"Send your men for a surgeon."

He opened his eyes wide in order to shoot her a glare. "You said you have experience with gunshot wounds."

"Yes, but I've never actually removed a bullet." Her face was drawn with fear, and yet he still detected a glow beneath her surface exhaustion.

He waved the objection aside. "I trust you and we have no other choice. If the Lords of Chaos find that I am wounded they will be like a pack of wolves on a lame ram. I won't survive the night—and neither will you."

He heard her huff, but her hand crept under his shoulder, urging him to rise. Then his men were there as well, a much stronger support. He could walk. He wouldn't be carried, damn it. Not in his father's house.

The stairs were tricky, the treads kept trying to trip him up, but they made it to the floor above. They trudged past the duke's rooms, and finally arrived at the duchess's rooms—the rooms that had once been his mother's.

He lay down in his bed with gratitude that nearly overwhelmed his senses.

"I will need a knife and a pair of tweezers or tongs if you have them," his wife said politely, almost apologetically.

"You trust this woman with a knife at your flesh, Your Excellency?" Ubertino growled in Corsican, even as Nicoletta trotted out of the room.

With effort Raphael opened his eyes and simply looked at his gathered servants, one by one, and said in English, "She is your mistress, your duchess, now. You will respect her. Do you understand?"

He heard his duchess draw in her breath.

There was a spattering of muttered agreement from his servants.

"I am not the one to whom you vow allegiance now," he barked.

Ubertino jerked his head to his fellow servants and turned to his wide-eyed duchess. The Corsican bowed low and said, "Your Grace."

She swallowed. "Thank you."

When she turned back to Raphael she was frowning, her brows lowered over those blue-gray eyes, like thunderclouds over a Yorkshire moor sky. A fanciful thought.

He didn't usually have fanciful thoughts.

Someone was unbuttoning his banyan.

He opened his eyes to see her, Lady Jordan, looking quite worried, with Nicoletta beside her. But that wasn't right, was it? She was the Duchess of Dyemore now.

"Bring me my mother's jewelry box," he ordered the maidservant.

Nicoletta hurried out of the room.

The bandages were being tugged away from his wound. He gasped at a shard of pain.

"I'm sorry," his wife whispered.

"Your Excellency." He opened his eyes to see Nicoletta holding out the jewelry box. There seemed to be a halo about her head, and he wanted to chuckle. Nicoletta was too sharp tongued by far to be a saint, surely?

"Open it," he said.

She took a key from a ring at her waist and inserted it into the lock, then opened the box and brought it close to him so that he could see the contents.

Raphael lifted his good hand—it felt uncommonly heavy—and stirred a finger through the jewels until he found the ring. His hand trembled as he lifted the ring from the box. "Lock it again and give the key ring to Her Excellency."

Nicoletta pursed her lips but did as he said.

His duchess merely looked bewildered on being handed a key to a treasure box.

"It is yours now," he said, his voice... Something was wrong with his breath. His gasped. "As my wife. As my duchess. This is yours as well."

He took her hand—so warm in his—and placed the heavy, chased ring on her finger. It wouldn't fit her ring finger—his mother had been a fragile creature with very thin hands. Instead he pushed it onto the smallest finger of her right hand. The sight of it there, glowing gold, the central round ruby burnished with the years it had guarded his mother's family, satisfied something within him.

His hands dropped to the bed like lead weights.

"Protect her," he whispered to Ubertino as the room darkened. Someone was weeping. Nicoletta? "Promise me. Protect her."

Iris's eyes stung, which was ridiculous.

She hardly knew this man, husband or not. What matter to her if he lived or died? He was arrogant, abrupt, and demanding—the *last* things she'd wanted in a husband.

And yet she wept for him.

She blinked, trying to clear her vision. Her fingers were stained with blood as she worked on the wound, the gold of the heavy ring Dyemore had placed on her little finger all but obscured by the gore.

She glanced at Dyemore and realized that his face had relaxed. Black lashes lay against his pale cheeks and his lips were parted softly, though the right side was still twisted even now.

He'd passed out.

For a timeless moment she stilled.

He was entirely at her mercy, this ruthless, violent, *powerful* man. This man who had saved her life and then demanded she marry him. He'd lain down and without hesitation or fear let her cut into him.

He trusted her—with his *life*, it seemed.

She'd never been so important to someone before.

She inhaled and picked up a small pair of tweezers—probably from a toiletry kit. The servants had brought a stack of cloths, a pair of scissors, water, a basin, a sharp knife, and the tweezers and laid them out neatly on a table beside the bed. They had also lit two candles on the bedside table to provide light in the otherwise dim room.

Carefully sliding the tweezers into the wound along the knife blade, she delicately probed. She was glad he was unconscious—she hated the thought of causing him further pain.

She moved the metal implement about in Dyemore's flesh, in his *shoulder*, as the blood continued to ooze out, staining his banyan and the sheets. Sweat slid greasily down the center of her back.

Finally—dear God, *finally*—she felt the tweezers clink against something. She tried to open the thin blades to grasp the ball, but there wasn't room.

"Damn," she muttered under her breath. It was terribly unladylike to swear. But then it was unladylike to have one's fingers in a gentleman's bloody shoulder.

She twisted her implement, trying to somehow capture the little bit of metal. For a moment she thought she had it, but then the tweezers slipped off the bullet.

Iris swallowed. She was so weary. She just wanted to correct the wrong she'd done to Dyemore.

Make him whole again.

Nicoletta murmured something and patted around the wound with a piece of cloth, wiping away some of the blood.

"Thank you."

Iris inhaled and closed her eyes. Working slowly, she felt for the bullet again. Caught the bit of metal...just there...and carefully withdrew the tweezers with the bullet and then the knife.

She blew out a breath, eyeing the nasty little thing, then reached for one of the cloths on the table. She wiped the bullet and examined it.

It was whole.

Thank God.

She set it down on the table and turned back to Dyemore. The wound was still oozing blood. She licked her lips and inhaled. She'd have to sew it closed.

There was no needle or thread on the table and she turned to Nicoletta. "Do you have a sewing kit?"

The maidservant nodded and hurried away.

That left Iris in the room with three big manservants. Ubertino knelt to stir the fire and put more coal on it.

Iris picked up a cloth, folded it into a pad, and pressed it against the wound. How much blood had he lost tonight? Dyemore was a big man, a strong man from what she'd seen—and she'd seen *all* of him—but even the strongest man could succumb to blood loss.

The door opened and she looked up to see that Nicoletta had returned with a basket.

The maidservant bustled over and opened the basket, revealing a sewing kit. She selected a sturdy needle and threaded it with what looked like silk.

"Thank you." Iris took the needle.

She lifted the soaked pad from the wound and hesitated. She'd seen bullet holes sewn up before, but she'd never watched closely.

Well. It wasn't as if they had any other choice.

She pinched the edges of the wound together, then laid the needle's point at his skin. It was harder than she'd imagined, piercing a man's flesh. The needle was slippery beneath her fingers and she almost lost her grasp.

Suddenly Nicoletta's hands were there as well, helping her by holding the wound closed.

"Thank you," Iris said again gratefully.

She stitched the wound together as best she could, but she was afraid it was rather a mess when she was done.

At least the bleeding had slowed.

Together she and Nicoletta bandaged Dyemore's shoulder. At one point the men had to lift the duke so that they could wrap the bandages around his back.

Even that didn't wake him.

When they were done, Iris found that her hands were trembling.

She blinked, feeling so weary she didn't know what to do next.

Nicoletta clucked and produced a clean bowl of water. Iris slowly washed her hands, watching the water turn pink from the blood.

She dried her hands and the maidservant gave her a glass of wine and a piece of bread.

Iris ate and drank mechanically, and then Nicoletta showed her the chamber pot behind a screen in the corner of the room.

She should be embarrassed, but Iris found she couldn't muster the energy. Instead she squatted and relieved herself.

When she emerged from behind the screen she found that

the duke had been tucked under the covers of the huge bed and that the other side was turned back.

Waiting for her.

She stopped dead.

It hadn't occurred to her...

Well, of course they'd *married*, but...

Oh, good Lord, Nicoletta and the manservants were looking at her expectantly.

Dyemore was injured. Surely she should sleep somewhere else? But what if there *wasn't* anywhere else prepared?

And she was so damned tired.

Iris made up her mind. The bed was more than big enough for two—even with such a large man as Dyemore—and she was exhausted. If she disturbed him in the night, she could always sleep on the floor.

She was that weary.

And besides—*someone* would have to make sure he was all right during the night.

She crossed the room, kicked off her ragged slippers, and climbed into the bed.

Oh.

Oh, *heaven*.

The light withdrew from the room and she heard the door close.

And then it was just her and this man.

Her husband.

Chapter Three

Now the elder of the stonecutter's daughters was tall, fair, and strong, and her name was Ann, but the younger was small, dark, and sickly, and her name was El. Soon after her twelfth birthday El took to her bed and lay, gray skinned and shivering. . . .

—From *The Rock King*

That same night the Dionysus sat upon his throne and watched the revels of his followers. Underneath the great arch of the ruined cathedral torchlight flickered, drawing macabre shapes on heaving bodies. Moans and the muted slap of flesh on flesh sounded in the night.

The screams had stopped hours before.

He was unaroused by the sights and sounds. These things didn't appeal to him. Actually, few things of the body appealed to him, truth be known, but this was, after all, a society of debauchery, so needs must.

Besides, they'd made him their Dionysus—their *king*. It was well to let his subjects celebrate this night.

The Dionysus smiled a little behind the smooth wood of his mask as he watched them. He knew who they were beneath those animal masks. Knew the respectable magistrate fondling the breast of his own sister. Knew the earl being buggered by a handsome youth. Knew the archbishop whipping a weeping woman.

He knew them, and they had no idea at all who he was because, unlike all the idiot men who'd been Dionysus before him, he'd made sure to gain his power without revealing his identity. He wasn't interested in mere rape and corruption.

While those earlier leaders of the Lords had thought only of pricks, arses, and cunts, he concerned himself with larger things.

He dreamed of *power.*

"Dyemore hadn't the right." The Fox had risen from the mass of bodies and was attempting to saunter toward the Dionysus's throne. He stumbled, though—his usual grace inhibited by the wine he'd drunk. "He flouts your authority."

"How so?" The Dionysus tilted his head, watching the Fox.

Like the animal he'd chosen for his mask, the man was sly and untrustworthy. But the Fox had also managed to live through the last six months of bloody upheaval that started when the old Duke of Dyemore—their Dionysus—had been murdered, leading first to a savage struggle for power, and then to the final catastrophe, when the Duke of Kyle discovered them and nearly destroyed their illustrious ranks. Few of the old guard in the Lords of Chaos had weathered the storm.

The Fox was one.

Which was why he bore watching.

"Took the woman, didn't he?" The Fox waved his arm, presumably to indicate where Dyemore had taken Lady Jordan. Or perhaps simply because he enjoyed waving his arm. "The woman was for *us*. For tonight."

The Dionysus sighed impatiently. "She wasn't the Duchess of Kyle. Her sacrifice would not have been the grand revenge against Kyle that I'd planned." He shrugged. "I made the decision to give Lady Jordan to Dyemore. It's done."

"It was a mistake—"

The Dionysus sat forward, the abrupt movement drawing several eyes in the crowd, among them those of the Mole, lurking alone under a broken pillar. "The *mistake* was in taking the wrong lady. That mistake was *yours*, I believe."

The Fox took a step back before he caught himself and stood his ground. "I wasn't the only one on that foray. The Mole and the—"

"Yes, but they're not here complaining to me now, are they?" the Dionysus asked. "*They* aren't questioning my authority and despoiling my enjoyment of the revelry."

"I...I only sought to warn you, my lord," the Fox said, his head lowered in submission.

"Of course," the Dionysus said, gentling his tone smoothly. "I know you are loyal to me."

"I am," the Fox said, raising his head cautiously. "Dyemore wants your throne."

The Dionysus sighed silently. Of course Dyemore wanted his throne. *Everyone* wanted his throne. Most, however, hadn't the brains or the ruthlessness needed to challenge him.

Dyemore, however...

If nothing else, the Dionysus liked to keep his enemies close under his eye to better understand their plans.

"You cannot trust him," the Fox said, his tone whining. He'd crept nearer. "Please, my lord, beware of Dyemore."

"Your concern is sweet." The Dionysus saw that the Mole was watching them from behind his pillar. "Come. Let us partake together. Bring a sacrifice and we will share."

"Oh yes, my lord," the Fox said eagerly. He darted away and was soon dragging back a drunken wench, her hair the color of burgundy. "Does this one please you?"

"Indeed," the Dionysus lied. He drew his finger down the woman's slack face—watching as her eyes widened in fear—and then drew the same finger down the Fox's freckled shoulder.

The Fox shivered at his touch.

Over by the pillar the Mole started forward, then froze.

The Fox thrust the woman down before the throne so that her face was between the Dionysus's legs, her task obvious.

The Dionysus sighed silently. His prick was limp—and would remain limp for her mouth or any other's were that the only thing available to stimulate him.

But needs must. A show was important—to him, the Fox, and, perhaps most importantly, the Mole.

So his fingers found the small dagger hidden in the side of his throne, and he palmed it in his fist and drove it into the inside of his right thigh, perilously close to where an artery ran just under the skin.

Pain blossomed and bright blood gushed over his fingers.

His prick awakened.

He took his bloodied fingers and daubed them about the stunned woman's mouth before meeting her terrified eyes. "Begin."

As she bent her blood-painted mouth to his genitals he dug his thumb into the wound, sweet, blissful agony shooting through his body.

The Fox was already grunting over her back.

The Dionysus glanced up once to make sure the Mole was watching, his fingers clenching the pillar, before he closed his eyes.

Yes, he'd have to look after Dyemore. Make sure he'd gotten rid of Lady Jordan.

And nullify him as a threat to his throne.

* * *

Iris awoke the next day to sunshine.

She blinked.

Sunshine seemed *most* inappropriate, considering the ghastly events of the night before, but there it was, all the same. A merry little beam of sunlight danced across the ancient wooden floor of the ducal bedroom, almost to the huge bed she lay in. She could see the window where the sun was coming in—made of stone, with a severely pointed top. The surrounding wood paneling was a dark, reddish brown, intricately carved into vertical points and honeycombs. The paneling continued all the way up to the ceiling. If she tilted her head, peering past the heavy purple canopy of the bed, she could just make out the edge of a carved medallion in the very center of the ceiling.

Iris let her head drop back on the pillow.

She could hear Dyemore breathing beside her, even and deep. It was actually rather comforting, knowing he was there with her. Knowing that he'd given so much to protect her.

Iris frowned at the thought. She really oughtn't to feel safe with Dyemore—she knew so little about him, and what she *did* know was suspect—and yet she did.

Carefully she inched from her side to her back, the sheets bunching around her waist and rustling horribly. She froze for a moment, but his breathing didn't hitch, so she rolled to face him.

Dyemore lay on his back, his lips slightly parted, his cheeks ruddy. From this angle his aquiline nose rose in sharp profile.

Iris propped herself up on her elbow.

Lines were drawn on his forehead, between his brows, and on the unscarred cheek from his nostril to the corner of his mouth. She didn't think they sat there normally. He looked as if he suffered in his sleep.

She gingerly laid the back of her hand against his brow. His skin was hot and damp and she frowned worriedly—had he started a fever?

He sighed and she snatched back her hand.

She might feel safe with him, but intellectually she knew she had no reason to do so. If she woke him, would he start ordering her about as he had last night?

Iris wasn't sure she wanted to submit to this man's rule. His husbandly right to do with her what he wished.

His right to *bed* her.

She shivered, staring down at him, forcing herself to examine the horrific scar that marred the right side of his face. The Duke of Kyle—Hugh, as she knew him—had been with her when she'd first seen Dyemore at that ball so many months before. He'd mentioned that there were rumors surrounding the scar. That there had been a duel between Dyemore and an enraged father because of a corrupted daughter. That Dyemore's own father, the old duke, had carved the scar into his son's face. Or that the scar was somehow the sign of a family curse.

That Dyemore had been born with half his face disfigured.

Her gaze dropped to the right side of his mouth, to the corner of his lip that was permanently pulled into a slight snarl by the edge of the angry scar, and then to the other side of his mouth, to the sensuous curve of his lips. She raised her hand, reaching out to touch that perfect curl. She stilled, her hand hovering, as the sunlight glinted off the ruby ring on her finger. It was a pretty little ring, delicate and made for a woman. In any other circumstances she would've worn it with happiness.

Here, though.... Well it was almost a mark of possession, wasn't it?

Iris inhaled and jerked her hand back before she made contact. This man might be her *husband* now—courtesy of a series of terrible events and his own stubbornness, but he was still a stranger.

A stranger she wasn't even sure she could entirely trust.

She shook her head and rose from the huge bed.

Hugh and Alf must be insane with worry. Iris had been taken from her carriage, but Parks, her lady's maid, the driver, and her footmen had been left behind. They would've notified Hugh of her kidnapping. There was also her elder brother, Henry, to consider.

Iris lived with Henry and his wife, Harriet, in their London house. Though she hadn't given them a specific date for her return from Hugh and Alf's wedding, surely Henry would be concerned over her continued absence by now. Hugh might even have ridden to London and raised the alarm over her disappearance.

She had to send word to them that she was still alive.

Dyemore had said the previous night that she couldn't be seen in the nearby village, but perhaps she could convince one of his men to ride with a note to Hugh or Henry.

Iris turned from the bed and froze.

At one side of the room a huge medieval fireplace took up most of the wall, blood-red marble veined in ivory framing the hearth.

Above the mantel was a portrait of a woman.

She was dark haired, wearing the rounded neck and long waistline of several decades before. Her complexion was so fair the artist had tinged it faintly green in parts. She was hauntingly beautiful, but it was the tragedy in the lady's light-gray eyes that made Iris stare.

Her eyes were the same gray as Dyemore's eyes.

Dyemore, however, never expressed such deep emotion—

or any emotion at all save for anger. At least Iris had never seen him do so.

His eyes were as cold as winter ice at midnight.

The woman in the portrait must be Dyemore's mother. Iris thought, but she couldn't remember hearing anything about her.

She glanced around. Besides the massive bed, the room was almost stark. There were a dainty chest of drawers standing on gilded legs in the corner, two trunks sitting on the floor beside it, a few low velvet chairs before that enormous fireplace, and the screen in the corner, hiding the commode.

She cast a worried look at the bed, but Dyemore slept on, so she hastily relieved her bladder and felt much better afterward. Unfortunately, now she could think about other matters—such as the state of her clothes and her person.

She needed a bath and to send word to Hugh, and Dyemore needed someone to nurse him.

Time to go in search of the Corsicans.

She opened the door as quietly as possible so as not to wake the duke, and ventured into the corridor. It was completely deserted, but she could hear the faint murmur of voices from below.

Iris strode down the corridor to the staircase. In the light of day, the abbey was better maintained than she'd thought from her impressions of the night before, but it still had an air of neglect. As she descended she noticed that the stairs were carpeted, but dust was matted in the corners of the treads. The paintings that hung on the walls, too, needed dusting, and motes danced in the sunlight that weakly struggled in from the few windows. There should be more candles lit, the marble banister should be polished, and the chandelier hung high above in the entry hall should be taken down and cleaned.

It was as if this house had been shut up and forgotten.

She frowned, following the voices back through the abbey into the servants' quarters. The hall became narrow and dark, and she followed a short set of servants' stairs leading down. She emerged into the kitchen, a large low-ceilinged room.

Ubertino, Nicoletta, and three other servants were sitting around the central table.

"Good morning," Iris greeted them as she entered.

"Good morning, Your Grace," Ubertino replied, rising and bowing.

He turned to the other manservants and said something sharp. They immediately rose as well, and Ubertino introduced them.

"This is Valente and Bardo, who brought the English priest last night."

The first was a gangly youth with thick black hair untidily clubbed back. He looked at her shyly from under extravagant eyelashes. The second was a scowling man in his thirties with silver threading his copper-colored hair. He wore a bright-red waistcoat that made his blue eyes seem almost unnaturally bright.

"And this is Ivo," Ubertino ended.

Ivo was the manservant who had brought her into the abbey last night. He was tall and rawboned and flushed blotchily at her attention.

"I'm pleased to discover your names," Iris said.

"They do not know the English," Ubertino replied apologetically. "But if you will, I can convey your words to them?"

"Of course," Iris said.

Ubertino murmured to the other servants in Corsican.

Only Valente—who smiled at her—changed expression.

"Are there no English servants here?" she asked curiously.

"No, Your Grace," Ubertino replied. "*Lu duca* sent away the English when we arrived. He does not trust the people in this place."

"Ah." Iris remembered Dyemore's saying something similar last night.

No wonder the abbey seemed deserted: usually an entire battalion of servants would be taking care of a house like this. One maidservant and two dozen men, most of whom apparently were on guard duty, were not nearly enough.

She nodded. "The duke is still asleep. I would like someone to attend him. But first, can you send a man on horseback to the Duke of Kyle with a letter?"

"Naturally I shall go directly to *lu duca*," Ubertino said gravely. "But I am afraid it is not possible to send a horseman to this Duke of Kyle."

"Whyever not?" Iris asked, trying for a smile. "I am, after all, your new duchess."

"Indeed, Your Grace, and I am most ashamed that I cannot help you, but His Grace has ordered all the men to stay here to guard you," Ubertino replied. "Until he wakes and gives a different order, we will do as he said."

Iris fought to keep her expression neutral as heat crept up her face. It was humiliating that the servants wouldn't obey her—no matter how apologetic Ubertino looked.

And more, she was irritated that she couldn't send word to Kyle.

She inhaled. "Then would it be possible to have a bath?"

"Yes, yes, certainly, Your Grace." Ubertino turned to Nicoletta and told her something in a flurry of words.

The maidservant scowled, shook her head, and snapped something back.

Ubertino insisted and finally the woman tutted and went to the hearth, where a kettle was already steaming over the coals. The other three manservants began filling large kettles with water from a cistern.

Iris raised her eyebrows in inquiry at Ubertino.

"Ah," he said, his face a little redder from his argument with the maidservant. "Nicoletta says that perhaps you will wish to partake of breakfast while the bathwater heats. She understands the English," he confided in a whisper, "but she does not speak it."

"That is good to know," Iris replied. "And yes, I'll have breakfast while I wait."

Ubertino looked relieved.

Nicoletta brought back an enormous stoneware pot of tea and plonked it down on the wooden kitchen table while Iris sat. Valente brought over a basket of bread and some hard-boiled eggs. Bardo offered a dish of butter and another of cheese, and Nicoletta poured the tea into a dainty china cup. Ivo was apparently in charge of the fire and heating the water.

Iris took a sip of the tea and nearly burned her tongue. The tea was strong enough to make her blink rapidly.

She smiled at Nicoletta anyway.

Nicoletta crossed plump arms under her bosom and lowered her brows, watching Iris.

Iris sighed silently and buttered her bread. She knew better than to offer food to the servants even though she sat in what was their domain—the kitchens. She might be in near rags, dirty, and in dire need of a bath, but she was the mistress of the house. As such she was forever apart from them.

She swallowed a bite of the bread. "Delicious."

Nicoletta—presumably the baker of the bread—didn't change her expression at all.

Perhaps the truce Iris had thought she'd struck with the maidservant the night before was over.

She sighed and addressed Ubertino. "Your English is quite good. How did you learn it?"

"Thank you, Your Grace." He bowed. "In my youth I was a sailor and my ship often came across other ships from different countries. When this happened the passengers of these ships became... guests on our ship. A large number of these guests were English."

He grinned again, rather roguishly.

Iris paused with her teacup raised to her lips and squinted at him. *Came across...?* Had Ubertino just confessed to having been a *pirate*?

Carefully she put her teacup down and glanced at the other manservants. Were they *all* former pirates?

Valente and Bardo stared back innocently enough.

She shook her head and picked up her teacup. "Ah... indeed. And do any of the other servants speak English?"

Ubertino shrugged. "Valente has some English. The others, not so much. But many are like Nicoletta and understand more than they can speak, Your Grace. They all know that you are the duchess now."

"Ah." Iris took another sip of her tea, remembering the duke lying so still in the bed, his scar angry and red. "Ubertino?"

"Your Grace?"

She hesitated, and then just asked her question. "Do you know how the duke got his scar?"

But Ubertino shook his head. "No, Your Grace."

Iris nodded, frowning as she wondered if *anyone* knew how he'd received that awful slash across his face. It must have been horrific when it had happened. The cut would've laid his face open from brow to chin. How painful it must've been. How awful the realization that he was so scarred for life.

She frowned, feeling uneasy at her sympathy for the duke. He didn't seem like a man who would like pity.

She finished her breakfast and pushed back from the table. "Thank you. The bread was lovely—fresh and with a nice crunchy crust."

Nicoletta sniffed and began clearing the dishes.

Ubertino rolled his eyes. "Nicoletta says she is gratified you enjoyed her food."

He blatantly ignored the fact that Nicoletta hadn't spoken at all.

The woman grunted and briskly snapped out some words to the manservants. Then she turned to Iris and made shooing motions with her hands.

This seemed to mortify Ubertino. His eyes widened before he smiled, made an elaborate bow, and said pointedly, "We are *all* happy to serve you. I shall come with you to the ducal chambers and the others will bring the water when it is hot."

Iris bit back a smile and led the way.

She'd expected Dyemore to have woken while she was gone, but he still lay in the bed when they entered the room.

Iris frowned.

"His Grace has usually risen by this hour," Ubertino muttered behind her, confirming Iris's fears.

He *was* still sleeping, wasn't he?

Her heart stopped in her chest for a moment. She crossed to the huge bed and bent over him.

There. She could see his chest rising and falling beneath the thin black silk of his banyan.

She exhaled, feeling light-headed with relief as she looked at him.

"*Lu duca* is too hot," Ubertino said from the other side of the bed. "I will fetch fresh cool water."

The Corsican slipped from the room, but Iris's attention was still on Dyemore.

He appeared to have pushed down the coverlet and undone the first few buttons of his banyan. Sweat had pooled below his throat, just at the junction of his collarbones, and she could see a few black hairs peeking up from the black silk. They were stuck to his chest with the moisture.

She'd seen this man *naked.*

She grew warm at the thought. He was so…so…*male*, even lying here, unconscious and wounded. She could feel the heat rolling off of him, could almost smell his musk, and she had a strange urge to touch that throat…

He has a fever.

Her heart fell at the realization. Fever could kill a man.

The door opened and Ubertino came back in, followed by the other servants. He carried wine, bread, and a jug of water. "I will see to His Grace while you bathe."

Valente carried a copper hip bath. Behind him were Bardo and Ivo, both holding huge jugs of steaming water, and last came Nicoletta with a pile of cloths in her arms.

Nicoletta marched across the bedroom to a connecting door, the others trailing obediently behind her.

Iris peered through the door and saw that a dressing room lay beyond. Nicoletta was already supervising the filling of the tub.

Iris turned back to the bedroom. She needed something to wear after she was clean.

She went to the chest of drawers and pulled the top out. Inside were handkerchiefs, stockings, and smallclothes. The next drawer down, though, contained shirts—*his* shirts. She took one out and held it up. It would be disgracefully scanty, of course, but it would cover her body from neck to knees. Rather like a chemise.

And it wasn't as if she had anything *else* to wear.

She took a pair of stockings as well, and then the servants trooped out of the dressing room—all but Nicoletta.

Iris clutched the shirt and stockings to her chest and entered the dressing room.

Nicoletta was waiting, hands on hips, the copper bath steaming gently beside her. There'd been only enough water to fill it a couple of inches, but that was enough.

Iris closed the door to the bedroom and set the clean clothes down on a chair. The dressing room held a small bed—presumably for a maid or valet—a tall cabinet with many small drawers, and two chairs.

Nicoletta bustled over without a word and began unlacing the back of her dress.

Something inside Iris relaxed. This at least was familiar. One didn't need a common language between mistress and maid to undress. The chore was the same whatever the country.

Nicoletta helped her out of her bodice, tutting over stains and a rip at the shoulder seam. The skirts were untied and fell to Iris's feet. She stepped out and stood still as the maid unlaced her stays. The stays were a fairly sturdy garment and as a result were still in good shape.

Underneath, her chemise was wrinkled and damp from her body. Iris sat on a chair to remove her shoes and stockings, and then hastily pulled the chemise over her head. She shivered as the cool air hit her bare skin.

Quickly she lowered herself into the little copper hip bath.

Oh, this is lovely. She simply rested for a moment in the hot water as Nicoletta moved about the room, muttering and shaking out her clothes, and thought about what the last twenty-four hours had wrought.

She was married. Again.

For a fraction of a second she let her face crumple, and then she smoothed it before the maid could turn and see. This... this wasn't how she'd wanted her life to be.

She'd hoped that after her marriage to James—a "good" match to a man nearly twenty years older than she—she could marry for love. Or barring love—for she wasn't such a romantic that she would hold out forever for an impossible dream—for affection. Iris wanted a gentleman who enjoyed the same pursuits as she—reading by a fire, attending the theater in winter, strolling in the country in summer.

Those sorts of everyday, simple things.

But most of all she longed for children of her own. A *family* of her own. At one point, months ago, she'd hoped that Hugh, the Duke of Kyle, could help make that family with her. But that was before he'd met Alf and they'd fallen in love. At that point Iris had told Hugh in no uncertain terms that really, a marriage between her and him just would not *do*.

She'd wanted a man to love *her*.

Because the thing was, she was alone.

Oh, she had friends, but none of them were close—not since the death of Katherine, her childhood bosom bow. She had her brother and sister-in-law, but they weren't *hers*.

All her life she'd wanted a close inner circle, a family that knew her intimately—all the good in her and all the bad—and loved her anyway.

A family in which she could be herself.

Instead she was married to a stranger—a violent, possibly *dangerous* stranger—who had also saved her life.

Iris was brought back to the present when Nicoletta bustled over and briskly began removing the pins from her hair. However careful Nicoletta was—and Iris could tell the maid was attempting to be gentle—her hair was hopelessly tangled.

Iris winced as her hair was yanked again and again.

When the pins were finally out, the maid placed her hand against the back of Iris's head and firmly pushed.

Iris leaned forward so that her head hung between her bent knees.

Warm water poured over her head. Nicoletta's strong fingers worked soap through her hair. It smelled of something nice—oranges, perhaps—and Iris let the movement of the maid's hands lull her.

Another splash of warm water over her head made her start. It felt good, though.

She pushed back her dripping but clean hair and set about washing herself. Scrubbing away the terror and exhaustion and trepidation. Letting fresh water rinse away the last couple of days.

And what might have been.

When she was done, Nicoletta held out a large drying cloth for her.

Iris stepped from the copper bath, feeling as if she had been born anew. She was the Duchess of Dyemore now, for better or for worse, and really she'd rather pick *better* if she had to choose. Perhaps...perhaps she could somehow build a family with Dyemore.

If Dyemore recovered from his wound.

She frowned as she rubbed herself dry and then found the clean clothes she'd set out on the chair. Lord, she hoped that he had only a light fever.

That he'd soon wake up.

Iris pulled the shirt over her head. It did indeed come down to her knees, and the sleeves fell over her hands. She heard a sound and glanced up in time to see Nicoletta covering her mouth with both hands, obviously trying to hide a smile.

She met the older woman's wide brown eyes, and for a moment they both froze.

Then Iris's lips twitched. "Yes, well, there wasn't anything else to hand."

Nicoletta clucked, said something in her native tongue, and then helped her roll up the sleeves. Iris pulled on the stockings while Nicoletta produced a comb from somewhere and patiently tamed the tangle of her hair. When the maid was done, she wove Iris's still-damp hair into a loose braid and tied the end with a ribbon.

"Thank you," Iris said.

Nicoletta didn't smile, but her face somehow softened. She dipped a curtsy and bustled from the room, her arms loaded with the dirty clothes. Hopefully she was off to find a way to clean and mend them, and not to discard the lot.

Iris, left alone, shivered as she looked about the little dressing room. A shirt really wasn't enough to wear. She should see if Dyemore had another banyan she could borrow. Or perhaps a coat.

But when she opened the door to the bedroom, the first thing she saw was her new husband, standing by the bed, his crystal eyes aimed at her.

"What," he said in his smoke-filled voice, "are you doing in my shirt?"

Chapter Four

"Is there naught we can do for El?" asked Ann.
"I fear not," the stonecutter replied. "For your mother gave birth to her in the rock fields, lured there by the flinty shades that haunt that place by night. Those shades stole El's heart fire the moment she first drew breath. And without that?" The old man shook his head. "She will not live to be a woman."...

—From *The Rock King*

Raphael clutched the bedpost, doing his damnedest not to sway. His duchess was poised upon the threshold like a startled naiad, one of his own shirts enveloping her form. Her hair had been braided like a girl's and hung over one shoulder, making the fine lawn of the shirt wet.

And transparent.

He fancied he could see the tip of one nipple, pink and pointed, and something tightened in his belly. *Christ*, she might as well be naked before him.

He dragged his gaze away from the sight and focused on her face. Her blue-gray eyes were wide and startled. She looked all of twelve.

Well, except for that damned nipple.

She blinked and seemed to come to her senses. "What are you doing out of bed?"

He raised an eyebrow. "I felt the need to piss."

Color bloomed in her cheeks, a pale rosy pink. He could spend days trying to duplicate that exact shade on paper and never lose interest.

"You have a fever, I think," she said tartly. "Perhaps you should return to your bed."

"I'm fine," he said, ignoring the sweat that rolled down the middle of his back. "My shirt?"

She clutched the front of the shirt between her fists as if afraid he might tear it from her. The fine lawn pulled tight, outlining her breasts in lewd detail. Was she doing it *apurpose*?

"I hadn't anything else to put on that was clean."

Her words brought him back to the conversation.

"Ah, of course." He should've realized.

Ubertino had informed him of her bath when the Corsican had woken him with wine and bread to break his fast.

He walked carefully to his chest of drawers. He must have something to cover her—for the good of his own sanity if nothing else.

Behind him, she said, "Is there someplace where I can procure suitable clothing?"

He turned with one of his banyans in his hands. "No. The only other woman in the abbey is Nicoletta, and she's hardly your size."

She took the banyan from him, looking hopeful. "The town where the vicar came from surely has a seamstress of some sort."

He was already shaking his head before she was done speaking. "It's far too dangerous for you to go into town without me. I don't want the Lords to realize that you're alive until I'm recovered."

"But surely—"

"No."

His harsh tone stilled her for a moment in the act of donning the banyan.

Her lips tightened. "Can I at least send a letter to the Duke of Kyle informing him of my safety?"

He frowned at the thought. "No."

She narrowed her eyes and finished pulling the banyan around her. The hem puddled on the floor, and the ebony color made her skin glow.

He really shouldn't mourn the veiling of her form.

"He'll be searching for me," she said with a clear hint of defiance. "He'll be *worried*. I can't think putting his mind at rest would do you or me any harm."

"Don't you?" he snapped. "And if the Lords of Chaos follow my man to Kyle—if they find out that you're alive while I'm still recovering from this wound?"

She knit her eyebrows. "Your men can guard both of us, surely."

"You don't understand how great the danger is." Raphael clenched his jaw, fighting dizziness, trying to convey the problem to her so she wouldn't do anything stupid. "The Lords of Chaos have held their revels in this area for decades. Their influence is deep with the local people. Indeed, my father led their society for years. The revel you were at last night was on my own lands."

"What?" She stared at him in what looked like horror. "You *invited* them to hold their debauchery on your property?"

"*No*," he snapped impatiently. "It's hardly as simple as that." His shoulder was a throbbing mass of heat, and he tightened his grip on the bedpost. "The Lords do as they please—and it pleases them to continue their revels at the ruined cathedral on my estate. My father enjoyed having them here. When I discovered that the Lords meant to hold the spring rite here, I realized it was in my own interests to let them continue with their plans."

"Your interests as a member of the Lords of Chaos, you mean." She was edging toward the door to the bedroom as if she could flee clad only in his shirt and banyan.

He wanted to laugh, but he hadn't truly laughed in years.

He took a deep breath and strode forward quickly, then grasped her shoulders.

She started and his head spun.

For a moment he thought he might vomit.

"Let me go," she said. "Let me go, or I'll—"

"You'll *what*?" He arched an eyebrow. "You've already shot me."

If he thought to embarrass her, he failed.

"Yes, I did." Her blue-gray eyes met his unflinchingly, and he could do naught but admire her spirit.

He squeezed her shoulders. The soap she'd used in her bath must've been perfumed with oranges, for the scent seemed to surround him. "I'm not a member of the Lords of Chaos."

"Then why were you there last night? Why were you nude and wearing a mask, ready to participate in their orgy?"

"Because I mean to infiltrate them," he gritted. The room was beginning to spin. "Find out who the Dionysus is and destroy him. Destroy them all."

She hesitated. "I... I don't know if I believe you."

"I don't give a damn," he lied, and fell heavily against her.

She cried out as his weight hit her, staggering back against the wall, but her arms came up to brace him. His face rested against her neck, his lips on soft, cool skin, and somehow his left hand had landed on her breast.

Most fortuitous, that.

No. No, such things weren't for the likes of him. He needed to resist. To pull away from her.

But he seemed unable.

"You're burning," she gasped.

"Then you ought not to touch me," he said seriously. "You'll be consumed."

"Too late," she muttered, and pivoted, trying to drag him, he presumed, toward the bed. "You're awfully heavy—"

"My soul is made of lead."

"—*and* you're delirious," she ended decisively. "I need to get help."

He stirred at that. "Don't leave."

Her eyes were so lovely. "I must find Ubertino."

He raised his head, staring into those storm-cloud eyes. "Promise me you won't leave the abbey." If she left him, all the light would leave as well.

She looked away and he knew she meant to lie.

"Promise," he said sternly.

Her gaze returned to his. "I promise."

"Good." And then he did the only thing that made sense.

He kissed her.

Iris gasped. Dyemore's mouth *burned.* Almost his entire weight had sagged against her—and he wasn't a small man—but it was the kiss that most startled her.

He…

She could *taste* him, the wine he must've drunk this morning, the scent of smoke in his hair, drifting about her face, the heat rolling off him in thick waves. He was so overwhelmingly *large*, so excruciatingly *masculine*.

She'd been married. She'd been kissed before—of course she had—but it hadn't been like this.

Nothing like *this*.

It was as if everything that made her female was being awakened and called forth by everything male in him. Her heart beat faster, her nipples drew tight, her sex grew wet, and she *felt*... everywhere.

He staggered and she abruptly came to herself, tearing her lips away from his. Her mouth slid clumsily over the side of his face and across the smooth skin of his scar.

She jerked back, startled at the contact. It seemed far too intimate somehow.

"We..." Her voice broke and she had to clear her throat. "You should lie down."

He grunted and she truly began to worry. Even at his worst yesterday he'd been articulate—more than coherent.

Now his head lolled against her shoulder, his face so hot on her neck she thought he might brand her skin. She half dragged, half walked him toward the bed. He stumbled, his arm wrapping around her shoulders, and she nearly went down with him. But she found the strength to lock her knees and remain standing. If they fell now, she'd never get him upright again. Where had Ubertino gone to? How dare he leave his master like this?

Iris gritted her teeth and hauled Dyemore the last few feet to the bed.

She pushed him at the bed, panting, and he fell against it. Fortunately, he had enough strength to crawl on top, but she could see his arms shaking.

Panic was beginning to fill her throat.

This couldn't be happening. He'd *survived* the gunshot. He'd been arguing with her only moments before.

Dear God, he couldn't die of infection now.

She yanked at the covers, pulling them out from under him, and then helped him climb underneath. He was shivering as if cold, but his touch was hot, and she could see sweat beading his forehead.

Perhaps...perhaps he'd merely overexerted himself by rising too soon.

But even as she was trying to convince herself, Iris was hurrying to the door. She flung it open and ran to the stairs, calling, "Ubertino! Nicoletta! Ivo!"

There was a clatter from below as she dashed down the steps. One of the manservants—she'd seen him last night but for the life of her she couldn't remember if she'd been told his name—met her on the stairs. He lifted a hand as if to stay her, his thick black eyebrows drawn together.

"No!" She struck aside his hand and swept past him, ignoring his shout.

The sitting room where they'd wed in that farce of a ceremony was on this floor. She banged open doors until she found it and hurried inside. There! The decanter of wine sat on a side table. She snatched it up and turned to see Ubertino at the door, gaping at her in confusion.

"Your Grace?"

"The duke—he's collapsed," she said. "Come with me."

Nicoletta was in the corridor, frowning suspiciously, along with Valente and Ivo.

Iris led them all upstairs.

She burst into the bedroom and a single glance at the bed told her that the duke was no better.

Nicoletta exclaimed something and brushed past her, hurrying to the sick man. The maidservant bent over him, touching his face.

The duke muttered in Corsican, but didn't open his eyes.

Nicoletta's mouth thinned. She straightened and barked orders to the men.

All three ran from the room.

Iris was already on the other side of the bed and, as if by common agreement, she and Nicoletta both began pulling back the coverlet. The duke's black banyan was wet with sweat, his chest rising and falling rapidly.

Between them they helped him sit up, and Iris tipped a little of the wine into his mouth. He drank and then turned aside his head, grimacing. His fingers were scrabbling at the buttons of his banyan.

Iris glanced up and met Nicoletta's black eyes. Nicoletta looked worried.

And that, more than anything else, terrified Iris.

She gently pushed Dyemore's hands aside and unbuttoned his banyan, then parted the fine silk, revealing his hot, sweating chest. She pulled his arm from his sleeve, gritting her teeth as he moaned at the movement.

The manservants returned. They carried jugs of water, cloths, and other items.

Nicoletta picked up a pair of scissors and cut away the bandage on the duke's shoulder. The outer layers were dry, but as the maidservant cut through them, it was apparent that the inner layers were sodden with blood and other fluids.

Iris wrinkled her nose.

The wound stank.

The smell reminded her of the times she'd attended the wounded after skirmishes on the Continent. It had been much against James's wishes, but there had been so many injured and so few to help that she'd felt it was her duty. As a lady she hadn't been permitted to do much more than bathe the faces of dying boys and men, write letters home for those who were coherent, and generally tidy up, but the sights, the sounds, and especially the *smells* of that time had been very hard to forget.

Nicoletta drew off the bandage and revealed a mass of swollen, angry red tissue. The stitches Iris had placed the night before were lost in the puffy mess.

Iris inhaled. She'd seen men die within days from infected wounds like this.

Nicoletta picked up a squat earthen pot and pulled the stopper out. She dipped a wooden spoon in the wide mouth and came up with a gob of glistening honey.

"Not yet." Iris stayed her hand.

The maidservant frowned and indicated that she wanted to put the honey on the wound.

"Yes, I know," Iris said. "But first..." She glanced around and beckoned Ubertino and Valente to the bed. "Come here."

"Your Grace?" Ubertino asked.

She looked at the manservant, seeing the concern in his bright-blue eyes. "I need you and Valente to hold the duke down while Nicoletta and I tend to him. It may hurt him and he mustn't injure himself more."

"Yes, Your Grace." Ubertino spoke to Valente and the men took up stances on either side of the bed, their hands holding down the duke's forearms.

Ubertino looked up at Iris.

Iris nodded at him.

Then she lifted the carafe and poured the wine directly onto the wound.

The duke shouted and tried to jerk away, but the manservants held him against the pillows.

His crystal eyes opened, staring accusingly up at Iris as she continued to pour the wine onto his festering skin.

"Cruel lady," he rasped, and she faltered.

The alcohol must burn him. Must hurt him terribly. But she'd seen the doctors do this when tending men with infected wounds.

Their patients hadn't always lived.

Finally the carafe was empty and she stepped back.

His gaze followed her even as Nicoletta leaned forward with the honey, carefully smoothing it onto the wound. He didn't move, didn't so much as wince as the maidservant worked, though that must hurt as well, for she was pressing the sticky stuff into the oozing flesh.

Instead he kept his eerie eyes locked on Iris.

And she couldn't do anything but hold his gaze, standing there as if she were a mouse hypnotized by a dying snake.

At last his eyelids closed, just as Nicoletta stepped back to stopper the jar of honey and wrap the spoon in a bit of cloth.

Iris took a breath and wondered at the ache in her chest.

She could hear the maidservant murmuring behind her, but she couldn't take her eyes from the face of the sleeping man. Such an awful face. Ravaged and scarred. She'd seen men horribly wounded in warfare. They wore bandages or scarves or hats to hide the worst of their injuries. Not Dyemore. He stood straight and met others' eyes squarely, unashamed of his scar.

She touched his hand, lying on top of the bedcovers. His fingers were long and elegant, the nails square and well shaped.

Nicoletta patted her on the shoulder, urging her to sit in a chair that one of the men had placed beside the bed.

"Thank you," Iris murmured.

Behind her the door shut, leaving her alone with the duke.

She dropped her head into her hands, only now realizing that she wore only a shirt and a banyan.

Iris stifled a hysterical laugh. Dear God. What had she gotten herself into? Married to a man who said he was waging war against the Lords of Chaos?

He moaned, moving restlessly against the sheets.

She looked up and touched his hand again—too hot under her fingers. All the complaining in the world wouldn't change her lot. She'd been married for three years to a man she hadn't loved.

Who hadn't loved her.

She'd survived that.

And she would survive this.

In the meantime she knew only one thing: she didn't want the duke to die.

His dreams were filled with flame and demons.

The demons danced on burning coals, their cloven hooves sending sparks into the smoky air. Long forked tongues flickered through the mouth holes in their animal masks, and dolphin tattoos swam over their naked skin. They called him their prince, and when he ran from them, they chased him through the abbey, pleading that they loved him and wished only to crown him their king.

He fled, his heart seizing with nameless dread, his lungs choked with smoke.

Everywhere he turned, the abbey corridors were filled with flames, and though he burned he was never consumed.

Behind him he could hear them crying, calling their terrible love, chasing him into the endless dark.

Until he came to the heart of the inferno, deep, deep underground. *He* was there, standing still with grapes in His hair and a smile on His unspeakable face.

He reached out long, stained fingers. "My sweet boy."

Raphael picked up the knife, for he knew what he must do...

He woke gasping, his throat so dry he felt he was choking.

The right side of his face burned, and for a moment he was still there, holding that awful knife.

"Here," a woman's voice murmured.

A cool arm slid under his neck, and for a fraction of a second he thought she was Madre, petite and dark and always so sad. But then she held a cup to his lips and he knew it was his duchess, practical and English, and with eyes that held the light after a storm.

The water was sweet.

He drank and then opened his eyes. "Iris."

She laid a cool hand against his brow. "Do you want more water?" Her voice was low, nearly a whisper, perhaps because it was night.

Perhaps because she felt the intimacy of this moment, just the two of them in the darkened room.

"No." He sank back into the pillows and fixed his eyes on her, sitting there beside his bed. The awful blackness seemed to loom so close behind her, but she held it back. The single candle made a nimbus around her face, so bright he had to squint.

"Shall I read to you?" She picked up a book from the table beside the bed, a small volume, and turned to a marked page.

He nodded.

She began reading, but though he could hear her voice, the words tangled themselves around his brain and disintegrated into dust.

He should try to understand what she read, but the effort seemed too large at the moment.

So he simply watched her, sitting by him, her pink lips moving, her voice trickling through him like sweet light. The room was quiet. The demons at bay for the moment.

The feeling was very much like peace.

And then he fell back into the dreams...

Chapter Five

"Well, then, we must steal El's heart fire back from the shades," Ann said.
"Ah, lass, if it were such an easy thing, do you not think I would've done it afore now?" cried her father. "'Tis said that no one but the Rock King can venture into the land of the flinty shades."
"Then I'll go and ask the Rock King," said Ann. . . .

—From *The Rock King*

The shout startled Iris awake, her heart beating as if it would shake itself from her chest.

The duke was arched upon the bed, head back, arms spread, as if he were being tortured.

She stared at him wide-eyed. He'd been restless before—they'd had to straighten the coverlet numerous times—but it had been nothing like this.

That *scream.*

He'd sounded as if he were a soul in eternal torment.

His body suddenly slumped to the bed, his limbs relaxing, and he lay still.

She exhaled shakily.

The fire had burned down to embers. The bedroom was in shadows, quiet and dark now. She might've imagined that terrible sound.

Except she knew she hadn't.

Iris winced as she straightened. She'd fallen asleep sitting in the chair beside the duke's bed, and her neck ached.

Her book fell to the floor as she moved, and she glanced quickly to the sleeping man.

He didn't stir, and for a moment her heart swooped.

Then she saw his chest move.

She picked up the book, straightening a page crumpled by the fall before setting it on a table by the bed. She rose and cautiously bent over Dyemore.

His black lashes lay against cheeks flushed from fever, his lips parted as he breathed heavily. Beads of sweat lined his brow. He looked the same as he had the evening before when he'd awakened for such a short time.

She bit her lip at the sight.

Just a day before, this man had been whole and strong, a vital, nearly overwhelming presence. It seemed somehow a sin against nature that he should be laid so low.

That *she* had laid him so low.

She closed her eyes, desperately praying that he might be well. That those strange, cold gray eyes might bore into her again while he argued with her and tried to order her about.

Abruptly she straightened from the bed and crossed to the fireplace. She knelt there and poked at the embers, adding coal to build the fire back up, and then she stood. By the clock on the mantel it was the middle of the night, but she was restless. Beside the clock was a candle and she lit it from the fire, then stood and glanced around the room.

Dyemore still slept.

The bedroom had two doors on opposite walls. One was the dressing room she'd bathed in. The other she'd not investigated yet.

She went to it now and tried the handle.

Locked.

Dyemore had told her on her first night at the abbey not to enter any locked rooms.

Iris bit her lip. The safe thing to do was to return to her chair. Forget about locked doors and whatever might lie beyond.

She darted another glance at the bed and the stranger lying there—her husband, who screamed in his sleep. She hardly knew anything about him or his motives.

She turned swiftly and crossed to the bedside table. A big ring of keys lay there—the ones that Dyemore had made Nicoletta give her after the wedding—and she picked them up.

She'd been so busy nursing Dyemore for the last day and a half that she hadn't had time to use them.

Until now.

But she was the mistress of the abbey, wasn't she? This was *her* house.

She tried key after key on the lock, wincing as the ring jangled loudly. The key to this door might not even be on the ring. Perhaps Dyemore had hidden it among his own possessions.

The lock clicked open.

Iris stared at it a moment before twisting the handle and pushing.

The door opened to reveal a sitting room, still and silent, as if waiting for someone to wake it.

Iris blinked and stepped into the room, nearly stumbling over a trunk sitting just inside the doorway. She frowned and held her candle high as she walked around the trunk.

Ivory-painted pilasters highlighted walls of the lightest pink imaginable, with a dainty carved bas-relief floral spray between each two pilasters. Gilt and moss-green chairs were grouped here and there. A small round table with gold inlay stood against one wall, and a painted fire screen was before the cold hearth. The windows were the same as in the bedroom—tall and narrow with pointed tops—but they seemed somehow to fit this room better.

Iris inhaled. This was a beautiful room—warm and welcoming—and it was entirely unlike anything else she'd seen in Dyemore Abbey.

It was also obviously feminine.

Iris knit her brows. That meant that the room Dyemore slept in was the *duchess's* bedroom, not the duke's.

How strange. Why would he not sleep in his proper bedroom?

She turned to go back into the duchess's bedroom again and saw the trunk.

Iris knelt and put down the candlestick before lifting the lid. Inside were piles of clothing.

She drew one out and saw that it was a dress in a style several decades old. The gown was quite ornate, with embroidery worked over the entire skirt, and a matching stomacher. This was no everyday gown. A woman would save it for very special occasions.

Iris gently laid the gown aside. Underneath it was a lovely primrose-yellow bodice and skirt. She held it up against herself. The skirt was inches too short for her, but the bodice might fit.

Excited now, she dug through the rest of the trunk. It was filled with a woman's clothing, all of it for a lady shorter than Iris but with a fuller bust. At the bottom she found a chemise and stockings and nearly wept at the thought of clean clothes.

Except these must be Dyemore's mother's clothes. She bit her lip. Why else would the trunk be in the duchess's sitting room? His mother was dead—she knew that much—

but when or how the woman had died she'd never heard. He might be very angry at her for donning his mother's clothing.

Iris shook her head. It was the dead of night and she wasn't wearing her stays in any case. In the morning she'd decide whether or not to use the dress.

She closed the trunk and, taking the yellow skirt and bodice along with the stockings and chemise, retraced her steps. She placed the clothes on a chair before locking the sitting room again.

Then she looked across the room to the dressing room.

The duke's room had to be on the other side.

With that thought she picked up the candle again and crossed to the dressing room. Inside, the copper bath had been removed. She held her candle higher and saw that another door was on the other side of the dressing room.

She went to it and tried the handle and was unsurprised to find it locked as well.

Outside she could hear faintly the wind whistling around a corner, but mostly it was quiet.

As if everything in this great house had died long ago.

She pushed aside the thought and concentrated on the lock.

On the third try she found the correct key.

The lock gave with a screech, as if reluctant to yield to her curiosity.

She pushed open the door and held up her candle.

The room was almost twice as large as the bedroom she shared with Dyemore. A massive bed on a raised dais stood in the center, and ebony pillars carved into twisted shapes held up drapes in a blood red so dark she at first mistook them for black.

She stepped in and glanced around. This had to be the

ducal bedroom, but everything was layered in dust—as if it'd been locked up after the previous duke's death.

Why hadn't Dyemore opened it?

The fireplace across the room was enormous, shielded in black marble. A large painting hung above it. Iris raised her candle to get a better look. Saint Sebastian stood tied to a tree, nude and dying horrifically. He was impaled by numerous arrows, the blood painting his white, writhing body.

She shuddered and turned aside.

Her hip bumped against a small table, knocking it over along with the things that had been standing on it. A marble bowl thumped to the carpet, rolling in a circle, spilling its contents, and a book of some sort slid to the floor.

Iris bent to look at the bowl and what it had held. She could smell the scent even before the candlelight picked up the thin curls of wood: cedar. The subtle, balmy fragrance filled her nostrils. She must've inadvertently stepped on some of the chips as she bent down. Carefully she swept as much as she could back into the little bowl with her hand and set it on the table again.

Then she knelt to reach for the book.

It was quite large, but thin, as if it might contain maps or botanical prints. She opened it curiously, only to find that it wasn't a printed book at all.

It was a *sketch*book.

On the inside cover were the words *Leonard, Duke of Dyemore*. Across from the inscription, on the first page, was a drawing of a little boy, perhaps seven or eight, standing, one hip cocked. It was a beautiful sketch, innocent and ethereal.

She turned the page and found another little boy, this one sitting, his legs skewed to the side. On the opposite page was a girl, her hair brushing her shoulders.

Iris flipped through the book. There were dozens of delicate drawings in black pencil and red crayon, page after page, all of them exquisite, all of them drawn by a master hand.

All of nude children.

They stood or sat or lounged, their soft limbs not yet formed into the muscle of adulthood. Several were facing away from the viewer, and from that angle it was impossible to tell if the model had been a boy or a girl. The bodies were done in intimate detail, but the heads were hardly sketched in—or, in some cases, missing entirely—as if the artist wasn't interested in his models' faces.

As Iris turned the pages with fingers that had begun to tremble she noted that the children seemed to be just on the cusp of puberty. The girls with barely budding breasts, the boys with hands and feet that had begun to grow ahead of the rest of their bodies. The children trembled on the cusp of metamorphosis. It made the drawings horrid somehow. As if the artist had caught this special, almost mystical moment in these children's lives and dissected it on the page.

As if they'd been caterpillars in the chrysalis, about to turn to butterflies, and he'd crushed the chrysalis to pulp between his fingers.

A teardrop splashed on the page, warping the elbow of a girl. Iris gasped and hastily wiped at her cheeks.

The last model was different from the others, although he, too, was nude. The drawing was of a small boy, no older than five or six. He sat with one leg drawn up, his elbow resting on his knee and his head in his hand. Unlike all the other children's, his face had been sketched in meticulous detail.

He was beautiful.

She stared at the little boy. It was hard to tell—a child was so different from an adult—but there was something in the lips, the set of the eyes...

She swallowed. She must be imagining the resemblance to her husband.

She *must*.

Except she knew she wasn't. This was Dyemore—her husband—and his face was beautiful and innocent and entirely unblemished.

There was no trace of a scar.

Iris slammed the book shut and thrust it onto the table.

Standing, she turned back toward the door to the dressing room. A man was staring at her from the shadows.

She bit back a scream—and then realized that it was only a painting.

A life-size painting.

She inhaled and walked closer, peering at the figure. It was obviously the last duke, judging by the cut of his purple suit. He had a red velvet robe lined in ermine flung over one shoulder and wore a full-bottomed wig powdered gray. In the portrait he appeared to be about forty years of age. He gazed out at the viewer with a sly smile on his red lips, one beringed hand resting on a gold snuffbox sitting on a table next to him.

Iris remembered what Dyemore had said: this man had led the Lords of Chaos. Such corruption should leave a trace on his countenance, surely? Some mark of his evil? She'd heard whispers about him—of depravity so terrible it could not be named.

This man had been notorious.

But the duke in the painting was unblemished, his face unlined. If anything, he was rather handsome.

Suddenly the room was too quiet. It seemed oppressive,

filled to suffocating with desires and emotions too black to have simply died along with the man who had engendered them. They lurked here like malevolent spirits, waiting to infect the living, drag them closer with skeletal hands, and breathe despair and hatred into their faces.

No wonder Raphael had locked this room up.

Iris rushed from the dreadful bedroom. Her hand shook as she locked the door, and then she nearly ran back to the room she shared with Raphael.

He still slept. She crept to the bed and looked at him. In her candle's light his scar stood out like a livid worm on his face, almost as if *he* bore the mark of evil his father did not. Dear Lord. Was that possible? Was his scar somehow *caused* by his father's sins?

When had it happened?

And who had scarred him?

Iris swallowed and tried to rein in her imagination. She touched one finger to his scar and traced the length. The skin was tight and abnormally smooth beneath her fingertip.

And it was slippery with sweat.

He was still terribly ill—perhaps deathly ill.

Whatever he had done, something inside her knew that Dyemore didn't deserve to die. Not when his father had lived a long life without consequence. Not when his father's face had been unmarred.

She inhaled shakily, feeling the hot splash of tears against her cheeks, and bent over him.

Gently she kissed his scar.

The next time Raphael escaped his nightmares, the bedroom was dark, but his duchess still sat beside him, candlelight softly lighting her face as she read her book.

The curve of her cheek, limned by the light, made him ache.

The fire in the hearth crackled, creating the only sound in the room besides her soft breaths and the turning of her pages.

She'd pulled her golden hair into a simple knot at the back of her head and found a rough-looking shawl to wrap about her shoulders. Perhaps she'd borrowed the garment from Nicoletta? She might've been an ordinary woman—a cobbler's daughter, a seamstress, or the wife of a baker—were it not for the way she held herself. So very upright, her spine straight, her shoulders level, her chin tilted just slightly so she could look at the book in her hands.

Even if she were in rags she'd be discovered as a lady at once—by her gait, her gaze, her speech, and the manner in which she sat.

His lips quirked at the thought.

She must have sensed something, for she looked up and met his gaze.

She smiled like the sun breaking through cloud cover. "You're awake."

He nodded.

She stood and poured him a glass of water, then sat on the edge of the bed to help him sit up to drink it.

He wrapped his hand around her wrist, feeling the delicate bones beneath her skin. The scent of oranges lifted to his face.

He swallowed the water gratefully.

She made to rise, but he stilled her.

"How..." He coughed and tried again. "How long?"

She knit her brows, looking at him warily. "What?"

He blinked, trying to focus his eyes, glancing about the room. Where were his men? Nicoletta? "How long have I been abed?"

"Yesterday and today," she replied calmly. "This is the

evening of the second day. You were feverish, your wound infected. The fever only broke this morning. Do you remember arguing with me before you collapsed?"

He let his eyelids close. His head ached and his limbs felt heavy. He grimaced in frustration. "You were wearing my shirt."

He remembered her nipple, small and pointed and pink.

"Yes." She pulled her hand from his and rose.

She took the one burning candle and lit several others around the bed, making the area brighter. As she did, the shawl slipped off her shoulders.

He squinted. She was wearing a yellow dress. "Where did you get that?"

Her eyes darted away from him. "I... erm... I found it in the next room."

He froze. "*Which* room?"

His voice had been quiet, but her gaze flew to him, clearly alarmed. "The sitting room. But I... I also went into the duke's room."

His lip curled as he looked away from her. He didn't want her to see the rage rising behind his eyes.

He kept his tone calm. "I *told* you not to go into any locked room."

"Yes, you did." Her voice was steady, though a bit high pitched. "But I'm your *wife* now. Don't you think I should be allowed to access rooms in your house?"

He turned to look at her then because she deserved it—and because he'd gained control of his expression. "No, I do not."

Her lips trembled, but she lifted her chin. "Would you prefer it if I'd continued to wear your shirt and banyan?"

Actually he'd quite liked her wearing his clothes, both because her breasts had been unbound and because it made something in him very, very content. The yellow dress, however, quite suited her. She seemed to glow in the candlelight, like a beacon of purity.

"Naturally not," he replied. "You may wear my mother's clothes if that is what you truly desire. But I don't want you to enter my...*father*'s room again."

He felt wild at the very thought. That room was steeped in evil.

"Why?" she asked.

"Because I *ordered* you not to." The words slid like ice from his lips.

She frowned, looking stubborn. "Whyever don't you sleep there instead of the duchess's room?"

He gazed at her and the scent of cedarwood seemed to drift through the room.

His stomach roiled.

That must be why he answered her with the truth. "Because walking in that room makes me want to vomit."

He closed his eyes and listened to her swallow.

"Oh."

Damn it. He hadn't wanted to argue with her. Nor reveal the worst parts of himself.

He sighed. "Thank you."

He felt her straighten the coverlet over his chest. "For what?"

"For nursing me." He opened his eyes with effort. "For not running away."

She frowned at him and then abruptly turned to pour more water in the cup. "I wouldn't leave a sick man, Your Grace."

Ah. He'd insulted her.

She held the cup to his lips again and he watched her as he drank. She looked tired. Weary and wary...of him?

Most probably.

As she should be.

She set the cup down by her book.

"What are you reading?"

"Polybius's *Histories*." She glanced at the book and then up at him, her brows knitting. "Don't you remember me reading to you?"

"Yes, but I couldn't understand you. The fever, I think." Polybius was rather an obscure chronologer of Roman history. He glanced at her curiously. "In Latin? Or Italian?"

"Neither." She cleared her throat almost as if she were embarrassed. "My Latin isn't particularly good—though I *have* read a Latin edition of Polybius before—and I don't know Italian. I found you had an English translation in your library."

"Ah." He nodded. "I was unaware of an English translation in the library, but I came across a record of my father's steward having bought the Earl of Wight's library when the earl was forced to sell on his father's death." He caught her puzzled frown. "Gambling debts."

"Oh." She glanced down at the volume in her hand, smoothing her fingers over the worn cover. "I see. Then the Earl of Wight's loss is my gain, I suppose."

"So it would seem." He watched as she swallowed and tapped her index finger on the book. Was she nervous? "Where did you read that Latin edition?"

She looked up as if a little startled at his interest. "My father's house in the country, where I was born."

He raised his eyebrows in question.

"It's in Essex," she said. "An old rambling sort of house that sits on a low hill with meadows all around. Much too big for our family's means now, I'm afraid. The Radcliffes—my family—have rather descended from our height in the time of the Tudors."

He realized that he knew very little about her, this woman he'd impulsively dragged into his darkness. "You were an only child?"

"Oh no," she replied. "I have an older brother, Henry. Seven years older, actually. Though he was sent off to school, so I didn't see him very much except at holidays. But I had a very good friend from the neighboring estate. Katherine." Her voice hitched.

"Katherine?"

She nodded and inhaled. "She died this last fall. Quite suddenly. It was...a shock." She looked up at him, tears pooling in her eyes. "She was married to the Duke of Kyle. That's how I became friends with Hugh."

He frowned at the name, his chest tightening. "You fell in love with your friend's husband?"

"No!" Her eyes had widened. "Good Lord, no."

"But you *were* going to marry Kyle," he said softly. "That's what everyone thought. That's why the Dionysus assumed you were the bride at the wedding."

She nodded. "Yes, we had a sort of understanding—nothing was ever said aloud, mind you—but we both knew that eventually he would propose to me. But then he fell in love with Alf—the woman he made his wife."

"Ah." He studied her, the still posture, the slim, white hands, the calm face. Had she not felt any regret when the man she'd thought would marry her turned to another woman? Jealousy? Rage?

Did it matter?

He had her now. She was his and he would not let her entertain other men—in body or thought.

Even if that made him a cad.

The door to the room opened and he turned to see Ubertino coming in.

The manservant grinned when he saw that Raphael was awake. “Your Grace! Praise God you’ve woken. I will tell Nicoletta to bring her soup and I will fetch some water.”

“Thank you,” Raphael said, and the manservant left again.

He turned to see that his duchess was stroking the cover of the book she still held.

“What part had you come to?” he asked.

She glanced up. “I beg your pardon?”

“Polybius.” He nodded at the book.

“You’ve read it?”

His lips twitched. “In Latin. And Italian, but a bad translation.”

“Oh.” She blinked. “I’m reading about the sack of Carthage. It was a brutal time. So many killed.”

“It was warfare.” He hesitated, but he was curious about what she thought. “Have you come to Hasdrubal’s wife?”

“Yes, I have.” Her pink lips drew down. “For a woman to do such a thing—to fling her two children into a fire and then jump in herself, cursing her husband? I think she must have been mad. Or much too proud.”

“You didn’t find her suicide noble?”

“No.” She stared at him. “Do you?”

He shrugged. “Carthage had fallen. The fate that awaited her and her children was rape and slavery. I can understand a proud woman choosing death over such a life.”

“And her husband?” she asked, leaning a little forward, her cheeks pinkened with passion at her argument. “What about cursing her husband, the father of her children?”

He felt his own face grow stony. “Hasdrubal surrendered to the Romans instead of fighting to the death. More, he begged for mercy. His wife had no obligation to stand by such a man.”

“Had she not?” his duchess asked softly. “By wifely

love or honor or simple decency? She took his children—took *herself*—away from him at the moment of his greatest defeat."

"Madam, I say *he* was a coward and *she* a noble lady."

"Then I return," she said softly, "that he was a man trying to live while she had given up all hope."

He stared at her. Where did she find such naïveté? His lips curved in a mirthless smile. "There was no *hope* to live for, only slavery, rape, and death. The honorable thing to do was what she in fact did: suicide."

"No." In her fervor she placed her hand over his on the coverlet, though he thought she didn't notice. "*No.* While there is life there is *always* hope. Where you see a coward begging for his own life, I see a man who *despite* his pride has decided to persevere. Remember that the siege of Carthage went on for three long years. Had Hasdrubal truly been a cowardly man he could have surrendered at any point during those years. Yet he did not. He fought. Only when the walls were breached and the city fallen did he throw down his sword. *That* is not the act of a coward."

"And his wife?" he asked quietly, "What of she? Should she have lived as a slave? Perhaps as some Roman soldier's whore?"

She lifted her chin. "Yes, I think so. To kill oneself is—"

He sneered. "You place Christian morality on a pagan queen."

"No, let me finish." She drew a breath, thinking, perhaps composing her thoughts. "In my view it is a waste to kill oneself, even if one is raped and degraded. Hasdrubal's wife was the mother of two sons. She was a person in her own right. Even in slavery there is always the prospect, however slim, of escape. Of rising up and rebelling against those who have hurt you."

He looked at her and wondered if she'd ever suffered in her life. Had ever found the thought of death preferable to the thought of living another day.

Dear God, he hoped not.

"And if she *did* escape slavery," he said gently. "In this hypothetical world where Hasdrubal's wife never flung herself on the fire, never sacrificed her children, let us grant her escape and let us grant her the impossible fortune of finding her husband again. Do you think that noble man, who begged on his knees from the Romans who had destroyed his city, would accept her back? Would he caress her face and never ask about the men who had rutted on her body when she was in captivity? Could he take to his bed again a wife so thoroughly defiled?"

"I don't know," she replied quietly, "but he should. Whatever might happen to her wouldn't be her fault." She looked him in the eye, her gaze gentle and ruthlessly earnest. "Just as if you had not rescued me from the Lords of Chaos, what might have happened to me that night would not be my fault. If I had been able to escape them afterwards, I would have. And I would *not* have taken my own life."

His heart stilled at the mere thought of her hurting herself.

He was a fool. Of course this debate harkened back to her recent capture. To her near rape. What must she have thought when she'd been kidnapped? When she'd been hooded and dragged before the Lords of Chaos and made to kneel in front of a sacrificial stone?

She must have been out of her mind with terror.

And yet she'd controlled her fear. *More*, despite her firsthand near experience, she now passionately argued that a woman ravaged and raped should never give up hope. Should fight to stay alive despite all odds.

He was amazed by her perception.

Awed by her bravery.

He turned his hand over and gripped her fingers. "Your pardon." It wasn't naïveté that had driven her argument. It was something far nobler. "I would never blame you, my duchess, if you were thus abused, and I would never wish for you to take your own life."

He lifted her hand and pressed his mouth to her palm, and as he did so he had a sharp, visceral memory: He'd kissed her before the fever had overtaken him. Her lips had been soft and yielding to the invasion of his tongue. She'd tasted of tea.

He wanted to taste her again. To lick across her prim little lips, make her open her mouth and moan.

But that was folly. He could not let himself slip, even a little bit. She was pure and he was not. He had to make sure his stigma never touched her.

He let her hand fall from his lips, looking down so that she might not see the lust in his eyes.

"Thank you," she whispered.

She started to say more, but at that moment Nicoletta entered the room. The maidservant held a dish of steaming soup and a cloth over her arm. Behind her was Ubertino with a jug of hot water.

The manservant beamed at the sight of him. "I think you will want to sit, Your Grace."

Raphael nodded as the Corsican helped him to sit up.

Nicoletta and his duchess discreetly retired to the dressing room.

Raphael unbuttoned his banyan, noting that it was stiff with blood at his shoulder. He wrinkled his nose in disgust at the mess.

He glanced at the dressing room door, making sure it was closed before he spoke. "How has my duchess fared?"

Ubertino brought the chamber pot to the side of the bed. "Her Grace has spent most of her time nursing you."

And sneaking into rooms where she didn't belong. "She hasn't ventured outside of the abbey?"

Raphael sighed as he relieved himself. He shook his prick and drew the banyan closed.

"No, Your Grace." Ubertino covered the pot and stowed it away behind the screen.

The door to the dressing room opened.

His duchess cleared her throat pointedly from the threshold. "If you spend your strength chatting with Ubertino, you'll not stay awake long enough for Nicoletta and me to wash you."

She proposed to put her hands on him herself? The mere thought had his belly tightening.

He turned to her, scowling. "I don't need to be bathed like a bloody babe."

He couldn't afford the temptation.

"Actually you do." She crossed to the bed and handed him the bowl of Nicoletta's savory beef soup. She smiled sweetly. "You haven't washed since the night I shot you. You've been lying in a bed with dried blood on your banyan and the bedclothes. You stink."

He narrowed his eyes and took a bite of the soup. He *could* have argued with her further, simply to impress upon her that it was *he* who was in charge, but he was tired. Weak and susceptible to her lure.

And besides. He *did* stink.

He ate half the bowl of soup in silence as Nicoletta bustled about the room, muttering to herself in a scolding voice.

When at last he pushed the bowl aside, Ubertino hurried over to take it.

Raphael caught his wrist. "Have there been any callers? Anyone on the grounds?"

"No, Your Grace," he replied. "The men walk around the outside of the abbey and have seen no stranger."

Raphael nodded and released him. "Good."

Ubertino bowed and left the bedroom.

He lay back against the pillows. This injury was ill timed. He needed to find a way to continue to burrow into the corrupted apple that was the Lords of Chaos. With the spring revelry over, they wouldn't have another meeting for months—not unless the Dionysus called a special meeting. Perhaps if he—

"Sit up a little," his duchess murmured in his ear.

He opened his eyes. She was close, her hands reaching for his arms. Apparently she was serious about this washing.

Foolish, foolish girl.

He pushed himself up, ignoring the stab of pain in his shoulder.

She placed several cloths under his head. "You can lie back."

He raised an eyebrow at her.

She merely pursed her lips and turned to wet a cloth and rub soap into it. When she faced him again, her shoulders were squared, her expression calm and determined.

She started with the left side of his face. The unscarred side.

Naturally.

He watched as her brows furrowed slightly, the warm, damp cloth moving gently over his cheek, across his jaw, up to his forehead.

She blinked and hesitated.

"The scars bother most people," he said softly. Stiffly. "It isn't anything to be ashamed of. Let Nicoletta do the other side. She is used to them."

"No." She inhaled and met his gaze, her blue-gray eyes resolute. "I'm not bothered by your scars."

She lied, he could tell, but somehow that made her insistence on doing this thing all the more...courageous? Yes, courageous. She didn't do it as some sort of penance or as an act of charity—he could tell by the set of her lips, the steadiness of her hand, the smoothness of her brow—but perhaps because it was simply the right thing to do.

He had married a woman far nobler than he.

He nodded and closed his eyes and suffered her touch again.

The cloth was cool now against his skin, stroking from the unmarred side of his forehead to where the scar started over his right eye. She didn't hesitate—he gave her that. The cloth swept over the scar and down his face. She must feel the snaking rope. The unnatural smoothness. Yet she continued, wiping down and over his mouth with its twisted lip to his neck. He heard her wring out the cloth and then it returned, wiping the soap from his face.

He opened his eyes and looked at her.

Her cheeks were pink. Did she sense his heat? The control with which he held back his limbs from seizing her?

She blinked. "We'd better do your hair next."

He raised both eyebrows. He had no notion how she and Nicoletta proposed to do that without setting the bed awash in water.

But they somehow wedged a basin, padded around the edge with a cloth, under his head.

His duchess caught the tip of her tongue between her teeth as she carefully poured warm water over his hair. Her lips were very pink. Plump, with a prominent Cupid's bow on the upper one. Her mouth gleamed softly with moisture.

His eyelids dropped as he considered what he wanted to do with that mouth.

She was working soap into his hair now with strong, slim fingers that massaged his scalp.

He clenched his jaw to keep from groaning.

She scrubbed backward through his hair, stroking, pressing, and he found his eyes closing like a lazy cat's. He'd not been touched like this by another since…

Well. Not for a very long time.

She lifted her hands away, and then the clean water was poured over his head. He felt her slick the excess water from his hair and then pat it with a cloth to dry it.

The basin was removed.

He opened his eyes to see her licking her lips nervously. "I…er… *We* should remove your banyan. At least the upper portion."

If he were a man given to mirth he might've grinned then. She was playing in the flames of his control. Did she not understand her own peril?

But her blush had deepened and she was deliciously out of sorts.

He simply could not resist—either his own urges or her innocent befuddlement.

He spread his arms and said gravely, "Be my guest."

Chapter Six

Now the Rock King lived so deep in the barren stone wasteland that few had ever seen him. In fact there were those who said he did not exist at all. The stonecutter pleaded with Ann not to go, for he feared she would never return. But Ann's love for El was strong and determined. In the end she set off with half a loaf of bread, some cheese, and a pretty pink pebble her mother had thought lucky. . . .

—From *The Rock King*

Iris swallowed. Dyemore's voice was rich and husky, his eyes mocking as he held his arms out in challenge to her.

Well, he was her husband, wasn't he? And an ill man besides. She'd spent the last two days tending to him with the help of Nicoletta. Bathing him was a simple necessity, nothing more.

At least that was what she told herself as she bent her head to the task of unbuttoning his banyan. She couldn't help but notice that however brisk and no-nonsense her mind's voice might be, her fingers trembled.

Perhaps that was only to be expected. It had been some time since she had last undressed a man.

Then, too, her late husband had been in his middle years, while Dyemore was a man in his prime, only a little older than she, if she had to guess, and of course he was quite, erm... that is...

Well.

He was quite *robust*.

Iris tried not to notice how *robust* Dyemore's chest was as she and Nicoletta pulled first his left arm and then, very gingerly, his right from the banyan sleeves. The coverlet was pushed to his waist, covering his lower half discreetly.

By the time they were done taking the upper portion of the banyan off him, his forehead was glazed with sweat and he was panting. She exchanged a worried glance with Nicoletta. Iris didn't want to exhaust him—he'd already been awake for some time, considering he'd been in an insensate fever for the last two days.

But she was concerned that the filthy sheets and the blood crusted on his arm would deter his recovery.

Best to get this over with as quickly as possible so that he might sleep again.

With that in mind she turned to the fresh basin of warm water that Ubertino had brought to the bedroom while she and Nicoletta had undressed the duke. She took a clean cloth and wetted it, then used the soap that the maidservant had supplied. It was the same soap that Iris had bathed with, and the heady scent of oranges filled the air.

She inhaled and turned to the man on the bed, eyeing him and his broad chest. There seemed to be quite a bit of bare skin laid out before her. She swallowed and decided to start with his good arm. She placed the soapy cloth on his shoulder, briskly stroking over smooth skin, trying not to notice how firm the muscles beneath her fingers were.

She kept her gaze strictly on her hand.

Still, it was impossible to ignore the elegant sweep of his collarbone, the bulge of his upper arm, the way a single vein ran along the inside of his forearm…

She realized that her hand had slowed along his arm. The room was very quiet. Nicoletta had left with the dirty water and Ubertino was somewhere, perhaps fetching more clean water. She and the duke were alone in the bedroom with her hands on his body.

She daren't raise her eyes to his.

She took his hand in hers and ran the cloth over the veins that roped the back. His fingers were long and strong, and they dwarfed hers, the nails square and pale. She carefully washed each one and then cupped his hand in hers to wash his palm. It was an intimate act. A…*caring* act. One a mother might perform for a child.

Or a woman might perform for her lover.

Iris caught her breath and straightened to rinse the cloth.

When she turned back her gaze caught his.

He was watching her, his crystal eyes half-lidded, his twisted lips parted.

She felt something inside her clench.

She looked away, hastily wiping his hand and arm free of the soap.

The bedroom door opened and Nicoletta entered, bringing fresh water.

Iris concentrated on her cloth as she soaped it again.

She nudged his arm to wash under it, where his dark hair grew in a swirl.

Where the scent of his masculinity was the strongest.

She shouldn't find this erotic. A *lady* shouldn't find this erotic.

And yet she did.

His lifted arm made the muscles over his ribs stand out in

intriguing ridges, and she wanted—rather badly, in fact—to lean down and inhale his scent.

She bit her lip.

Nicoletta poured the dirty water out of the basin, the sound bringing Iris out of her reverie. She glanced up to see that the maidservant wasn't even looking in her direction.

Evidently Nicoletta hadn't noticed anything amiss.

Thank God for that.

Iris couldn't meet Dyemore's eyes again. Her awareness was too volatile. If she caught his gaze she might combust.

For the first time the thought of sharing a marriage bed with this man seemed not only possible, but also something she could look forward to.

Nicoletta began washing the duke's wounded arm and shoulder as Iris turned to his chest.

She gulped as she looked down.

He had nipples.

Naturally.

All men—and women and children and even babies—had nipples. It was just that normally ladies didn't *see* a gentleman's nipples, and before, when he'd been wounded, she hadn't had the time to stare.

Iris cleared her throat and rubbed in small circles on his upper chest, moving downward, toward one of those nipples. They were just little bits of flesh, weren't they? A deeper color, certainly, than the surrounding skin, and creped, but nothing out of the ordinary.

Her breath caught as she swept over his nipple with the cloth. Did he feel that? Did it feel any different from the rest of his skin? Did he feel as she did when cloth brushed over her bare nipples?

She dared to peek from under her lowered eyelashes.

His nostrils were flared, his eyes mere slits.

And his nipple was erect now, a sharp little peak on his chest.

It might've been from the cold of the water and the air.

Perhaps.

She washed down his side and to his waist where the coverlet lay, watching as he sucked his stomach in at her touch. There was a whorl of black hair about his navel that trailed into the depths of the sheets.

She swallowed.

He was covered, of course, but she knew what lay beneath the sheets—she'd seen him entirely nude at the Lords' revels. She had the image burned into her memory: a proud, thick penis, heavy sac, and curling midnight hair. If the coverlet slipped just a little bit downward, she would see the upper edge of that nest of black hair.

The thought made her press her thighs together under her dress.

Did he know how his body affected her?

Hastily she forced her hand to move—*away* from that dangerous coverlet. She worked her way back up, over that flat plain, over ribs, to his chest. She washed the hair in the center of his chest and then gently circled his right nipple, feeling her insides heat and melt even as the bit of flesh grew hard and dark.

Suddenly her wrist was caught. "Enough."

She straightened guiltily.

His cold eyes met hers. "Are you done?"

She tugged her wrist, but even weakened by illness, his grip was firm. "Your back and the rest of your—"

"I think you are done for now, my duchess," he rasped, his voice deep and hard.

Had he noticed her too-intent attention? Had she offended him? She searched his face, looking for anger or condemnation, but could find neither. In fact it was almost impossible to read any expression there. He didn't reveal anything of himself, she suddenly realized. He kept all his emotions, all his thoughts hidden behind crystal eyes and a scarred face.

He simply watched her.

It was maddening.

She licked her lips. "I think you'd rest better if your bath were finished."

"No doubt." He let her wrist go. "Ubertino can help me with the remainder."

"And Nicoletta?" She glanced at the maidservant. Nicoletta was carefully washing around the bandages. She had her head down, but Iris wasn't so silly as to think that the maidservant wasn't paying sharp attention to her master and mistress.

"I'll send her to you when she is done." He looked at her, his eyes cold as the North Sea. "I have no further need of you. Go."

She fought to keep herself from flinching. That was a dismissal. A *rude* dismissal.

They were *married*. Surely it was permissible for a wife to help with a husband's bath? But one look at his forbidding expression put paid to that idea. He acted as if he could no longer stand her touch.

As if he might be *repelled* by her touch.

Iris raised her chin, trying not to let her hurt show.

She met his eyes and said, "Nicoletta, please go to the dressing room. I would like a word with my husband."

The maidservant froze, her hands hovering over the duke's chest. She looked between Iris and Dyemore.

Dyemore nodded.

Nicoletta dropped her washrag into the bowl of water and hastily left the room.

Iris waited until the dressing room door shut and then turned to the duke. "I'm your *wife*, sir, not your dog. I will not be sent away as if I'd soiled the rug."

Raphael watched Iris. She held herself stiffly—*proudly*.

He admired her daring even as he felt his ire rise at her questioning him. He didn't wish to be tempted by her anymore. Arguing with her would hardly help the matter.

"I beg your pardon if you think I addressed you as if you were a bitch," he said with gritted teeth. "But my protest remains the same. You needn't wash me."

"And if I want to?" The color was rising in her cheeks, and he couldn't help but think how lovely it made her. She looked like a woman in passion.

That was not a productive thought. "This discussion is—"

"Why don't you want me to touch you?" she demanded.

"Why should you wish to?" he asked bluntly. His patience was wearing thin. "My face is disgusting. I saw how you flinched—please do not deny it, madam."

"I'm sorry if I flinched," she whispered. "I don't find your scar disgusting. I don't find *you* disgusting. And since that is the case, it seems to me that I should be able to touch you if it pleases me."

He sneered. "I don't know why touching me would please you."

"Don't you?" Her blush had grown rosy. She was obviously embarrassed by this discussion, but she still held his gaze. "I'd think you'd be happy your wife was interested in your body. After all"—her voice lowered—"we will share a bed as man and wife."

His stomach plummeted and he looked away from her.

"We *will* be sharing a bed, won't we?" she demanded, and her voice was closer.

She'd stepped nearer to him.

He raised his eyes, pinning her with his gaze. She had a hand half-raised, reaching to touch him again.

He caught her hand in his just in time.

"Of course we'll share a bed," he replied, his voice hard. He couldn't afford to show weakness here. "But we will do nothing else."

She blinked, looking confused. "You mean—"

"I mean you'll not be *bothered* by me," he gritted out. Did she have no idea how tenuous his hold on his control was? He held himself in check only by the merest thread. Had he not been weakened by the fever, he might grab her and pull her into his bed, into his *lap*. Lick across her lips and down her tender neck. Pull the fichu from her bodice and trail his teeth across the pretty swells of her breasts. And then...

No.

No.

He'd vowed that he wouldn't corrupt her, and he'd *keep* that vow no matter what it cost him.

"I...I don't understand." She sounded *hurt*, as if he'd insinuated that the problem lay with *her*. "You married me. Why would you do that if I disgust you so much you won't even *bed* me?"

He should correct her. Tell her that she had it completely—*comically*—wrong. But to do so would result in her asking more questions.

Questions he most definitely did not want to answer—now or ever.

Perhaps it was better this way.

"I married you to save your life," he lied, his voice flat, and even as he did so he could feel the ice forming over his skin, chilling him to the bone. Making his heart still. "Nothing else."

She staggered as if he'd run a sword through her belly. "But... but you kissed me. Surely—"

"I was feverish," he drawled. Blackness shrouded his soul. "Not in my right mind."

She stared at him a moment, her blue-gray eyes devastated, and then she drew herself up, proud and strong. "I see. If you'll excuse me, then, I'll go fetch Ubertino."

She turned and swept from the room.

Taking all light with her.

Iris blinked back tears as she left the bedroom, which was, frankly, pure foolishness. She hardly knew Dyemore—had been married to him only a matter of *days*. There was no reason for her to take his rejection of her so much to heart. He'd married her to protect her. She'd married him because she'd had no choice.

It was all quite logical, really, and had nothing whatsoever to do with sexual desire—or lack thereof.

She fought down an impulse to kick a side table as she passed by.

The problem was that she had thought, when she and Dyemore had discussed Polybius, that they might find some common thread of friendship. That this marriage, however hastily and badly begun, might have a chance of becoming palatable.

A marriage she could be content with.

Now she was thrown back into uncertainty. If he didn't desire her—if he was actively *repulsed* by her—what chance that their marriage would be a happy one?

How could she live with a man who had rejected her so curtly?

How could she live without the children she so longed for?

Damn him!

Iris paused before the kitchen door, taking a moment to settle herself. Then she walked into the kitchen and discovered Ubertino picking up two steaming pitchers of water.

"The duke is ready for you to finish his bath and to shave him," she said.

"Yes, Your Grace." Ubertino hurried out of the room.

Two servants remained in the kitchen—Bardo and the one with the bushy eyebrows, whose name she still didn't know. They'd been sitting at the kitchen table, evidently finishing their supper, and had risen when she'd entered.

She nodded at them and turned to go.

"*Donna*," Bardo said.

Of course. He picked up the candelabrum from the table and waved her on. The manservants had taken to trailing her about the castle—obviously on the duke's orders. Evidently he felt she needed bodyguards even inside the abbey.

She shivered at the notion, then shook herself and set her mind firmly on the task of changing the duke's filthy bed linens.

She squared her shoulders and looked at the two men, summoning a smile. She pointed at Bardo and said, "Bardo."

He looked puzzled, but he bowed and said, "*Donna*."

She moved her finger to Bushy Eyebrows and raised her own eyebrows.

"Ah!" the manservant said, smiling broadly. He was homely, but the grin made what would otherwise be an intimidating face quite likable. "Luigi."

She nodded. "Luigi." She looked at both men. "Do you know where the linens are kept?"

Luigi and Bardo exchanged a puzzled glance.

"Linens?" For a moment Iris contemplated how to mime *linen*, and then simply gave up.

She was tired, it had been a long day, and linens were generally the purview of women.

She sighed and turned around in the kitchens. If there was some sort of cupboard used for linens it would probably be in the housekeeper's room. And the housekeeper's room was oftentimes off the kitchen.

Iris started for an arched doorway across from where she'd entered.

She stopped, making both Bardo and Luigi look at her in confusion. It was odd to think of all the people who had been living in this house until Dyemore came. The housekeeper, the butler, the maids, the footmen, and all the many, many servants needed to keep a great house like this one running even when the master was not in residence.

No wonder the abbey seemed dead—it had been gutted of people.

Iris shivered at the thought, remembering a rather vicious nurse telling her the gory story of Bluebeard. She'd been seven and had nightmares for months afterward.

Good Lord! She suddenly realized that like Bluebeard's poor wife, she'd been given the keys to the abbey and had stolen into a locked room. Except these locked rooms contained only dusty furniture and strange paintings, not bodies.

Iris took a breath and shook her head at her own silliness. Dyemore had let the servants go; nothing sinister had happened. He'd *said* he didn't trust the local people. Just because he'd recently rejected her was no reason to look for more ominous actions from him. Ridiculous to stand here making up stories to scare herself without evidence. She wasn't a ninny just out of the schoolroom. She was a grown woman, a widow of eight and twenty years, and far too sensible for this nonsense.

With that thought she continued through the low doorway. Beyond was a short hall and then steps leading down into a wide cellar. She peered down. It looked to be a larder or wine cellar or both. In either case, linens would hardly be kept there—they'd become moldy.

She retraced her steps with the manservants trotting behind and went back out into the hallway that led into the kitchen. Ah! Here were several other doors. She tried the first and found it locked.

Fortunately she'd tied the key ring to her waist with a bit of string. Several minutes later she pushed the door open, just as the sound of Nicoletta's heels came along the corridor. The maidservant joined the little party.

Iris looked inside.

The room contained several cupboards, chests, and shelves, and they held what was probably everything that the housekeeper would keep under lock and key. Spices, sugar, medicines, beeswax, nuts and dried fruit, the silver, and the good linens.

Iris crossed to the largest cupboard and opened the door, revealing stacks of snowy white linens. She couldn't help an exclamation of satisfaction as she inhaled the scent of cedarwood.

She had started to gather some of the linens when Nicoletta said, "No."

Startled, Iris turned to look at her.

The maidservant shook her head emphatically and went to one of the chests to open it, then rummaged among what looked like older linens. She grunted finally and straightened with two sheets that, while clean, were frayed at the edges.

Iris stared. The sheets Nicoletta held looked as if they had been kept only to be used as rags. But the older woman was moving to the door with her burden. Perhaps she had a use for them other than for the duke's bed?

"No, wait," Iris called.

Nicoletta turned, frowning.

Iris quickly took several of the clean white sheets from the standing cupboard. "We'll need these for the duke's bed."

But Nicoletta shook her head again, holding out the old sheets in her hand. She said something—very vehemently—in Corsican.

Iris couldn't understand what the problem could possibly be, but she was tired. "I'm sorry, but I'm using *these* sheets."

She swept by the maidservant and the men and continued, ignoring Nicoletta's cries behind her.

By the time her procession had reached the upper floors and the duke's bedroom Nicoletta had grown silent, but Iris could practically feel the woman seething behind her.

Iris sighed. She felt sad for the loss of whatever goodwill she'd gained with Nicoletta in the last few days, but she couldn't let the older woman think she could rule her. *Iris* was the mistress of this house, and if she had to make that point clear, it was best done early in their relationship.

So she didn't bother with any conciliatory smile toward the servants when she paused to knock on the door to the bedroom.

Besides, she was more nervous about her reception from her new husband.

"Come," Dyemore's voice called from within.

Iris entered with Nicoletta as the two manservants bowed and turned away.

Dyemore was out of the bed, sitting in one of the chairs before the fireplace in a clean black banyan. The duke's inky black hair fell to his shoulders, drying with a slight wave.

With his scar and his hair worn loose he looked like a brigand. Well, an ill brigand—his cheeks were still more flushed than usual.

"You've finished with your bath?" Iris asked briskly. She was determined not to let him know how distressed she'd been by his rejection.

Ubertino was busy doing something with the duke's chest of drawers.

Dyemore raised an eyebrow sardonically. "As you see."

Damn him. She cleared her throat and said a bit stiltedly, "Yes, well. I'll just change the sheets, shall I?"

She went to the bed and began stripping the richly embroidered coverlet off with Nicoletta's help. Fortunately, the coverlet hadn't been stained at all. The sheets, however, might never recover.

She frowned as she threw them to the floor.

"I thought..." She glanced quickly at the servants.

"Yes?" he asked from behind her.

"That is..." She inhaled and mentally rolled her eyes at herself. *Ninny! Get on with it.* "Since you're ill I thought it best that I make up the bed in the maid's room so that you could rest comfortably in the bed by—"

"No."

"Yourself..." She trailed away and straightened from tucking a sheet in at the side of the bed.

She turned to look at him.

He was facing her quite calmly, but with an implacable expression on his face. "You are my duchess. You will sleep in this bed with me."

She felt her lips part in confusion. He'd just told her that he couldn't stand her touch. What was he thinking? Cautiously she said, "You're still recovering. I don't want to disturb you."

"Your presence does not disturb my sleep."

"Don't you think we should discuss this?"

He cocked his head. "I was under the impression, madam, that that was what we were doing."

"No." She realized that she'd balled her hands into fists and quickly let them relax. She couldn't let him distress her so. "*You* made a decision and stated it. *That* hardly constitutes a discussion."

"Bickering will not change my mind," he said with breathtaking arrogance. He stood and Ubertino hurried over to help him. "Now, if there is nothing else, I think I shall retire."

Oh, for goodness' sakes! She really ought to tell the man that this was no way to conduct a marriage—and she would've had it not been for the drawn expression on his face.

Tomorrow would be soon enough to inform Dyemore that he was going to be in for something of a shock if he thought she was going to simply roll over and show her belly every time he stated his mind.

Tonight she pressed her lips together and turned to help Nicoletta finish spreading the coverlet.

"Thank you," Dyemore said from very close.

He loomed behind her and she froze a moment before sidling rather awkwardly along the bed to give him room to get in.

She cleared her throat. "I'll just change in the maid's room."

Behind her there was a choking sound.

She turned, puzzled.

He was half on the bed, as if caught somehow in the act of crawling in, his down-bent face obscured by his long hair.

"What—?"

Dyemore gave a whistling wheeze, and suddenly Iris knew something dire was happening.

She ran to his side to place a hand on his shoulder, and looked into his face.

His eyes were white rimmed and his lips were turning blue.

"Dyemore," she said. "*Raphael.*"

He didn't seem to hear her. He just stared fixedly and made that terrible whistling sound. His body felt like stone.

Then Nicoletta was beside her, pulling her away and shouting for Ubertino. The manservant wrapped his arms around his master and bodily lifted the taller man from the bed, half dragging him away, nearly across the room, toward the fireplace.

Somehow that broke the spell.

Dyemore drew a rattling breath and rasped, his face gray, "Get it out. Now. Get it out. *Get it out.*"

"What?" Iris asked, stunned by his rage, the ice in his eyes.

"*Cedarwood.*"

She stared at him. He leaned against the mantel as if he might fall at any moment, and she didn't understand. Cedarwood? What—?

He bared his clenched teeth and with one broad stroke swept everything from the mantel. The gold clock, a vase, two china shepherdesses, and a pot of spills fell to the floor with a crash.

Dyemore glared at her and snarled, "*Now.*"

She jumped at his fury and spun to see Nicoletta already tearing the bed apart. Iris just had time to snatch up the new sheets before Nicoletta took her arm and dragged her from the bedroom, then shut the door behind them.

Panting in the corridor, eyes wide, Iris looked at the maidservant, expecting a smug expression. Nicoletta had tried to warn her not to use these sheets. She'd known something about this.

But instead the Corsican woman merely stared back with sad eyes. She shook her head and then did something entirely unexpected.

Nicoletta leaned forward and patted Iris's cheek gently.

The maidservant shook her head again and, after taking the sheets from Iris, trudged away.

From within the bedroom Iris heard a crash and her husband shouting in Corsican.

For a moment she simply stood there in the dark corridor, her heart stopped, the duke roaring huskily behind her like some beast out of one of her childhood nightmares.

Despair wrapped chilly fingers around her throat.

Then she brought her hand before her face and looked at the ruby ring on her little finger. Delicate. Lovely. Eternal.

She breathed again.

Dyemore was no beast. No Bluebeard. No fairy-tale nightmare.

He was a man—a man in pain.

And she was going to pull herself together and *help* him.

She was already moving toward the stairs.

He hadn't liked the sheets. Something to do with the cedarwood scent had driven him to this crisis. Nicoletta had tried to give her the worn-out sheets—the ones *not* stored in the cedarwood cabinet. Therefore she needed to go down and find *those* sheets and return to her husband.

Because they were married now, and that meant she was tied to this man until death decided to separate them.

No, it was more than that.

Dyemore had saved her at great risk to himself, and she'd rewarded him by shooting him. He'd nearly died from that wound—continued to be ill from that wound. She owed the man.

And more still.

It didn't matter that he was maddeningly autocratic, unsmiling, and abrupt. Or even that she found him to be the tiniest bit frightening. He'd asked her about her childhood. Engaged her in discussion. Was interested in her opinions on Polybius's *Histories*—and even when he didn't agree with those opinions, he'd respected them.

His cool gray eyes as he'd watched her face during their debate had been intent and focused, as if *she* was the only thing he cared about at that moment. She'd had his entire attention.

And that? That was worth fighting for.

Even if they never had a real marriage.

She rounded the corner to the kitchens, only to almost run into Nicoletta.

The maidservant rocked back on her heels, and Iris saw that she had the worn sheets in her arms—the ones not scented by cedarwood.

Iris held her arms out.

Nicoletta looked at her...and then smiled and gave her the unscented sheets.

"Thank you, Nicoletta."

The maid was already turning away, back to the kitchens.

Iris retraced her steps until she was once again at the bedroom door. She raised her hand to tap, then thought better of it and simply pushed the door open.

She halted when she saw the duke. His pose was eerily familiar, though she couldn't quite place in what way.

Dyemore was still by the fireplace, sitting on the floor, his back against one of the chairs. One knee was drawn up, his elbow resting on it, his hand propping up his head, his hair draped over his down-bent face. He should've looked weak, a fallen man. Yet even in extremis he reminded her of nothing so much as an ancient hero, battling overwhelming odds. He'd been knocked to his knees, but he would struggle upright again soon, pick up his shield and sword, and march back into the conflict.

She frowned at her own fanciful thought. How terrible it would be if the duke was always at war, never resting.

She shook her head and glanced at the debris of Dyemore's wrath, scattered on the floor.

Ubertino was across the room with a glass of wine in his hand. The manservant frowned at her entrance.

Iris hurried to him. "Come. Help me to make the bed again."

She held out the sheets, and though he looked dubious he set down the glass of wine and did as she indicated.

When the bed was remade she took the wineglass and approached Dyemore. "Your Grace, the bed is ready and I have a glass of wine here."

She waited, but there was no answer.

It wasn't to be as easy as that, then.

She retraced her steps to place the wine by the bed and then knelt by his side. "Dyemore."

His raven hair obscured his features, and his broad shoulders, clad in black silk, slumped as if he bore a great weight. At that moment he looked so much like Hades, forever alone and exiled, it made her heart ache.

Hesitantly she touched his shoulder.

He started, then stilled.

She swallowed and whispered, "Raphael."

"You came back." His voice was hoarse—from the shouting?

"Yes." She bit her lip. "Come to bed."

"I cannot," he said so low she had to bend closer to hear. She saw that his eyes were squeezed shut. "Cedarwood. The smell of it. I cannot."

"No," she said. "I'm sorry, I did not know before, but now I do."

"Is it gone?" he husked.

"Yes."

One gray eye opened, staring at her warily. She felt as if she were looking at a wild thing—some animal much more powerful than she, deciding whether to trust her or to devour her.

He must have made a decision, one way or the other, for he placed a heavy hand on her shoulder and stood. His face was gray, highlighting the livid scar, and she wondered what had happened to make him so wounded—both on his face and on his soul.

She rose as well, keeping her shoulder under his arm, wrapping her smaller arms around his waist to steady him. "Come. It's only a little way to the bed, Your Grace."

"I prefer that you call me Raphael." When she was this close, pressed against his side, his voice seemed to resonate through her.

She glanced at him, startled, but he had his head up, his eyes straight ahead. "Then I will, if that is what you wish."

She waited for a sarcastic retort, but he merely shot her a sideways glance before climbing into the bed. He hesitated for a fraction of a second as he was laying his head on the pillow. Had she not been watching—had she not seen the breakdown only minutes before—she would have thought nothing of it.

Then it was over and he lay still. "Will you come to bed with me?"

She caught her breath, glancing quickly at him, but his

eyes were closed now. Had this been any other circumstance she might think that an invitation....

Since it so obviously *wasn't* an invitation, but was instead a very straightforward and simple question, she should stop waffling and answer the man. "Yes. I'll just...erm...ready myself in the other room."

She let herself into the maid's room, closing the door behind her. Iris blew out a breath, feeling like a fool. The fact was, she'd spent the previous night in the chair, and the first night when she'd slept with him in the bed, they'd both been near dead to the world.

Tonight felt very different.

But after his bad turn earlier she didn't want to argue the matter.

Her lips twisted as she reminded herself—*firmly*—that he'd made quite plain that he wouldn't touch her. There was nothing to be nervous about—nothing to be *frightened* about. Even if *she* still had some lingering attraction from the sponge bath, she thought bitterly, *he* wouldn't be moved to consummate their marriage.

Quickly she took down her hair, brushed it out, and undressed, leaving on her chemise—which had been mended very competently by Nicoletta.

She opened the door to the bedroom and saw that Ubertino had left and only one candle still burned in the room. She tiptoed around the big bed to the side that was apparently hers and got in as gently as she could. The duke—Raphael—didn't move.

Perhaps he was already asleep.

She blew out the candle and settled on her side, very near the edge of the bed, facing away from him.

In the darkness she heard his voice. "Good night, Wife."

Her eyes drooped, her mind spinning away drowsily.

Until her thoughts lit upon the way Raphael had been sitting when she'd first entered the bedroom.

He'd sat in the same pose as the little boy in the old duke's sketchbook.

He lay awake and stared at the fire's embers, keeping the dreams at bay.

Cedarwood.

It clogged his nostrils still, acrid and sharp, making his head ache, seizing the breath from his lungs, tearing sanity from his mind.

Cedarwood.

The linens had always stunk of it, and his father's room had reeked with the scent.

She must think him insane. Or a weakling.

He was, in a way. He'd not finished what he'd set out to do so many years ago. By his own estimation that made him a coward.

Cedarwood.

Once, sitting down at a dinner party, he'd happened to smell it on the clothes of the man next to him. Raphael had staggered out of the room and barely made it into the garden, where he'd vomited into the shrubbery. And left without apology to his host. He hadn't been able to bear returning to that room and that scent.

He could hear his wife's gentle breaths behind him. She'd edged as far away from him as possible in the big bed. Perhaps she feared him. Or was disgusted by him.

He should have let her sleep in the dressing room.

But something proud within him couldn't do that. She was *his* duchess. Even if he was tainted, even if theirs might never be a normal marriage, he wanted her here.

With him.

In the room that had belonged to his mother. The only room in the abbey in which he'd felt safe as a boy.

He turned finally, moving slowly, his shoulder aching. She'd sewn the wound closed, Ubertino had told him, and he wouldn't be surprised if his movements earlier had torn something open. At the moment he didn't care.

He only wanted to rest.

And not to dream.

He lay on his back and turned his head, letting his eyes adjust to the darkness until he could make out her shoulders sloping down to the indent of her waist and then the curve of her hip. He found himself matching his breaths with hers.

Inhaling.

Exhaling.

Keeping the dreams away.

But of course they came anyway.

Chapter Seven

Three nights and three days Ann journeyed through the rocky wastes, clutching the pink pebble for protection. No animal moved, no bird sang, no color broke the endless gray stone. Only the wind whistled endlessly.
And on the morning of the fourth day Ann came upon a tower made of that selfsame gray stone....

—From *The Rock King*

Iris stood on the parapet of Dyemore Abbey the next morning, looking not at the front drive but at what lay behind the abbey. It was a jumble of ancient wings, towers, and ruins. Close to the main building was a wide green that might in summer have a garden—there were certainly steps leading down into a paved area circled by boxwoods. Dark-green shoots were coming up in the grass, and she thought she saw a bit of yellow, but from this height she couldn't tell what flowers they might be. Bracketing the green were two wings of the abbey—she wasn't even sure they were open to habitation. One looked as if it might be a gallery. Farther on was a round building, looking almost medieval. Perhaps in its time the crude tower had been a fortress for the people of the area? In the distance, but still quite visible, were the skeletal arches of the old cathedral, ruined no doubt in some forgotten war.

She'd thought that night when they'd driven away from the Lords of Chaos's revels that they'd been miles away. Now she could see that had they wanted to they could've walked from the old cathedral ruins to Dyemore Abbey.

Iris shivered. How ghastly to realize that evil was so very close to where one slept.

And yet...

She turned, the breeze catching a stray lock of her hair and blowing it against her face. Dyemore Abbey itself wasn't such a bad place. From up here, high on the roof, she could see for *miles*. There was a copse of trees close by to the west, but the rest was rolling hills, turning bright green with spring. It was lovely country—*gorgeous* country. No wonder the Dukes of Dyemore had built here.

Why, then, had the present duke lived most of his life in exile?

Iris turned to make her way back inside the abbey as she pondered the question. Hugh had said there were rumors that Raphael's father had scarred him. She shivered as she remembered the sketch of Raphael as a nude, beautiful boy. Something had happened here—something terrible—but she wasn't sure what.

She wondered why Raphael had stayed away from the abbey—from England—for so many years. What would make a man exile himself from his home?

Except...Raphael didn't seem to look upon the abbey *as* his home. He'd locked up the ducal chambers, he kept to only one bedroom, and as far as she could see, he hadn't made any changes or improvements to the abbey.

As if he was simply using it as an inn.

He seemed to have no fondness at all for the manor he'd presumably grown up in.

And she was beginning to have a terrible inkling of why

Raphael so loathed the estate. Perhaps she ought to be contemplating a different question altogether: what would make Raphael return to the abbey in the first place?

She shook her head and carefully made her way down the worn stone steps that spiraled from the corner of the rooftop to a hidden door on the uppermost floor of the abbey. The walls here were bare and cold, and she shivered as she felt her way in the dark, her fingers trailing on pitted stones. How many other women had passed along here? Had they, too, had trouble understanding their Dyemore husbands?

The thought made her smile a little wryly.

She opened a little door and stepped out into a narrow corridor on the topmost floor of the house—she suspected the servants' quarters lay just on the other side.

Iris picked up her skirts, hastening to the stairwell.

She came out into the hallway of the third floor and began walking toward the main staircase at the front of the house. The abbey seemed eerily empty, and she shivered. There was a lush carpet on the floor and small, exquisite paintings hung on the walls, but even so, there was a sense of loneliness.

Of loss.

On the ground floor she noticed that no one was guarding the front entrance—usually one of the Corsicans sat on a chair beside the door.

Now it was empty.

Iris stopped and glanced quickly around. She was alone in the hall.

And she hadn't been properly outside in *days*.

Quickly she ran to the door. It had an old-fashioned bar, presumably left over from medieval times. She lifted it and was out the door in a minute.

The front steps were deserted and she let out a breath.

On the night that she'd been brought here she'd had the idea that the abbey was closed in by trees. Now she could see that a little green stood on the other side of the gravel drive. Yellow flowers were in bloom here as well—a veritable carpet of them.

She walked across the drive, heading toward the flowers.

Daffodils. They were daffodils, *thousands* of them. Iris knelt in the grass and inhaled the faint perfume. A breeze passed by and all the bright-yellow trumpets nodded as one. How could this be? Had someone patiently planted each bulb?

But no. The daffodils weren't in soldierly rows. They bloomed in drifts and clumps. They must be wild.

She drew in her breath in wonder. How amazing that such beautiful ephemeral things could bloom here in this house of death and decay.

But perhaps she was wrong. Perhaps the abbey wasn't dying.

Perhaps it merely waited, sleeping, for joy and life to return to it.

She bent forward to inhale from a blossom.

"Iris!"

She startled badly at Raphael's shout.

Before she could respond, rough hands grasped her and pulled her to her feet.

She turned and oh, his face was hard and cold, his scar a red brand, and for once she could read the expression on his face.

He was *furious.*

"Have you no sense?" he snarled. "I tell you that you are *in danger* and to stay inside the abbey, and that causes you to go tripping about the countryside?"

She tried to step back. "I merely—"

"*No.*" He yanked her into his chest, his face within inches of hers, his breath hot on her lips. "No explanations, no excuses. I've had enough of your carelessness, madam."

Her eyes widened and for a second she was almost afraid.

Something in Raphael's face twisted and changed. "What you *do* to me—"

He slammed his mouth onto hers, forcing her lips apart and thrusting in his tongue.

She mewled helplessly as he bent her back over his arm. Her senses were filled with the taste of coffee and the scent of cloves and she couldn't *think.*

He lifted his mouth from hers so abruptly she could only stare up at him, dazed.

Then she heard the sound of wheels on gravel.

A carriage jolted down the drive at a fast clip and halted in front of the house.

Raphael swung her to the side and partially behind him, his grip on her arm still firm.

A half-dozen Corsicans stood on the front steps and for a moment Iris felt embarrassed at the idea that they'd seen their master reprimand her and then embrace her so savagely.

Then the carriage door opened and three gentlemen emerged: two who might be brothers, they looked so alike, and a third, slightly shorter man.

There was a stunned moment while she and Raphael stared at them, and they stared back.

Then one of the brothers swept her a low bow before saying, "Lady Jordan. How... *surprising* to find you here."

Iris felt her breath catch in fear even as Raphael went rigid beside her. These men were strangers to her, and yet here, far from London, they knew who she was.

Which could mean only one thing.

They were members of the Lords of Chaos.

Raphael stared at the intruders on his land, only his iron self-control keeping him from herding Iris into the abbey.

He could feel fine trembles shake her hand.

How *dare* these worthless cowards invade his territory?

Frighten his *wife*.

"Oh dear, did we arrive at an inauspicious time?" Hector Leland—the man who had been Raphael's first contact with the Lords of Chaos—mockingly drawled the words. Leland was a short man with unpowdered reddish brown hair clubbed back at his neck.

"Ubertino," Raphael called without taking his eyes from the three men.

The Corsican hurried to his side.

Raphael made sure his voice was clear and loud. "Escort my duchess to her room, please."

Ubertino bowed and extended an arm, indicating to Iris to precede him.

Raphael was taking a chance, of course. She might decide to disobey him at this crucial moment. He had, after all, been berating her when the men arrived.

But it seemed that his wife had at last understood the danger she was in. Without a word she walked into the abbey. Ubertino followed with Valente and Ivo on his heels, and Raphael was glad he had such loyal men.

They would protect her.

He turned to his unwelcome guests.

They looked quite harmless and were all of nondescript countenance. They might be any group of aristocrats gathered at a coffeehouse or salon.

Save for the fact that all three were members of the Lords of Chaos.

Raphael prowled toward them.

Gerald Grant, Viscount Royce, the eldest of the invaders, cleared his throat. "Dyemore. I had no idea you were contemplating marriage. We came to—"

He cut himself off as Raphael kept walking and all three men were forced to back up a step.

Raphael halted and stared at them. "Why are you on my lands?"

"We come on the orders of a mutual friend," Royce said with significance.

The Dionysus had sent them—most probably to find out if Raphael had killed Iris. He should have expected this. It was simply bad luck that Iris had been outside when they arrived. If she hadn't been, Raphael might've been able to stay the news that she was still alive for another couple of days—time enough to fully heal.

But it was no use mourning what might have been. If nothing else, this would be a good opportunity to question these men about the Dionysus.

Having made up his mind, Raphael jerked his head toward the abbey. "Come inside."

Andrew Grant, the younger brother of Lord Royce, swallowed with an audible clicking sound and said carefully, "Most kind, Your Grace."

Raphael turned without comment and walked to the steps of the abbey.

"Luigi," he said to one of the men on the steps, and addressed him in Corsican. "Tell Nicoletta to bring a tray of tea and whatever food she might have to the sitting room."

"Yes, Your Excellency," the man replied, and trotted into the abbey.

"You both come with me," he said to the remaining Corsicans, and as he passed, followed by his guests, his men fell in behind.

He led the procession up the stairs and into the same sitting room in which he'd married Iris. He walked across the room to the fireplace.

"Thank you for inviting us in, Dyemore," Leland said from behind him.

"I don't remember *inviting* you to the abbey, Leland." He turned finally to face the three men. "*Any* of you."

"Naturally we don't mean to intrude, Your Grace," Andrew said. "We are on our way to London. We just stopped to see you. Had we known..."

His voice trailed away as Royce shot him an irritated glance. The brothers might've been twins, they were so alike, both with slightly pointed chins and noses, a faint scattering of freckles across each one's fair complexion giving him a boyish air.

He'd seen what these *boys* did by torchlight. In fact, he'd known both since childhood.

After all, the Grant estate was adjacent to his own.

And of course their father, like his own, had been a member of the Lords of Chaos.

"You might want to heed our mutual *friend*," Royce said with heavy emphasis.

Raphael lifted an eyebrow. "*I* heed no one."

"No?" Leland said. "And yet you wish to join an exclusive company. One with a definite leader."

Raphael met Leland's eyes. He'd never seen the man alone—Leland always trailed one or both of the Grant brothers. Raphael had always assumed the man was a sycophant, yet now he seemed the least fearful of Raphael's presence.

Interesting.

Bardo entered the sitting room and turned to hold the door for Nicoletta, who bustled in with a huge tray of tea and little cakes. She darted Raphael a cautious glance as she set the tea upon a table beside the settee and poured four cups before curtsying and leaving the room.

Andrew piled several cakes on a plate and took a cup of tea.

The other two men ignored the offering.

Raphael threw himself onto a chair. "Tell me why you've disturbed my peace."

"We were sent by the Dionysus himself to see if you'd fulfilled your promise," Royce hissed like a cat splashed with water. "And a good thing, too—you were ordered to *kill* her, yet we find Lady Jordan here and, what's worse, you've gone and *married* her."

Raphael shrugged, picking up a teacup and sipping. He'd never much liked tea, but it was a drink the English were fond of. "I changed my mind."

Andrew laughed. "You changed your mind?" The younger Grant brother took a seat across from Raphael, shaking his head. "He'll kill you, you do know that?"

"Will he?" Raphael cocked his head, feeling the fire, never banked for long, leap within him. "He's certainly welcome to try."

Andrew looked puzzled. "But you gave your word on your *honor*."

"*Honor*." Raphael arched an eyebrow. "In that company? With torches all around, standing with our cocks out, masked and afraid to show our faces." He leaned forward. "How many victims were there that night, hm, Andrew? How many were *children*? Don't talk to me of bloody *honor*."

Andrew's eyes lowered to his lap, where his hands twisted together.

Leland, however, wasn't as cowed. "He made it plain that you were to dispose of Lady Jordan," he murmured. "He considers her a liability to the Lords—especially because she's a friend to the Duke of Kyle."

"More fool he for kidnapping her in the first place, then." Raphael said, lounging back. "But tell me, the Dionysus sent you here himself? You saw him unmasked?"

"He left a note." Andrew looked up, his watery eyes anxious. "You know he never shows his face to anyone."

"He must show it to someone," Raphael murmured. "Someone knows where he came from and who he is."

"No one." Leland shook his head quickly.

Raphael watched him. "Then how does he communicate? How did he know you were still in the neighborhood? Where to leave the note?"

"Does it matter?" Andrew asked. "We were at Grant Hall. Presumably he must've been nearby for the revelry. The note was sealed and left at the door."

Raphael's eyes narrowed. "How are you to report your visit to me?"

"A note in—" Andrew began, but his brother cut him off.

"Why do you need to know? What would you do with the information?" Royce demanded. "You seek to bring down our Dionysus, don't you? You want to take his place."

"If I do?" Raphael asked softly.

Royce took a step toward Raphael, his face twisted with anger, but he hesitated on his retort a beat too long.

Royce feared him.

"This Dionysus is strong," Leland said quickly. "The Lords haven't had such a fine leader since your father was killed last fall. The man who attempted to become the Dionysus immediately after your father was too obsessed with his own fortune."

Raphael sneered at the mention of his father. The prior Duke of Dyemore had been a roué of the worst sort and a man completely without honor. In no way had he been *fine*.

"This new Dionysus has magnificent plans," Leland continued. "Plans that will make us all wealthy and powerful. No one will back you if you try to overthrow him."

"No?" Raphael looked at them intently. "Not even if I pledge to share the power of the Dionysus?"

"What do you mean?" Leland asked.

Raphael shrugged. "When I become the next Dionysus, naturally I'll reward those who helped me to achieve that position—perhaps permanently. Why, after all, should there be *one* leader of the Lords?"

"This is dangerous talk," Andrew murmured uneasily.

"It's ridiculous talk," Royce scoffed. "You have no idea who he is—*what* he is."

"I'm sorry, Dyemore," Andrew whispered. "We cannot back you." He lowered his head when his brother sent him a glare.

Royce turned to Raphael. "You and your new duchess won't have long to live if you continue on this mad course, Dyemore. Quit it and leave well enough alone. Perhaps if you grovel, the Dionysus will forgive you and let you live."

Raphael's brows rose. "I don't grovel."

"Then you're insane and doomed," Royce said, sounding exasperated. "What possessed you to marry Lady Jordan anyway?"

"Why, Royce, don't you believe in fairy tales?" Raphael drawled. "Perhaps I saw the former Lady Jordan at a ball months ago and fell in love with her at once."

Leland snorted, Andrew simply looked at him thoughtfully, and Royce bit off something foul. "Don't mock me,

Dyemore. You're the one who'll soon be dead, not me. You *and* your duchess."

He felt the fire overrun his barriers.

Raphael rose and Royce started back.

"Get out," Raphael whispered.

They scurried from the room like rats.

He strode to the door and up to his bedroom.

He threw open the door, startling Iris, who was sitting by the hearth.

She rose, twisting her hands together. "What is it? What did they want?"

"You," he snapped. "Pack what you need. We leave for London in an hour."

That afternoon the Dionysus smiled behind his mask at the Fox. They sat in a private room in an inn not far from Dyemore Abbey. The Fox had procured a room for the revels and the Dionysus had asked him to stay afterward on a whim.

A decision that, as it turned out, had been most fortuitous.

"My lord," said the Fox. "You know I am at your disposal."

"Are you?" The Dionysus studied him, for the Fox of course wore no mask.

He was a man of medium build, red haired—though his pate was covered now with a white wig—and green eyed. He came from an old family and was handsome enough to have caught himself an heiress wife, though not so handsome that the wife's dowry could satisfy all the debts his father had put the family estate into. The Fox was entirely amoral and entirely in thrall to his own sexual appetites, which were far from what was considered tasteful.

Oh, and he wanted desperately to regain the fortune his father had lost.

It made him biddable.

"You know I am loyal," the Fox said.

"So you have said," the Dionysus replied, tapping his fingers on the arm of the chair he sat in. "But have you ever proved yourself to me? I think not."

"Then set a task for me." The Fox was on his feet now, his green eyes wide, his face filled with fervor. "Tell me what to do and I shall do it so that you will know my loyalty once and for all."

"Very well." The Dionysus inclined his head. "Dyemore has defied me. He gave his word to me and then broke it. He is dishonorable. He is rebellious. He is dangerous. Rid me of this traitor and his wife and you will not only be held to my bosom as my most trusted friend, but I shall also reward you monetarily."

The Fox's eyes lit. More at the mention of money than at talk of being held to his master's bosom, but then the Dionysus was a cynical man. He'd take whatever means motivated his pawns.

"I vow I'll do this for you," the Fox said with satisfying fervor.

"Good," said the Dionysus, and began telling him how he wanted Dyemore—and his wife—killed.

Chapter Eight

The tower was round and squat, made without mortar, the stones simply fitted together. Ann circled it until she found a door, and there she knocked.

The man who answered was tall and lean, gray and craggy, stern and unsmiling. He was, in fact, exactly like the barren rocky wasteland.

Ann looked at the Rock King and raised her chin. "I need you to save my little sister."

The Rock King stared at her, unblinking. "How?"...

—From *The Rock King*

In the late afternoon of that same day Iris watched her husband from across a carriage as it bumped along a country road. He was pale, his lips pressed into a thin line, but held himself sternly upright as if he could overcome the lingering effects of his fever by sheer force of will alone.

And perhaps he could, she thought with a wry smile. This was, after all, the man who had sent three members of the Lords of Chaos fleeing with their tails between their legs. Who had declared open warfare against the Dionysus of the Lords of Chaos—and by extension the Lords themselves—without hesitation or qualm.

Hades was a man other men were wary of—and with good reason, it seemed.

He turned at that moment and his crystal gaze met hers. He arched a brow. "What do you smile at?"

She shrugged. "I was just remembering how swiftly our guests left the abbey."

"I've no doubt they went running straight to report to the Dionysus that you still live." He glared at her. "And that we're married."

"I thought his identity was secret?" That much she'd learned from Hugh.

"It is." For a moment she thought he'd stop there; then he seemed to come to a decision, his eyes intent on her. "Apparently the Dionysus has been communicating via notes with the Grant brothers. They didn't tell me, but I have no doubt that they have a way of sending a message to him in return. He probably knows you're alive right now."

She couldn't help her muscles' sudden tightening, an instinctive reaction like that of a rabbit freezing before a fox.

Then she drew a breath. "That's why you insisted we decamp for London so precipitously, isn't it?"

He nodded. "The sooner London society knows we are married, the sooner you'll be safe." He gazed out the window, tapping his forefinger against his lips as if thinking. "And, too, they were no doubt headed for London, as the Dionysus will be. That's where I'll catch him. That's where I'll *destroy* them." He shook his head. "I'd thought that I'd be given more time before the Dionysus discovered that you were alive so that my wound would entirely heal, but it seems that hope is not to be."

Iris cleared her throat, feeling vaguely guilty that the Grant brothers and Mr. Leland had seen her. "At least in

London you can call upon the Duke of Kyle for help with the Lords of Chaos."

He glanced at her, black brows drawn. "Why would I need Kyle's help?"

She felt her jaw sag. "You *can't* take down the Lords of Chaos alone."

"I can and I will."

Was he that arrogant—or merely mad? Hugh had thought he'd destroyed the Lords of Chaos this last winter, and yet like the many-headed Hydra they'd lived. How could Raphael prevail against such a powerful enemy—especially if he refused help?

He sighed. "I'm truly sorry you were thrown into the midst of this war, but my plans remain the same: I will find the heart of the Lords of Chaos, I'll tear it out, and I'll burn them all to the ground."

"But why must you do it yourself?" She leaned toward him urgently. "And all alone?"

His lips pressed together and he looked out the window. "Because my father was their Dionysus. Because I knew all these years what the Lords of Chaos did and I never moved against them." He looked back at her and his crystal eyes had iced over. "This is *my* battle, my penance for what I let happen."

"But..." Iris shook her head. "Your father's actions aren't your fault."

"Aren't they?" His lips curled in a sneer, but she thought it was aimed at himself. "I could have stopped him. I could have *killed* him and destroyed the Lords of Chaos years ago."

"You would have been hanged for murder if you'd done that," she whispered. "It would've been suicide."

He held her gaze. "A principled man would've done it and damned the cost."

She stared at him, sitting so calmly—so *still*—as he spoke of violence and turmoil. He was dressed all in black like Death himself, his glossy ebony hair left unbound about his shoulders, his cold gray eyes watching her without emotion.

But *were* they entirely without emotion? Or was it a mask like the one he'd worn on the night she'd shot him? Because the thing was, she was at a crossroads. She could let him dictate the terms of this marriage. Could let herself be set gently aside while he went on his destructive way—alone, furious, and suicidal—or... *or* she could try to break through all that ice and pain and find out what lay beneath.

She could try to make this a *real* marriage, with or without sex. Only a tiny percentage of a marriage was spent in the bedroom, after all.

How a husband and wife got along all the time they *weren't* in bed was perhaps, in the end, much more important to their happiness.

Iris bit her lip. "And after?"

His eyes narrowed. "I'm sorry?"

"After you burn the towns and salt the earth of your enemy," she said. "What will you do then?"

"What do you mean?" His brows knit. "I will be done."

"Done with your mission, certainly, but with the rest of your life? I hardly think so. You can't be more than five and thirty—"

"I'm *one* and thirty," he interrupted, his tone as dry as dust.

"Are you?" she said brightly. "I'm eight and twenty. But the *point* is that you have years yet to live."

He cocked his head, watching her a moment, then said, "It doesn't matter what I do afterwards. All that matters is the downfall of the Lords."

He means to die. She knew it suddenly and completely.

He wasn't thinking beyond the defeat of the Lords because he didn't think he would live past the conflict. Why was he doing this? What was driving him to destroy the Lords and himself at the same time?

She was suddenly unaccountably angry. How *dare* he?

"Humor me," she said with a hard little smile. "Imagine a world without the Lords. A world in which we have newly married. What would you do?"

He stared at her for a very long moment, his face expressionless, and she thought he would refuse her request. Would turn aside and lock her out.

As she watched him, with the light from the window on the unmarred side of his face, it occurred to her that had he not been scarred, he would've been the most handsome man she'd ever seen.

Then he opened lips both beautiful and ugly. "I think I would defer to my wife," he murmured. "What would you have me do? What is this fairy-tale life you insist we explore?"

Iris fought the urge to roll her eyes. What an incredibly stubborn man. "Do you like the country or the city?"

He shrugged. "Either."

She grit her teeth. "*Choose.*"

He eyed her a moment. "Very well. The country."

"Good. The first thing a newly wedded couple must decide is if they will spend most of their time together in the country or in the city."

"Is that what you did in your first marriage?" he asked, his voice flat.

She blinked, taken aback, but she should have remembered: he wasn't unsophisticated in the art of verbal dueling. "No. James was an officer in His Majesty's army. The first years of our marriage were spent on the Continent."

"And after that?"

"I lived in his town house in London," she replied, her voice steady.

"Without him?"

She lifted her chin. "Yes."

His eyes were ice gray, but they watched her with his full attention. "Was that his decision or yours?"

"I..." She glanced down at her lap, trying to order her thoughts. "It was a mutual decision, I think, though we never discussed it. The marriage was not... a fond one. He was twenty years my senior." She looked up at him and smiled, though her lips trembled. "My mother was so happy when he proposed. It was considered a very good match for me. James was titled and rich—at least richer than my family."

"I see." His voice was deep. Calm. Certain. "I would much prefer that you live with me. Always."

"As would I." Her smile widened in genuine happiness. Suddenly she felt much more sure of herself. "So." She cleared her throat. "I like the country as well. Perhaps we could refurbish the abbey—bring in new servants from London if you don't want to hire the local people—and then we can live there."

He frowned. "I have other estates. One in Oxfordshire and one in Essex. Both houses are in disrepair, though."

"Indeed?" Iris leaned a little forward in excitement. "Then perhaps we should make a tour of your estates first before deciding on which to live at?" She suddenly thought of something. "That is... Oh, I beg your pardon. I'm assuming your finances allow for the repair of your estate houses?"

Raphael waved that worry aside. "My grandfather was in debt. My mother's dowry settled the Dyemore fortunes. My father just never bothered to have the estates properly repaired. Don't worry. I have ample funds."

"Oh, lovely," Iris murmured. "I *do* enjoy decorating."

"And that is what you'd like to do?" he asked curiously. "Spend your life in the country refurbishing my manors?"

"Oh, we'd do much more than that. Part of the time we'd spend in London, visiting friends." She ignored the fact that he didn't seem to *have* any friends. "I'm very fond of reading and collecting books and I'd like to frequent the booksellers to build a library, with your permission?"

He nodded.

She smiled. "Edinburgh is also known for its booksellers. I'd like to travel there, and perhaps to the Continent, to Paris and Vienna."

He stirred. "It would depend on the state of the conflicts between the governments there."

"Yes, of course." She waved that concern aside. "Once we've repaired and redecorated one of your estates, we can spend most of the year there. I'd like to plan a garden. Build a library. Go on walks and riding. Oh, and"—she glanced at him a little shyly—"I'd like to have a dog if I may. A little lapdog."

"Naturally," he said, staring at her intently. "But I don't understand. If you wish for a dog so dearly, why don't you have one now?"

"I live with my brother, Henry, and my sister-in-law, Harriet. They're both very kind to let me live with them. James's estate was naturally entailed. He left me a small portion, but to have my own establishment would have stretched my funds." She inhaled and smiled ruefully. "Harriet doesn't like animals."

"Ah." His eyelids had half lowered over his gray eyes. "I assure you, you may have as many canines as you wish. An entire pack."

"Thank you." She sighed happily.

He cleared his throat and she looked up.

"I have one other estate," he said softly. "A house on Corsica."

Corsica. Where his servants came from. Where *he* seemed to have come from.

"Will you tell me about it?" she asked.

"It lies high above a bay on the south of the island," he said, "built on white cliffs by my mother's grandfather. He was from Genoa and we have lands there, though I've never seen them. There is white sand on the bay and I swam there as a boy—a young man, really. Rode my horse there as well. The sea is a different color in Corsica, clear and green blue. The sky is wide and sunlit. On my estate we grew chestnuts, and I used to walk among the trees, dipping in and out of the shade and the sunlight."

His words enthralled her. "Why did you leave?"

He looked at her. "To finish it."

She didn't dare ask what "it" was.

"I would like..." He paused. "If it is possible—after it is over—I would like to travel to Corsica again."

For some reason her eyes stung. "I would like that, too."

The carriage was silent a moment as they rumbled along the road.

Then Raphael tilted his head. "And is that it? A decorated country house, dogs, books, and travel? This is all you wish for your life?"

"I'm afraid I'm not a very complicated woman." She half smiled. "I don't need jewels and carriages or parties and scandal. A fire and a dog on my lap while I read and I'm perfectly happy."

He snorted. "I've married a dormouse."

She bit the inside of her cheek. He'd brutally refused her before, but surely now...

She cleared her throat. "I…I'd also like what any other woman wants from her marriage…"

He cocked his head in inquiry.

Oh, for goodness' sake! The man couldn't be so obtuse.

She forced a trembling smile. "Children."

He stiffened, and any hint of the camaraderie they'd found fled. "No."

He'd spoken too sharply to her.

Late that evening Raphael watched his duchess as the carriage drew into a large inn for the night. They'd barely exchanged two words for the rest of the day after he'd cut short their conversation about children. She had done her best to act as if nothing were wrong, but he could see that she'd lost the light that shone in her eyes when she'd discussed decorating his houses and building a library for herself.

He looked away from her pensive face. What had she expected? He'd already made clear his terms. Surely she didn't want to mate with such as he? With the blood that ran in his veins, with the stain that shadowed all that he was? She wasn't aware of the latter, but surely she'd understood what his father was?

What the Dyemores had been for generations?

Better by far to end his filthy line with himself than to continue the corruption any further. To risk what his father had done—

No.

He blinked, shaking his head to push the thought away. For a ghastly moment he imagined he smelled cedarwood, but that was madness.

He set his jaw and realized that she was watching him, her brows drawn together.

No. No, better to end it here.

His duchess opened her lips to speak and he stood and slammed open the carriage door, startling Valente, who had been setting the steps.

Raphael jumped to the ground and turned to hold out his hand to his duchess. "Come. Let us find rooms for the night."

For a moment she sat and eyed him thoughtfully and he wondered if she would disobey him. But then she stood and took his hand and he was relieved. He grasped her fingers and had the insane notion that he'd never let her go.

She stepped down from the carriage, looked around the inn yard, and murmured, "Your men are causing a commotion."

He glanced up as he tucked her hand firmly in the crook of his arm. "Are they?"

His Corsicans were mounted to protect the two carriages—the one he and Iris rode in and another carrying baggage and servants. His men circled their horses in the muddy inn yard as hostlers shouted and ran back and forth, trying to handle all the horses while the Corsicans swore at them.

"You travel like some Ottoman potentate," his duchess said with a hint of disapproval.

He couldn't help it. He bent low over her golden head and whispered into her ear, "No. I travel like a duke."

He heard a snort from her, but chose to disregard it as he led her into the inn. Ubertino had already spoken to the innkeeper, and the man met them in the entryway.

The innkeeper was bewigged and smartly dressed in a brown suit and looked rather like a prosperous merchant. He had a broad smile on his face, and he began a low bow that faltered when Raphael walked into the light.

"Your... Your Grace." The innkeeper swallowed and recovered, although his smile was less enthusiastic and his gaze seemed fixed on the right side of Raphael's face in horrified fascination. "We are honored by your presence. I've made ready our best rooms for you and your duchess. If you'll come this way I'll show you to a private dining room."

"Thank you," Iris replied, and the innkeeper shot her a grateful smile.

The man led them past a common room and into the back of the inn. There he bowed them into a small but comfortable room with a crackling fire and a polished table. They'd hardly sat down before maids started hurrying in with platters of food.

The table was laid, the maids stared at his face and whispered, and then they were gone again.

Leaving him alone with his wife.

Raphael cleared his throat and reached for the bottle of red wine. "Will you have some wine?"

She leaned forward, her expression determined. "Do you mean to sleep with me tonight?"

He looked at her.

She was like a dog that would not leave a bone. She sat across from him in his mother's old yellow dress—the same dress she'd worn ever since he'd risen from his sickbed. He couldn't wait to clothe her in brocades and velvets. To present her with everything she deserved as his duchess.

Now her rose-pink lips were pressed into a line as she awaited his answer, her brows drawn together. She watched him very seriously.

And *dear God*, he wanted to kiss her. To pull her from her chair and taste her sweet mouth again. To make love to her until she gasped and panted.

Instead he poured wine into her glass and said calmly, "I will share your room, certainly."

"And my bed?"

His eyes flicked to hers, so stormy. "If that is what you wish."

Her lips crimped together and she lifted her wineglass to take a sip.

He filled his own glass.

She put hers down. "Do you like women?"

"What?" he growled, impatient.

She took a deep breath. "Do you prefer men?"

"Ah." He understood what she asked now. He watched in amusement as her cheeks pinkened, but she kept her gaze determinedly on his. "No. I prefer women."

"Then please explain to me why you won't bed me," she said.

"I have no wish to continue my line." He clenched his jaw. "To continue my father's blood. You *know* what he was. Do you really want children of his bloodline?"

"But—"

"Have some chicken."

"Raphael—"

"I do not want to discuss this matter."

"I am your *wife*."

"And I am your *husband*." Raphael found himself on his feet, leaning across the table, breathing in his duchess's face. Her lips were parted, her eyes wide. He closed his own eyes. *No*. This was entirely unacceptable. "Your pardon."

He pushed back his chair with a horrible scraping sound. He could not remain in this room with her. This line of discussion had stretched his control thin.

"Where are you going?" she called behind him, sounding anxious.

"For a walk," he muttered. "I need air."

He yanked open the door to the room and found Valente and Ubertino outside. He nodded to them. "Keep guard over her. Don't let her out of your sight."

"Yes, Your Grace," Ubertino answered for them both.

He strode through the inn, past a maidservant who stifled a shriek at the sight of his face, out through a knot of locals in the front room, and into the cool night air, several yards away from the entrance.

God.

Raphael tilted his face up to the heavens. The moon hung high in the sky. They'd driven late into the night because the journey to London was several days and he wanted to get there as swiftly as possible.

He turned, gravel grinding beneath his boot heels as he walked. The stables were beside the inn, and he could hear his men's voices.

Bardo looked up as he entered. "Your Excellency."

Raphael nodded. "You've found enough room for the men?"

"Yes, Your Excellency."

"Good man." Raphael clapped him on the shoulder before moving down the row of horses and Corsicans.

Ubertino had helped him choose his men, and most of the Corsicans had been with him for several years. He knew each by name, and he felt a little calmer now that he was walking among his men. Some were still grooming or watering their horses, but a few had finished and were sitting on barrels with lit pipes.

Raphael made sure to stop and say a few words or give a nod to each man. He paid them generously, but it was important that they see him and know he took care of them as well.

They were guarding her life.

It was an hour later when he finally made his way back to the inn. He looked for her first in the private dining room, but it was empty. She must have already gone up to their chamber.

He mounted the stairs and found Valente and Ubertino sitting on stools outside the room. They stood when they saw him.

He halted. "Is my duchess inside?"

"Yes, Your Grace," Ubertino said. "She retired half an hour ago."

Raphael nodded. "Have you eaten?"

Ubertino grinned. "I sent Ivo to get us some dinner. Bardo said he'll send men to relieve us at midnight."

"Good." He pushed the door open.

The room was dimly lit, only the fire and one candle on a small table providing light, and for a moment he didn't see her.

Alarm raced through his veins.

Then he noticed the mound in the bed.

Softly Raphael shut the door and slid home the bolt. He walked to the side of the bed and looked down at her.

Iris lay there, her eyes closed, her golden hair spread on the pillow, half-turned toward him.

She must've been exhausted to have fallen asleep so swiftly.

The candlelight sent shadows spilling from the tips of her eyelashes, made her brow and cheeks glow, and left the valley between her breasts in darkness. She was so lovely it felt like a hook digging into his heart, tearing a jagged hole.

He turned and went to his traveling trunk, then knelt to open it. Inside, under a layer of folded banyans and pairs of breeches, he found his sketchbook and pencil case. Then he picked up a straight-backed chair and set it down next to the bed.

And began to put on paper what he couldn't say in words.

Iris woke to the sound of a rooster crowing.

She blinked, for a moment confused at the unfamiliar bedroom, until she remembered that they'd stopped at an inn.

At the same moment she felt the weight of an arm slung over her waist, the heat of a body—an obviously *male* body—against her own. Raphael might not want to bed her during the day, but his body betrayed him in sleep: she could feel his erection against her hip.

She inhaled, but before she could even think of what to do he was moving away.

"We should rise," Raphael said, his voice deep with a morning rasp. "Best we resume our journey as soon as possible."

She sat up and turned to see him pulling on his breeches, his broad back bare, the muscles in his shoulders shifting as he worked. Had he slept next to her in only his smalls?

She shivered at the realization and mourned her foolishness in not having woken earlier.

He scooped up a pile of clothes and his boots before finally turning to look at her, his jaw shadowed by morning stubble, his crystal eyes unfathomable. "I'll dress in the next room."

And then he was gone.

Well.

Iris rose and set about her meager toilet with the help of one of the inn's maids, who arrived with hot water, all the while contemplating her husband and his possible reasons for not wanting children. Then she went down into the private dining room and ate a solitary breakfast of eggs, buns, and gammon. The meal was probably quite good, but she couldn't taste it. Instead she sat staring at the ruby ring. She put aside her fork and took off the ring, laying it on the table. It was so small—a thing easily lost. Perhaps she should give it back to Raphael.

Perhaps she should stop tilting at windmills.

No.

She could not give up her dream of children—of a *baby*—without a fight. Previously she'd thought that he was physically repulsed by her, but that kiss he'd given her among the daffodils had put paid to that notion. Raphael might not want to admit it, but he wasn't at all repelled by her. That meant her only problem was simply that he didn't want children.

He said he didn't want to continue his line, but that was ridiculous. His father might've been a disgusting, dissolute roué, but *Raphael* wasn't. As far as she could see there was absolutely no reason he shouldn't father children, if that was his only argument.

Really their marriage would be much more content if Raphael took her as a husband should a wife. Certainly *she* would be much more content.

Now she only had to convince *him* of that fact.

Iris put the ruby ring back on with a decisive twist.

When she went out to the inn yard she was disappointed to find that Raphael had decided to ride with his men. She spent the morning all by herself in a jolting, lurching carriage.

But after they'd stopped at midafternoon for luncheon at an inn, he met her at the carriage.

He bowed as she neared, and held out his hand to help her into the carriage. "I hope you found the luncheon to your liking, ma'am?"

She smiled sweetly as she took his big hand. "I did indeed."

Since she'd dined alone she'd had plenty of time to think.

And *plot*.

As if sensing her thoughts he eyed her smile a trifle cautiously as he handed her up. "I'm glad to hear it."

He stepped inside, knocked on the roof to signal the drivers, and sat across from her.

Iris busied herself settling a lap blanket across her knees as the carriage lurched into motion.

Then she looked up and beamed at her husband. "Have you had many lovers?"

His crystal eyes widened. "I... *What*?"

"Lovers." She gestured airily with one hand. "I'm given to understand that many gentlemen sow their wild oats, as it were, before marriage—or indeed afterwards, though I do hope you shall not, for I do disapprove of infidelity. It leads to deep unhappiness in most cases, I think."

His black brows were knitted, rather as if she were speaking in a foreign language he was trying to decipher. "I don't plan to break my marriage vows."

"*Lovely*," she said. "Neither do I. I'm so glad we're in accord on that subject."

He cocked his head and said in a voice that sounded very like a growl, "Are you *mocking* me?"

"Oh, I would *never*," she said very earnestly. "But you haven't answered my question."

"Which was?"

"Lovers? How many?"

He stared at her for a very long moment. "None."

Oh... this was unexpected. She kept herself from showing surprise only by the strongest of self-control.

She cleared her throat delicately. "You're a virgin?"

"No," he snapped, "but the women I've bedded would not fall into so romantic a category as lovers."

"Ah." Iris could feel heat on her cheeks, but determinedly kept her gaze locked with his. Her *marriage* depended on this conversation, and she wasn't about to be put off by missishness over the subject matter. "And were there many?"

He arched an eyebrow. He looked rather formidable, sitting so motionless across from her, his eyes frosty and his arms folded across his chest.

"B-because." She lurched into speech when it became evident that he wasn't going to answer her. "I wondered if you'd perhaps had a bad experience with an unwanted pregnancy?"

"No." The single word was without inflection. "I made very sure the women would not have my children."

How? She was dying to ask, but didn't quite dare.

A woman with less courage—or perhaps with more sanity—would have given up at this point.

Not she.

"That's quite interesting," she babbled. "I myself have never taken a lover, even when I was widowed, so my experience in such matters is rather limited, as you can understand. But my friend Katherine had a different view on the subject." She inhaled, shoving down the part of her that was terribly scandalized that she was *talking* about this with him. They would never have a normal marriage if she couldn't make herself be brave. "Katherine took many lovers and she used to enjoy telling me about...her escapades to try and shock me."

"And did she?" He was lounging back against the squabs, listening to her with as much polite interest as if she were discoursing on literature or the weather. Good Lord, why hadn't he stopped her yet?

"Sometimes." She raised her chin, suddenly feeling as if he'd challenged her. "When she described a lover's genitals. I'm afraid Katherine could be quite, *quite* crude, you see. She did like to see me blush. She called it a man's *cock*."

His eyes narrowed on the word.

Her voice lowered as if she were imparting secrets. "We would take tea in her sitting room and she would describe her latest lover's cock—what it looked like erect. How his cock felt in her hands. How his cock felt in her mouth." Her voice had become a bit breathless. "I'm afraid I was quite naive. When she first told me about putting a man's cock in one's mouth—of licking the head and playing with the foreskin—I was appalled. I'd never imagined such a thing. But over time I became accustomed to the idea. I even thought..."

She stopped and swallowed, for her throat was suddenly dry.

"You thought what?" His voice was a whisper of dark smoke.

She inhaled, feeling hot. "I thought that someday, when I married again, I might want to do that with my husband. Take his cock between my hands. See what it feels like." Her breath was coming faster, but she met his half-lidded eyes—and then let her gaze drop to the bulge between his legs. She had the idea that it might have grown larger. "I've never done that. Never studied a man so closely. Never touched a man's cock with my lips. Never held him on my tongue."

Her eyes darted back to his face as she waited anxiously for his response.

He closed his eyes and swallowed. His hands had fallen to his lap. "Why are you telling me this?"

"I..." She cleared her throat, beating down the disappointment that threatened to overwhelm her. She had to *try*. "I wanted you to know that I don't have very much in the way of experience in that area. But I would like to. I would like to find out how to please a man. I would like to discover what makes bedsport so enjoyable that Katherine took many lovers. I would like to do that with you." She inhaled and made her voice firm. "I would like to do *everything* with you."

He opened his eyes, but his head was turned. He looked out the window, refusing to meet her gaze. "I cannot do this."

The mortification and disappointment that washed over her at his rejection—his *third* rejection—was near all-encompassing.

Still she kept her head held high. "*Why?*"

"I've *already* told you why I choose not to have an heir. My reasons are—"

"Your reasons are patently ridiculous!" She'd raised her voice, but she couldn't find it within herself to care. "You say you desire women, you *kiss* me twice, you have no struggle in becoming hard—"

He closed his eyes again, and a muscle jumped in his jaw. "Madam. Quit this line of questioning *now*, I beg of you, for if you do not, I shall not be responsible for the consequences."

Iris watched him and saw a man with his temper barely leashed, his jaw hard as a rock, the muscles in his arms and shoulders bunched, his entire aspect so frozen he nearly shook.

He'd told her to stop. And she had—twice before. "I cannot quit my questions—I'm *married* to you. I have no other choice but you if I want to have children—and I *do*—therefore please explain to me *why* you won't bed me. Why you think we shouldn't make a child together."

She had known that he could move quickly. Still it was

a shock when she found herself pressed against the back of her seat, his face inches from hers.

"God's blood, woman, how much control do you think I have?" he whispered, his clove-scented breath brushing her face. "You must think me a saint by the way you harangue me despite my warnings. Listen and listen well: *I am no saint.*"

"But I don't need a saint," she breathed, her voice trembling. "I don't *want* a saint. I want *you.*"

"God forgive me," he snarled, and pulled her mouth to his.

His kiss wasn't gentle. He opened her lips with his tongue, invading her angrily. Passionately. How had she ever thought this man uninterested in bedding her?

His big, hot body pressed her against the seat and he scraped his teeth over her bottom lip.

But just as she felt herself melting, he was gone.

Iris opened her eyes to find him banging on the carriage ceiling, signaling for it to stop. He was out the door before they'd even properly halted.

The carriage started again.

Alone once more, her body cold after his warmth, Iris put a single fingertip to her lip.

It came away stained with blood.

Chapter Nine

"The flinty shades have stolen my sister's heart fire and she is dying," Ann said. "You must wrest it from them."

"What will you give me in return?" asked the Rock King.

Ann's eyes widened. It had not occurred to her that she would have to pay the Rock King for his labors. All she had was the pink pebble.

He raised a brow. "Have you riches?"

"No," she replied....

—From *The Rock King*

Raphael shut the door to the inn bedroom and strode to the stairs that night. He'd ridden the rest of the day after fleeing the carriage. Tomorrow he'd have to start the day on horseback—he saw no other solution. Not if he didn't want to spend a third day arguing with his duchess. He wasn't sure how much longer he could last with her constantly by his side. Constantly *tempting* him to do more than simply *kiss* her.

God. She'd tasted of oranges and honey and he'd felt her shake beneath his hands. He'd wanted to strip her right there in the carriage with his men riding outside.

She was driving him mad. He couldn't look at her anymore without feeling the pull. And yet he could not send her away—everything inside him rebelled at the thought. She had to stay with him so that he could protect her.

So that she could illuminate his darkness just a little.

She must think him a foul, unnatural beast by now.

He made the lower floor and turned toward the back of the inn, slamming his fist into the wooden beam of a doorway as he strode through. *Damn it!* What was he supposed to do when she started talking to him like that? Speaking of *cocks* and her tongue with those pretty pink lips? He'd been hard. He'd wanted her. *And he couldn't have her.*

He found himself in a dark passage that led to the kitchens, where he startled the maids. They stifled shrieks and pointed the way to the stables. He nodded his thanks, ignoring their stares, their whispers.

He had long been inured to the reactions to his face.

At last he stepped out the back door and into the night air, which cooled his temper a little.

He tilted his face to the moon and the stars overhead.

He'd sworn, on all that he believed in, on all that he loved, on his very *soul*, that he'd never become his father. And yet today he'd argued with his duchess. Had threatened her. Had made her go pale.

Was he no better than an animal?

Worse.

Was he no better than his *father*?

Raphael shook his head and made for the stables, a low building enclosing the yard on three sides. He ducked to enter under the ancient, thick wood lintel, inhaling the scent of horses, hay, and manure. Most of his men still tended to their horses, and Bardo called a greeting. Raphael nodded to his men as he walked along the rows of stalls, stopping to caress a glossy equine neck now and again. The stables were lit with flickering lamplight, but as he walked along he came to an unused portion with empty stalls that was dark. He paused and then found another door to the yard.

Here, away from the lights of the inn, the stars lit the sky the brightest, glowing like pearls strewn on black velvet. He threw back his head, gazing, all thought pushed from his mind for the moment.

Almost at peace.

And then he heard a rustle and turned just in time to see the glint of a knife descending.

Iris glanced around the inn room wearily. She wasn't sure she could endure another day of arguments followed by abandonment in that carriage.

She went to the table where a maid had put a hearty supper earlier and sat down. Roast chicken and vegetables swimming in gravy lay before her, but she hadn't any appetite. A glass of red wine was by the plate and she took a sip.

She'd lived three years with her first husband, hardly talking, watching as he walked away whenever the discussion became uncomfortable for him. It had been a miserable marriage. James had been kind and good—and had hardly noticed her at all. She might have been one of his hunting dogs—left to the care of his gamekeeper, taken out whenever he remembered her and felt the urge for a ramble at his small country estate.

Otherwise forgotten.

He'd never loved her, never cherished her, and never spoken to her as an equal. She hardly held out hope for the first two from Raphael, but he'd spoken *with* her, not to her. Surely that was something she could build upon?

Hugh had been the husband of a friend and then a friend in his own right. She'd considered marriage to him because of his motherless boys and because she liked him.

She hadn't thought about her *own* wishes with either man. With James she'd married for her mother. With Hugh she'd thought about marriage for his boys and their dead mother, her best friend.

Now... *now* she wanted something for *herself*. She wanted children. She wanted a husband she could talk to without arguing. She wanted long morning walks and evenings by gentle fires and *companionship*.

And *damn* it, she wanted a physical relationship with Raphael.

Maybe she was being selfish to want all those things. To place her desires above any other's.

Certainly her stance couldn't be called modest or what most people considered feminine and ladylike. And yet... she would stand by her desires and feelings and *needs*. Was she not as deserving as anyone else of happiness? Why should she dutifully push aside her dreams simply because *it was not ladylike*?

Feeling exasperated and restless, she rose from the table. Perhaps she should call for hot water and change for bed. But she really wished to wear something fresh. Raphael hadn't seemed to mind her borrowing his shirts before. She crossed to his trunk and opened it, carefully pushing aside silk banyans, searching for a shirt.

Her fingers touched the edge of something hard.

Puzzled, she drew out a book—a sketchbook—very like the one she'd found in the ducal chambers in Dyemore Abbey.

For a moment she could only stare, her body frozen.

Then she opened it.

A minute later she flung open the door to the room and found Ubertino and Valente outside. "Where is he?"

"Your Grace." Ubertino smiled hesitantly as he rose from his chair. "The duke said we were to guard you."

"Good," she replied, marching past them, "then you can take me to him."

"I do not think he will like this," Ubertino muttered.

She ignored him, continuing down the stairs and forcing the two men to follow her. She felt as if she might *explode* soon. "Where did he go?"

"We don't know. Perhaps we can escort you back to your rooms?"

"No indeed," she said. "He mentioned going out for air. We'll try the inn yard." She paused impatiently. This inn was larger than the one they'd stayed in the night before. The corridor had several doorways. "Which way is it, do you know?"

Ubertino exchanged a glance with Valente and sighed. "This way, Your Grace."

He led her along a narrow passage and into the kitchens, bustling with activity at this time of night.

"Your pardon," a maid gasped as she trotted by, a huge tray laden with full tankards on her shoulder.

Iris stepped aside, momentarily distracted.

She heard a shout from outside.

Her heartbeat sped up.

She picked up her skirts, hurrying to the back door. It was probably only a fight between hostlers, nothing to worry about, nothing to concern her.

Behind her, Ubertino called, "Your Grace!"

She burst out into the cool night air.

The inn yard was large and square, enclosed on three sides by the stables, with the inn on the fourth side. An ancient arched tunnel led to the side of the inn and the road. A few lanterns were hung by the stables and by the door where she stood.

As she watched, a mass tumbled from the deep shadows

at one end of the stables, rolling into a pool of light and spilling apart into two men.

Raphael and a man with a knife.

Raphael uncoiled into a crouch.

Men flooded into the courtyard, fighting with fists and knives.

The masked man attacking Raphael staggered up and immediately leaped at him. But Raphael was already flowing to the side, his left hand flashing out to grab the other man's knife arm. Raphael lunged, wrapping his right arm around his opponent in a vicious hug, knocking his legs out from under him.

They both went down.

Iris couldn't see them in the melee. She darted to the side.

A gun exploded nearby.

She flinched.

Someone jostled her, and she turned to see a man with a kerchief over his mouth.

She opened her mouth to scream—

Valente hit the man hard in the belly, shoving him away.

"Come inside, Your Grace!" Ubertino shouted.

"No!" She pulled her arm from his grasp.

The men had parted, and she could see Raphael on top of his attacker.

He lifted the knife man's hand and smashed it into the ground.

Once.

Twice.

A third time and the knife spun away as the knife man lost his grip.

The attacker arched up, white teeth snapping at Raphael's face, his wig askew, and the fingers of his left hand scrabbling at Raphael's throat.

Raphael jerked his head back. The attacker tried to wriggle from his grasp.

Raphael growled, baring his own teeth in a savage snarl, and slammed his fist into the side of the other man's head.

Iris heard a distinct *crack*, and the masked man lay still.

She stared, horrified. He wasn't...?

Ubertino took her arm and said gently, "Come away now, Your Grace."

The fighting had died down in the yard, and she could see now that the duke's men had prevailed against what looked like nearly a dozen attackers.

She turned on Ubertino angrily. "Why didn't you help him? Why didn't you save your master?"

"My duty is to protect you." Ubertino looked at her gravely. "Had I or Valente left you, the duke would have dismissed us. Had you been hurt, he would have had us whipped."

Iris stared at him, appalled. Then she shook her head and hurried to Raphael.

He still knelt by the man who had attacked him. Raphael held the edge of his palm beneath the man's nose.

"Is he...?" Iris asked.

"Dead." Raphael frowned at her as he rose. "What the hell are you doing out here? Ubertino?"

Her guards had caught up with her.

"They've been with me the entire time," she said hurriedly.

"That doesn't explain why they let you wander out into an attack," Raphael growled, eyeing poor Ubertino and Valente.

"Your Grace—" Ubertino began.

"No excuses," Raphael snapped, looking quite frightening in the lantern light, a smudge of blood on his forehead and a terrible scowl on his face. He seemed to loom over the other men. "If my duchess had been harmed, I would have both of your *heads*. How can you—"

"*Raphael.*" Iris gingerly touched her husband's arm. "He couldn't stop me."

"He bloody well could," Raphael said without taking his eyes from his red-faced men. "If he can't keep you safe, then I'll assign another in his place."

"No, *don't*," Iris exclaimed, and he finally looked at her. She took a breath to steady herself. "This is my fault. I'm not a dog, and I don't respond well to commands. Blame me if you need to blame someone."

He gave her a look. "You should go inside to our rooms. This is distressing."

She narrowed her eyes at him, feeling anger ignite low in her belly. "Yes, it is, but probably not for the reason you think. And I'm not going anywhere."

"As you wish." He turned to the manservants. "Ubertino, take Valente and see who is hurt and if any of our men are missing. Have the men take any live brigands to the corner of the stable yard. Mind their hands and ankles are tied tightly."

Ubertino nodded and hurried to obey Raphael's orders.

Raphael crouched by the man who had attacked him and took off his mask and wig.

The face revealed was of a man in his early thirties with an upturned nose and thin lips, in all ways ordinary save for the fact that his hair was a bright orange.

Iris winced. The man had blood on his temple.

Raphael grunted. "Of course."

She leaned closer. "You know him?"

"Not here," her husband murmured.

He withdrew the dead man's right arm from his coat sleeve and rolled the shirtsleeve up past his forearm.

There on the inner elbow was the tattoo of a dolphin.

The sign of the Lords of Chaos.

"What goes on here?" The shout came from the innkeeper, belatedly peering from his back door.

"My men and I have been assaulted in your yard by brigands." Raphael slowly rose to his full height. "Is this the business you do? Luring rich travelers into your inn and murdering them for their money?"

The innkeeper's face went so white it was nearly green. "N-no, Your Grace, indeed not! I can only apologize for this tragic occurrence. Please. I'll send for a doctor immediately to tend to your men."

"See that you do so at once." Raphael waved aside the man's continued stuttered apologies as he backed into the inn.

Raphael caught Iris's elbow. "Come. I want to see the faces of the other assassins."

He strode to the side of the inn yard where his men had already dumped five dead foes. Iris hurried to keep up. She glanced once at the dead men's faces and then quickly looked away again. But Raphael spent some minutes gazing at each.

When he was finished he straightened and beckoned Ubertino over. "How many hurt?"

"Ivo has a cut to his cheek and Andrea a broken arm. Otherwise it is merely bruises and scrapes. There were many more of us than them."

Raphael nodded. "Good." He gestured to the bodies at his feet. "Have Bardo and Luigi strip the bodies and look for a tattoo of a dolphin. Do the same to the prisoners."

He went to the four attackers who had survived the assault. Again he studied their faces, but finally he shook his head.

He pulled Iris toward the kitchen door of the inn.

"You didn't recognize any of them?" she asked, only slightly out of breath.

"No." Raphael glanced at Valente and gave a small jerk of his chin.

The Corsican inclined his head and stepped back into the yard.

The innkeeper opened the kitchen door and started on finding Raphael right in front of him.

"Y-Your Grace." The innkeeper swallowed. "I've sent for two doctors and ordered that rooms be prepared for your men."

"Excellent," Raphael said. "My duchess is weary and I find myself ready to quit this sordid yard. We'll retire now."

"Of course, Your Grace, of course!" The poor man bowed as he held the door open, his face shining with sweat.

A minute later Raphael led Iris back into their room. The fire had been stoked, and fresh plates of food were waiting for them. Warm water was already steaming in pitchers on washstands beside the bed.

"Would Your Grace care for more refreshments?" the innkeeper asked. "Some sweetmeats for your lady?"

"No," Raphael replied. "That will be all." He turned to both the innkeeper and Ubertino, who had followed them up the stairs to the room. "And no one shall enter this room after this save my men. Is that clear?"

"But... but the maids—"

"No one."

"Y-yes, Your Grace." The innkeeper bowed himself out.

Raphael waited until the door was closed and then looked at Ubertino. "I want two men at the door at all times tonight and two below the window. Two at the front of the inn and two at the back. Two more in the common room. Make sure they are rotated so that no man becomes fatigued and falls asleep. There will be no more attacks. Not with my duchess close by."

Ubertino came to attention, his bright-blue eyes flashing. "No, Your Grace. I will see to it on my honor."

Then he too left.

Raphael began taking off his coat. "Shall I send for a bath for you?"

"No, thank you." Iris frowned at her husband. "You were terrible to the innkeeper. That poor man thinks that you blame *him* for the attack in the yard."

She caught the silver glint of his eye as he glanced at her. "Better that than he accuse me or my men of murder."

"But you and your men were only defending yourselves." She wrapped her arms about her waist, remembering the horrible scene.

"Yes, but I don't wish to have to explain that to some provincial magistrate," he said as he sat to remove his boots. "And besides, I wanted the innkeeper out of the yard in order to give Valente a chance to search the bodies."

"Why did you order him to do that?"

"To see if he could find any information, obviously," her husband replied in what sounded like a very patient tone. "The man who attacked me wasn't a common brigand."

"Well, *that* much I'd gathered when you found the dolphin tattoo on his arm." She sat in a chair across from him, watching as he shrugged out of his waistcoat. He was favoring his right shoulder again. "Who was he?"

"Lawrence Dockery." He glanced up at her. "Judging by his red hair and the placement of his dolphin tattoo, I suspect he was the one wearing the fox mask on the night you were brought before the Lords of Chaos."

She shuddered at the memory. "Do you think the Dionysus sent Mr. Dockery to kill you?"

"Most likely. Although..." His brows drew together, pulling at the scar on the right side of his face.

"What?"

He glanced up at her and shook his head. "It's just that if the Dionysus *did* send Dockery to assassinate me, it was an uncommonly foolish move on his part."

"Why?"

"Because," he said, rising and moving toward a washstand, "I'd already overpowered the Fox easily on the night of the revelry. He wasn't exactly a proficient assassin, even with hired bullies. And, too, there was always the chance that matters would play out exactly as they have—leading to my discovering Dockery's identity. It gives me a way to track the Dionysus—Dockery must have some connection to him."

He gingerly pulled his shirt over his head.

For a moment Iris was entirely distracted by the movement of the muscles across his bare back. The wings of his shoulder blades glided gracefully beneath smooth skin as he lowered his arms, and his spine made a sort of hollow in the small of his back, just where it disappeared into the waistband of his breeches. She found the entire sight unaccountably fascinating and couldn't help but wonder if he intended to continue stripping off his clothes.

So it was a beat or two before she processed what he'd said. "That means you might be able to discover the Dionysus."

"Perhaps." He poured warm water into a basin. "But my visitors yesterday morning told me that the Dionysus communicated with them via letters. None of them actually knew who the man beneath the mask was."

"Oh." Iris slumped in her chair in disappointment.

He glanced over his shoulder at her as if he'd heard all her dismay in that one word. "I'll still question Dockery's friends and acquaintances once we reach London. Perhaps the Dionysus has made a mistake."

"Mm." She stifled a yawn against the back of her hand. It had been a long day filled with travel and too much excitement.

"You are weary," he said in that voice like smoke. "You should prepare yourself for bed."

She looked at him speculatively—that wide, muscled back, the stubborn set of his jaw—and thought of the argument they'd had before in the dining room. Of the words she'd meant to say to him when she'd stormed through the kitchens.

"Actually, I had something important that I wanted to discuss with you first."

He stilled as if he knew what was coming. "What is that?"

She rose and crossed to the bed. A black banyan had been tossed across the end, and she moved it aside to reveal the sketchbook. She picked it up and opened it to the first page.

To a sketch of her.

Sleeping.

For a moment she studied the sketch. It had been done in pencil and the artist was very skilled. The single sharp line that edged her nose, the delicate shading on her bottom lip, the suggestion of light reflected off her forehead.

In the sketch she lay asleep and peaceful—and beautiful. Iris had never thought of herself as beautiful. That word was for the lauded belles of society. The women who walked into ballrooms and made conversations stop.

But in this sketch she was beautiful.

And in the corner were the initials *R.d'C.*

This was how he saw her.

When she looked up at him he was watching her, his crystalline gray eyes wary.

"I found this," she began, "in your trunk. It's yours, isn't it?"

He inclined his head.

She stepped closer to him. "These sketches are very good. Who taught you?"

He swallowed. "My father."

She nodded. "I saw his sketchbook as well."

At that his eyebrows snapped together. "What?"

"When I went into the ducal bedroom. His sketchbook was there." She inhaled. "I didn't like his drawings, but I like yours." She glanced up at him. "Even if they all are of me."

He didn't answer. He stood there like a solid block of ice and said nothing. If he hadn't been watching her, she would've thought he wasn't listening.

His very serenity maddened her.

"This entire book is full of sketches of me," she said again, her voice tight. "Horseback riding, walking, dancing. Laughing and simply smiling. Profiles and full face." She looked down at the book, turning the pages. "You had to have been following me. Following me for *months. Why?*"

He blinked. *Blinked.* "I met you at a ball in which I'd gone to rendezvous with members of the Lords of Chaos. I...was worried for you."

"Worried?" She threw up her hands. "*Worried* doesn't explain page after page of my face in your book."

He turned, putting his back to her. "I found you an interesting subject."

"Don't lie to me!" She went around his back to face him. His nostrils were flared, his mouth pressed into a thin line. He tried to retreat, but she followed. "You made me think that you were indifferent to me. That I was a burden that you never wanted to take to your bed. When all along," she whispered. "All along you had a sketchbook full of pictures of me. A man doesn't do that because of *worry* or an *interesting subject*."

By the time she'd come to the end of her rant she was right up against his bare chest, searching those icy eyes—except they weren't very icy at the moment.

Not at all.

She stretched on tiptoe and pressed the sketchbook to his chest, holding it there with the flat of her palm. "Tell me the truth, Raphael. *Now.* Tonight. No more evasions and lies. What is it you feel for me? Is it affection—or merely indifference?"

He finally moved then, snatching the sketchbook from her hand and tossing it to a chair.

He wrapped one arm around her waist and fisted her hair with the other hand, bending over her until she had to grasp those broad shoulders or fall. "Believe me, Wife, the last thing I feel for you is *indifference*."

Then his mouth was on hers, *devouring* her, his hot tongue demanding that she part her lips and let him into her depths.

Chapter Ten

"Have you strange knowledge?" asked the Rock King.
"No," Ann whispered.
"Have you magic?" mocked the Rock King.
"No." Ann closed her eyes. "All I have is myself."
"Then you will have to do," he said. "Do you promise to be my wife for a year and a day if I bring you your sister's heart fire?"
Ann swallowed, for the Rock King's black eyes were cold and his voice hard. "Yes."...

—From *The Rock King*

Iris tasted of red wine—the red wine she must have drunk at dinner—and all the reasons he shouldn't do this fled his mind. A vital chain broke in his psyche and everything he'd held back, everything he'd restrained with all his might, was suddenly set free. He surged into her mouth, desperate for the feel, for the *taste* of her, his wife, his duchess, his *Iris*. She was soft and sweet and warm and he wanted to devour her. To seize her and hold her and never let her go. The deep unfathomable well of his urges toward her frightened him, and he knew that if she became aware of them, they would frighten her as well.

But that was the thing—she *wasn't* aware of them. She thought she was simply consummating their marriage or some such rot, God help them both.

She gripped his naked arms and the beast within him shuddered and stretched, claws scraping against the ground.

Dear God, he wanted this woman.

But he had to remember—to keep that human part of his mind awake and alive—that he mustn't seed her.

Must never do as his cursed father had done.

He broke from her mouth, feeling the pulse of his cock against his breeches, and trailed his lips across her cheek to her ear. "Come with me, sweet girl."

She blinked up at him, wide blue-gray eyes a little dazed.

He covered her mouth again before she could speak—either to consent or decline—and drew her slowly backward, step by step, toward the bed, until he hit it with the backs of his legs. He broke the kiss, looking down at her, her wet ruby lips parted, her cheeks flushed pink.

She looked edible.

"Raphael," she whispered, his name on her lips like a plea, and something within him broke.

This wasn't what he wanted. This wasn't right. But it was the only thing possible and it would have to suffice because it was all he could do.

And trying to resist was killing him.

He traced a hand up her arm, over her shoulder, to her neck, and from there touched her bound golden hair. "Will you take down your hair for me?"

She gasped—a small, quick inhalation—and nodded.

He watched as she raised her arms, her stormy eyes locked on his, and withdrew the pins from her hair one by one until the heavy mass fell like a curtain around her shoulders. He bent then and gathered the locks in his hands, burying his face in her neck, inhaling her.

His woman.

He felt her tremble against him and then her fingers speared through his hair. "Raphael."

He lifted his head.

Her hands fell away and she began undressing, her head bent down as she unhooked her bodice. He saw that her fingers fumbled and he knew that a better man would turn aside. Would give her privacy to collect herself and disrobe with modesty.

But he wasn't such a man. He wanted *all* of her—her mistakes and her private moments, her shame and her worries—everything she held back from the rest of the world. As he wanted *this*. This moment of fumbling.

This moment of intimacy.

She pulled the bodice from her arms. Untied her skirts and let them pool around her feet before kicking them aside. Glanced up at him and then worked at the laces to her stays.

Her unbound hair fell over her shoulders, nearly to her waist, thick and swaying gently as she moved.

Beautiful.

She was beautiful.

She pulled her loosened stays off over her head and stood in chemise, stockings, and shoes. The tips of her breasts peeked out from beneath the thin cloth.

She began to bend for her shoes, but he stopped her. "No. Let me."

He grasped her by the waist and lifted her to the bed.

Carefully he drew off her slippers, letting them drop to the hardwood floor before running his hand up her left calf. The room was so quiet he could hear each breath she drew. She watched him as he reached under her chemise, into that warm spot behind her knee, tugging at the ribbon of her garter.

Her breath hitched.

He glanced up at her as he found bare skin. Hot, so hot under her skirt. He could almost imagine he smelled her, standing between her bent legs. He pulled the first stocking off and moved to her other foot, smoothing his thumb over her arch, over that high instep, that sweet, delicate ankle. The curve of her calf—one of the loveliest curves in nature—elegant and perfect. Someday he'd like to draw her nude.

The faint, almost inaudible whisper as he pulled the ribbon off raised the hairs on the back of his neck. His nostrils flared and he couldn't wait any longer. He lifted her bodily, moving her farther up on the bed, placing her head and shoulders against the pillows, and then pushed up her chemise, crawling between her spread thighs and settling to enjoy what he'd found.

There. There she was, her pretty, pretty pink cunny, all coral lips and wispy dark-blond curls. He hiked her trembling legs over his arms, ignoring her gasp of shocked surprise. He glanced up once and saw wide, wondering eyes gazing back at him. Her gentlemanly first husband had evidently never done this to her.

More fool he.

Then he bent and feasted.

His nose pressed into her mound, inhaling her woman's scent, his cock grinding hard into the bed, his tongue licking into tart and salt and *her*.

Oh God, *her*.

She squealed at his first touch and tried to squirm away, but he held her fast with his hands on her hips. He almost smiled against her tender flesh, his teeth scraping oh so gently. She might be startled, might be outraged and shocked, but she *liked* it.

Perhaps even loved it—what he was doing to her.

She was moaning now, low in her throat, making little mewling sounds, so erotic and sweet, her hips twitching against his lips, trying to get more. He opened his mouth, covering her, breathing over her. He stiffened his tongue and speared into her as far as he could reach, his jaw aching. She cried out at that and he felt fingers tangling in his hair.

He withdrew his tongue and moved to her clitoris, taking the small bit of flesh gently between his teeth and pulling. She froze, trembling all over, and he could hear her gasping breaths. He opened his mouth and licked her. Softly. Tenderly.

Thoroughly.

And at the same time he shoved two fingers into her, feeling her wet walls contract against his knuckles, smelling the rise of her arousal.

She arched under him, her soft thighs thrashing restlessly, making no sound, but he knew.

He knew.

He curled the fingers inside her and stroked her wet, silky inner walls as he pulled them back.

Then he shoved them again into her, hard and firm, repeating the motion as he suckled her clitoris.

She moaned—loud in the quiet room—and pushed against him, and he felt her tremble and suddenly grow wetter. She shuddered helplessly and he was drunk on her release, his cock a heavy, near-painful throb.

He turned his head and kissed the inside of her soft thigh, listening to her pant.

Then he knelt up, there between her spread legs, and tore open the placket of his breeches and smallclothes. Reaching down, he smeared his fingers in her juices and wrapped his hand around his erection.

He stared at her—her face, open and a little dazed in the aftermath of her orgasm. Her breasts were vulnerable, veiled only by that thin chemise, her legs were spread lewdly, revealing her ravished cunny.

And he stroked himself.

Feeling the build of heat, coiling in his bollocks, the edge of sweet pleasure teasing along his nerves. He spread her wetness along his prick and fisted himself hard, his foreskin rubbing against the rim of his cockhead.

But it wasn't until he saw her open her eyes—those blue-gray eyes, those stormy eyes, those too-knowing eyes—and look at him that he felt his seed boiling up.

He gritted his teeth, throwing his head back, his own eyes slitted but watching her still.

Even as his come exploded out of him and splattered across her ivory thighs.

Iris lay awake and listened to Raphael's deep, even breathing.

He'd made love to her, brought her exquisite pleasure—pleasure she had never felt before—but he hadn't entered her.

He'd spilled his seed on her but not *in* her.

She stared into the dark, thinking, trying hard not to weep.

He'd told her he didn't want children. He'd been most frank on the subject. And yet she realized now that somewhere in a corner of her mind she'd held out hope that when he came to the point, his animal urges might overcome him.

What a fool she.

She inhaled very slowly, careful not to make a sound.

The thing was... Well. The thing was, she *yearned* for children. Desperately. A child at least. A single babe to hold in her arms, to cradle against her breast. She'd be content with just the one, really she would. It was one thing to be married and childless through no one's fault. While married to James she'd resigned herself to childlessness. She was his third wife and he had no children. He'd suffered a riding injury that made it difficult for him to achieve fulfillment in the marital bed sometimes. She'd simply assumed after the third year...

She sighed. She wanted this. She wanted a marriage with Raphael and she wanted his children.

She just didn't how she was going to achieve her dream.

The next morning Iris woke alone in bed—actually, alone in the *room*. Raphael was nowhere to be seen.

She frowned to herself, but was distracted by a maid knocking on the door with fresh hot water. After making a hurried toilet and dressing herself, she opened the door to find both Ubertino and Valente outside on guard.

Ubertino bowed. "Good morning, Your Grace."

Iris nodded. "I'm in search of breakfast."

"Ah, then let us escort you," Ubertino said solicitously.

He led the way while Valente followed, and Iris realized that they intended to guard her.

She sighed silently. Raphael had been worried about attack even before the assassination attempt by Mr. Dockery. She understood the need for protection, but she couldn't help but think that being shadowed by two large men might become tedious after a bit.

She'd hoped to find Raphael in the private dining room, but he was absent.

Iris shook her head and ate alone—a cold meal of ham, cheese, and bread.

When her guards walked with her out to the waiting carriage, she rather expected it to be empty as well.

And she wasn't wrong.

However, she wasn't to travel alone.

Ubertino made an apologetic face. "I will be sitting with you, Your Grace."

"Of course," Iris said, trying to sound gracious. After all, it wasn't the *manservant's* fault that her husband was apparently avoiding her.

She huffed in exasperation as she climbed into the carriage. Was he going to avoid her for the rest of the trip to London? They had at least another day and night before they made the capital. She frowned at the thought. Good Lord, would he take a separate bedchamber from her tonight?

The thought was a melancholy one. She'd *enjoyed* herself last night—and she was under the impression that he had, too. True, she wasn't terribly sophisticated in the matter, but she *had* been married for three years.

Raphael had gone to sleep looking very pleased.

Then why leave her to ride alone today?

She pondered that question off and on for the rest of the day, in between chatting with Ubertino and reading from the books she'd borrowed from the abbey library. Although it was hard to concentrate enough to read when she had no idea what her husband was thinking.

By the time the carriage stopped for the night at an inn, Iris was tapping her fingers on her knee—a nervous habit that her old governess would've rapped her knuckles for. Raphael had even managed to eat with his men during luncheon.

It was with a bit of relief, then, when Ubertino escorted her to her room for the night and she found her husband already there.

Raphael turned around from the fireplace and nodded to Ubertino. "Thank you, you may go."

The Corsican bowed himself out.

Iris raised her eyebrows. "Are you to stay with me tonight?"

"Of course," he said with a small frown, as if he couldn't understand her sharp tone.

She very much felt like rolling her eyes. "I'm afraid it was not obvious to me, since you never spoke to me today."

He grimaced. "Iris—"

A knock at the door interrupted him, and the inn maids tromped in bearing their supper. The maids briskly arranged their meal on a small table before the fire and then curtsied and left.

Raphael looked at her and pulled out one of the chairs at the table. "Please."

She sat down, watching as he took a chair opposite.

There were two plates of roast beef with gravy and potatoes, as well as bread and butter and spiced stewed apples. To the side was a bottle of wine, and Raphael picked it up and poured her a glass.

"Thank you," Iris said, and took a fortifying sip. The wine was atrocious, but that really wasn't important right now. "Do you mean to live apart from me?"

He had picked up his knife and fork and begun to cut his meat, but he paused at her question. "No, of course not."

She pursed her lips, eating a bite of the beef—that at least was quite good. "Then why did you stay away from me today?"

He sawed away at his beef, but then threw down his cutlery with a sigh. "I don't want to argue with you. I stayed away because I can't withstand your temptation, as was most obvious last night."

She inhaled and shoved aside her first impulse: to be hurt. "I thought last night was nice."

He glanced up at her, his eyebrow cocked. "*Nice?*"

She could feel the heat creeping up her cheeks. "Spectacular, actually." She cleared her throat. "I'd really rather do it again—or something else." He stiffened, opening his mouth to object already. She hastened to add, "Not *that*. Not...not anything that would lead to children."

He looked at her, his face expressionless. "And you would be content without *that*?"

"Not exactly. I think I might always want a baby, but since you are so vehemently against it..." She closed her eyes—this was such an intimate conversation! "I want a true marriage." She opened her eyes and said softly, "I want to be with you however you wish. I want that closeness. And I want that joy."

She lifted her chin and met his gaze—even with her cheeks aflame.

Something softened in his face. "I think you deserve much more."

She shook her head. "No. We may not have married in the conventional way—I may not have chosen to wed—but I choose *you* now."

A corner of his lips quirked up. "Then I'm content to take you to bed tonight, madam."

She arched an eyebrow at him pointedly. "*Content?*"

His lips curved even more. "Honored, thrilled, excited." He hid his mouth behind his wineglass. "There. Have I answered to your expectations?" He sipped his wine, but kept his crystal eyes on her over the rim.

She felt a jolt between her legs. He was so... *compelling* when he let the ice melt in his eyes. When he let himself relax into that half smile. She wondered suddenly what Raphael would look like if he ever laughed aloud.

But he still waited for her response. "You answered most excellently, I think."

"Good." He set his wineglass down. "Then let us enjoy this meal. The wine is terrible but the meat is good."

She smiled at him shyly at that. "Corsica is very warm, is it not?"

He swallowed a bite of the beef. "Certainly warmer than England."

"Do they make wine there?"

"Oh yes." He took another sip of his wine and winced. "We make very fine wines because we have knowledge from both the Italians and the French. There is a small grape field on my land, and though we don't harvest much, it is enough to make our own wine."

"Really?" She couldn't conceive of one's own wine—though she supposed it wasn't much different from having a brewery on one's land—something that many aristocrats had. "I should like to taste your wine."

"I'd like you to drink my wine," he said softly. "You could sit under the chestnut trees with wine and bread, a picnic of sorts."

Her brows drew together. "We'd sit together, surely?"

"Of course." He glanced down as he poked the lone potato on his plate. He cleared his throat. "We'd sip the wine and I'd show you the white cliffs overlooking the ocean."

"That sounds lovely," she whispered.

He looked up again, his gaze intent. "Iris..." His voice was a smoky rasp, deep and sinful.

She loved his voice.

She stood and went around the table.

He pushed away from the table, obviously intending to rise, but she placed a hand on his shoulder, halting him.

She sat on his lap and laid her palm on his scarred cheek. "Will you kiss me?"

Something flared in his eyes, and then he leaned down and brushed his mouth against hers. Lightly. Tantalizingly.

Her lips parted and he bit the lower one before taking her mouth with his. He licked into her mouth, his tongue rubbing against hers until she captured it and sucked.

His arms wrapped around her, pulling her close.

She felt sheltered, his broad shoulders shielding her, his hands hot and certain on her back.

She squirmed, feeling a rising excitement. She wanted *more*.

And he'd given her permission.

She broke their kiss and leaned back, plucking at his coat. "Take this off."

Her voice was husky.

"Get in the bed," he said, unsmiling.

She rose and took several steps back, but instead of immediately climbing in the bed, she began to unhook her bodice.

He slowly stood, watching her without blinking, and stripped off his coat.

She shrugged out of her bodice and laid it carefully on the chair.

Her hands moved to the ties on her skirts as he began unbuttoning his waistcoat.

He took off the waistcoat and then stood waiting as she struggled out of her skirts. She deposited them on the chair and glanced at him.

He was taking off his neckcloth.

She unlaced her stays as his strong neck was revealed. He began on his shirt buttons and her breath caught as the sides parted to show curling black hairs.

She shrugged out of her stays.

He pulled his shirt off over his head, and for a moment

she simply stared at that wonderful chest. His wound was healing, she noticed absently. Soon she'd have to take out the stitches.

She mourned that he would have a scar on his otherwise smooth skin.

Then she bent to her slippers.

Out of the corner of her eye she saw him sit and draw off his boots and stockings.

He paused when she lifted her chemise to untie her garters.

She looked up to see that his face had darkened and his gaze was fixed on her thighs.

She rolled off one stocking as his fingers moved to the falls of his breeches.

Her second stocking came off as he slid his breeches down.

He stood in only his smalls, the fabric over his groin tented.

Her breath was coming faster and heat was climbing up her breast.

She bent to grip the hem of her chemise.

He unbuttoned his smallclothes.

She pulled her chemise over her head and stood nude before him.

He kicked off his smalls and she could see the dolphin tattoo on his left hip. He prowled toward her, his cock swinging as he came. It was partially erect.

And she knew what she wanted.

"Lie down," she said, and she couldn't recognize her voice. It sounded slow and languid and low, as if it were warm honey.

She felt the place between her legs heat.

He cocked his head at her, and for a moment she thought

he wouldn't obey her. He seemed a god of the darkness, scarred and black haired and gray eyed. He was tall and lean but with ropes of muscles down his arms and legs. A formidable creature. A creature accustomed to wielding power. Did such as he follow the commands of mortals?

But he humored her, crawling onto the bed and settling himself in the very middle, sprawled against a pillow like an Ottoman potentate.

She walked to the side of the bed and reached up and began taking the pins from her hair. Drawing one out at a time, letting them drop to a china dish on the table beside the bed, each making a small plink in the quiet of the room.

He stared at her breasts and then lower, at the curls between her legs.

She saw him swallow.

Her hair uncoiled down her back in a mass. She shook it out, running her fingers against her scalp to relieve the tension from her hair's having been pulled taut all day.

Then she climbed on the bed.

She crawled right between his spread legs and curled up there, leaning down to examine all that made him male.

His penis jerked as she watched, and she couldn't help a smile. Katherine had described all sorts of cocks to her. Thin ones and fat ones. Cocks with drooping foreskins, cocks that leaned to the left or the right. But even though Iris hadn't the same experience, she still thought that Raphael must have the most beautiful cock. It lay to the side, in that line that separates the hip from the stomach on a man—or at least a *lean* man.

Beside his cock was the dolphin tattoo, no bigger than her thumb. She traced the black ink embedded in his skin and then turned to what interested her more.

His penis was straight but with roping veins outlined over

the shaft. It was widest at the middle, lovely and thick, and led to a reddened head. His foreskin had drawn a little back, letting the tip peep through, wet and shining.

She touched that wet tip with her finger and he jerked again.

Her gaze darted to his face.

He was watching her, his mouth in a thin line, save for where the scar curled it. He looked as if he barely held himself in check.

She smiled, slowly leaning forward, and licked his penis.

He inhaled sharply.

She looked down at her prize and said, "What do you like?"

"Anything," he rasped. "Anything you want to do."

She scowled at him. "But what would *you* like?"

He closed his eyes as if she tested him sorely. "Wrap..." He cleared his voice and started again. "Wrap your hand around my cock."

"Like this?" Oh, he was hard under the skin! She'd had no idea *how* hard a man could be. And at the same time his skin was so soft and hot.

"Now pull up," he said.

She darted a look at him, a little alarmed, his penis pulsing in her hand. "Won't that hurt you?"

His lips twitched. "No."

"But my mouth?" She looked down again and missed the expression on his face when he sighed.

"You can lick if you wish," he said softly. "But you don't have to. It's the sort of thing courtesans do. It isn't considered very ladylike."

That spurred her on.

"Isn't it?" she asked, looking up at him as she bent her head again.

She caught the flare of his nostrils, his lips parting, and then she concentrated on putting him into her mouth.

She licked all around the head, not tiny licks anymore. Broad licks with the flat of her tongue while she tightened her lips around him.

He tasted...hm...Well, he tasted like skin mostly. But the aroma here, near the center of him, was rich. Musky and male, and she felt almost heady with it.

That probably wasn't ladylike, either.

She popped her lips off the head and kissed down the ropy shaft, tonguing him, mouthing him. She wanted to shove her nose right into the black hairs at the base, but she thought that might be too much, so she licked up the other side of him, making him quite wet.

His hips jerked and then stilled as if the movement had been involuntary.

She glanced up and saw that he'd thrown an arm over his eyes.

"Dear God," he muttered. "You're going to kill me."

Which made her giggle.

He looked at her under his arm and groaned, letting his head fall back to the pillow. "Can you...?"

"Hmm?" she hummed a question around the head of his cock. If she was very careful with her teeth she could suckle him.

"Oh God," he moaned. "Just...rub up and down with your hands. Please. God, please. And keep sucking."

He sounded as if he were in duress, and it made her press her thighs together.

She did as he asked, using both hands to squeeze and pull his shaft, all the while tonguing and sucking at the head.

His hips began to move, thrusting gently, shoving his cock in and out of her mouth.

She glanced up and saw his head tilted back, the tendons of his neck drawn taut, and suddenly his hand was in her hair, pulling, trying to make her move away.

But she didn't want to. She had such power now and she was drunk on his taste and scent. She sucked strongly, moving her hands up and down that gorgeous shaft, feeling as he thrust his cock against her tongue.

He groaned as if he were in pain and his hips shuddered.

And she tasted hot, bitter liquid in her mouth.

Semen. His semen.

She swallowed without thinking and then winced, but since it was done she decided not to worry about it. Instead she gently touched his cock. It was reddened and still rather hard.

"Come here." His voice was brimstone and gravel.

She glanced up and saw him watching her, his eyes half-lidded, and something in her gave a leap. It wasn't sensual. It was sort of a thrill of affection for him.

Or possibly more.

She rose and went to the table, trying to be sophisticated and not care that she was nude. There she took a long drink of the not-very-good wine, refreshing the taste in her mouth.

She turned, the glass still at her lips, and his eyes were on her, nearly glowing. He held out his hand.

She swallowed and went to him, climbing into the bed and lying down next to him. Hesitantly she laid her cheek on his shoulder—his *good* shoulder.

But then his fingers were under her chin, tilting her lips up to meet his.

He kissed her openmouthed as if he would devour her.

"Straddle me," he whispered against her lips, and sat up against the headboard.

He pulled her into his lap and trailed kisses down her throat, making her nipples peak with the sensation.

One hand came up and cupped her breast and then he was drawing her nipple into his mouth, sucking strongly.

Oh. Oh, that was lovely.

Her head lolled against her shoulders as he moved to the neglected nipple and suckled it as well.

Both of his wide hands were on her hips now, squeezing gently. Then he lifted her and repositioned her with one leg between his.

With his knee cocked up between her thighs as she straddled him.

He guided her down so that she was pressed against him, his knee right in her softness, her lips spread on him.

Her eyes widened.

"Rock," he said, watching her.

She grasped his thigh and slowly rubbed against him, her breasts trembling.

"Do you like it?" he asked, looking quite sinister.

"Yes." She licked her lips. "Yes, I do."

"You look like you like it," he murmured low. "Your cheeks are rose pink and your lips are red and swollen." He stared down to where she was wantonly rocking against him. "And you're wet. I can feel your slickness on my skin. Are you close?"

She shook her head. "I...I don't know."

"Have you ever pleasured yourself?" he asked.

And she opened her eyes wide in shock. She never...To discuss aloud such things!

His eyes were knowing, as if he'd seen her, lying in her virginal bed long ago, fingering herself.

"Show me," he growled. "Show me what you do."

She swallowed and trailed her right hand down, burrowing her middle finger into where she was hot and wet.

Oh! She couldn't catch her breath. Doing this in front of

him as he eyed her dispassionately. As he *ordered* her to display herself for him. She was on the point, so close, so close, her finger working faster and faster as her scent rose in the air between them.

Her mouth opened wide and her hips stuttered against him, sweet heat flowing through her, infusing her limbs, making her light-headed.

He caught her and drew her against him, pressing kisses into her mouth as he murmured, "So beautiful. So beautiful."

He sat up to pull the covers over them both and then he took her into his arms as he lay back down.

The fire crackled and the few candles still lit guttered and she thought, as her mind began to drift, that perhaps her feeling for her strange, dark husband might be more than just affection.

Chapter Eleven

The Rock King retreated into his tower, and when he came out again, he wore a strange sort of armor. It was entirely black and seemed to be made from a sort of thin rock. The armor lay on his body like jagged slabs, reflecting no light, and clinked like dry bones as he moved.

"You may stay in my tower while I am gone," he said to Ann, and then turned to the north....

—From *The Rock King*

The next night Raphael glanced out the carriage window as they jolted into the outskirts of London.

He cast a glance at Iris. Her face was delicate in profile, lit now and again by lanterns on the shops outside. She'd been quiet but seemingly happy for the ride today, spending some time reading from Polybius.

It baffled him still that the lady sitting across from him, so upright and prim, was the same woman who had taken his cock into her mouth last night.

When he'd woken this morning, her soft limbs entangled with his, he had spent long minutes simply gazing at her in wonder. Her lips were a dark pink and parted softly, and her eyelashes lay against her cheeks like moth wings. She was beautiful and she was determined and he hadn't thought that marriage to her would result in this intimacy. He'd wanted her near, true, for he was a selfish, wicked man, and he didn't particularly like the dark that he lived in. She was to be company—nothing more. But it seemed he'd deceived himself, both about the power of her lure and about his own savage desires.

The last thought made him uneasy.

Had he frightened her? Had his lovemaking over the last two nights been too... carnal? Too crude for her?

He grimaced, looking away from her. He hadn't much experience with gentle ladies, truth be told. Not with a face like his.

Not with a past like his.

When his baser instincts could no longer be put off, he bought his relief.

But if he *had* shocked or repulsed Iris, perhaps that was for the best. She wouldn't be so quick to seek him again, which should make his own resistance easier.

Except that even now he found himself leaning infinitesimally toward her as if his body, having once tasted of her fruit, now not only understood hunger, but could be satiated by her and her alone.

He closed his eyes.

He'd practiced self-denial before and he could do it again. Giving in to this lust was dangerous. Not only because *she* was dangerous to him and to what he knew about himself and about his blood, but because her allure interfered with his mission.

It was as if she'd spellbound him like a fairy-tale hero lulled asleep by some fay creature for a thousand years. He was in danger of forgetting the real world and all he owed it.

He couldn't let that happen. He was in London to find out who Dockery's friends had been. Who had ordered him to assassinate Raphael.

To discover and destroy the Dionysus.

"We've reached London," she murmured, interrupting his thoughts.

"Yes."

She glanced at him worriedly. "You know I must contact Kyle and my brother as soon as I can."

He had a base urge to keep her to himself, but he knew she was right. "Naturally, but I suggest you wait until tomorrow. It's already late tonight."

Her brows knit over those blue-gray eyes. "By now Henry must have had word from Hugh that I was kidnapped. I wouldn't be surprised if all of London knows. I should think it would be best to tell him I'm alive and well as soon as possible."

He had a fleeting wish that they could've stayed at the abbey.

But that was folly—both because he couldn't keep her hidden forever and because he had a duty. "Then write them both letters tonight and I'll escort you to see your brother tomorrow."

"What shall I say to them?" She bit her lip, hesitating. "I think the truth won't do for Henry, at least. If word gets out that I was at an orgy, it will hardly do my reputation good, duchess or not."

"No." Nor would it do to announce his involvement in the Lords of Chaos. If he made the secret society known, it would end his chances of infiltrating them. "Very well, what story do you suggest?"

"I think we cannot avoid the fact that I was kidnapped," she said slowly. "After all, the news of it would be everywhere by now."

He inclined his head.

"But perhaps...you rescued me? Not from the Lords,"

she added hastily. "But from highwaymen. You rescued me and brought me back to the abbey. And then you realized that my reputation would be in tatters and proposed marriage."

"How chivalrous of me," he drawled.

She cocked her head, a smile twitching at her lips. "Well, that's more or less what you actually did. You insisted on marriage to save me. So yes, it was indeed quite chivalrous."

He glanced away from that little smile. It wouldn't do if Iris started having romantic notions about him. He was no fairy-tale prince—far from it.

The carriage was pulling into the square where his family's London town house lay.

"We're here," he said quietly.

Chartres House took up the entire north side of the square, a solid mass of dark-gray stone, intended to impress or intimidate anyone who saw it. He'd spent very little time here as a child, which meant that Chartres House hadn't the same memories as Dyemore Abbey.

That, at least, was a blessing.

The carriage rolled to a stop.

His duchess turned to him. "This is it?"

"Yes," he said. "I'll show you in and then I must go out again."

Her brows snapped together. "Why?"

He stifled his impatience. "I have business to conduct."

The carriage bounced as the footmen jumped down.

"You're not going to investigate the Lords *now*, are you?" She looked almost fearful. "Raphael—"

The door was flung open and Ubertino bowed.

Raphael couldn't help but be grateful for the interruption.

He descended the steps and held out his hand to help Iris from the carriage. "Welcome to Chartres House."

She tilted her head back to survey the massive house before her. "It's...quite large."

"My grandfather wasn't a man who believed in parsimony." He tucked her small hand into the crook of his elbow and led her to the front door.

Standing there was a tall, spare man in an impeccable wig and silver-and-black livery. "Your Grace, welcome back to Chartres House."

"Thank you," Raphael said as he ushered Iris in. He looked down at her, watching her examine the entrance hall. "This is my butler, Murdock." He glanced at the butler. "Murdock, my duchess, your new mistress."

The only surprise the butler showed was in a single blink. "Your Grace." Murdock's bow was so low his nose nearly swept the floor.

When he rose, Iris smiled warmly. "A pleasure to meet you, Murdock."

A reddish tinge crept up the man's craggy cheekbones. His wife could enthrall a badger, Raphael thought a bit sourly.

He cleared his throat. "Is Donna Pieri home?"

Murdock snapped to attention. "My lady is in the Styx sitting room, Your Grace."

"Good."

He felt his duchess's sharp gaze as he led her to the staircase at the back of the hall. Red marble imported from somewhere exotic made up the treads and the heavy sweeping railings. The walls were lined with his unsmiling ancestors—they had a tendency to be dark and draped in an excessive number of jewels.

On the upper level the stairs ended in a long gallery, running the width of the landing. He brought her to tall double doors painted pale gray and opened them.

Inside was a petite woman, her dark hair streaked with

white. A neat little lacy cap covered the top of her head. She sat at the edge of a chair upholstered in gold brocade, her back straight, her shoulders level, her hands held before her as she pulled a thread through an embroidery hoop, peering through small gold spectacles.

His chest warmed at the sight of her.

She glanced up at their entrance, raised an eyebrow, and said with only a hint of an Italian accent, "Ah, Nephew, I am glad to see you alive."

Iris blinked, rather alarmed at the woman's greeting. She'd never thought about Raphael's possessing living relatives, yet here was his aunt.

And apparently she thought it was notable that Raphael was still alive.

Iris turned quickly to look at her husband, but he'd regained his icy reserve. *Damn it.* What exactly had he intended to do at the Lords of Chaos's revel if she'd not been there? Had he planned something that would've gotten him killed?

She knit her brows at that appalling thought and glanced back at the petite elderly woman, sitting in profile.

Donna Pieri was all alone in the enormous sitting room done in shades of black and gold: white-painted walls were divided by black marble pilasters topped with gold Corinthian capitals. The delicate chairs, scattered here and there, were upholstered in gold brocade, and at one end of the room was an elaborate black marble fireplace mantel.

The ceiling was painted. But instead of the usual gods or cherubs cavorting in clouds, this was a scene of the River Styx with a rather muscular Charon ferrying the newly dead into Hades. Iris couldn't quite repress a shiver. The artist had been quite fond of vermilion.

Though she supposed this room fit with her initial impression of Raphael—it was an appropriate setting for Hades.

She brought her gaze back to Raphael and watched as he bent and kissed his aunt's cheek. It was a show of affection all the more astounding from a man who hardly ever displayed emotion.

He straightened. "There's no need for dramatics, Zia. Of course I'm alive."

She peered at him shrewdly. "I truly did not know if you would return alive from your trip north. If my worry is dramatic, then so be it."

Raphael frowned. "Zia."

"We will not talk about your obsession with these Lords now." She waved her hand. "Tell me instead who this lady is."

"This is my wife." He turned to Iris, his crystal eyes glinting in the candlelight. "My dear, may I introduce you to my late mother's elder sister, Donna Paulina Pieri. Aunt, my wife, Iris."

The older woman stood, and as she did so she turned and Iris saw her face in full for the first time. Donna Pieri's upper lip was split on the left side. A harelip.

Iris made sure that her own smile didn't falter as she sank into a curtsy. "*Donna*, I'm so glad to meet you."

"The pleasure is mine," Donna Pieri said in her lovely accent as she rose from her own curtsy. She came only to Iris's chin. Donna Pieri arched a fine eyebrow at her nephew. "I confess myself surprised—both by the suddenness of your marriage and because I never thought to see the day Raphael would wed."

Something passed between them, a communication that Iris was unable to decipher, before Raphael bowed again. "I beg your pardon, but I fear I must leave again. I have to see an old... friend."

Iris's eyes narrowed. He must be going to investigate something about the Lords of Chaos. Perhaps Dockery? She'd hoped that they'd settled the matter when she'd expressed her dismay at his "business" in the carriage.

She should have known better. Raphael *was* obsessed with the Lords. He let nothing stand in the way of his revenge.

"Really, Raphael?" Donna Pieri tutted. "Why, you've just arrived. You haven't even taken off your cloak. Your poor wife must think you a savage. At least stay long enough for supper."

"I'm sorry, but my business cannot wait." Raphael's gaze flickered to Iris's, confirming to her that his meeting had to be about the Lords of Chaos. "If the hour is not too late when I return, I shall join you. If not, I shall see you again in the morn. Ladies, farewell."

And with that he strode out of the room.

Iris fought to keep a pleasant expression on her face.

"*Tch.*" Donna Pieri shook her head as she gathered her embroidery silks into a little box inlaid with mother-of-pearl. She took off her gold spectacles and hooked them onto a fine chain at her waist. "He has terrible manners, my nephew. But then I suppose it is my own fault. After all, I raised him after his mother died. The poor boy was only ten years old."

"I hadn't realized his mother died so young," Iris murmured.

"Oh yes." The older woman looked up at Iris, her tea-brown eyes inquisitive. "My sister was delicate both in health and in mind. But come. You must be tired and famished from your journey. Let us sup and you can tell me how you met my nephew and how you came to be married to him in such a scandalously short time. Would you like to be shown to your rooms first to wash?"

"Yes, my lady, that would be lovely," Iris said with real gratitude. They'd stopped for luncheon, but that had been hours ago. She felt rumpled and not a little grimy.

"Of course." Donna Pieri picked up a small bell on the table by her golden chair and rang it.

A maid appeared at the door almost at once. "My lady?"

"Bessy, please take Her Grace to the ducal chambers." Donna Pieri turned, her brows knit. "I hope that meets your approval? I can have the duchess's rooms aired during dinner."

"Thank you, but I prefer the ducal chamber." Iris smiled and followed Bessy out into the hall.

They climbed the stairs to the third level of the mansion, the maid leading her down a wide hall lined with ornate mirrors and more portraits. At the end was a set of double doors.

The maid opened one and curtsied. "His Grace's rooms, Your Grace."

Iris walked in, gazing about curiously. The bedroom was wide, with several windows that must overlook a back garden, though they were covered now by long dark-gold curtains. A tall four-poster stood in the center of the room, draped in heavy black textured velvet. The walls were paneled in carved dark wood, as was the massive fireplace. Several chairs sat before the hearth, upholstered in red velvet, their arms and legs gilded. Under one window was a beautiful table, the top a deep bloodred marble with cream veins running throughout.

She turned and nearly started. On the wall by the door was another portrait of Raphael's father. In this one he wore a pale blue suit. His hand was raised, gesturing to a scene in the background. It looked like the ruined cathedral at Dyemore Abbey.

Iris shuddered and looked away.

By the bed, on the wall, hung a small framed sketch.

Iris wandered over to peer at it, thinking it might be one of Raphael's drawings. She caught her breath, however, when she looked closer. The sketch was done in red chalk and showed the head of a woman in profile, her features strong and classic, her eyes downcast, her hair merely a few strokes and the hint of a wrap about her head. The small artwork was obviously a preliminary sketch for a painting—and also obviously the work of a master.

It occurred to her suddenly that this was her new home. *She* was the duchess here.

It was an odd thought—that the grandeur was the right and proper setting for *her*.

"There's fresh water on the stand, Your Grace." Bessy's voice came from behind her. Iris turned to see the maid readying a washbasin. "I can act as your lady's maid if it's your wish."

Iris cleared her throat, smiling. "Thank you, that would be lovely." She had a lady's maid, of course—left behind in the carriage when Iris had been kidnapped—but Parks never dressed as grandly as Bessy.

Iris took off the cloak she'd found in Raphael's mother's trunk. Bessy was well trained—she didn't even blink at the state of the new duchess's clothes, but helped her to wash her face and neck and comb out her hair and then gather it into a loose chignon.

"Might I have some writing materials?" Iris asked when she was dressed.

"Certainly, Your Grace." Bessy showed her how a small

table inlaid with multicolored wood unfolded into a desk with paper, quills, ink, and sand.

"Thank you," Iris said. "If you wait a minute, can you take my letters to a footman to be delivered?"

"Yes, Your Grace."

Iris sat and thought a moment before writing short notes to both Henry and Hugh with an identical story of how she came to be married to Dyemore. The story differed from the truth in several key points, but it would have to do for now. Iris was aware that neither man would be content until she could see him herself and explain where she had been for a fortnight.

She folded, sealed, and addressed both notes before rising and handing them to Bessy.

"Shall I show you the small dining room, Your Grace, before I give these to the footmen?" Bessy asked.

"Please."

The small dining room turned out to be on the level below and was not small at all, which made one wonder about the *large* dining room. Donna Pieri sat at one end of a wide, dark wood table with huge squat legs, her back to a roaring fire.

She looked up as Iris entered, and beckoned. "Come, sit by me so that we can converse."

A footman held a chair out for Iris at Donna Pieri's right hand, where a place setting was already laid.

As soon as Iris sat, a footman appeared at her elbow and offered her a tureen of soup.

She inhaled gratefully as she ladled the broth into the bowl in front of her.

"Now then," the older woman said after the soup was served, "how did you meet my nephew, eh?"

Iris carefully swallowed her spoonful of soup before she began the story she and Raphael had worked out between the two of them in the carriage today. "It was quite exciting, actually. I was returning from the wedding of the Duke of Kyle when my carriage was attacked by highwaymen."

"Is this so?" Donna Pieri straightened, looking appalled, and Iris felt terribly guilty for lying to the woman.

Although the truth was far worse.

Iris inhaled, some of the memories of her real kidnapping coming back to her—the shouting of her men, the gunshots, the horrible feeling of helplessness and fear.

She tried a smile, but found it didn't quite work. "They put a hood on me and one took me onto his horse and they all started galloping. Naturally I was quite frightened. I have no notion how long they rode with me, but then...*then* Raphael's carriage came upon us, from the other direction." She took a sip of her wine to steady herself. "He and his men fought the highwaymen off, but I confess to being shaken. Dyemore Abbey was close and Raphael kindly offered us refuge. The rest...Well, I think you can guess. After staying several days with him in his house, recovering, Raphael said it was only right that he discourage any rumors that might arise. He sent for the local vicar and we were married."

She glanced down, biting her lip. The problem was—and she really couldn't help thinking this *wasn't* a fault of personality—she had always been a dreadful liar.

"How very romantic," Donna Pieri said.

Iris made the mistake of looking up.

The little woman next to her was watching her with narrowed eyes.

Iris swallowed. For the life of her she couldn't think how to answer. "Erm..."

"And you say *my* nephew was worried about propriety?" Donna Pieri sipped her wine.

Iris winced. Actually, Raphael *didn't* seem the sort to worry about propriety. "Yes?"

"Hmm."

Iris had never been so grateful for the sudden removal of a soup bowl. A second footman placed a platter of buttered fish fillets on the table.

She cleared her throat as she watched the older woman select a filet. "Raphael told me he grew up on Corsica?"

Donna Pieri merely looked at her, and for a long moment Iris thought she wouldn't respond to the change of subject. Then the older woman's lips twitched as if she found Iris's ploy amusing. "Not grew up there. Not exactly, you understand, for he only came to live on Corsica when he was twelve years of age. Before that we lived in England, at Dyemore Abbey."

Raphael's father had sent his heir away at *twelve*? How very odd. Most aristocrats wanted to have some say in the education of their sons.

"Why—" Iris began, but the older woman shot her a stern glare and continued speaking.

"Corsica is a beautiful island. A paradise. England is so cold and dreary, but when Raphael said he must return I knew it was my duty to come with him." She shuddered delicately. "But now I think we will not be here for very long. My nephew is too obsessed with revenge. It is not at all healthy."

"Revenge?" Iris laid down her knife and spoke delicately. "You are aware of Raphael's plans for... revenge?"

"*Tch!*" Donna Pieri looked scornful. "You know as well, then, about these Lords of Chaos?"

Iris nodded.

The older woman shook her head. "When we received word that Leonard had died, I told Raphael that he must return and claim the dukedom. This was his right, after all. But then we landed in London and he found out almost immediately that the Lords were still using the abbey's cathedral for their revelry. He realized that they were still alive."

"He thought they'd disbanded?"

"Indeed." Donna Pieri took a sip of wine. "And now he thinks he must destroy the Lords—*all* the Lords. That this is his duty." Her lips twisted. "It is nonsense, that. He has suffered enough from the Lords—from his beast of a father. He should forget all this and come with me back to Corsica."

Iris raised her eyebrows. Donna Pieri must know how unlikely *that* was; Raphael had set his course and was determined.

She cleared her throat and decided to change the subject. "You lived in Corsica with Raphael?"

"Yes, of course," Donna Pieri said. "I am after all his closest living relative. In Corsica the ocean is the color of turquoise—a bird's wing—not the dull gray it is here. We have mountains and beaches, skies kissed by the sun. When he was a boy Raphael used to ride horses bareback like a wild savage. He'd disappear into the hills for weeks at a time and I'd despair of him ever returning to our home, ever becoming the aristocrat he was born to be. He was so angry. So very angry." Her voice had dropped to a whisper, as if she spoke to herself—or maybe to her memories.

Iris contemplated that revelation. What had made Raphael so angry as a child? She frowned, feeling a sort of dread as if she didn't want to know the answer.

She took a sip of the wine and asked, "You said you were Raphael's closest living relative?"

Donna Pieri blinked and straightened again, her bearing proud. "I am the daughter of a *conte*. He ruled lands in

Genoa. My estates in Corsica were given to me by my mother. My sister, Maria Anna, was also given land in Corsica. So you see Maria Anna had no need to marry Raphael's father. No need at all. She could have come to Corsica with me and lived there. We would have been very happy." She shook her head, reaching for her wineglass.

"How did your sister meet the Duke of Dyemore?" Iris asked. Genoa seemed a very long way away to hunt for a bride.

"He said he was on his grand tour." The older woman shrugged expressively. "Leonard came and courted my poor sister and she was won over by his elegance and his foreign ways. My family knew nothing of him. Of his reputation. Of why he did not seek a bride amongst his own people. She should have never married him. *Never.* He was truly a monster."

Iris felt her heart beating faster at Donna Pieri's words. At the hatred there. The shame and grief.

She thought about the portrait of the old duke that she'd seen—the handsome, ordinary face—and the sketchbook of naked children.

And that last drawing—the one that resembled Raphael.

She shuddered.

Then Iris asked the question that hadn't left her mind since the first night she'd seen Raphael de Chartres, the Duke of Dyemore: "Who scarred Raphael?"

But the older woman shook her head. "That isn't my story to tell. You must ask Raphael himself."

A half hour later Raphael lifted the brass knocker on the Grant town house and let it fall. He glanced around the darkened neighborhood as he waited for an answer. The Grant brothers lived on a semifashionable street, but in a rather small house in an older style. If they were profiting from their association with the Lords of Chaos, they weren't showing it.

At least not yet.

The door drew open and a butler with watery, bloodshot eyes looked at him. "Yes?"

"The Duke of Dyemore to see Viscount Royce."

The butler straightened on hearing his title. "I'm sorry, Your Grace, but my lord is not in."

"Then Mr. Grant."

"This way."

The butler led him back through a dark corridor and up a narrow, barely lit staircase. On the upper level was a dining room.

Andrew Grant was seated by himself at the long table, eating a dinner of roast beef. The fire was down to embers in the grate and the room was lit only by two candlesticks.

Parsimony or apathy?

Andrew glanced up on their entrance, starting when he saw Raphael. "Dyemore! What are you doing in London already? When we last saw you I had the impression that you were to stay at the abbey for a while."

Raphael shrugged, taking a seat without waiting for an invitation. "I'd always planned to come back. Business concerns."

Andrew took a gulp of his wine. "And your new bride?"

"What of her?"

The other man shook his head, keeping his eyes on the thick slice of beef on his plate as he sawed into it. "I thought with your marriage you might decide to stay longer in the country. As a sort of honeymoon."

Raphael raised an eyebrow, simply watching the other man.

Andrew chewed and swallowed and at last was forced

to meet his eyes when the silence became prolonged. "Yes, well. I should've remembered what a cold bastard you are. Course you weren't always, as I recollect. As a boy you were quite sweet. Your father certainly changed that."

Raphael ignored the sly probe.

"Whom did you see after you called upon me and before you set out for London?" he asked Andrew.

"No one. Would you like some wine?" At Raphael's impatient nod, the other man motioned for a footman, then continued, "We were already on the way to London when we stopped to see you at Dyemore Abbey."

Then how had the Dionysus known to send an assassin after him? But perhaps the murder attempt had nothing to do with his marriage to Iris. Perhaps the Dionysus had had his men watching Raphael all along.

Or perhaps Dockery had acted on his own.

"Why do you ask?" The footman set a wineglass before Raphael, and Andrew filled it.

Raphael looked at him. "I was attacked on the way to London."

Andrew's eyebrows rose as he sawed at his beefsteak. "Highwaymen?"

"Lawrence Dockery and nine hired ruffians."

The other man froze. "*Dockery?*" He glanced at the footmen, abruptly waved them from the room, then waited until the doors closed before turning once again to Raphael. "Dockery the redheaded ne'er-do-well who married a horse-faced heiress?"

"Yes."

"I wouldn't have thought him capable of murder." Andrew shook his head. "What happened?"

Raphael twisted the stem of his wineglass. "We'd stopped for the night at an inn. Dockery and his men attacked in the stable yard. Dockery himself tried to stab me in the back."

"He always was a sneaky thing." Andrew shook his head and sat back. "I take it he was unsuccessful."

Raphael inclined his head.

The other man looked nervous. "And where is he now?"

"Hell," Raphael replied succinctly.

"Damn me," Andrew muttered, the blood draining from his face. "He must've been acting on the Dionysus's orders."

"Obviously."

"We did try to warn you."

Raphael shrugged and took a sip of wine.

Andrew watched him, his eyes wide. "Good Lord, man, aren't you frightened? He can have half a dozen men sent to kill you without lifting a finger."

"The Dionysus is a man like any other," Raphael said. "Which means he has to communicate with his assassins in some way. Could either your brother or Leland have sent a message to the Dionysus after you saw me?"

"I...I don't see how..." Andrew frowned as his voice trailed away. "Of course we did stop for meals and for the night at various inns. It wasn't as if I kept a constant eye on them. We didn't even share a room." He swallowed, staring down at his half-eaten beefsteak. "I've never liked staying in the same room with Gerald. Not since we were boys." He glanced up, his eyes not quite meeting Raphael's gaze. "Well, you know why."

Raphael felt his chest contract as if a hand were squeezing his lungs.

Carefully, slowly he lifted his wineglass again to his lips.

He couldn't taste the wine.

"Perhaps you don't remember," Andrew was saying now, his voice soft, almost a whisper. "You left when you were only a boy. Right after the initiation. But I had to stay with them, my father and brother and the Lords. For *years*. Until... until I grew too old, I suppose." He grabbed for his wineglass and gulped the contents before refilling the glass and shooting a shaky smile at Raphael. "But that's all in the past, isn't it?"

Raphael stared at Andrew, wondering if he looked as broken as that.

He set his glass down. "So either Gerald or Leland could've sent a message to the Dionysus."

"Yes... possibly." Andrew had his brows drawn together, thinking. "It doesn't make sense, though, does it? The Dionysus would then have to contact Dockery and send him after you. It seems terribly unlikely. Even if he traveled by horse, it would've taken him days to catch up, surely." He looked up. "What night were you attacked?"

Raphael frowned. "The second."

Andrew waved a hand. "There, you see? I can't comprehend how it could have been done."

Raphael narrowed his eyes. "Unless one of you is the Dionysus."

The other man's mouth curved in a wobbling smile. "You jest. Gerald isn't the Dionysus and Leland is a follower, not a leader. As for me..." Andrew's face gave an odd twist. "Well, it's ridiculous, isn't it?"

"Is it?" Raphael watched him closely. "Why? The Dionysus must be someone who longs for power. Someone who behind the mask is powerless. You fit that notion rather nicely."

Andrew blinked rapidly. "You're joking."

"Have you ever seen beneath the Dionysus's mask?"

"No, of course not," Andrew answered automatically. "No one has."

Raphael nodded. "And are you with your brother at the revels? Or with Leland? Are you ever separated?"

Andrew looked away, nervously fiddling with his wine-glass. "I don't attend with Gerald. Ever. But yes, I often see Leland. He wears the mole mask. Gerald is the Stag... though I didn't see him at the last revelry..." The other man's brows were drawn together as if he was considering for the first time if his elder brother could really be the Dionysus.

It would take a man with steady nerves, a man cunning and sly, to deceive his own brother.

But then Raphael knew that the Dionysus, whoever he was, was a particularly clever and evil man.

"And you?" Raphael asked.

"What?"

"Your mask. What do you wear?"

"The rat." Andrew glanced down, a corner of his mouth quirking up. "Our father gave Gerald and me our masks, and they reflected his differing opinions of us." He looked up, and his entire face seemed to fall for a moment. "Father never thought I would amount to much, and Gerald has the same opinion."

Raphael felt his jaw tighten as he looked at the other man's broken eyes. The scent of cedarwood seemed to drift in the air, and he was moving before he gave it conscious thought.

His chair screeched against the hardwood floor.

Andrew jerked his head up.

Raphael nodded. "It seems I need to talk to your brother."

"Wait—" Andrew called behind him.

But Raphael was already striding out.

He could no longer stay in that room, hemmed in by the memories of a broken boy.

Chapter Twelve

Seven days and seven nights Ann stayed at the tower. She found within it a pot that always bubbled, full of stew, and a jar that always stayed full of sweet, cool water. In the morning she would walk around the tower, searching the horizon to the north, and finally on the eighth day she saw the Rock King returning....

—From *The Rock King*

Iris sat in the duchess's chambers, which, oddly, appeared to have an Elysian fields theme. The walls were painted with murals of vaguely Grecian people lounging about in meadows strewn with flowers.

Well, it could be worse. She supposed she should be grateful the walls weren't painted with Sisyphus rolling his boulder up a mountain in Tartarus.

She'd had a lovely bath and was wearing a *clean* chemise borrowed from Bessy until she could get her own clothing. After this last fortnight she vowed to never, *ever* take clean clothes for granted again. Her hair was brushed out and falling around her shoulders, a small indulgence.

The wine-red chair she was curled in was large and the cushions soft, and she was having a hard time keeping her eyes open as she stared into the fire, but keep them open she must.

Because she was waiting to talk to her husband.

There were questions she should've asked days ago.

Ah, there it was.

Boot heels in the hall outside. The opening and shutting of the door in the duke's room next to hers. A murmur of voices. Quiet again.

She stood and went to the connecting door and opened it.

Raphael looked up. He was in his shirtsleeves and was just taking off his boots. "Iris. How may I help you?"

His voice was as cold as hoarfrost, his eyes empty as glass. She hadn't seen this Raphael for days, and for a moment she thought about stepping back.

She didn't understand this side of her husband—was he sad or angry or in despair? Or was he simply bored? She couldn't tell, and really it was beginning to alarm her. Wasn't a wife supposed to be her husband's confidant?

Except James had never been that emotionally close to her. He'd made sure to hold her apart from himself.

She didn't want another marriage like that.

That decided the matter. She walked into Raphael's room and closed the door behind her.

She'd expected paintings on the walls or ceiling of his room, but there weren't any. Instead they were painted a dark red, the color of dried blood. Gold was etched along the panels and into the pilasters lining the walls. The ceiling was entirely gold, in swirls and intricate patterns, like something from an Ottoman's palace.

"Iris?" He was still watching her, waiting for her to say something.

Perhaps to explain why she'd invaded his territory.

She walked to a chair in front of the fireplace and sat. "Where did you go tonight?"

The good side of his mouth turned down, giving him an

oddly lopsided appearance. "I went to talk to Lord Royce. He wasn't home, however, so I settled for speaking with Andrew."

He set his boots outside the door and returned without saying anything else.

Iris frowned in irritation. "And?"

He sat, unbuckling the knees of his breeches to reach the tops of his stockings. "And I asked him about Dockery."

He didn't look at her as he threw his stockings aside.

She glanced at his feet. They were big, with long toes. Generally one didn't think of a man's feet as handsome, but his were.

He huffed. "What do you want, Iris?"

Her gaze snapped to his face. "I want to know why you've suddenly grown cold."

He was in profile to her, and she saw the movement of his Adam's apple as he swallowed. He clasped his hands between his knees, bowing his head. "Andrew…I knew Andrew when we were boys."

Her brows knit. How was that…?

Then her eyes widened in sudden realization. "Did your father draw him?"

"What?" He turned to look at her, and now there was an expression on his face: puzzlement. "No, of course n—" He cut off his own speech and twisted his mouth and made a sort of cawing sound.

He was…Oh, dear God, that was a *laugh*. Iris recoiled in horror.

But he wasn't paying attention. "Maybe. Yes. No. I don't know. My father could have indeed sketched Andrew. He was…" He shook his head helplessly and then closed his eyes. "You should go. I'm no fit company tonight."

She inhaled. If she left now she had the feeling that they

would stay the same—he would keep her at arm's length always.

She couldn't let that happen.

Iris folded her hands in her lap, straightened her back, and looked him in the eye. "Who scarred you, Raphael?"

His head jerked back as if she'd slapped him. "No."

She surged to her feet. "*Yes.* How . . . how do you expect us to live together, to make a *life* together, if you won't share what you are with me?"

He was shaking his head as he stood and strode to a chest of drawers. "You don't want to know."

"I do," she said, following him across the room. "*Please.*"

He turned, catching her in his arms, thrusting his face into hers. "Why not simply listen to the gossip? Choose one: A duel because I besmirched a lady's honor. My father cut me because he could not stand the sight of me. The Dyemores are cursed from birth. Are the tales—the *endless* rumors—not enough for your curiosity? Enough to assuage your need to *know*?"

She reached up and pulled his head down to hers. Placed her lips against the top of the scar, where it split his eyebrow, and, kissing, trailed downward, over his eyelid, over the ridge of his cheekbone, over the edge of his permanently curled lip, to the divot in his chin.

"Please," she whispered against his ruined flesh. "*Please.*"

He groaned, deep in his chest, and buried his face in her hair. "Iris."

"Please."

His shoulders tensed, his breathing grew ragged.

His voice sounded like broken obsidian when he spoke. "I did it." He inhaled as if the words were burning his throat. "I scarred myself."

Her heart stopped.

Of all the possibilities, she'd never even *imagined* that one. Dear *God*.

"How..." She had to stop to clear her throat. "How old were you when you did it, Raphael?"

"Twelve."

And then she knew what it was to have one's heart break, for she could feel a sharp ache inside her, a well of grief and shock and horror. "Why?"

He shook his head against her, his face still hidden.

But she'd come too far. This was important. She could feel it.

"*Why*, Raphael?"

He bent and lifted her, one arm under her legs, one under her back.

Iris clutched at his shoulders as he took two steps to the bed and carefully laid her on it. She watched him as he stripped himself of breeches, smalls, stockings, and shoes, until he was naked. Beautiful and strong and without shield. And then he climbed in beside her.

She opened her arms to him and he gathered her close again.

Her cheek was against his warm chest and she could hear his heartbeat. She was still, breathing next to him, wondering if she would have to give up her questions for the night.

Then he spoke.

"My father adored me when I was small. He called me beautiful. I was his prince. Cosseted. Spoiled. Stroked and petted. You know that he was the Dionysus. That he..."

His breathing was uneven again.

Very, very carefully she shifted until she was holding him and stroked his hair.

His head was a heavy weight upon her breast.

He swallowed, his throat clicking. "He liked children,

though I didn't know it at the time. How could I? I was too young, too sheltered to even conceive of such a thing."

She inhaled, suppressing any sound, though she wanted to exclaim.

To perhaps scream.

If he could speak this horror aloud—for *her*, because she had asked it—then she could listen.

"My father didn't touch me in that way until I was twelve," Raphael said, his voice hoarse. "I was to be initiated into the Lords of Chaos. It was to be a great honor."

He gasped as if a hand were tight around his throat.

She closed her eyes, trying to keep her fingers from shaking as she threaded them through his hair.

"First..." He inhaled. "First there was the tattoo. It would hurt, but I was determined not to weep—and I didn't. I was absurdly, *naively* proud. Then he took me to the revelry and there were..." He swallowed again, loud in the silence of the room, and when he spoke again his words were stark. Staccato. "I was confused. They were hurting children. Women. But they gave me wine to drink. My father. And then. My *father*....Brought me. Back to the abbey. To his room." He wrinkled his nose, opening his mouth as if to refrain from inhaling a scent. "Father's room always smelled of cedarwood. He said there was one more step to the initiation."

Iris bit her lips to keep from crying aloud. Oh no. No, no, *no*.

But her silent denials couldn't stop his broken, rasping voice. "He told me. *He* told me. He *said* he loved me. I was his beautiful prince. Then he pushed my face into the pillows—his cedarwood-scented pillows." He breathed heavily. As if he were gasping for air that wasn't there. "And buggered me."

She sobbed—a loud, awful sound—and laid her cheek against his as if to brace him.

As if to give them both strength for his next words.

He turned his face into her breast and said in a rush, "When it was done he rolled off me. He fell asleep. I...I fled. I ran to the kitchens. I was half-mad. All I could think while he was on me was that this must not happen again. He'd said I was beautiful."

"Oh, my darling," she whispered, her heart aching. Her eyes were blinded by her tears now.

He shuddered, his entire body quaking as if a giant hand shook him. "If I could make myself *ugly* then he wouldn't do it again, would he? I found the sharpest carving knife. I held it with both hands. And I put it against my eye. I meant to cut it out."

"Oh *God*," she moaned. How must he have felt—such a little boy in despair and fear, doing that? It was a wonder that he hadn't killed himself.

She traced over his scarred cheek with her fingers. He still had the eye. He hadn't done that, at least.

"I obviously didn't succeed," he said, "but my plan did work. The cook found me in the morning. When my father saw me—saw the great gash I'd carved in my face—he was disgusted. Aunt Lina took me to Corsica the next week. I never came back."

"I'm so glad she was there to take you away," she whispered, choking on her sobs.

He was still, breathing against her, and then he raised his head and looked at her.

His eyes were perfectly dry and his face was blank.

For some reason that made her sob anew. She knew now that the ice covered a wound so awful, so terrible that it would never completely heal.

He sat up and found a handkerchief on the table beside the bed.

"Hush," he said, sounding weary, drying her cheeks. "It happened a long, long time ago."

She closed her eyes. But it *hadn't*, not really. This injury was always with him. He lived with it, *aching*, every day.

She shook her head, gently touching the corner of his mouth where the scar distorted the line of his lips. "I'm so sorry, Raphael. Oh, my darling, I'm so terribly sorry."

He stroked her face with his thumbs. "You understand now why I cannot continue my line."

Her eyes widened in shock. "What?"

"I carry *his* blood in my veins." His nostrils flared as if he scented something rank. "Filthy, deviant, disgusting blood. Are you not repulsed by my story? Surely you can see why my line needs to be stopped with me?"

"I...I'm repulsed by what your father did to you," she said slowly, carefully. She mustn't say the wrong thing now. "And I'm repulsed by your *father*. But Raphael, you're not your father."

"It doesn't matter." He shook his head. "Better my family die with me than another monster be born. Another like my father."

She looked into his eyes, still crystal gray, still icy with resolve, but all she could see now was the pain he hid so well. "Raphael..."

"No." He placed his palm against her cheek. "My mind is made up. I have known my fate since I was twelve, and I will not be persuaded from my decision. Can you not leave your argument, just for tonight? Let us not be at odds tonight."

She shouldn't give in to him. Shouldn't let his weary words win her over.

But he'd let her see the black ichor that lay at the heart

of his past. He'd bared it for her, though she knew he was ashamed and hated it.

She nodded—what else could she do? He had confided in her, despite the pain it must have caused him. This was not the time to rail against him, to give him more pain by arguing.

This was a time to comfort.

"Very well," she whispered. "I, too, have no wish to be at odds."

She knelt up in the bed and leaned to look at him. His wide brow, his Roman nose, those too-cold eyes, and the lips that in another life—another, better world—would still have been beautiful.

This man was her husband. He was intense and intelligent, arrogant and vulnerable, dark and strange.

The more she found out about him, the more she thought that perhaps she might fall in love with him, Raphael de Chartres, the Duke of Dyemore.

What was more, he was *hers*.

Hers to take care of.

And in that she would not fail.

She bent and brushed her lips over the divot in his chin. Kissing again his scar, now that she knew how it had been made. The memory, the mental anguish it represented was terrible. But this scar? It was just skin. A bit more knotted than his other skin, true, but skin nonetheless.

She told him so with her lips, her tongue, her breath. Licking the permanent sneer of his upper lip, tracing the path of the knife up his cheek, pausing to kiss his closed eye and give thanks, and ending at his bisected eyebrow.

She cupped his dear, mysterious face and drew back to examine him.

And when he opened his frozen eyes and looked at her,

she quirked a smile and kissed him. She closed her eyes and brushed her lips against his, feeling the silk of his mouth, the slight bump where the scar cut across the corner. She licked his bottom lip, teasing with her tongue, feeling as he tensed beneath her.

He hugged her and slowly rolled her over so that now she was below and he above as he took control of the kiss.

He caught her bottom lip between his teeth for a moment. Giving it a gentle tug before he pressed against her lips with his tongue.

And she yielded.

Maybe that was why she opened her mouth, because she'd asked and he'd answered. Because he'd suffered for her. For her *curiosity*. Such a small thing, and in the end, did it make any difference?

She couldn't say.

Except she knew now. She *knew*. And even though the memory was horrific, she was glad she knew. She wanted to understand this man. *All* of him, both the good and the bad.

No matter how shattering.

So she opened her lips and let him in, and when he thrust his tongue into her mouth, she sucked on it softly.

Yielding to his desire.

Yielding to his wants.

Yielding to the heat rising between them.

Trying to tell him that she wanted to give him everything he needed.

He threw one leg over her hips, holding her trapped as if he never wanted to let her go.

She could feel the press of his penis through the thin layer of her chemise, pulsing as he came to erection. He caught her thighs between his legs, pressing them together, and he moved...

Oh. He was so close to where she wanted him to be! She could almost feel him. Feel his bare skin. Her chemise was becoming damp from the slick wetness growing at her core. She tried to arch up. To widen her legs. To get his cock where she *needed* him, but he was stronger than she.

He would not bend.

She whimpered in frustration and he twisted a hand between them and pulled the ribbon free from her chemise. The bodice was merely gathered at the neck and it fell open, giving him access to her breasts.

He lowered his head and sucked one nipple into his hot mouth.

She moaned, twisting under him, panting, wanting something he would not give.

And then he was moving to the other nipple, and he sucked it as well until she thought she would scream from the tension.

He licked, flicking her nipple with his tongue on one side and his fingers on the other, and at the same time he ground down on her, shoving her chemise into her pussy, rubbing against her clitoris, until the silk was sodden with her wetness. Until she could hear the soft, slick sounds he made, his body on hers, him pleasuring her, while he would not let her move.

He wasn't gentle. But then perhaps he didn't know *how* to be gentle, and the thought made something inside her weep, even as he drove her up that peak. Maybe this was all he knew: flesh and liquid heat.

Maybe that was all she would ever have from him.

She wasn't certain it was enough.

But it didn't matter now because she was at the cliff, racing straight over the edge. Falling into space.

It was almost painful, this physical jolt, this sudden heaving of her heart, and for a moment she hung frozen in space and time, unbreathing, unmoving. And then she came back to life, her limbs flooding with warmth and sweet lassitude, the backwash of that height of pleasure.

She opened her eyes and saw him rise over her spread body and thrust between her thighs, separated from her flesh by only the wet silk.

Once.

Twice.

Once more.

And still. His lips twisted, his eyes hollow and almost pained.

Staring at her as he came between her thighs.

Raphael walked into the breakfast room at the unfashionable hour of half past nine the next morning and kissed his aunt on her soft cheek. "Good morning, Zia."

"Up at last," was her tart reply as she peered at him over her gold spectacles.

The remains of Zia Lina's breakfast was already on the table, and he knew well that she'd probably been awake for over an hour.

"Perhaps I've grown soft," he said, sitting across from her.

Or perhaps he'd woken to silken limbs and a tangle of golden hair and simply wanted to linger for a while in that warm feminine embrace.

But then the memory of what he'd told her—the *shame* of what he was—had flooded him, and he'd fled the room.

He wasn't yet ready to gaze into her blue-gray eyes and find out how she looked at him in the light of day now that she knew.

His aunt humphed to herself as she sorted through the

morning mail. "You have many invitations for a recluse. I can't think why."

"Perhaps it's the title," he replied drily, pouring himself some coffee.

A footman entered, bringing plates of sliced meat and shirred eggs.

"It must be," his aunt decided. "Because it's certainly not your charming wit."

He let his lips curl for a second before they fell again, then helped himself to eggs and several slices of gammon. "From whom are the invitations?"

His aunt looked up sharply. "There are only two in this batch, but I have a stack on my desk. Shall I send for them?"

"Please."

She signaled a footman and made the request.

He felt her eyes on him as they waited for the footman to return with the invitations and he ate his breakfast.

"I never thought I'd see you married," she said softly. "I am glad."

He kept his gaze on his gammon. He wasn't entirely certain Iris would wish to remain with him after she thought about what he'd told her. "Are you?"

"Yes. I think she will be good for you."

He had a far-too-sarcastic rejoinder on his tongue—for he doubted *he* was good for *Iris*—but the footman arrived at that point.

"Ah," Zia Lina said, gathering the stack of papers in front of her. "Let me see. Do you want to look through them yourself?"

He shook his head and then swallowed his bite of gammon. "Read them to me."

"As you wish." She held up the first invitation. "An afternoon musicale to—"

He held up his hand. "Pardon me, but I think only evening events."

"That will eliminate several of these." Zia Lina paged through the invitations, setting aside the invitations that didn't meet the requirement. "Here is one—you are invited to a ball given by the Countess of Touleine in honor of her granddaughter's introduction to society."

"Not that." He cut a piece of gammon.

"Hmm. An evening masquerade at the home of Lord Quincy?"

"I don't think so."

"Another ball—this one being given by Lord and Lady Barton."

"That's the one."

She looked up, her eyebrows raised. "Indeed? It's in only two days."

"Nevertheless." He took the invitation from her and read it. This would do. If he remembered correctly, Barton's wife was a good friend of Viscount Royce's wife. Royce was bound to be at the ball. Raphael could corner the man when he wasn't expecting an assault and ask about Dockery and the Dionysus. It would be interesting to find out if Royce had a different story from his younger brother.

He looked up at his aunt, who was watching him with too-shrewd eyes. "Can you respond for me? I'll be attending."

"With Iris?"

"Naturally." Assuming she didn't change her mind about him when she awoke.

He rose from the table. He needed to see Ubertino and find out if his Corsicans were settled in their quarters.

"She'll need a ball gown," his aunt said with not a little asperity, "and something to wear to the dressmaker."

He glanced at her, frowning. "Yes?"

His aunt raised her eyes to the ceiling as if asking for patience. "I will take her shopping and see if my lady's maid has something she can wear."

"Thank you." He hesitated. "And when you return I'll take her on a second errand."

"Oh?"

"To see her brother—and announce our marriage to him."

The Dionysus watched through guileless eyes as the Mole nattered on about horses over his coffee.

They sat at their leisure in a London coffeehouse, crowded with gentlemen of all walks of life: here the city banker, intent upon his secret moneymaking, there the member of Parliament arguing fiercely about the breeding of hounds with his opponent from across the aisle, and over there the country squire on his annual trip to the city, the clots of mud not yet shaken from his boots.

Gossip and news swirled here almost as fast as the youths who ran back and forth from the counter, delivering coffee to the customers. At the counter a large man in an apron stoically produced tankard after tankard of hot, black brew.

Though of course none of these fine fat pigeons knew anything about the real news in the world.

The Mole sent him an uncertain look, perhaps realizing his companion's attention had wandered.

The Dionysus leaned forward and smiled.

The Mole smiled back, reassured.

The Fox was dead—he'd had the news yesterday. The Dionysus might mourn the man's death were it not for the incompetence of his assassination attempt. Better on the whole that Dockery be killed than captured alive.

Though really Dockery could not have told Dyemore anything about the Dionysus that he didn't already know.

Still. It would have been easier had Dockery managed to succeed in killing Dyemore and his new duchess. Now Dyemore had followed him to London and was probably stalking him like a rabid wolf. Which meant the Dionysus would have to think of his next move. Something Dyemore wasn't expecting. Something that would hit him in his soft underbelly.

It was a pity. In another life they might have been . . . Well, not *friends*, for the Dionysus didn't have friends, but perhaps allies.

They did have so very much in common, after all.

Chapter Thirteen

The Rock King arrived at the stone tower, his brow bloodied, but his gaze steady. In one hand he held a strange little cage made from a round carved rock. Inside the hollowed core glowed a rainbow light.

"Here is your sister's heart fire," said the Rock King. "Take it to her and restore her health, but forget not your promise to me." . . .

—From *The Rock King*

"We are very lucky," Donna Pieri said that afternoon as she and Iris stepped from the most exclusive dressmaker on Bond Street, "that Madam Leblanc had several gowns partially made up and ready. I do hope that you felt you had an adequate selection to choose from?"

"Oh yes." Iris sighed happily.

It was so nice to be able to afford a dressmaker of such skill. While Iris's wardrobe was by no means inadequate, she'd always been quite frugal with her gowns, making sure she could wear them for several seasons and taking very good care of them. Today, with Donna Pieri by her side, she'd ordered a half-dozen new dresses besides the ball gown.

The peach gown she'd chosen was the color of the sunrise, the rippling watered silk seeming to subtly change from rose to pink to nearly orange in different lights. She'd fallen in love with it at once.

"Thank you for coming with me," Iris said as they strolled along the busy street.

Behind them Valente and Ivo were constant, close shadows. Iris hadn't thought she needed bodyguards on *Bond* Street of all places, but the Corsicans had been quite insistent that they must come along, apparently at Raphael's orders. It had been easier in the end to accept their presence than argue further.

Nevertheless, the spring day was sunny, and all of London seemed to be out, promenading and examining the wares set out by shopkeepers. They'd had to leave the carriage around the corner in order to avoid causing a blockage in the road.

"I enjoyed the trip," replied the older woman in her lovely accent. "I am fond of Raphael, though he makes it hard sometimes, I think. He does not suffer affection easily."

"I've noticed that." Iris glanced at the other woman meditatively.

Raphael had said that his aunt had spirited him away after his father had...

She mentally flinched from the thought.

After Raphael had cut himself. Was Donna Pieri aware of why he had done such a thing?

The older woman tucked her hand into Iris's elbow. "He was always thus—a quiet child. A child who watched and made his own decisions. My sister used to write that he hoarded his smiles like a miser."

Iris frowned at the thought that even as a child Raphael had rarely smiled. How strange. "You sound like you were very fond of your sister."

"I was." Donna Pieri turned and met her gaze, her brown

eyes calm and a little sad. "My nephew is the closest relative I have left now." She faced forward again as they moved around a pair of swaggering young bucks laughing raucously and taking up far too much of the walkway. "There was only my sister and I in my family. We had an infant brother, but he died of a fever before he was out of leading strings. We were close, Maria Anna and I. She was very pretty and had many suitors when we were young, while I—" She shrugged and motioned to her upper lip. "I had none."

Iris was not entirely sure what to reply to that. She wanted to say she was sorry, but Donna Pieri's demeanor didn't call for apology. Indeed, the other woman was calm and proud.

Perhaps she had weathered so many negative comments upon her harelip throughout her life that she no longer wished for *any* comments, not even sympathetic ones.

They came to a cross street, where two ragged boys skipped up to them, spinning brooms and demanding coin to sweep the road for them.

Donna Pieri opened her purse and took out two pennies to give them—a prudent action, since the child street sweepers were known sometimes to deliberately flick muck onto the skirts of those who refused to pay them.

They crossed the street and Donna Pieri continued, "Raphael was the apple of Maria Anna's eye. She would write me long letters about him, about how he was growing, what he ate, when he first walked, when he first rode a pony. She loved him dearly. I could read it in her letters." She pursed her lips. "She never wrote me of her husband. I knew this was a bad sign, but I did not know how bad until I received the letter informing me that she had died."

Iris knit her brow, sorting through the other woman's careful words. "Your sister's death was sudden?"

Donna Pieri's mouth turned down, her eyes bright and angry with old sorrow. "Yes. I had no notice that she was ill beforehand. Naturally I immediately began my journey to England, but by the time I arrived, my sister had already been buried. Her husband told me that her health was not good. The English weather did not suit her. She had a fever of the lungs and failed very quickly."

"I'm so sorry," Iris said. How horrible it must have been for the other woman—alone in a strange country, bereaved of a beloved sister, not even allowed to mourn properly at her funeral.

Donna Pieri nodded curtly in acknowledgement. "I was not yet proficient in your language and I did not like my sister's husband, but I felt it my duty to stay so that my nephew would know of his mother's family."

Iris shivered, thinking how awkward it would be to live with a man one hated. A man one suspected of abusing a beloved sister.

"That must have been difficult."

The older woman shrugged. "Yes and no. Dealing with the old duke was tedious, but Raphael..."

"What was he like as a little boy?" Iris asked.

"I first saw him sitting bent over a table, drawing with a pencil. His black hair was clubbed and it fell in curls down his back. When I called to him, he looked up, and I was struck at how much he looked like Maria Anna: big gray eyes, red mouth, his face a perfect oval. He was handsome." A small smile curved Donna Pieri's lips. "As I got to know him I discovered that Raphael was a joy, so small and solemn and clever. He could draw faces and horses so well I was astonished. And he clung to me when I first arrived, though he could not have remembered who I was. No doubt I reminded him of his dead mama." She sighed, her smile dying. "I hoped to help him. To protect him. In that I failed."

Iris looked down, feeling her eyes fill with tears so that the ground before her blurred before her eyes. "He told me that you took him to Corsica after he cut himself. Surely that saved him."

The older woman was quiet as they strolled along.

"I did what I could," Donna Pieri finally said. "It was not enough and it was too late, but it was all I was able to do at the time."

Iris inhaled. "I think you were very brave."

"Thank you." Donna Pieri stopped and looked up at her. "He will try to push you away, you realize. This is something he does. You must not allow it."

"I understand." Iris swallowed, suddenly realizing that the other woman's tale had been much more than a recitation of memories. It had been a handing over of care. "I won't let him chase me away."

They turned the last corner and Iris looked up to see their carriage. There behind it was another carriage.

And standing beside both was her brother Henry.

Raphael watched out the window as his carriage rolled slowly along Bond Street. He was to meet Iris here after her shopping trip with Zia Lina, but the road was so crowded he was making little progress.

The carriage rolled to a stop.

He pushed open the window to see what the matter was, and saw Zia Lina and Iris standing up the block. Iris appeared to be in conversation with a man, and though Valente and Ivo were hovering nearby, Raphael decided he should find out who the gentleman was.

He opened the door and jumped down.

Ubertino, sitting in the driver's seat, called to him in Corsican, and Raphael waved to him and pointed to the ladies before jogging to the sidewalk.

He strode swiftly down the street, dodging the other pedestrians until he came close enough to hear the gentleman exclaim, "You *what*?"

Zia Lina was looking displeased, while Iris had a pleading expression on her face.

Raphael felt a protective instinct rise in him and stepped between the ladies, taking Iris's arm.

The gentleman, wearing a white wig and nut-brown suit, turned to glare at him. "And who are you?"

When the man looked at him, Raphael recognized the blue gray of his eyes, even though they were narrowed in anger. This had to be Iris's brother.

He bowed. "Raphael de Chartres, the Duke of Dyemore. And you are?"

"Henry Radcliffe." Iris's brother tilted a pugnacious chin. He looked to be nearly forty, and a head shorter than Raphael, yet he wasn't backing down.

Raphael couldn't help but approve.

"I'm pleased to meet you, then, but perhaps we should confer in private? I don't particularly enjoy discussing my affairs in front of an audience." He tilted his head to the gathering crowd whispering among themselves.

Radcliffe's eyes widened when he noticed their watchers. "Very well. Would you and Iris care to join me in my carriage?"

He waved to the carriage standing behind Zia Lina's vehicle.

"Thank you." Raphael turned to Zia Lina. "Do you mind journeying home alone?"

"Naturally not." She sniffed as if the entire episode were beneath her and, after giving Radcliffe one more glare and saying her farewells to Iris, turned and stepped into her carriage with Valente's help.

Raphael nodded to the men to accompany his aunt home and then turned to Iris. "Shall we?"

"Yes, of course," she replied, though her voice trembled a bit.

Raphael's lips tightened. Had her brother been bullying her?

He handed Iris into the carriage and sat beside her, his hand still on her arm.

Radcliffe followed them in and sat on the opposite seat. Although the other man pointedly stared at Raphael's hand on Iris, he said nothing.

The carriage ride was made in silence, and Raphael could feel Iris growing more and more tense as the journey went on.

Five minutes later they rolled up in front of a neat but unassuming town house.

Raphael stepped out of the carriage and assessed the street and house.

They were not impressive.

He helped Iris down from the carriage and waited for Radcliffe to descend. They followed Radcliffe up the front steps, where a young maid opened the door.

She goggled at his scar.

"Please stop gawking, Sarah," Iris said to the maid.

Radcliffe cleared his throat. "Bring a tray of tea to the study." He turned to Raphael. "This way."

Radcliffe's study turned out to be on the upper level in a far corner, a rather cramped room stuffed with ledgers, papers, and books. Unlike many an aristocratic study, this one was obviously used for business, and Raphael remembered that Iris had mentioned something about her brother's remaking their family fortune.

He looked at Radcliffe with a bit more respect.

"Please. Have a seat," Radcliffe said gruffly, motioning to two chairs before his desk.

Raphael saw Iris settled in her chair before he took one.

"Is it true?" Radcliffe demanded, staring at his sister. He waved what appeared to be a letter. "I thought this letter was a forgery when I received it last night. Are you bamming me, Iris?"

"Hardly," she replied, her chin lifted stubbornly. "As I told you in the letter and again on Bond Street, Raphael and I married only a week ago."

"When, precisely, were you going to inform me of that fact?"

Raphael cleared his throat. "I planned to bring Iris to visit you today so that she could explain the matter to you. That was why I arrived on Bond Street when I did."

"Humph." Radcliffe frowned and looked at his sister again. "What about Hugh? There's rumors all over town that he married some nobody."

"The nobody's name is Alf," Iris replied drily. "They had a lovely wedding. And I thought you knew I never intended to marry Hugh when I left London."

She might have not intended to marry the Duke of Kyle, but her voice softened each time she said his name. The thought made him want to punch something. Perhaps Kyle.

"Good Lord," Radcliffe muttered, rubbing his jaw. "You know I only want to see you happy, Iris."

"Oh," Iris said in a little voice, almost as if she *hadn't* known.

Raphael sighed. "Radcliffe. I'm honored that Iris agreed to marry me."

Radcliffe clasped his hands in front of him, his brow wrinkled. "Your Grace . . . I . . . Ah, this is unexpected."

He looked very grateful when the maid interrupted with the tea.

Five minutes later a corner of his desk had been cleared for the tea service and Radcliffe was looking a little more relaxed.

Iris poured a cup of tea and handed it to her brother. "It's not very complicated," she said with amazing aplomb, and proceeded to tell Radcliffe the fairy tale they'd conceived together on the journey from Dyemore Abbey.

Raphael noticed that she'd made several embellishments since.

He watched his new brother-in-law's skeptical expression. Radcliffe knew something was amiss with the story—he appeared to be a smart man. He sipped his tea and listened to his sister and once in a while darted a shrewd glance at Raphael.

At the end of Iris's recitation there was a silence.

Iris had handed Raphael a teacup, but he hadn't bothered drinking. He met the other man's eyes, waiting.

Radcliffe inhaled. "Well, it seems that the marriage is a fait accompli." He looked at Raphael. "Might I know your sentiments toward my sister, Your Grace?"

Raphael nodded. "I hold Iris in the highest regard. There is no other reason I would make her my wife."

The other man waited, but when Raphael said nothing else he sighed. "Then I hope you have a long and happy marriage, Iris. I'll inform Harriet. I've no doubt she'll want to have a soiree or musicale or some such to celebrate your nuptials, however abrupt."

Iris stood and walked around the desk. She bent and hugged her brother, appearing to surprise him. "Thank you, Henry. You know how much that means to me."

"Oh, well," was all the man seemed able to say as he patted her back awkwardly, a small smile on his face. "Perhaps you'll want to go on up to your rooms to see about packing. Thought I'd have a word with His Grace."

She darted an alarmed glance at Raphael.

Which amused him. Did she think he could be routed by a middle-aged banker?

She merely nodded and, with a last look between the two of them, left the room.

He turned to see what threat Radcliffe would deliver.

The other man's smile had left his face. "I didn't believe a word of that."

"As well you shouldn't," Raphael drawled.

"Will I be hearing the true story?"

"No."

Radcliffe pursed his lips. "Did you debauch my sister?"

Raphael looked him in the eye. "No."

The other man seemed a little taken aback by that answer, and now he was puzzled. Obviously he couldn't work out why else Raphael would marry her on such short notice.

Well. That was no problem of Raphael's.

Radcliffe finally shook his head. "No matter. I may not be titled or rich, but duke or no duke, I will make sure you regret it, sir, if you harm my sister in any way."

"So noted." Raphael inclined his head. "I expected no less." He rose and offered his hand to Radcliffe. "I intend to spend my life cherishing Iris."

Radcliffe looked a trifle startled at his words, and then something seemed to relax in his face and he smiled as he stood to shake Raphael's hand. "I'm glad to hear it, Your Grace."

* * *

Iris watched her husband an hour later as they traveled back to Chartres House in the carriage. "What did Henry want to talk to you about?"

Raphael looked at her for a moment, his eyes fathomless. "Your brother wished to make sure that I would take care of you."

She frowned. "That was all?"

He shrugged. "Yes."

She had a sneaking suspicion that there had been more between them, but she also suspected that Raphael wasn't about to tell her about it.

In any case Iris was rather pleased—and surprised—by how concerned Henry had been about her abrupt marriage. Henry was seven years older than she, and though they got on, they had never been particularly close—at least not in a demonstrative way. It was lovely to know that he did truly care for her.

The carriage drew up before Chartres House, and Raphael helped her out before tucking her hand in his elbow and climbing the steps with her to the front door.

"I have something I want to show you," Raphael said as the door opened.

"Your Grace," Murdock the butler said, bowing to Iris. "You have a guest waiting for you in the Styx sitting room."

Raphael's brows snapped together. "Who is it?"

Murdock's eyes widened. "He gave his name as the Duke of Kyle, Your Grace, I—"

"Oh, it's Hugh!" Iris lifted her skirts and rushed up the stairs to the upper level.

"Iris!"

She heard Raphael's shout from below but didn't stop.

Hugh must've been so worried for her after hearing the news that she'd been kidnapped.

She threw open the doors to the Styx sitting room.

Hugh turned.

He looked as if he'd been pacing in front of the fire. He had shadows under his black eyes and his big frame was held tensely. Two of his men—former soldiers—lurked on opposite sides of the room.

"Iris," Hugh said. "*Thank God.*"

She went to him, and though he was normally quite circumspect with her—almost ridiculously formal, considering they'd once thought of marrying one another—he opened his arms to her.

She wrapped her arms about his waist as she felt his arms encircle her in a warm hug.

"Alf has been half out of her mind with worry for you," he rumbled above her.

Iris looked up into his face. "Is she here?"

He shook his head. "She stayed to guard the boys. When you were kidnapped—"

"Iris," came a low, smoky snarl from the doorway. "Come *here*."

She felt Hugh's arms tighten around her as she glanced over her shoulder.

Raphael stood on the threshold, Ubertino, Bardo, and Ivo behind him. Her husband's eyes were so icy a gray that from where she stood they nearly shone.

Oh.

His gaze flicked from her to the man holding her. "Unhand. My. *Wife.*"

Raphael's face was set and stern, entirely frozen over, and it occurred to her—strange thought at the moment!—that she'd never heard him really laugh. He'd made only that cawing sound—not joyous laughter at all. Had he ever laughed since he was a boy? Or had his father destroyed all laughter in Raphael that night?

It was a terrible thought.

Out of the corner of her eye, Iris saw Riley and Jenkins, Hugh's men, sidle closer to her and Hugh.

Raphael tracked their movement.

The potential for violence seemed suddenly very high.

She looked up at Hugh and patted his chest. "It's all right."

Carefully she extracted herself from his arms and went to Raphael.

Her husband gripped her arm while never taking his gaze from Hugh. "What do you want, Kyle?"

Hugh appeared relaxed, but Iris could see the way his shoulders were bunched even beneath the black coat he wore. "To find out how you came to be married to my friend Iris. The letter I received last night told me nothing."

Iris cleared her throat. "Perhaps we should have some tea?"

Raphael glanced down at her for the first time since she'd come to his side and murmured sotto voce, "I feel I should tell you for the future harmony of our marriage that I loathe tea."

She smiled up at him sweetly. "I'll certainly keep that in mind."

Ten minutes later she, Raphael, and Hugh sat in uneasy truce around an enormous platter of dainty cakes and tarts. She eyed the offering uncertainly. Iris hadn't had time to meet Raphael's cook yet, but if he or she considered this an adequate repast for gentlemen, perhaps she should have a gentle word.

The Corsicans and Hugh's men had taken opposite sides

of the room in what might be a comical standoff were it not so very serious.

Iris poured a dish of tea for Hugh and handed it to him, belatedly remembering that *he* wasn't fond of tea, *either*.

Well, if the men insisted on this sort of ridiculous jostling for power, then they'd both have to drink their tea and like it.

She handed a cup to a frowning Raphael and sat back with her own dish of tea, hot and milky with just one small lump of sugar. She sipped. Perfect.

Iris selected what looked like a lemon curd tart.

"Well?" Hugh demanded, ruining her enjoyment of the tart.

Raphael's mouth twisted up rather horribly. "Iris was kidnapped by the Lords of Chaos under the mistaken impression that she'd married you. They were seeking revenge against *you*. Pity you failed to entirely destroy them."

Oh dear.

"What the *hell* do you mean?" Hugh started forward, and for a moment Iris was worried that he would stand and attack Raphael in his ire at the Lords' continued existence.

"Exactly what I said," Raphael drawled. Was he *trying* to make Hugh hit him? "You were careless. The Lords are as strong as ever and they have a new Dionysus."

"*Christ.*" Hugh did rise at that, but it was only to pace across the room and back. "I'll need to inform His Majesty, send Alf and the boys to the Continent." He winced. "She won't like that. But *God*, I don't know if I can stand them being threatened."

He suddenly looked at Raphael.

"How do you know so much about the Lords of Chaos?" Hugh's eyes narrowed. "How did you find her?"

"I was at their revelry." Raphael paused to take a sip of the tea he loathed, which *obviously* was for effect—and to further rile Hugh. "They planned to rape and kill her."

"You're one of the Lords?"

Hugh's incredulous question came at the same time as Raphael said, "I rescued her."

The men stared at each other like dogs about to battle.

Iris cleared her throat, drawing the attention of both men. "And then I shot him."

Hugh looked appalled. "Why did you do that?"

"I didn't *know* he was rescuing me." She decided it was prudent not to mention the nudity. No need to go into pointless details. "At the time I, too, thought he was a member of the Lords—which he *isn't*, by the way. He's only pretending to be one of them to get closer to them."

"It was very brave of her," Raphael said unexpectedly. "And it was a good shot. It nearly killed me."

"That pistol pulls to the right," Ubertino chimed in, breaking the pretense that all the servants weren't in actuality listening to the conversation. "Had it not, you most certainly would have been dead, Your Grace."

Strangely, he sounded approving.

Hugh frowned, blinked, and shook his head. He looked at Raphael. "And then you *married* her."

Raphael spread his hands. "How could I not?"

They stared at each other for a long moment.

And then each reached for a tart.

Hugh sat. "What were you doing at the revelry?"

"Attempting to rejoin the Lords so that I might bring them down." Raphael took a bite of his tart, watching Hugh all the while. "My father initiated me many years ago, but I never truly joined their ranks as I was brought up in Corsica. Now I hope to infiltrate the Lords and destroy them."

"That's my job." Hugh frowned. "I'm glad that you were there to save Iris, but there's no need—"

"Had I wished for your opinion, I would have asked for it," Raphael interrupted silkily, brushing a crumb from his knee. "Actually it *is* my job to bring down the Lords of Chaos." His cold gaze flicked up to Hugh's face. "My father led them for decades. My right of battle far precedes yours."

"I've the Crown's approval and backing," Hugh said.

"Do you?" Raphael drawled. "It didn't help you much last time, now did it?"

Hugh glared. "I'll be mounting my own campaign against the Lords—a campaign you are welcome to join. I would like your help, frankly. If we work together—*without pride*—we're far more likely to bring down the Lords of Chaos."

Raphael rose slowly, extending a hand. "It's been a pleasure to meet you, Your Grace," he said with patent dishonesty.

Hugh grimaced, stood, and shook his hand. "Think about it, Dyemore."

He jerked his head at his men and strode from the room.

Iris blew out her breath and looked up at Raphael. "You will accept Hugh's help, won't you?"

Her husband held out his hand to her. "No."

She didn't take his hand, staring up at him instead. "But if you work together, won't your chances of bringing the Lords down improve?"

He shrugged. "I don't care. I work alone."

"*Raphael.*" She felt tears of anger and frustration start in her eyes.

It was foolish for him to refuse to work with Hugh. The other man had spent months chasing the Lords of Chaos and had the backing and resources of the Crown.

On his own Raphael stood a far greater chance of failing.

On his own Raphael would *die*.

She wouldn't be able to bear it if anything happened to Raphael—anything at all. He might be stoic and grave and nearly stone-like, but she knew now that under that frozen exterior his emotions roiled like molten lava.

She wanted him safe. She wanted him to simply *be* with her. To learn to be happy.

To learn to laugh.

And all he seemed to care about was his stupid revenge.

She stood, still ignoring his hand. "Please, Raphael. Please, for me. Let Hugh help you. There's no need for you to risk yourself like this."

"Come with me, Iris," he said quietly.

"Don't you hear me?" She gripped the sides of his coat. If she'd been strong enough, she would've shaken him. "*I don't want you to die.*"

"You're making yourself upset for no reason," he said, and a trace of impatience finally cracked his facade.

"You've set a course of *suicide*," she said, her voice rising. She no longer cared if she sounded hysterical. "I assure you I'm mad with worry for a very good reason."

He looked away, his mouth crimped in irritation. "I've told you this is my battle—"

"Fine!" She threw her hands up in the air in exasperation. "It's your battle, the only important thing in your life, but why do you have to die to accomplish it?" Her voice lowered as tears bit at her eyes. "Tell me, Raphael. Please. *Why* do you have to leave me alone in order to bring down the Lords of Chaos?"

"*Iris*," he snarled.

She started at the sound. He'd raised his voice. He never raised his voice.

Raphael inhaled, looking down and then up at her. "Because it's the only way to lay him to rest."

Her eyes widened in horror. "*Him?* You mean your father, don't you? Raphael, his sins don't require your death. Is *that* what you think?"

He stared at her, his brows drawn, and for a moment she thought she had broken through to him. Thought he might answer the question and come back to her.

But then he looked away. "I'm not trying to kill myself, but if I die you won't be alone. You have your brother, your friends, *Kyle*."

She looked down and dashed at the tears with the back of her hand. As if any of those people were the same as *he*.

"Please," he said, his voice like drifting smoke. "I don't want to argue with you. Won't you come with me?"

She didn't want to argue with him, either. It made her heart ache and left her weary and sad. She took his arm because she didn't know what else to do.

He led her out of the sitting room and up the stairs, and she wondered if there was any argument she hadn't used. Anything she could say to stay him from his course of action.

Raphael stopped suddenly, and she looked up and saw that they'd come to the duchess's chamber.

She frowned and peered up at him.

His eyebrows were still drawn together, as if he wasn't sure what her reaction might be. As if their fight had made him sad as well. "Do you remember that I said I had something to show you?"

Back when they were entering the house. Before she'd seen Hugh. Before their argument. "Yes?"

He pushed open the door to her bedroom. "Look."

She went inside and saw Valente sitting on the floor in

front of her fireplace with a basket. He had a silly grin on his face.

She glanced over her shoulder to Raphael. "What—?"

Her husband tilted his chin toward Valente and the basket. "Go and see."

At the same time she heard an animal whimper.

Her lips parted and she picked up her skirts to hurry to the basket. It was lined with a soft blanket and inside was the sweetest little blond puppy, looking very sorry for itself.

Iris stared, torn. Did Raphael think a *puppy* would be an adequate substitution for him?

The moment the puppy saw her it began whimpering and yipping, trying to climb from its wicker prison, but its legs were too short to make the attempt and it ended by falling backward, revealing that it was female.

It was hardly the puppy's fault that she was angry with Raphael.

"Oh," Iris breathed, sinking to her knees on the carpet opposite Valente. "She's perfect."

Somehow the words made tears start in her eyes again.

She picked up the puppy, which wriggled in Iris's hands until she held the small animal against her chest. The puppy promptly began licking Iris's chin with a tiny pink tongue.

Iris looked up at Raphael through her tears. "What is her name?"

He shook his head. "She has none that I know of. You must give her one."

Iris stood, cradling the still-squirming puppy carefully, and went to her husband. "Thank you."

She stood on tiptoe and kissed him on the lips, trying to convey all she'd said before. All he'd pushed aside.

Stay. Stay. Stay.

Raphael took her arms gently and kissed her, angling his face over hers. He embraced her as if she were a lifeline.

As if he wished to remain with her forever.

The puppy yelped and he took a step back, breaking their kiss.

Drawing away from her without effort.

He walked out of the bedroom.

Iris closed her eyes to keep her sorrow and tears in. She kissed the top of the puppy's silky head and whispered in her ear, "Tansy."

Chapter Fourteen

So Ann set off with El's heart fire carefully cradled in her hands. She walked through the barren wastelands for three days and three nights until at last she came once again to her father's hut. El lay still, gray, and cold, only a whisper of breath leaving her lungs, but when Ann held the stone cage near her, the heart fire flew from the rock walls and disappeared into El's chest. At once she took a deep breath....

—From *The Rock King*

The night of the Bartons' ball, Iris stepped carefully into the carriage with the help of her husband and settled back onto the squabs. Her peach watered silk gown had turned out beautifully. It was a robe à la française with cascades of white lace at the wrists and pinked rosette ruffles down the skirt front.

She watched Raphael opposite her in the carriage. He seemed as cold and aloof as when she had first met him at that ball so many months ago, but she could see beneath that mask now. He was focused, his eyes on his prey, intent on the hunt.

She shivered and turned to the window. She understood now why he was so obsessed with the Lords of Chaos, but her understanding didn't make her any happier.

In fact it frightened her—that he would give up so much in pursuit of justice. Why did *he* have to be the sacrifice?

She watched lantern lights pass outside.

They had only slept together last night—nothing more. And while Iris was glad that she hadn't had to make love with Raphael while she was angry with him, a part of her missed their closeness.

It was hard to sleep with a man and not become... attached to him. Her friend Katherine had moved from lover to lover, as free as a butterfly, but it seemed Iris was not made of the same essential material.

Or perhaps it was simply she and Raphael. The volatility of their combination.

The carriage pulled to a stop in front of a new town house made of white stone.

"Come," Raphael said, helping her down.

There was the usual crowd outside—the carriages dropping off guests, ladies and gentlemen trying to make their way to the door, and liveried footmen jostling each other.

Inside, the crush continued up the narrow stairs to the ballroom.

They were announced, and for a moment it seemed as if everyone in the room was silent.

Iris looked out over the brightly colored crowd and took a deep breath to steady herself. This was her first public event as the new Duchess of Dyemore. She could see people whispering together throughout the ballroom and she couldn't help but wonder if it was *she* they were gossiping about. Just today she'd found out that the news of her wedding had spread throughout London.

Apparently she and Raphael were the scandal of the season.

She swallowed and pasted a serene smile on her face as they strolled into the ballroom.

Iris nodded to a trio of ladies she knew vaguely and smiled at Honoria Hartwicke, a friend of Katherine's. Honoria gave her a wink, and Iris began to relax. This was just like any other ball, after all. The important point was to parade about, showing off one's finery, and be sure to nod to the correct people.

She'd done this innumerable times.

"Shall I find you a glass of punch?" Raphael murmured in her ear after ten minutes or so of perambulating the hot room.

"That would be delightful," she said gratefully.

"Perhaps you'd care to take a seat?" He indicated a group of chairs in a small window alcove.

She nodded gratefully—she wouldn't mind a moment to herself before braving the eyes of the crowd again. Raphael seated her before he left.

Almost immediately her hopes of a respite were dashed when a pair of ladies strolled over. Iris knew one of the ladies very slightly—Mrs. Whitehall was a matron and staple of society events.

Iris rose when it became apparent that they meant to converse with her.

"Your Grace," Mrs. Whitehall exclaimed, "may I present Miss Mary Jones-Thymes? Miss Mary Jones-Thymes, Her Grace the Duchess of Dyemore."

Iris inclined her head as Miss Jones-Thymes, a lady of middling years with suspiciously red hair, curtsied.

"The news of your marriage is quite the talk of the town, Your Grace," Miss Jones-Thymes said carefully.

Iris smiled. "I'm not surprised, it was so sudden." She told them the fictitious tale about the highwaymen and

Raphael's gallant insistence on marriage to save her good name.

"What a terrifying story," Mrs. Whitehall said when she was done with the recitation. "You must've been very frightened."

Iris agreed without any deceit on that account.

Mrs. Whitehall pursed her lips into a little moue. "It's just too bad that your brother was unable to help you with the decision to marry. Negotiating the marriage contract should always be done by a gentleman who has the best interests of the lady involved. I find that every woman needs the level influence of masculine counsel, especially when making such important decisions."

Iris's smile grew a trifle stiff. "I think I made an adequate decision all on my own."

"But did you, Your Grace?" Miss Jones-Thymes asked gently. "I'm not at all sure that you were aware of all the facts when you made such a precipitous decision."

Iris narrowed her eyes. "What facts are you referring to?"

The ladies before her exchanged a look.

Mrs. Whitehall cleared her throat. "There are rumors, my dear. Rumors that, had you or your brother been aware of them, might have made you more cautious about leaping so rashly into matrimony with His Grace."

Iris firmed her lips. "I find I have no interest in rumors."

"No?" Miss Jones-Thymes purred. "Not even that the Duke of Dyemore enjoys the company of little boys?"

Lord Barton's house was too small for a ball, Raphael thought irritably. The refreshments were well away from the dancing room, and already the passages in between were filled with sweating bodies. He edged past two elderly gentlemen in full-bottomed wigs and came face-to-face with Andrew Grant.

"Dyemore." Andrew glanced quickly over his shoulder. "I had no idea you'd be here.

Raphael raised his brows. "It seemed time to introduce my duchess to society. Are you attending alone?"

Andrew had an uneasy look in his eyes. "I... I—"

But before he could answer, his elder brother loomed behind him.

Viscount Royce's thin mouth was twisted with irritation. "What's kept you, Andy, I've—"

He cut himself short when he saw Raphael. "Your Grace." He darted a glance at his brother. "I had no idea you were in London."

"My wife and I only arrived a few days ago," Raphael said smoothly. He didn't mention that he'd already seen and spoken to Andrew in London. "Although we were attacked at an inn on the way down. You don't happen to know anything about that, do you?"

"Why would I?" Royce glared.

Raphael shrugged. "Our mutual friend—"

"Pardon, pardon." A young man in a lavender suit pushed past.

"This isn't the place for this discussion," Royce hissed. "Follow me."

Raphael barely had time to incline his head before the other man was turning and shoving his way through the crowd, his brother behind him. Raphael followed. Interesting that Andrew hadn't told his elder brother that he'd talked to Raphael. Perhaps he could find an ally there? Andrew had certainly endured the worst the Lords of Chaos were capable of.

Royce led them through two corridors and finally to a hidden door at the end of a hall. The viscount opened it and gestured Raphael in ahead of him and his brother.

It seemed to be a small study or sitting room, but it was dimly lit—there was no fire in the hearth.

Hector Leland rose from a chair as they entered.

"What took you—" He cut himself off when he saw Raphael.

Leland's eyes widened and darted quickly behind Raphael as if signaling a message.

Raphael turned, but he couldn't tell which brother Leland had been looking at.

In any case, Leland had recovered by the time he glanced back at him.

"Why did you bring him here?" Leland hissed. He was definitely speaking to Viscount Royce now. He sidled nearer the brothers as if seeking their protection.

Royce grimaced and abandoned both Leland and his brother to walk across the room to a side table where a decanter stood. He poured himself a large measure and took a sip. "Dyemore was discussing Lords business—out there where anyone could overhear."

Even here, in a room far from the crowd, Royce's voice was low and careful.

Leland shook his head at Raphael. "To what purpose? Are you trying to goad the Dionysus into killing you?"

"He's already tried once," Raphael drawled. "I have nothing to lose by inciting him further."

"That's not exactly true," Andrew said quietly.

The three other men turned to him.

Andrew blinked as if being the center of attention made him nervous.

"What do you mean?" Raphael asked.

Andrew licked his lips. "Well, there must be people you care for? You *did* save the former Lady Jordan—and even married her. That must mean something, surely? And don't you have an aunt? Some sort of female relation, anyway. I know you're a cold brute, but if she turned up floating in the Thames or hanging from a tree in Hyde Park, wouldn't that make you twitch just a little?"

Raphael's veins felt as if they were filled with ice, but he hadn't time to feel dread. To take in the bone-deep fear for both Zia Lina and Iris.

Pack animals attacked when one of their own was wounded or showed fear.

He couldn't afford weakness here.

So he went on the offensive.

He stalked right up to Andrew, making the shorter, slighter man back into Leland. "You seem to know an awful lot about the Dionysus's thoughts," Raphael snarled into the other man's face. "How he plans. How he takes revenge. Even how he kills. So much so, in fact, that I can't help but think you must be the Dionysus himself." He wrapped his hand around Andrew's throat. "And if that is the case, I can stop looking and settle our argument *now*."

He hadn't actually tightened the hand around Andrew's throat, but the other man was scrabbling at his hand with his fingers. "No! You d-don't understand... I... I'm not—"

"Don't be ridiculous, Dyemore," Royce drawled, still by the decanter and sounding bored. "My brother isn't any more the Dionysus than Leland over there is. *None* of us are the Dionysus. We don't bloody know *who* he is."

"Don't you?" Raphael said softly. He let go of Andrew, who scampered to Royce's shadow. "How do you explain the attack on my men and me, then, at an inn on the road to London?"

"What attack?"

Raphael turned at Leland's voice and saw that his brows were drawn together.

"Lawrence Dockery tried to stab me in the back at an inn on the road to London," Raphael said. "I killed him."

"Killed him?" Leland went white.

"Then you know who Dockery was," Raphael said flatly. "I thought only the Dionysus knew all the members' names."

"I..." Leland blinked rapidly. "Well, but everyone knew Dockery was the Dionysus's pet. He had no fear—he had even taken off his mask at the revels." He shivered and looked down. "Really, it's no wonder he's dead."

"You don't sound regretful," Raphael said softly.

Leland raised his chin. "Should I be?"

"For God's sake!" Royce growled behind them. "What is the point of all these questions, Dyemore? By this time a month from now you'll be dead and the Lords of Chaos will continue as they always have. Now. You'd better check that your wife is still where you left her, hmm?"

Raphael lifted his lip, but he couldn't disregard the threat. In a crowded ballroom Iris could be taken and no one would be the wiser.

He strode to the door, brushing roughly past Leland on the way.

"Watch it!" the other man cried, catching hold of his arm. Leland whispered, "My house tomorrow."

"Let go of me," Raphael said loudly, without any indication that he'd heard.

He strode into the corridor, pushing past overdressed bodies.

What did Leland want with him? Was he ready to join with Raphael, perhaps help him gain leadership of the Lords of Chaos? Raphael had always thought that Leland was too much of a coward to move without the Grant brothers by his side, but perhaps he'd misjudged the man.

Or it was some sort of trap.

By now the mass of people and the thousands of candles burning in order to light all the rooms had heated the house so that it was as if they were all bubbling in a stew of smells: sweet perfume in overabundance, the stink of body odor, and the wax from dozens of wigs and thousands of candles.

Raphael gritted his teeth and, with the greatest of effort, refrained from simply shoving rudely through the throng. More than one person flinched at his face, but he ignored the stares and mutters.

That is, until he heard a whisper.

"Boy lover."

Iris had been searching for Raphael for at least fifteen minutes, her hunt made harder by the press of bodies. Lady Barton would be thrilled; her ball was a crush—a sure sign of success. But Iris felt her chest tighten in a near panic. She needed to find Raphael and talk to him quietly alone. Inform him of the nasty gossip in private.

Before he heard it, if at all possible.

She was beginning to think she was on a hopeless errand. She heard snippets of the rumor everywhere she went. The gossip was spreading like wildfire throughout the ball.

And she still hadn't seen Raphael.

Where was he? She'd been to the punch room and not found him. Could she have missed him on his way to her? Should she go back to the seat in the alcove—or perhaps return to the punch room?

She left the ballroom and went back out to the grand staircase instead, because it was the only place she hadn't yet looked.

There was a crowd at the top of the steps, but the staircase itself held only a few people—none of them Raphael.

Iris turned in despair and bumped into a lady in an

atrocious orange-and-green-striped dress that hurt her eyes. She felt herself stumble, and as she did so someone shoved her hard from behind.

Toward the stairs.

She felt herself teetering, her toes at the very edge of the top step.

Nothing to hold on to…

And then someone caught her, pulling her firmly back against a hard chest. "*Iris.*"

She gasped and looked up.

Raphael was staring at her with blank crystal eyes, his mouth set, his scar standing out on his face like a brand. "You nearly went down the stairs. You could've broken your neck."

"Someone…" She gasped, beginning to tremble as she realized just how close to falling she had been. "Someone pushed me."

His head instantly came up, and he searched the crowd. "Who?"

"I…I didn't see."

His attention snapped back to her. "We need to leave."

She could only nod shakily. "Y-yes."

He took her elbow and began ushering her down the stairs.

The murmured gossip behind them didn't stop.

If anything, with Raphael right there, it became louder.

At the bottom of the steps ladies waiting for their wraps stared and whispered behind fans.

Gentlemen frowned and shook their heads or tutted.

Matrons hurriedly ushered their unmarried daughters away.

Raphael never changed his expression. He looked forward, cold and aloof, a slight sneer on his twisted lip.

If she'd not known him, not spent days talking with him and sharing her body with him, she might have believed the gossip.

Oh, but she didn't.

Not even for a minute.

What was more, she knew now what these horrid rumors were doing to her husband. Beneath his frozen mask he must be aching inside.

They finally made the entryway, which wasn't as crowded as it had been before. Raphael barked an order to one of the footmen waiting by the door and then helped Iris into her wrap as they waited for the carriage to be pulled around.

His hand was a vise on her upper arm and Iris knew she would have bruises later, but she didn't want to say anything.

They waited in silence, Iris leaning against his comforting strength.

When the carriage finally arrived, after what seemed like hours, he marched her toward it.

She just had time to see Ubertino in the driver's seat before Raphael bundled her inside.

Iris sat and watched her husband as the carriage lurched into motion. He sat so stiffly and he wouldn't meet her eyes. He was withdrawing into himself, icing over, almost as if he thought she would believe that...

Something poked her in the hip.

She shifted absently and felt a sharp jab.

What...?

She put her hand down to feel her skirts. Perhaps a wire in her panniers had broken. Her hand touched something metal, and hot pain sliced across her last two fingers.

"Oh!"

Raphael looked up, his gray eyes narrowed. "What is it?"

"Something in my skirt cut me," she said.

He moved swiftly across the carriage. "Let me see."

She raised her hands.

Gingerly he sifted through her voluminous skirts and then paused. Iris felt a tug and then he was holding a long thin knife in his hand. The light from the carriage lantern glinted off the blade.

She tried to make sense of what she was seeing. "What...?"

He turned to her and the light shone off his eyes as sharply as it had the blade. "Someone tried to kill you in there. When you nearly fell down the stairs. That was an attack. Somehow they missed and the knife was caught in your panniers." He shook his head. "But the fall most likely would've killed you in any case."

"Except you were there." She felt steadier now, even though the shove had obviously not been an accident. "You saved me, Raphael."

"I wasn't there when whoever it was tried to stab you." His eyes were frozen. "Had the knife gone through, you'd be dead. There would be nothing I could do about it."

Iris opened her right hand. The last two fingers were daubed with what looked like black liquid in the lamplight.

It was one thing to be aware that an enemy wanted to kill you, but it was something entirely more visceral—more immediate—to see that death had nearly claimed you.

"What is that?" Raphael growled. He took her hand and pulled it closer to the light.

Now the blood was clearly red.

He stared at the blood on her fingers for a moment and then picked her up bodily to place her in his lap, his strong arms wrapped around her. He pulled off his neckcloth and wrapped it around her hand.

She didn't even think to protest, simply laid her head

against his chest. "I wasn't stabbed. I didn't fall down the stairs. I'm safe." She could hear his heartbeat, slow and strong, beneath her cheek. "I'm safe with you."

His arms tightened around her as if in answer.

That was how they rode the rest of the way back to Chartres House.

Even when the carriage stopped and the door was pulled open to show Ubertino's face, Raphael didn't let go.

He looked at the Corsican. "They've tried to kill my wife."

The smile on Ubertino's face was wiped away. His eyes narrowed, and suddenly Iris could see this man as a pirate on the Barbary Coast. "I will set guards. On my life, this will not happen again, Your Grace."

Raphael nodded.

Then he gently set Iris down on the carriage seat, stepped from the carriage, waited for her to stand, and then swept her up in his arms again.

She might've given an unladylike squeak.

He mounted the front steps.

She cleared her throat. "I can walk."

The door opened and Murdock's eyes widened.

Raphael ignored the butler. "No, you can't."

He strode past two footmen, through the entry hall, and up the grand staircase, all without even breathing hard.

Iris clutched his waistcoat with her unbound hand, feeling the muscles bunch and relax under her fingers. His face was set.

They reached the ducal chamber finally, and Raphael shouldered open the door. He crossed the room and set her on the bed and then climbed in after her, shoes and all, and pulled her to his chest.

The room was dark, save for a banked fire.

She could hear his breaths in the silence, even and steady.

"I'm not," he said, so suddenly she started.

She licked her lips. "Not what?"

"An abuser of little boys. Or little girls. I swear to you on my mother's grave, on my soul, on everything I hold dear in this life or the next that I've never, *never* touched or looked at or thought about children in that way. I—"

"Raphael." She struggled to face him, for he wouldn't unlock his arms from around her. "*Raphael*, please listen."

He stopped, his breathing uneven now.

She tested his hold and found she could sit up and turn around and look at him.

He lay staring at the canopy of the bed, his eyes iced over and blank.

She had to make that look stop.

"I *know*," she said to him, and took his face between her palms. "I know you would never do the things they were whispering. I know they're all lies. I believe you, my darling. I believe *in* you."

He closed his eyes.

And when he opened them the ice had melted. He was looking at her with tears in his crystal eyes.

"Iris, my Iris," he whispered, and drew her lips to his.

He kissed her like a man dying. Like a man taking his last breath.

As if he cherished her.

And something in Iris blossomed open and expanded in her chest and seemed so full it would make her burst. She wasn't sure she could contain this feeling, this emotion, she had for him.

Her husband.

She *cared* for this man—rather a lot. Perhaps even *more* than cared for him.

The thought should frighten her, but all she felt was happiness.

Happiness.

"*Iris.*" He sounded desperate. Undone. And she realized his hands were shaking as he held her.

He rose up suddenly and turned her, so that she lay on the bed. He pushed up her skirts, found the ties to her panniers, and yanked them off and threw them to the floor.

Then he was on her again, trailing his mouth down her neck, biting at her collarbone.

She ran her fingers into the hair at the back of his head, grasping, trying to hold on as he moved on her so intently.

He'd always been in control when he'd made love to her. Now he seemed moved by a sort of compulsion.

An animal need.

The thought made her shudder with arousal. Made her clutch at his shoulders.

She felt his hand on her leg above her garter, on bare skin, urgent and hot. She was still fully dressed, as was he, but he didn't seem to want to take the time to disrobe. His fingers covered the curls at the tops of her legs possessively, and he raised his head.

"Spread your legs for me," he said, his eyes implacable.

She inhaled and felt liquid heat pool low in her belly even as she was already moving.

She felt enthralled by him, enthralled by her own sexuality. He bared something in her that she hadn't even known was there before she married him.

Something base, primal. Had it always been there, this fierce drive to *feel*? Or was it something that had been engendered by his touching her?

Her touching him?

She knew that she should be wary of this part of herself.

Ladies were often exhorted to ignore any animal urges. To be polite. Formal. Cold.

But the flames of her desire, meeting and burning higher with his compulsion, were intoxicating.

It felt *wonderful.*

Too good to ignore. Too good to give up.

And when his fingers traced into the wetness of her vulva, into the depths of her pleasure, she cried out, her eyes still caught with his.

He smiled, crooked and sinister because of his scar, but a smile nonetheless. A smile that wasn't exactly nice or gentlemanly.

But a smile that was all for her.

Only her.

No man—no *one*—had ever looked at her so before.

She arched beneath him, her hips shoving up, trying to get more of that hand, more of that gaze. He lowered his head and covered her mouth, thrusting between her lips as he slid a finger into her softness.

She trembled beneath him, moaning as he kissed her so deeply she thought she might lose her senses.

He was rubbing his thumb over her clitoris now, fast and hard, and he broke the kiss to murmur in a voice dark as hell-fire, "Wet my hand. Show me your desire. Show me all that you are. Let me look at your sweet cunt, swollen and rosy for me. I want to make you weep. I want all your pleasure, Iris, all your pain, everything you are. You are the light in my black night. Come for me."

And she felt herself bow with the stark white bliss of her epiphany, the shattering realization of his words and his hands and his mouth. She was gasping for breath, shaking, lost, unseeing. The center of her being pulsing with pleasure.

She lay limp and heard him curse, sounding desperate, and then felt his weight on her.

She opened her eyes and saw that his face was hard and his gaze riveted on her.

"Raphael," she moaned, begging. Wanting. "*Please.*"

"I can't," he said. "God, I *can't.*"

She felt his hips meet hers and realized that the placket of his breeches was open. She felt his cock, hard and hot against her inner thigh, and her heart bounded.

Despite his denial, he was so close and she knew he wanted her. By the wild look in his no-longer-cold eyes. By the uncontrolled stuttering of his hips.

He wanted her.

"Please," she whispered, tilting her hips up in invitation. So close. He was so close. "*Please*, my love."

He closed his eyes as if he was pained. As if a great sword had been driven through his chest, impaling heart and lungs and liver. His hips settled more firmly on her, and she felt him against her folds.

Oh God, she wanted him to fill her.

She pressed her palm to the side of his face.

He turned his head and kissed her palm... and at the same time thrust inside her.

She gasped at the sudden invasion. At feeling his cock inside her at long last. At the stretch and the fullness and the glory.

He thrust again and was fully seated, as far inside her as it was possible to be. Her legs were stretched open to accommodate his hips, and he was pressed deeply, intimately into her.

He pushed up on his arms and held himself there as he pulled his cock nearly all the way from her body and then drove back in again.

She opened her mouth, panting, holding his crystal-gray gaze. His hips were working now, driving into her at a hard pace, filling her again and again.

She'd never…

It had never been like this before.

So intense. So intimate. So devastating.

His nostrils flared just a little bit, and the lines bracketing his mouth grew deeper. He snarled with his beautiful, twisted lips and she thought, half on the edge of falling again, she thought he looked like a demon making love to her. A demon fighting for life or light or possibly redemption.

But now his hips were pistoning in a nearly out-of-control movement, driving both him and her higher and higher. He lowered his head and glared at her from under his eyebrows, baring his teeth.

And suddenly she knew what she had to do.

"Come for me, my husband," she said. "Give me all that you are. Give me the dark and the light. I accept them both. I want your cock in me. I want *you*."

He shouted, flinging his head back, the tendons on his neck straining as he pumped his hips into her, convulsing.

The sight sent her into a glorious warm wave of pleasure. She gripped his buttocks—still clad in his breeches—and ground against him, seeing stars.

He gasped great breaths of air and let his head fall to her shoulder, his raven's-wing hair hiding his face as he opened his mouth against her throat. She was still shuddering, small aftershocks of pleasure rippling through her.

She felt exquisite.

He breathed against her, lying half-on and half-off her body, and she thought that he might be too heavy before long, but not yet. Not quite yet. She wanted to linger like this, secure in his heat.

Secure in his affection.

She felt tears prick at her eyes. He'd made love to her—*finally*. Now they were truly married.

Now they were truly joined.

Joy flooded her being. She was so happy with this man. This, this was what had been missing from her former marriage—indeed, from her entire life.

A sense of belonging.

A sense of peace.

She loved him. The realization was a wonderful glow within her.

She loved Raphael.

Too soon she felt him shift. Felt that sublimely sad moment when his flesh slipped away from hers. He rose from the bed.

She rolled to watch him.

He was standing still, his back to her.

Iris knit her brows. "Raphael," she called softly, and felt a flush when she heard how husky her voice was. "Come back to bed."

He turned.

His face was white, his scar a scarlet snake on his skin. "No. No, I..." He stared at her as if she were something catastrophic.

As if she were disgusting.

Iris felt herself shriveling. *Dying*. "Raphael?"

He strode from the room.

Chapter Fifteen

Now El quickly grew strong again, her cheeks pinkened, her eyes sparkled, and her laughter filled the little hut. She rose from her bed and was able to do all the work she could do before and more.

And then Ann told her father and El that she must return to the Rock King and be his wife for a year and a day....

—From *The Rock King*

Raphael stood in the room adjacent to the duke's rooms—a dressing room—and tried to button his falls.

He'd...

Dear God.

He'd penetrated Iris. He'd *come* in Iris.

His hands were shaking and his breaths were harsh. Absently, in a small corner of his mind, he thought he sounded like a bear about to charge.

What the hell had he done?

He could *smell* her on him—some flowery perfume and the scent of her cunny, arousing and dear to him now.

He gasped as if he'd been punched in the gut.

After *that* had happened. After his father had ruined him for all living things and cast him into solitary darkness, he had been a being without sex for a very long time.

He had not touched himself save to do what needed to be done to keep himself clean.

He had not looked at others with lust.

He had not thought of bodies at all, except with the utmost revulsion.

Indeed, had he been of the correct faith he would have made an exemplary initiate to the priesthood.

But then, in his sixteenth year, things slowly had begun to change. He'd seen a girl and his eyes lingered on her breasts. He no longer ignored the erections he got at night—and, more and more often, during the day.

He'd grown to his full height in the next several years.

He'd mastered horseback riding to the point that he needed neither saddle nor stirrup and could guide the animal by his thighs and heels alone.

He'd learned to fight and once, when roaming alone on a deserted part of the island, knocked to the ground a man who had meant to rob him.

He'd learned Italian, Corsican, Latin, Greek, and French.

He had became a man.

And in his twenty-first year he lay with the widow who did the laundry in his house. Her hands were rough, but she was a gentle soul, ten years older than he, and not a promiscuous woman by any means. He met with her thrice more and gave her a cottage and enough money to buy an oven and begin selling bread.

He'd had two other women since.

None had been lovers.

And he had not penetrated them. He had not penetrated *any* woman.

Until Iris.

God. What had he done? He'd made a vow to himself that

he'd never have children. That he wouldn't continue his father's cursed line.

He'd forsworn himself because of her.

She'd destroyed all his defenses.

"Raphael?"

He stiffened at her voice and then turned.

She hesitated in the doorway. She'd undressed and wore only a chemise and wrapper, her hair down about her shoulders.

She *shone*.

Her light hurt his eyes and he shut them against her radiance. "*Leave.*"

"No."

Her simple word made him look up.

Her lips trembled, but she stood brave and tall in the doorway, refusing to go. Refusing to leave him in his broken ruin.

"Raphael," she said, "what is the matter?"

He stared at her. Could she truly be so unaware?

"I...I've made a mistake," he said, trying to keep his voice level. Trying to keep from shouting. This wasn't her fault.

The fault—the *weakness*—lay with him.

"What..." She licked her lips. "What do you mean?"

He shook his head. "You *know* what I mean. I told you innumerable times."

He heard her quiet inhalation. "You didn't want a child. Yes, you said that to me, but would it really be so awful if—"

"Yes!" He'd lost the battle not to shout. "Dear God, *yes*. My father was a *monster*. I cannot risk having a child like him. Can't you see—"

"I see that you aren't your father." She took a step toward him. "If—"

"How do you know?" He gripped his own hair. He felt as if his sanity were leaking out of his pores. "How the hell can you tell? I have his blood in my veins. I have his words and actions in my brain. He raised me to be *his*. Don't you see—can't you understand—that I am just as much monster as he?"

"No!" She rushed to him and wound her arms around his neck, holding him when he tried to pull away.

He couldn't injure her. Not even now.

"No," she said again, her face inches from his. He could see the storm in her eyes, the desperation in her face. "You are not him, Raphael. You will *never* be him."

"I cannot risk it," he said, his voice low. "It's too much. I cannot."

Her arms fell from him and she stepped back, swallowing. "And if it's too late?"

He shook his head, turning away. "I don't know."

He looked at her, so beautiful with her golden hair around her. With her light shining bright from within her.

He'd never deserved her. It'd been folly to tell himself otherwise.

He inhaled and said it, severing whatever might have been. "I only know that this can never happen again."

Her lips parted and she simply stared at him a moment. He had the odd hope for a second that she would argue further. That she would somehow convince him otherwise.

But in the end she simply left him there.

Alone, cold, and in utter darkness.

He couldn't stand it. He'd been in her light too long.

Raphael slammed out of the dressing room and into the hall. He passed a startled Ubertino, standing guard outside the ducal bedroom, and kept walking.

"Your Grace!" the Corsican called behind him.

Raphael ignored the shout and ran down the stairs.

Valente and Ivo were at the front door. He held up a hand as Valente stood and opened his mouth.

Both servants stood aside as he made the door.

Raphael walked out into the night.

Leaving everything light behind him.

The Dionysus sat in front of a roaring fire that evening, drinking a very good brandy. He held up his glass and watched the amber glow of the firelight behind it.

"Dyemore is getting close," the Mole said from a chair nearby. "And the attempt on his duchess's life will make him even more determined."

The Dionysus ignored him. Other than for the very fine brandy, the Mole was of little use to him.

Something the Mole had apparently forgotten.

"Will you send another assassin?" the Mole asked.

Obviously he was worried that he would be the next assassin chosen. "I mean, of course Dyemore needs to be killed, but I don't know if it wouldn't be better to simply pressure him to return to Corsica."

The Dionysus raised his eyebrows and slowly turned to the Mole. "You've been talking to my brother."

"*No.*" The Mole's eyes widened in what looked like fear. "No, I wouldn't, my lord. I'm loyal to you. *Only* you."

"Are you?" the Dionysus asked with genuine interest.

"Yes!" The Mole was sweating. Perhaps because of the proximity of the fire, but more likely because of the proximity of the Dionysus. "I... I just think that now you've spread the rumors about Dyemore, he'll be less likely to stay in England. Who, after all, would associate with him? You've isolated him most admirably."

The Dionysus nodded. It was the truth. He narrowed his eyes at the Mole, feeling in a playful mood. "Yes, Dyemore has lost any allies he might have had, but that's not enough. He must be destroyed." He sipped his brandy, watching the other man over the rim of his glass. The Mole looked nearly ill with fear. "Only the most loyal of my followers can be trusted for such a mission. Do you have any candidates?"

"I... That is..." The Mole took a handkerchief from his coat pocket and blotted his forehead. "Perhaps the Bear?"

The Dionysus raised his eyebrows.

"Or... or even the Badger."

"Not my brother?" the Dionysus asked, simply to find out what the Mole would say.

"Do you trust your brother?" the Mole asked, which was rather brave of him.

The Dionysus smiled. "No."

The Mole winced, and the Dionysus enjoyed watching him slowly realize.

"I can do it," the Mole said, as if it were his choice. "I'll kill Dyemore."

"Lovely." The Dionysus smiled at him and listened as the Mole came up with a plan.

The Mole was a treasonous bastard, he decided. Or perhaps simply cowardly. Or the Mole's face had taken on an ill-starred aspect.

Whatever the case, the Dionysus no longer favored him. The Mole was not his friend nor his brother nor his pet.

He would have to be cast out.

Dyemore would also have to be cast out. Out, out, out into the far reaches of hell. Out of this life entirely. But first the Dionysus would have to steal away Dyemore's salvation and his life.

For if the Dionysus was not allowed salvation, then neither should Dyemore be.

It was only fair.

The sun had long risen by the time Raphael woke the next day. He winced at the sunlight streaming into the room—he'd gone to sleep in one of the guest bedrooms of his house, avoiding both the duke's and the duchess's chambers.

He wasn't certain he'd be able to resist Iris again.

He rose slowly, careful of his aching head. He'd gone to several taverns last night, and while he'd not been exactly drunk when he'd returned in the early hours, he hadn't been entirely sober, either.

For a moment Raphael sat on the side of the bed and held his head. She'd looked so hurt. As if he'd stabbed her through her heart and the blood was only beginning to flow from the wound.

Had any other person put that look on her face, he'd have killed them. But it had been he who had hurt Iris so awfully.

He'd been the one wielding the knife.

The mere thought made his stomach lurch.

God, what was he going to do? He couldn't live with her, not now that he'd obviously shown he couldn't resist her. But what if she was with child?

He sighed, standing like an old man, and looked at the clothes at his feet. Bending, he picked up his coat, and a scrap of paper fell out of the pocket.

He stilled.

He didn't remember having put anything in his pocket the day before.

Raphael picked up the paper and unfolded it. In what looked like hastily scrawled handwriting it said:

He isn't what he seems

Raphael narrowed his eyes. *Who* wasn't who he seemed? The Dionysus? When had the note been placed in his pocket, and by whom?

He began to wash and dress as he considered the matter.

The tavern he'd been drinking in last night had been nearly empty. The maid serving him his drinks could've slipped the paper into his pocket had she been particularly adept, but that seemed unlikely. And he hadn't met anyone walking to or from the tavern.

That left the ball.

The problem was, almost anyone could have slipped a note into his pocket last night at the ball. The crowd had been pressed so closely together, and he'd moved through it several times, encountering innumerable people.

Among them Andrew, Royce, and Leland.

He'd met both Andrew and Royce in the crowd, but they'd been facing him at the time. Of course there was a slight possibility that he'd walked by them or Leland at some point in the mass of guests and not realized it. If he had, any one of the men could have passed the note to him during that time.

Then, too, when Raphael had initially entered the small study to talk to them, both Andrew and Royce had stood behind him. He didn't think anyone could slip a paper in his pocket without his noticing, but obviously someone *had* at some point…

And finally, Leland had bumped against him as he'd left the room to whisper that instruction to come to Leland's house today. He might've slipped the note to Raphael at that point.

Always assuming that someone else entirely at the ball hadn't put the note in his pocket.

Raphael blew out a breath in frustration.

In any case the note was not at all useful. It didn't mention a name. Whoever had scrawled it had been in a hurry and fearful—the Ts had been crossed twice.

Raphael pondered that point as he pulled on his shoes.

If the note had been written in the study, perhaps it was a warning about one of the other men: he wasn't as innocent as he seemed.

Or the note could've been written by the Dionysus himself or an agent of the Dionysus purely to confuse him.

Raphael's mouth twisted sourly on the thought. If that was the case, the note was working admirably.

Regardless of the note, he was willing to take Hector Leland up on his invitation to talk. Leland was always about, always on the fringes, but never spoke without Andrew and Royce nearby. Alone, Leland might be more forthcoming—about Dockery and the Dionysus.

He'd go to Leland's house... but not without his Corsicans.

Having made that decision, Raphael finished dressing and descended the stairs. He met neither Iris nor Zia Lina, but that wasn't surprising. They were probably breaking their fast together.

A braver man would bid the ladies good morning.

But he'd already demonstrated his inability to resist Iris.

Best to stay away.

So Raphael called for three horses to be brought to the front of the house and then found two of his men.

Fifteen minutes later, he was mounted and riding to Leland's town house.

London was wet and dreary, matching his mood as he rode, Valente and Bardo trailing behind on their own horses. The streets were crowded and the journey slow.

By the time they came to Leland's house—wedged into a cramped corner of an older street—Raphael had the feeling that he had missed his opportunity to question the man.

An elderly woman stood on the step of the house, talking with a man who, judging from his bobbed wig and the black case he carried, must be a doctor. Beside them was a sobbing maid who couldn't yet be twenty, and an elderly butler, white faced and shaking.

Raphael dismounted. "Wait here," he murmured to his men, giving Valente the reins of his horse.

He approached the tableau on the steps.

"Who might you be?" asked the doctor, peering over tiny spectacles perched on the end of a pointed nose.

"I am the Duke of Dyemore," Raphael said coolly, "and a friend of Hector Leland."

"Then I'm afraid I'm the bearer of very sad tidings," said the doctor. "Mr. Leland met with an accident while cleaning his dueling pistol this morning."

"Wretched boy," said the elderly lady. She wore a huge lace cap tied under her chin. Her mouth was an unpleasant, lipless line, and her eyes narrowed to unlovely slits. "And my poor niece Sylvia with two babes and another on the way. What a wicked thing to do. I did tell her that she shouldn't marry Hector Leland. 'He's a bounder through and through,' I said, and now look what it's got her. Disgraceful, is what it is."

Two houses down, a door opened, and a maid stepped out to openly gawk.

"I'd like to see him," Raphael said.

"He's dead," the doctor said bluntly.

"Nevertheless, I insist."

"You won't thank me for it. Gunshot makes a terrible mess."

Beside them, the maid shrieked, and the older woman tutted and led her rather brusquely inside, the butler trailing.

The doctor watched them, then turned to peer at Raphael suspiciously.

Whatever he saw in Raphael's face seemed to make up his mind. The doctor shrugged. "Very well. Be it on your shoulders." He led the way back inside. "You'll see soon enough why I have no doubt of the cause of death."

Leland's study was on the first floor at the very back of the house, overlooking a meager garden.

"The maid found him there"—the doctor pointed to a desk holding blood-splattered papers—"and I moved the body here after I was called to the house."

"Here" was a table, probably brought in from another room. Leland was stretched out, wearing his nightshirt and stockings and with half his shaved head blown away.

"Dead," repeated the doctor. "Told you so."

"Mm." Dyemore looked over the body. "You're sure he did it himself?"

The doctor's bushy gray eyebrows flew up his forehead. "Slumped at his desk, pistol in his hand, shot in the side of his head. All the house's doors locked and no outcry in the night. Nothing at all in fact until early this morning, when the maid came to clean the grate."

A letter on the desk caught Raphael's eye. The contents weren't interesting—it appeared to be addressed to Leland's father-in-law begging for more money—but the handwriting was.

All the Ts in the letter had been crossed twice.

Beside him the doctor was continuing his monologue. "You don't think his lady *wife* would do such a thing, do you? It beggars belief. Only reason we're saying 'cleaning his dueling pistol' is to save her sensibilities. You ought to know that, man."

Raphael glanced at the window and went to it to look down. The brickwork of the house was laid with regular ornamental indentations beginning about six feet off the ground. An agile man could climb it easily if he had a ladder to start.

He turned back to the room and approached the body.

"Nasty business," the doctor said, almost sounding cheerful. "Be a job to clean the gore from the wall." He gestured to a spatter on the wall directly behind the desk.

"Mm," Raphael murmured and bent over what was left of Leland. There was a piece of paper sticking out of the man's right sleeve.

He plucked it out.

"What have you there?" The doctor was at his elbow, peering at the paper.

On it was a dolphin, crudely drawn, but quite recognizable.

The doctor snorted. "A fish. Whyever would he draw that?"

Raphael ignored him and turned the paper over.

And then his heart stopped.

An iris was drawn on the other side. The doctor was muttering about flowers and fish and other nonsense, but Raphael heard none of it. There was a dark X over the iris, drawn with such venom that the pencil had scored the paper. Beside the crossed out iris was a bunch of grapes.

Dionysus was the god of wine and grapes and debauchery.

Leland hadn't drawn this. The Dionysus had—and the message was plain: Iris was in danger. The Dionysus had threatened his *wife*.

It was as if he'd been hit in the head. There was a ringing in his ears and his vision was washed with red. How—*how*—could he have let himself become so enthralled with

Iris that he'd let his pursuit of the Lords of Chaos and the Dionysus slow? She'd almost been murdered last night by one of them and what had he done?

He'd taken her home and lost himself in fucking her.

She was a distraction. A siren, singing only to him. He had no defenses against her, and while she sang her song so close to him his attention would always be diverted. The next time he fell in thrall to her, the next time he turned from his mission, the assassin the Dionysus sent might not be so incompetent.

She might die.

He had to get back to her.

Raphael turned to the doctor. "Thank you."

The doctor was still commenting behind him on daft aristocrats when he left, but Raphael hadn't the time to respond.

The Dionysus had already killed Leland.

His sights were set on Iris now.

Raphael had to send Iris away—to keep her safe and to save his own sanity.

Chapter Sixteen

"Do not go," said the stonecutter to Ann. "The Rock King is an evil spirit. Once you're in his grasp, he'll never let you free."
"He seemed but a man to me," said Ann.
"Oh, stay!" cried El. "How is it fair that you save me and then must give your life away?"
"It's only a year and a day," Ann replied. "Besides, I promised him."
And she set off into the wasteland, a small sack of clothes on her back and her mother's pink pebble in her fist....

—From *The Rock King*

Chartres House had a lovely garden, even when it wasn't yet in bloom.

Iris stood in the gravel path with Donna Pieri. It was late morning and she hadn't seen Raphael since their argument the night before. She hadn't told Donna Pieri about the fight, but she had the sense, from the way the older woman studied her with a pitying air, that Donna Pieri suspected a falling-out.

Iris sighed and looked down at Tansy. The puppy was sitting in the middle of the path and crying piteously, refusing to take a step farther.

Donna Pieri cocked her head as if examining an insect

she had never seen before. "And you say Raphael got this dog for you himself?"

The older woman had to speak rather loudly because Tansy's whining had risen in volume.

Iris shook her head and gave in to the dog's begging, bending and picking her up.

Tansy wriggled frantically, licking Iris's face in thanks as if the puppy had been saved from perilous waves.

"Yes, I think so," Iris replied as they continued their walk. She frowned down at Tansy, who had settled, tucked into her elbow, and was now enjoying the view. "He didn't say, but he presented her to me in a basket."

"Amazing," Donna Pieri murmured.

Tansy yawned, shaking her little head with the effort.

Donna Pieri smiled, her eyes crinkling behind her gold spectacles. "It is a very pretty little dog."

"Yes, she is," Iris said, and stroked Tansy's silky head.

Tansy licked her hand. For some reason the puppy's affection made her lips tremble. She wasn't sure after the night before if she could fix what was between her and Raphael. If he'd ever accept her—accept their *marriage*—and let them live together as they should.

As man and wife.

His face last night had been so horrified. So angry and cold. And it had been cruel, just when she thought they'd overcome their problems, just when she thought they'd finally become *one*, for the whole thing to be smashed because of his fear.

If he never relented, could she live like this?

She wasn't sure. She blinked, gazing at her ruby ring as she held Tansy. Somehow the sight of the ring made her eyes blur.

The door to the house slammed.

Both women turned.

Raphael was striding down the gravel path. "Come inside."

"What has happened?" Iris asked cautiously.

"Inside."

She jolted at his tone and was already hurrying up the path with Donna Pieri beside her. Raphael was tense, his face stony, and she had trouble meeting his eyes.

She could see no similarity between this man and the one who had made love to her so sweetly last night.

He ushered them inside Chartres House and into a small back sitting room, gesturing for her and Donna Pieri to sit in a far corner—well away from the windows.

Raphael waited until they were seated before stating, "I'm sending both of you away."

"What?" Iris rose and stepped toward him. *He can't do this.* "What are you saying?"

He stared at her coldly, no emotion at all in his face. Was he punishing her? "Hector Leland is dead. Shot this morning, supposedly a suicide, but I think it's the Dionysus."

"Oh, dear God," she whispered, horrified. Tansy was still in her arms, asleep now, and she stroked the puppy's soft ears. She'd *met* Mr. Leland. He was a member of the Lords of Chaos, true, but he'd been a person.

"How does that affect us?" Donna Pieri asked.

Raphael looked at her. "Threats were made against you and my wife last night and again this morning. I should have sent you both away at once, but I was...distracted. We cannot wait another minute."

Iris sucked in her breath at being called a distraction. Was that how he truly saw her—*them*? As something that got in the way of the more important things in his life?

Donna Pieri nodded. "I will go pack, then."

Iris watched her leave and then turned to Raphael. "I'm not leaving you."

His eyes were so cold she thought she must've imagined their ever thawing. "You will. Both you and Zia Lina. I'm trying to keep you safe."

"Is the danger really so great?" she asked.

"Leland's head was blown away," Raphael said without a trace of emotion. "Yes, the danger is great."

She sucked in a breath at his blunt words, and suddenly she was at that dark revelry, the torches flickering all around as she waited to die.

She truly did not want to die.

Iris shook her head and looked at her husband.

His eyes narrowed, and with his scar he looked like the very devil. How could she want to be with the devil?

Except he wasn't. He wasn't at all.

"Nothing will stop me from ensuring that you're safe," he said. "Not even you."

"But how can you keep me safe away from you?" she asked, and was upset when she felt the prick of tears in her eyes. She couldn't lose her composure now. She had to remain as cold as he so that she could *fight* this.

He closed his eyes as if she pained him. "The Dionysus is after *me*. He will stay in London if I am here. Therefore you and Zia Lina must leave."

She felt her lips trembling. "If the Dionysus could send an assassin to kill you on the road, what is to stop him doing so again? Let me stay."

"No." He was already shaking his head. Had he even heard what she'd said? "I will send my Corsicans with you and Zia Lina. You will be guarded well."

She was desperate. Last night she had felt a change in

their marriage. They *had* been growing closer before he'd left her bed. She hadn't imagined it.

She just needed time to make him see the happiness she saw could be in their marriage.

But if he sent her away now, she was afraid that every gain she'd made thus far would be destroyed.

"Raphael," she said softly, moving toward him. "Please. Please don't send me away."

But he turned from her as if he couldn't stand her touch. As if he couldn't even *look* at her. "Do not beg me. I cannot bear it. I cannot bear *you*. You tear down my walls, take away my reason and purpose. Iris, you have to go. I can't do what I must do with you here." He held out his hand to his side, fingers outstretched as if to push her away. "I've made up my mind. We don't have time to waste like this."

She walked around him—walked around that damned hand—so that he was forced to face her.

There were tears on her cheeks now, true. She was humiliated. Devastated. But she had to at least *try*.

And what mattered her pride now?

She looked at him, her husband. At his eerie crystal eyes, at his raven's wing–black hair, at the scar that he'd carved into his own face. Out of fear but in bravery. She looked at all of him and she knew. "I love you."

He closed his eyes, shutting her out. "I made a mistake last night."

"Don't say that." She felt as if she'd been hit in the chest. She couldn't inhale. "*Please* don't say that."

He opened his eyes, clear gray and completely without emotion. His gaze was that of a dead man. "But it was a mistake. *My* mistake. What is done is done. With luck there will be no consequence, but I would be a fool to continue to court disaster."

She held out her hand, *pleading*. "Raphael—"

"No."

She sobbed angrily, uncaring of her wet face. "I am not a disaster. *Our child* would not be a disaster. On the contrary, if I am so lucky as to be with child I will rejoice. It will be a blessing. Do you hear me, Raphael? A *blessing*."

He flinched at her words. "Not to me. Never to me."

He might as well have struck her. She felt as if she were wounded. As if she were dripping blood on the floor.

She raised her chin. "If you send me away now, I will never forgive you."

He bowed his head. "So be it."

Iris turned and left the room without another word, pressing Tansy to her face.

Half an hour later she descended the front steps to a carriage driven by Ubertino. Five other Corsicans were on the carriage, either in back or beside Ubertino on the box. They were all armed.

Raphael was nowhere to be seen.

Bardo helped her inside and then slammed the door, standing back to wave the carriage on.

Donna Pieri sat opposite her.

The older woman eyed her as the carriage jolted away. "He is worried."

Iris shook her head. She couldn't talk. If she did, she might burst into tears.

Tansy was in her basket on the seat beside her, asleep under a blanket.

Iris stared out the window with aching eyes and wondered if they could ever resolve this break. Or if this was the end of everything.

Would she ever hear him laugh in honest joy?

It was two hours later and they'd left London when she heard the boom.

The carriage shook and swayed and then jolted to a stop. Donna Pieri fell to the floor, as did Tansy's basket.

Gunfire exploded outside, like fireworks in the sky, except this was no happy occasion. The shots were fast and close together. She couldn't even count them.

A man shouted in Corsican and then stopped midword.

Iris threw herself to the floor and opened the seat, searching for the pistol. Surely it had been replaced? Her scrabbling fingers found metal and she drew out the pistol. Checked to see if it was loaded.

It wasn't.

A small hole exploded near the window on her side of the carriage.

"Stay down," she said to Donna Pieri.

The other woman nodded calmly.

Iris dived back into the seat compartment and found a bag with the bullets and powder. She knew in theory how to load a gun, but it had been a while since she'd seen it done.

The shooting stopped.

Iris poured the powder in the gun, her hands shaking, the powder spilling onto the carriage floor.

Someone wrenched at the door.

The ball was already wrapped in wadding. She shoved it down the barrel.

A man in a mask—a terrible mask, the mask of a young man with grapes in his hair—climbed into the carriage.

She pointed the pistol at him, straight armed, from her position, kneeling on the floor.

He laughed and kept moving toward her.

She pulled the trigger, but of course nothing happened.

She'd not had time to pour the gunpowder in the priming pan.

The Dionysus laughed and roughly pulled Iris to her feet. He dragged her, stumbling, from the carriage. Iris just had time to catch a glimpse of Donna Pieri's white face and then the door was slammed behind them.

Outside there were at least a dozen men surrounding the carriage. Iris could see a few of the Corsicans still on their feet, but many were on the ground, lying still. She couldn't tell who had fallen—who was still alive and who was dead—before the Dionysus shoved her into another carriage.

Iris fell, her palms scraping across the carriage floorboards.

"You know what to do," she heard the Dionysus say behind her, and Iris's blood froze. Had he just ordered the death of Zia Lina and the remaining Corsicans?

Before she could do anything but get to her knees, he had climbed into the carriage and seated himself.

"Now then, Your Grace," he said in a soft voice. "Let us have a pleasant chat."

Late that afternoon Raphael stood at the window of his study, looking out over the back of his garden. He could see small blue flowers blooming along the gravel paths, but for the life of him he could not recall what their name was.

Somehow he knew that Iris would be able to name the tiny blue flowers.

He pushed the thought aside. He'd lived over thirty years without Iris in his life and never felt the lack. Yet now she was gone merely hours and he was gazing out the window, mooning after her.

He could shove her from his mind.

He *must* shove her from his mind.

But he still saw her tearstained face. Heard her pleading with him. Remembered her saying, "I love you."

He closed his eyes.

She was haunting him.

It was as if she were in his blood now, a part of him as surely as the veins running under his skin, the lungs that let him breathe air. She'd permeated him until he could no more separate her from himself than tear the heart from his body.

She was essential to his life.

He opened his eyes and turned back to his study, trying to distract himself from his pain.

It was a strange room. His grandfather had seen fit to decorate it in murals of the dead being sorted in Hades. Demons danced on one wall, driving cowering souls, while on another the souls were naked and being lashed by hoofed monstrosities. None seemed to have found peace in death.

Perhaps the lesson spoke to him especially today because he was at an impasse in his mission.

He'd gone to Lord Royce's town house only to find both him and his brother gone and not expected back for some time.

Their butler had informed him that they'd not told him where they were going.

Which left Raphael with what? Leland? He supposed he could go back to the dead man's house and beg leave to investigate the man's papers. Perhaps Leland had been stupid enough to leave evidence of the Dionysus.

Or perhaps it was time he found another way of discovering who the Dionysus was. If he—

"Your Grace."

Raphael turned at Murdock's voice.

The butler's face was white. "You must come at once, Your Grace."

Raphael strode to the door, an impending sense of disaster mounting in his chest. The butler led him to the front steps. His carriage was there. The carriage he'd sent Iris and Zia Lina off in that morning.

Only one man was on the box. Valente tilted sideways, his arm obviously wounded. Beside him sat Zia Lina, stiff and upright.

She turned her head slowly to look at him, her eyes glittering with banked tragedy. "Raphael."

There were bullet holes in the carriage door.

Raphael heard a shout, and then he was wrenching at the carriage door.

Inside…

Dear God.

The Corsicans he had sent with his family to protect them lay on the floor of the carriage. Gangly Ivo, his long legs sprawled. Luigi with his eyes open, looking surprised. Andrea, who had most of his head blown off. Others whose faces he couldn't see.

They were dead. All of them were dead.

Numbly he saw that his men had fought well. Their bodies bore terrible wounds. They had died bravely.

And on the top of the pile…

Ubertino lay on the top of the pile. One eye had been obliterated by a bullet, but the other stared, blue and blank, up at the ceiling of the carriage. Raphael couldn't breathe, his lungs had stopped.

Slowly he climbed into the carriage and reached for the body of his oldest friend.

He closed Ubertino's eye and laid his hand on the Corsican's already cold cheek.

Then he stood and climbed down from that charnel house.

He walked to the front of the carriage and held out his arms for Zia Lina.

He picked her up—she was as light as a child—and carried her to the house.

"Where is Iris?" he asked as he climbed the front steps. His voice was steady, his bearing calm, but his chest was frozen solid.

"He has her," Zia Lina said in a hoarse voice. "He sent me back with a message: Meet him at dusk, at the ruins of Saint Stephen's Church on the outskirts of London. He will discuss the matter there with you."

He nodded, carrying her into the house.

"It is a trap," his aunt said sadly, her voice nearly broken. Had she screamed when they took Iris? Had they hurt her, his tiny, brave aunt? "You must not go, my son. The devil knows how you feel about your wife. He tries to use your feeling against you. But she is already dead."

He stopped and looked down at Zia Lina, feeling the first stirrings of a terrible rage. "Did you see my wife die with your own eyes?"

"No," she said.

"Then there is hope." He continued walking. "While there is hope I will fight."

"That man is mad," she said, sounding desperate. "He will kill her and then he will kill you. He had many men. More even than your Corsicans. You are one man, Raphael. You cannot win against him."

He shouldered open the door to her room. If Iris died, he would as well.

She was in his blood. A part of his bones.

But he merely said, "You are right."

Iris sat very still in the strange carriage and watched the madman across from her hold Tansy. His men had found the puppy in her carriage and the Dionysus had laughed and demanded she be brought to him.

Now Tansy was squirming and licking his hand, and he was *playing* with her as if he were a normal man.

But she'd seen this man, whoever he was, send Donna Pieri away in their carriage filled with the bodies of Raphael's Corsicans.

Tansy nipped at the Dionysus's fingers and Iris tensed.

But the madman only laughed gently.

Ubertino had been among the dead.

Iris looked down, for she didn't want him to see the tears that suddenly welled in her eyes. She wouldn't show weakness to this creature.

"She's a dear little thing, isn't she?" the Dionysus said.

Iris looked up at him.

He had lifted Tansy up in front of his masked face and she was trying to paw at the painted surface. "Oh no, darling one, or Father will have to beat you. At least that's what mine did to me. Though I never knew why."

Iris cleared her throat. "I'm sorry. That...that sounds horrible."

The Dionysus lowered the puppy to his lap and said as if he'd not heard her, "Fathers are so capricious, don't you think? It's why one should really always stay away from them."

His fingers tightened his hold on Tansy's neck.

Iris gasped, stifling the urge to snatch the puppy away from him. "She's bothering you. Why don't you give her to me?"

The puppy whined and tried to twist from his grip. He didn't seem to notice. "I *did* try to tell Dyemore this—and really, he of all people should have known since his father was the Dionysus—but he would not listen." He bent his head to Tansy and whispered. "No one listened."

Iris stared at him. *He of all people*... It almost sounded as if the Dionysus *knew* what had happened to Raphael. But how could he know unless...

"I'm listening," she said carefully. "What were you trying to warn Raphael about?"

The Dionysus shook his head. "*He* was pampered and kept in ignorance. *I* wasn't. How could I be? They took me to my first revel when I was eight."

"That's... that's awful," Iris said, though she wasn't even sure the man was talking to her. "A child should never have to endure that, don't you think?"

"I shall *make* Dyemore listen when he comes for you."

Tansy gave a sharp yip.

Iris saw that the Dionysus had pressed her neck to his leg so that she could not move her head at all. She was frantically pushing her paws against his hand, trying to get away, but of course she hadn't the strength.

One twist and he could break her neck.

Iris knew she shouldn't, but she couldn't help it. "Please don't hurt her."

Chapter Seventeen

When Ann arrived at the rock tower it appeared deserted, so again she knocked at the door.
The Rock King answered, and when he saw her he blinked.
She raised her eyebrows. "You seem surprised to see me."
"I am," he replied. "In seven hundred years seventy maidens have pledged to be my wife for a year and a day. None but you have ever returned to serve their time."...

—From *The Rock King*

The town house was magnificent. Grand enough for even the son of a king.

Raphael ran up the front steps with all but two of his remaining Corsicans behind him—over a dozen in all—and pounded on the door.

It was opened by a regal butler, white wigged and red nosed.

"Where is your master?" Raphael demanded before the man could speak.

The man's mouth dropped open.

"Show me now," Raphael snapped before the idiot could start some protestation.

The butler turned and led him and his men into the town house.

Up stairs, through halls, until he arrived at a library.

Kyle was there with three of his men.

He rose, his expression wary, at the sight of Raphael and his Corsicans in his domain. His men spread out around him. "What is this?"

"I need you," Raphael said. "You and your men. Get your weapons and follow me."

Kyle didn't move. "I don't take orders from you."

Raphael remembered why he disliked the Duke of Kyle so very much.

"Damn you." Raphael gritted his teeth. "*Please.* He's taken Iris. I need you to help me get her back alive."

It was late afternoon now and the carriage was growing dark. Iris was curled in a corner with Tansy safe in her arms. The madman had grown tired of the little puppy after a while and simply let her go.

Now the carriage was stopped, the Dionysus sitting across from her doing nothing.

Outside, Iris could just make out a stand of trees and the arch of a church. The rest of the building had either fallen down or been cannibalized for the stone.

They hadn't traveled very far, so they couldn't have gone much beyond London.

Iris wondered if Donna Pieri had made it home safely. She'd seen Valente driving the carriage past with Donna Pieri on the box beside him. Valente looked as if he had been badly wounded in the shoulder. Would he be strong enough to control the horses until he could get help?

What if he fainted and the horses bolted?

She sighed and examined the carriage again. She could see no weapons. If she was left alone she could check the seats to see if they hid a pistol, as Raphael's carriage did.

It seemed unlikely, however.

"Have you ever pondered on the nature of fate?" came the Dionysus's voice in the darkness.

He held a pistol loosely in his lap now, handed to him earlier by one of his men.

Iris eyed it, wondering if she could grab the gun before he shot her.

"No, I haven't," she replied tartly, even though she knew by now that the man needed no partner for his soliloquies.

"For instance," he went on, proving her thought correct, "had *I* not had you kidnapped and brought to my revels, *you* would not now be the Duchess of Dyemore. You should thank me."

"You'll forgive me if I don't," Iris muttered.

Good Lord, the man was insane.

"Of course I will also be the agent of your death," he went on. "but that is an entirely separate and different affair."

He closed his eyes and was silent for several minutes, and she began to think that he'd gone to sleep. If he loosened his grip on the pistol…

Then he spoke again, dashing her hopes. "But there are deeper matters in fate than you. I think sometimes of what I would be had I not had the father I did. I *might* have been an entirely normal man. You might have liked me, Your Grace. Imagine that."

Iris shuddered. "I sincerely doubt it."

She could not imagine in any world liking this man.

"Oh, come now, Your Grace," he said. "I am not so very different from your husband, after all. Both our fathers loved the revels. Both our fathers loved *us*. The only difference is that he escaped and I did not. Am I to be blamed for this? I was but a boy. Should the dog, having been beaten every day of its life, when it finally turns and savages its master, tearing out his throat, feasting on his blood, gobbling his innards, should that dog be blamed for its madness? The dog began an innocent creature."

Iris swallowed, feeling sick from his words. If he was speaking the truth and she understood him correctly, then he'd been abused as Raphael had, only the Dionysus had never been rescued by a loving aunt. He'd been left to suffer—and this was the result.

"So you see why I have this interest in fate." The Dionysus's voice interrupted her thoughts. "Had I had a normal or even an unconcerned upbringing, perhaps this would be an entirely different carriage ride. Perhaps you would be *my* loving bride instead of Dyemore's. Wouldn't that be strange?"

Iris felt her breathing slow like a small animal in the presence of a predator. She didn't like the direction in which his thoughts were turning.

"But I am already married," she said steadily. "I rather wonder about you. Have you a wife? A fiancée? Someone you love?"

"Do you think your husband would mind terribly if we pretended, you and I, that we were wed?" the Dionysus asked mockingly, entirely ignoring her questions. It was as if she were mute.

Iris remembered that conversation she'd had with Raphael—it seemed so long ago now—about rape and the choice to live or not. She'd been so blithe in her insistence that life was always the better choice. That there was never reason to despair.

To give up and take one's own life.

Now, though, facing an insane man, not knowing if Raphael even knew that she was in danger, not knowing if he could get to her before she was raped and killed...

Well.

Things looked rather bleak.

But she raised her chin defiantly. She still believed that there was hope as long as one lived. No matter what might happen.

No matter what this madman might do to her.

She looked at the Dionysus coolly and said, "You are not a tenth the man Raphael is. You could *never* hope to replace him."

Raphael gripped the mare with his thighs as she galloped, her neck strained and flecked with foam. The gallop was reckless on the carriage road. They might come upon a pedestrian or a herd of sheep at any moment. But he'd grown impatient as they rode through London. In the city they'd been able only to trot and sometimes canter, all the while wondering if they'd be in time.

If *he* would be in time.

The moment they'd made the country roads, Raphael had kneed his horse into a gallop.

Beside him, Kyle was on a big bay gelding, and behind them were their men—his Corsicans, Kyle's trio of former soldiers, and over a dozen soldiers—the King's men—hastily gathered by Kyle. How he'd been able to summon the King's men on such short notice, Raphael wasn't entirely sure. But that ability was, of course, why he'd sought Kyle's help in the first place.

The sun was beginning to set, the sky turning a fiery orange as night fell.

All he could see was Iris's face. Her eyes blue gray and stormy. Hurt. Because he'd sent her away. He'd not even said farewell.

If she should die...

He would not consider the notion.

He gripped the reins so tightly they cut into his palms even through the leather gloves he wore.

She was alive. As long as she was alive, *no matter what*, all was not lost.

He would find her and save her. He would apologize. He would go on bended knee if it would make this right again. He would spend the rest of his life doing *anything* to make her happy.

Even if that meant letting her go if that was her wish.

She just needed to live.

Because a world without Iris was a world without light.

Chapter Eighteen

So Ann became the Rock King's wife, although there was not much involved in the job. The pot was always full of stew, so she need not cook. There were no chickens to feed nor cows to milk nor wool to spin. At night the Rock King would turn down his rough bed and let Ann climb in first. Then he would blow out the candle and she would listen as he undressed and entered the bed bedside her.

His arms were strong and warm....

—From *The Rock King*

Iris stumbled as she walked behind the Dionysus in the church ruins, a sleeping Tansy cradled in her arms. The sun had set only minutes before and dark had descended, fast and ominous.

Over two dozen rough-looking men surrounded them, the Dionysus's hired toughs. Two of the men carried a large chest between them.

Her wrists were bound in front of her and she feared for her life. She couldn't help thinking that she was back in the nightmare that had begun all this: the Lords of Chaos's revelry with their Dionysus presiding over all.

Save for the fact that today was not part of a revelry. Today the Dionysus meant to kill her husband and then her.

She knew this because he'd explained it all to her with great relish before they had left the carriage. If the Dionysus had ever been sane, he'd long since lost the battle to keep his mind.

"Now here we will meet your husband and here we will lay his bones," the Dionysus said, stopping by the arch of the ruined church. The two men with the chest set it down with a thunk. "A fitting place for the last of the Dyemores, I think, in the ruins of this forgotten church." He turned to her and cocked his head. "Would you like to be buried next to your husband?"

Her fingers were trembling in Tansy's fur, but she remembered, all those days ago, vowing to not to let this man take her dignity.

She saw no reason to change her vow now.

Iris lifted her chin. She was a lady from a family that traced its roots nearly to the time of the Conqueror. And now she was Raphael's wife as well. A *duchess*. "Eventually, but not tonight."

The Dionysus shook his head. "I'm afraid it will indeed be tonight, Your Grace." He turned and pointed to where the road ran along the side of the church ruins, disappearing around a curve. "There is the London road. Naturally, we should be expecting Dyemore to come from there. But your husband, being a sly sort, will no doubt try a different way. I think... Yes, I do believe he will try *that* way." The Dionysus pointed to the darkened woods beside the ruins. "What a very good thing, then, that I've placed sharpshooters in the trees."

She licked her lips. "I thought you wanted to talk to Raphael? Didn't you want to tell him about all that you suffered while he was away?"

Tansy woke up, and Iris set her down on the grass.

"I no longer feel the need," the Dionysus replied carelessly. "You shall be a lovely lamb staked out for our wolf."

The Dionysus took his pistol from his pocket and examined the weapon, sighted down the short barrel, and then cocked it.

He turned to her. "It shouldn't be long now. We'll be done by sundown and back in time for supper—or at least *I* will be."

"Back where?" she asked.

"Oh, you know well enough," he answered, kicking the chest. Something inside seemed to groan. "Grant House."

Tansy finished her business and trotted over to investigate the chest, sniffing interestedly all around the bottom.

Iris stared at the chest in dawning horror.

She glanced back up at the Dionysus.

His face was turned to hers, and she could almost see his eyes behind that awful mask staring back at her. "Dogs do have the most wonderful sense of smell."

One of the Dionysus's men jogged up to him. "Someone's comin' though the trees."

The Dionysus nodded. "Very good."

His man turned away.

And Iris knew she couldn't let Raphael walk into a trap.

She ran at the Dionysus and seized the arm with the gun, trying to twist it to the side. But he was stronger, of course.

The pistol exploded between them.

They had a plan and it was a good one, but when he heard the shot, Raphael started running toward the old church ruins.

The earth flew up around him as shooters fired on him

from the trees, but it was all but impossible to hit a running man.

Behind him Kyle cursed.

Raphael could hear gunfire and shouting in the woods. Kyle and the soldiers were taking care of the hidden shooters.

His Corsicans had but one order: save their duchess. Raphael had made plain that nothing else was more important than that.

He burst from the cover of the trees and saw Valente and Bardo fighting fiercely with four men. Farther away, Iris was in the Dionysus's arms and...

There was blood on her face. He nearly stumbled at the sight.

A burly man came at him from the side.

Raphael roared and elbowed him in the face.

Iris staggered and fell.

The Dionysus turned to meet him. Opened his mouth to say something.

Raphael knocked him to the ground.

All around them there was blood raining down. Gunshots and screams. A war encapsulated.

Raphael stepped over the Dionysus and grabbed his wife. "*Iris!* Where are you hurt?"

He frantically ran his hands over her head, trying to find the wound.

"Raphael!" She took his hands. "The shot blew off part of his ear. It's not my blood."

"*Thank God.*" He held her a moment, staring into her beloved face. Then he pushed her to the ground. "Stay *down.*"

The Dionysus was trying to crawl away.

Raphael straddled the monster—the *thing* that had dared to take Iris from him. He drew back his arm and hit the man beneath him in the throat.

The Dionysus made a strangled sound and tried to buck him off.

Raphael hit him again. And again.

A tiny knife flashed in the Dionysus's hand.

Raphael knocked it away.

And continued hitting.

Until he could no longer feel his knuckles.

Until the thing underneath him no longer moved.

Until small palms pressed to his face and a voice said in his ear, "My love. Raphael. *Stop.*"

And he obeyed.

He looked up and Iris was kneeling beside him, blood smeared over her beautiful face, her eyes swimming in tears.

He wanted to pummel the thing again for putting those tears there.

Instead he reached out his own bloody hand and touched her cheek. "I told you to stay down."

She smiled. "I don't take orders well...even from you."

He gathered her into his arms and held her, his sweet wife, as he looked over the abbey ruins. Bardo was kicking a downed man who was no longer moving, while Valente slapped another Corsican on the back and laughed. The fighting had ended. His men looked to be whole.

Kyle stood overseeing his men as they tied up prisoners.

As Raphael watched, Kyle met his gaze and nodded.

Raphael inclined his head. He owed the man. He owed the man more than he would ever be able to pay.

His arms tightened around Iris at the thought.

"He killed Ubertino," she said, and sobbed. "Oh, poor, poor Ubertino!"

He stroked her hair. He didn't know what to say, so he said nothing.

Valente suddenly appeared. He had a nasty gash on the

cheek and he still favored his wounded arm, but his coat bulged as if he hid something inside.

The young Corsican knelt in front of Iris and smiled tentatively. "Your Grace."

He opened the top of his coat and the puppy's head popped out.

"Oh!" Iris said. "Oh, Tansy. Thank you, Valente." Iris tried to wipe her cheeks. She merely smeared the gore and her tears around with a bit of mud, but Raphael wasn't going to tell her that. She reached for the puppy. "She ran when she heard the gunshot. Thank you for finding her. She would have been lost if you hadn't. Tansy might have died."

She hugged the puppy to her bosom and sobbed anew as the tiny animal licked her face.

Valente looked at Raphael, his eyes wide with alarm.

Raphael shook his head to reassure him. "The duchess is fine. You did well in finding her little dog. She is very appreciative, but she is also tired and frightened from her ordeal. Gather the men and we will return to London and Chartres House."

"Yes, Your Excellency," Valente replied, and for a moment Raphael's chest seized.

He was used to giving Ubertino these orders. Soon he would have to decide which of his men to put in Ubertino's place.

Raphael rose and helped Iris to stand.

Kyle saw him rise and walked swiftly over. "Are you all right, Iris?"

She nodded shakily. "I will be, I think. Thank you, Hugh."

He smiled at her and then looked at Raphael. "We have them all rounded up, I think." He glanced at the pile on the ground. "The Dionysus?"

"Yes." Raphael didn't bother to look.

Kyle crouched to pull off the mask.

Andrew Grant lay with his right ear blown off and his eyes half-lidded. He was quite obviously dead.

Kyle looked up at Raphael. "What about his brother?"

Before Raphael could reply, Iris said, "I think you should look in the trunk, Hugh."

Kyle glanced sharply at her and then moved to the trunk and opened the lid. "God's blood!"

He knelt and put his hand inside.

Raphael walked over to look, shielding Iris from seeing inside.

Viscount Royce lay naked in the trunk. Judging by his state, he'd been in there for many hours. Blood was clotted in his hair and bruises covered his body.

"Is he alive?"

"Barely." Kyle stood and waved one of the soldiers over. "Get my man—the one with the gray hair."

The soldier nodded and jogged away. Kyle turned back to the trunk. "This is the brother?"

"Yes," Raphael said grimly.

"Were they leading the Lords of Chaos together?"

"No, only Andrew led the Lords," Iris said. She had her face buried in Tansy's fur. "And… and Lord Royce had abused Andrew when they were younger, along with his father. I think Andrew hated him. Lord Royce was probably not even aware of it."

"How do you know this?" Raphael asked softly.

"He talked a lot," Iris answered. "On the way here." She looked up suddenly. "Donna Pieri! Is she all right?"

"Yes," Raphael said. "She's fine, though in a temper." He examined Iris. She was pale and swaying in his arms. He needed to get her home.

Raphael looked at Kyle. "Will you and your men be able to handle this?"

"Yes." Kyle nodded and then sighed. "Now that we know who the Dionysus is, I'll need to search his house and begin finding the rest of the Lords of Chaos." He glanced warily at Raphael. "I expect you'll want to help with that."

"Yes." Raphael looked down at Andrew, realizing that his sense of urgency had diminished now that he'd destroyed the Dionysus. Still. It was important to clean out all the Lords of Chaos. "Thank you."

Kyle's eyes darted to Iris, who was half-asleep, her head on Raphael's shoulder. He smiled. "No thanks are necessary."

Raphael opened his mouth to argue...and then simply nodded.

Perhaps he didn't *entirely* dislike Kyle.

With a nod Raphael swung his wife into his arms and headed for the carriage.

Chapter Nineteen

One day a man knocked upon the tower door. He told a desperate tale of a mangled soul and shale demons. He vowed he'd give the Rock King all his worldly possessions if only the Rock King would kill these demons and bring back the torn soul.

Ann watched as her husband donned his stone armor and strode off into the wasteland. The Rock King was gone a fortnight, and when he returned, his arm hung broken and bloody....

—From *The Rock King*

Iris woke early the next morning in the duchess's bedroom at Chartres House. She held herself very still, trying to think what she'd heard to wake her. Raindrops pattered against the windows, but that wasn't loud enough to alarm her.

There was another crash.

She jumped up from the bed at the same time that Tansy whined. Iris ignored the puppy to run into the dressing room.

The door to the ducal bedchamber was ajar.

Cautiously she opened it and looked inside.

The bedroom was a shambles. The bed torn apart, glass shattered on the floor, and drawers pulled from a dresser.

Raphael stood by the fire in shirt, breeches, and coat, watching it roar. He was barefoot. His black hair lay long and silky about his face, and his unmarred side was to her. From this angle he might be a poet lost in unearthly thoughts.

He turned to her and the illusion was broken.

She went to him and saw that the flames were consuming a sketchbook.

"He was a monster," Raphael murmured, his smoky voice husky from sleep or something else. "Even more of a monster than Andrew Grant. My father not only preyed upon the innocent, he turned them into monsters."

He walked to the table by the bed and pulled out a drawer. Inside was a knife, and Iris's heart leaped with alarm.

Raphael took the knife and went to his father's portrait. He raised the knife high above his head and thrust it into the painted face, gashing the painting. He tore through paint and canvas, slashing to the frame at the bottom. Then he began cutting along the edge, ripping the painting into pieces. He threw them onto the fire.

The fire began to smoke.

Then he froze.

"Raphael?" She went to him, laying her hand gently on his arm.

He was staring at the frame. Inside, between where the painted canvas had been and the backing sealing the frame, was a thin book, wedged into a corner of the frame.

Raphael took it out and opened it.

Iris peered at the book. She was prepared for something awful. Perhaps more sketches, perhaps something worse.

Instead there were tidy rows of names with dates next to them and notations.

She leaned to look over Raphael's shoulder.

The first line read:

Aaron Parr-Hackett Spring 1631 Badger d. 1650

Iris drew in her breath as she scanned the list. There were dozens of names.

"It's the ledger of names for the Lords of Chaos," Iris said. "Hugh thought he'd found it before, but obviously the list of names he had wasn't complete."

Raphael paged through the book. There were hundreds of names, some of them shocking. The dates marched forward until he came to blank pages.

The last entry was dated "Spring 1741."

"I told myself I never knew the Lords of Chaos were still in existence," Raphael whispered, staring down at the ledger. "But of course I was lying. How would they have died? All that evil doesn't simply waste away on its own. I should have come back sooner. Burned them away while my father still lived. Confronted him. But I was a coward." He closed the book. "I *am* a coward."

"No, you're not," Iris said fiercely. "You saved me. You brought down the Dionysus. You—"

He looked at her, the corner of his mouth—the side not scarred and twisted—curling up in what looked like self-disgust. "The Dionysus was one man. Not even a very large one. He was Andrew Grant, who was raped and beaten by his father and his brother again and again until he went mad from it. Killing such a weak man isn't the act of a hero. It's the act of a coward."

He set the ledger down and walked out of the room.

Iris gaped for a minute before hastily following him, clad only in her chemise. "Where are you going?"

"Back to Corsica," he said.

She stumbled to a halt. "At once?"

He didn't even turn as he started down the stairs. "Yes."

"But I have no clothes," she said stupidly.

He paused, but still did not face her. "You are not coming with me."

He continued down the stairs.

She stared after him in shock. But they'd come so far...She'd been kidnapped—*again*—and he'd *saved* her and he'd *killed* two men.

For a moment she simply wanted to sit down and cry. It wasn't *fair*.

She shouldn't have to fight this battle again.

Love shouldn't be this hard.

But Raphael was nearing the bottom of the stairs now, and if she didn't move he would be out of sight.

And she might lose him.

She couldn't let that happen, no matter how hard or how stubborn he might be.

So ran down the stairs after her husband. And when she saw that he'd opened the back door—the door to the garden—and was walking out into the rain, she stepped out into the deluge, too.

"Wait," she called. "Wait!"

He turned. Rain was running down his face. "Go back."

She shook her head, raindrops splattering off her nose and chin. "No. Where you go, I go, too."

He closed his eyes and tilted his face to the sky as if this was one thing more to bear. As if his shoulders were bowing under terrible pressure.

"Iris," he said, "I'm tainted. He fucked me, Iris. My father fucked me. Look what that did to Andrew Grant. Do you want to wait until the day I go mad?"

"But you won't," she said, bewildered.

He shook his head. "I can't breathe when I smell cedarwood. Is that how a sane man behaves?" He opened his eyes and looked at her. "I forced you to marry me. I was selfish. Now I let you go. You can have my houses, my estates, my English monies. I'll never bother you again. Just let me go to Corsica."

"I can't let you do that," she said, exasperated. "You're my husband. I'm your wife. I *married* you. Don't try and wriggle out of it now."

"I can't stay here with you," he said starkly. "You are too much temptation. You've proven it already."

She held out her hand, the palm filling with rain. "Then give in to temptation."

He looked away. "You make it sound so easy. But it's not. You don't understand."

"Then *make* me understand," she cried in desperation. "Why? Why can't you be with me?"

"Because *I* am the evil," he shouted. "It's passed from father to son, on and on, ad infinitum. Would you wait, never knowing if I would attack a child of ours? *When* I might attack our child?"

"You wouldn't attack a child," Iris said, shocked. "Raphael, I *know* you wouldn't."

"Why not?" He held his hands up to the thundering sky. "Why not? I have the blood of monsters in my veins. He loved me." He dropped his arms. "He *loved* me."

He took a ragged breath.

"And I... I loved him."

Her heart broke. Iris's eyes filled with hot tears that spilled over to mingle with the cold rain on her cheeks.

She watched as Raphael sank to his knees on the muddy ground, his shoulders bowed, his hands lying open in the mud. "He was my father. I couldn't kill him. Even after he did that. I couldn't kill him." He peered up at her through the strands of his sodden hair. "You can't trust me, Iris. I am a beast. A demon. Send me back where I belong. Send me to hell."

She sobbed and sank to her knees, facing him, wrapping him in her arms and laying her forehead against his. "You are not a demon or a beast. You are my beloved husband. I *know* you, and you are not your father. You are good and kind and valiant. You are stubborn and intelligent and sometimes very witty. You will never hurt a child of ours, I promise."

His head was bowed against hers, rain running from his brow to her cheeks and dripping off both of their chins.

He loved her, he knew that now. *That* was what this longing, this never-ending want was.

How she believed in him—despite all that had happened, despite all that he was—he did not know, but he was grateful.

He angled his head, taking her sweet lips with his, drinking her succor, her faith in him. She was his light, his hope, guiding the way out of the depths of his Stygian despair.

"Iris," he murmured against her wet lips, "my radiant wife, my love, my life. I promise I will try to live up to your belief in me. I do not think I can do otherwise, for I would repine and die were I to leave you. I would be blind and alone, howling in the darkness. I would go mad without you."

He captured her mouth again, forcing her lips open, sliding his tongue into her, claiming her as his own.

Dark to light.

She tore herself from him, gasping, her cold wet fingers against his jaw, raindrops beaded on her eyelashes. "Will you believe me, Raphael? Can you accept our marriage and a family?" She stared at him with her storm-blue eyes, terrible in her certainty of him. "Will you be my husband in truth?"

"Yes," he vowed, and swept her into his arms.

Chapter Twenty

The Rock King gave the man his torn soul, glowing white in a stone cage, and the man was beside himself with gratitude.

Ann watched the man leave and then asked her husband, "When will he return with the riches he owes you?"

The Rock King sighed. "He won't. They never do."

She stared at him, gray and stern, save for the red of the blood on his arm. "Then why do you help them?"

His black eyes seemed a little less cold. "Because someone must."…

—From *The Rock King*

Raphael carried Iris back through the garden door and up the staircase with all his forbidding ancestors watching.

She didn't care.

She clung to his neck, staring at his face as he climbed, feeling as if this was their true wedding night. He carried her down the corridor and to their bedroom, shutting the door firmly behind him.

Then he stood her before him and took her sodden clothes from her body until she was naked and shivering.

He found cloths in the dressing room and dried her carefully and then insisted she climb into their bed under the covers.

She watched as he stripped off his clothes. He rubbed the cloth roughly over himself and then threw it aside. Nude he stalked to the bed, his penis heavy between his thighs.

She sat up, looking at that utterly male part of him and then in his eyes. "Let me."

He paused at the side of the bed.

She reached out and took him in her palm, feeling the soft skin. The warmth. He was filling as she watched, lengthening between her hands, pulsing under her fingertips. She saw his foreskin stretch and the eye of his penis, red and wet, begin to show.

"Iris," he growled above her.

But she ducked, looking closer as she encircled his girth and slowly stroked up his length. Under the skin the muscle was hard, so hard, and veins snaked along the shaft. She thumbed the head, feeling the wetness there, and, on an impulse, brought her thumb to her mouth and licked it.

She was suddenly on her back, Raphael above her, his crystal eyes staring into her own.

"What you *do* to me," he rasped, and opened his mouth over hers.

She arched up, feeling all that bare skin, warm and alive. The hairs on his chest tickled over her nipples, teasing them into points as he kissed her. His thigh was between her legs, pressing insistently into her. Making her widen her legs and gasp.

She clutched his shoulders, feeling his muscles shifting beneath his skin. Feeling a sense of wonderful freedom. *This*, this, must be what it was to be truly happy.

To be happy in love.

She opened her eyes.

He shifted, lifting his head. Kissing along the underside of her jaw. "Are you ready now?"

She tilted her head back. "Yes."

"Then put my cock in you now, Wife."

She widened her legs and reached down, grasping that heated length of flesh. Placing it at her entrance where she was wet.

She looked up at him. "I love you, Raphael."

He gazed into her eyes and thrust into her, burying himself to the hilt with one movement. When he was fully seated, his flesh in hers, linked to her as intimately as it was possible for a man to be with a woman, he paused and said, "You are my wife and my love, Iris. Without you I die."

He lowered himself so that he lay completely on her, his body covering hers, and he began to move. Gently rocking. Hardly thrusting at all.

The movements so subtle and yet so right that they nearly drove her insane.

Iris gasped and twined her legs around his, locking his body to hers so that they moved together.

Grinding.

His shoulders shone with sweat. His eyes were feral and he gritted his teeth as he worked his cock into her. Seeking her pleasure and his.

She moaned, long and low, wanting to arch, to thrash, to scream. Instead she opened her mouth and bit his shoulder, tasting salt.

Tasting want.

Then she gasped. "Please."

"What do you want?" he whispered in her ear, an incubus, dark and alive and in her. "Tell me. What do you need?"

"I..." Her mouth opened, wordless.

"Tell me," his smoky voice curled around her.

"You."

He chuckled, dark and low.

"This?" He thrust short and hard into her, the impact sending jolts of pleasure through her body. "Yes, that," he murmured to himself as if pleased, and did it again.

And again.

Until the heat between them combusted. Until she felt hot liquid wash over her limbs. Until she looked up and wondered why she'd ever thought his gray eyes emotionless.

He was watching her with passion. With lust.

With so much love.

She felt tears in her eyes.

He groaned above her, his hips jerking without rhythm, but all the while he watched her with those eyes.

And when he at last stilled and rested his sweaty forehead against hers, he whispered, "I love you."

Epilogue

Now the days went by and time trundled on until at last it came to be that a year and a day had passed.

Ann took the few things she had brought with her into the barren wastelands. Everything fit into a small sack. All but her mother's pink rock. That she held in her hand.

She turned to the Rock King. "I'll away, then."

He sat by the door to his grim tower and he didn't look up. "Indeed."

She hesitated. He'd never shown her affection, but his arms had been warm in the night. "Will you bid me farewell?"

"Farewell, my wife."

She took a step, but then whirled to face him again. "You could come with me!"

At last he looked at her, his black eyes grave. "No, I cannot."

Ann frowned. "Why not?"

"Because I am cursed to remain here," he replied simply.

She looked at him, this stern, gray man. Looked at the ugly black tower and the surrounding barren landscape.

Then she looked to where she knew her father's hut lay. "I'll come back."

"No," he said gently, "you won't."

And she wanted to argue, but she knew he was right. No one came back to him.

At that moment her heart broke for him.

Ann dropped her little sack. "Then I'll stay with you."

For the second time only she saw surprise in his eyes. "What?"

She nodded. "I'm staying here with you as your wife."

He stood, his fists clenched. "For how long?"

"For always." And she held out her mother's pink pebble to him.

As she said the words the ground trembled beneath her feet. The tower shuddered and fell, rocks tumbling down to be swallowed by the earth. All around them green grass, verdant trees, and blue streams billowed up from the ground, overwhelming the dull rock. Where once the black tower squatted, a shining gold-and-white castle stood. The doors opened and a crowd of people swarmed out, soldiers and ladies in fancy dresses, farmers and townspeople, children and old crones.

Ann turned to look in astonishment at the Rock King, but he had changed as well. Where before he had been dreary gray and black, now his hair was a burnished brown, and his eyes glowed clear blue. He wore fine velvet clothes in shades of red and green and purple, and she fell to her knees before him, for she knew him to be a king.

But the Rock King smiled and drew her up to

stand before him. "Sweet Ann, my wife, my queen. You have broken a seven-hundred-year-old curse, one that bound me, my people, and my lands. In all my many cursed years I have never known anyone as kind and loving as you. Will you stay by my side and rule my kingdom with me as my beloved bride?"

"Oh yes," Ann said. "And I think, if you agree, that we ought to have at least a dozen children and live happily ever after."

"Wise woman," said the Rock King, and kissed his queen.

—From *The Rock King*

FIVE YEARS LATER...

"Did you know they bloomed here?" Iris asked her husband.

It was spring and they stood on the banks of the small river that ran beside the ruins of the old cathedral at Dyemore Abbey. The stone arch rose into a clear, blue sky and below, the scattered stones that had once made up the cathedral were carpeted with yellow. Hundreds of thousands of daffodils, wild in this part of England, had taken over the old ruins and made a home for themselves. The view was gorgeous. The daffodils rolled in a yellow-dotted wave right up to the stream itself and splashed over onto the opposite bank, disappearing into the little wood there.

"No," Raphael said. "Or if I did, I don't remember."

He lifted his face to the sky, a smile curling his lips.

He smiled more now—not frequently, to be sure, but

often enough for Iris to know that he was happy with their love and what it had brought.

A sharp bark made her turn her head. Tansy came racing through the flowers, almost taller than she, her jaws wide in doggy joy. Behind her, and much slower on chubby legs, was the Earl of Cyril, better known as Johnny, aged nearly three and the apple of his papa's eye.

"Mama," said Johnny when he at last made her side. "Fwowers."

He held up two daffodils much the worse for wear.

"How lovely, darling," Iris replied, taking the offering. "Wherever did you find them?"

Johnny, who was a terribly serious child, turned and pointed to the vast sea of daffodils. "Dere."

And Iris heard the most wonderful sound in the world: a deep, rich chuckle, coming from beside her. She turned and smiled at her husband.

He still had times when he was moody, and once in a while dark thoughts seemed to consume him, but especially since the birth of Johnny those times had been more and more infrequent. And when he had started laughing—just before Johnny's first birthday—Iris had known true joy.

They were still rare enough, Raphael's laughs, that she cherished each one. Was thankful for each one. Because she knew what a journey her husband had had to make to come from despair to happiness.

"Papa, hungwy," announced Johnny, and held his arms up imperiously to his father.

Iris raised her eyebrows. Johnny had inherited his father's height and was a sturdy little boy. She could no longer carry him—not in her condition—and she was secretly amused that Raphael indulged him enough to carry him all the way back to Dyemore Abbey.

But he bent and lifted their son, setting him high on his shoulders, where the similarity between the black curls on the little boy's head and the man's ebony locks was unmistakable.

Johnny settled with the complacent satisfaction of a child who knows he will be taken care of.

Raphael turned to Iris and glanced at her swollen belly, his eyebrows drawing together. "Are you sure you can walk back to the Abbey? We should not have come so far today."

She rolled her eyes at him. "I'm fine. The baby won't come for another two months at least."

"Very well," her husband decreed, "but we shall go slowly, and I want you to take my arm over the rocks."

"Of course." Iris stood on tiptoe and kissed him beneath the interested blue eyes of their son.

And then, with Tansy bounding by their side, they went home for tea.

Don't miss Hugh and Alf's story. Turn the page for an excerpt of
Duke of Pleasure

Chapter One

Now once there were a White Kingdom and a Black Kingdom that had been at war since time began....

—From *The Black Prince and the Golden Falcon*

JANUARY 1742
LONDON, ENGLAND

Hugh Fitzroy, the Duke of Kyle, did not want to die tonight, for three very good reasons.

It was half past midnight as he eyed the toughs slinking out of the shadows up ahead in the cold alley near Covent Garden. He moved the bottle of fine Viennese wine from his right arm to his left and drew his sword. He'd dined with the Habsburg ambassador earlier this evening, and the wine was a gift.

Firstly, Kit, his elder son—and, formally, the Earl of Staffin—was only seven. Far too young to be orphaned and inherit the dukedom.

Next to Hugh was a linkboy with a lantern. The boy was frozen, his lantern a small pool of light in the narrow alley. The youth's eyes were wide and frightened. He couldn't be more than fourteen. Hugh glanced over his shoulder. Several men were bearing down on them from the entrance to the alley. He and the linkboy were trapped.

Secondly, Peter, his younger son, was still suffering nightmares from the death of his mother only five months before. What would his father's death so soon after his mother's do to the boy?

They might be common footpads. Unlikely, though. Footpads usually worked in smaller numbers, were not this organized, and were after money, not death.

Assassins, then.

And *thirdly*, His Majesty had recently assigned Hugh an important job: destroy the Lords of Chaos. On the whole, Hugh liked to finish his jobs. Brought a nice sense of completion at the end of the day, if nothing else.

Right, then.

"If you can, run," Hugh said to the linkboy. "They're after me, not you."

Then he pivoted and attacked the closest group—the three men behind them.

Their leader, a big fellow, raised a club.

Hugh slashed him across the throat. The leader went down in a spray of scarlet. But his second was already bringing his own club down in a bone-jarring blow to Hugh's left shoulder. Hugh juggled the bottle of wine, seized it again, and kicked the man in the balls. The second doubled over and stumbled against the third. Hugh punched over the man's head and into the face of the third.

There were running footsteps from behind Hugh.

He spun to face the other end of the alley and another attacker.

Caught the descending knife with his blade and slid his sword into the hand holding the knife.

A howling scream, and the knife clattered to the icy cobblestones in a splatter of blood.

The knife man lowered his head and charged like an enraged bull.

Hugh flattened all six foot four inches of himself against the filthy alley wall, stuck out his foot, and tripped Charging Bull into the three men he'd already dealt with.

The linkboy, who had been cowering against the opposite wall, took the opportunity to squirm through the constricted space between the assailants and run away.

Which left them all in darkness, save for the light of the half moon.

Hugh grinned.

He didn't have to worry about hitting his compatriots in the dark.

He rushed the man next in line after the Bull. They'd picked a nice alley, his attackers. No way out—save the ends—but in such close quarters he had a small advantage: no matter how many men were against him, the alley was so cramped that only two could come at him at a time. The rest were simply bottled up behind the others, twiddling their thumbs.

Hugh slashed the man and shouldered past him. Got a blow upside the head for his trouble and saw stars. Hugh shook his head and elbowed the next—*hard*—in the face, and kicked the third in the belly. Suddenly he could see the light at the end of the alley.

Hugh knew men who felt that gentlemen should never run from a fight. Of course many of these same men had never *been* in a real fight.

Besides, he had those three *very* good reasons.

Actually, now that he thought of it, there was a *fourth* reason he did not want to die tonight.

Hugh ran to the end of the alley, his bottle of fine

Viennese wine cradled in the crook of his left arm, his sword in the other fist. The cobblestones were iced over and his momentum was such that he slid into the lit street.

Where he found another half-dozen men bearing down on him from his left.

Bloody *hell.*

Fourthly, he hadn't had a woman in his bed in over nine months, and to die in such a drought would be a particularly unkind blow from fate, god*damn* it.

Hugh nearly dropped the blasted wine as he scrambled to turn to the right. He could hear the men he'd left in the alley rallying even as he sprinted straight into the worst part of London: the stews of St Giles. They were right on his heels, a veritable army of assassins. The streets here were narrow, ill lit, and cobbled badly, if at all. If he fell because of ice or a missing cobblestone, he'd never get up again.

He turned down a smaller alley and then immediately down another.

Behind him he heard a shout. Christ, if they split up, they would corner him again.

He hadn't enough of a lead, even if a man of his size could easily hide in a place like St Giles. Hugh glanced up as he entered a small courtyard, the buildings on all four sides leaning in. Overhead the moon was veiled in clouds, and it almost looked as if a boy were silhouetted, jumping from one rooftop to another...

Which...

Was insane.

Think. If he could circle and come back the way he'd entered St Giles, he could slip their noose.

A narrow passage.

Another cramped courtyard.

Ah, *Christ.*

They were already here, blocking the two other exits.

Hugh spun, but the passage he'd just run from was crowded with more men, almost a dozen in all.

Well.

He put his back to the only wall left to him and straightened.

He rather wished he'd tasted the wine. He was fond of Viennese wine.

A tall man in a ragged brown coat and a filthy red neckcloth stepped forward. Hugh half expected him to make some sort of a speech, he looked that full of himself. Instead he drew a knife the size of a man's forearm, grinned, and licked the blade.

Oh, for—

Hugh didn't wait for whatever other disgusting preliminaries Knife Licker might feel were appropriate to the occasion. He stepped forward and smashed the bottle of very fine Viennese wine over the man's head.

Then they were on him.

He slashed and felt the jolt to his arm as he hit flesh.

Swung and raked the sword across another's face.

Staggered as two men slammed into him.

Another hit him hard in the jaw.

And then someone clubbed him behind the knees.

He fell to his knees on the icy ground, growling like a bleeding, baited bear.

Raised an arm to defend his head…

And…

Someone dropped from the sky right in front of him.

Facing his attackers.

Darting, wheeling, spinning.

Defending him so gracefully.

With two swords.

Hugh staggered upright again, blinking blood out of his eyes—when had he been cut?

And saw—a boy? No, a slight *man* in a grotesque half mask, motley, floppy hat, and boots, battling fiercely with his attackers. Hugh just had time to think: *Insane*, before his defender was thrown back against him.

Hugh caught the man and had another thought, which was: *Tits?*

And then he set the woman—most definitely a *woman* although in a man's clothing—on her feet and put his back to hers and fought as if their lives depended on it.

Which they did.

There were still eight or so of the attackers left, and although they weren't trained, they were determined. Hugh slashed and punched and kicked, while his feminine savior danced an elegant dance of death with her swords. When he smashed the butt of his sword into the skull of one of the last men, the remaining two looked at each other, picked up a third, and took to their heels.

Panting, Hugh glanced around the courtyard. It was strewn with groaning men, most still very much alive, though not dangerous at the moment.

He peered at the masked woman. She was tiny, barely reaching his shoulder. How was it she'd saved him from certain, ignoble death? But she had. She surely had.

"Thank you," he said, his voice gruff. He cleared his throat. "I—"

She grinned, a quicksilver flash, and put her left hand on the back of his neck to pull his head down.

And then she kissed him.

Alf pressed her lips against Kyle's lovely mouth and thought her heart might beat right out of her breast at her daring.

Then he groaned—a rumbling sound she felt in the fingertips on his nape—and tried to pull her closer. She ducked away and out of reach, skipping back, and then turned and ran down a little alley. She found a stack of barrels and scrambled up them. Pulled herself onto a leaning balcony and from there shinnied up to the roof. She bent low and tiptoed across rotten tiles, some broken, until she was nearly to the edge of the roof, and then lay flat to peer over.

He was still staring down the alley where she'd disappeared, daft man.

Oh, he was a big one, was Kyle. Broad shoulders, long legs. A mouth that made her remember she was a woman beneath her men's clothing. He'd lost his hat and white wig somewhere during his mad dash away from the footpads. He stood bareheaded, his coat torn and bloodied, and in the moonlight she could almost mistake him for a man who belonged in St Giles.

But he wasn't.

He turned finally and limped in the direction of Covent Garden. She rose and followed him—just to make sure he made it out of St Giles.

The one and only time she'd met Kyle before this, she'd been dressed in her daytime disguise as Alf, the boy who made his living as an informant. Except Kyle had wanted information on the Duke of Montgomery, who had been *employing* Alf at the time.

She snorted under her breath as she ran along the ridge of a rooftop, keeping Kyle's shorn black head in sight. Insulting, that had been—him thinking she'd inform on the man paying her. She might not be a lady, but she had her honor. She'd waited until he'd bought her dinner and outlined what he wanted to hire her for—and then she'd turned the table over into his lap. She'd run from the tavern, but not before thumbing her nose at him.

She grinned as she leaped silently from one rooftop to another.

The last time she'd seen Kyle, he'd worn potatoes and gravy on his costly cloak and an angry expression on his handsome face.

Down below, his stride was increasing as they neared the outskirts of St Giles, his boot heels echoing off the cobblestones. She paused, leaning on a chimney. There were more lanterns set out here by the shopkeepers. She watched as Kyle crossed the street, looking warily around, his sword still in his hand.

He didn't have need of her to see him home to whatever grand house he lived in. He was a man well able to look after himself.

Still, she crouched there until he disappeared into the shadows.

Ah, well. Time to go home to her own little nest, then.

She turned and ran over the shingles, quick and light.

When she'd been a child and first learned to scale buildings, she'd thought of London as her forest, St Giles her wood, the roofs her treetops.

Truth be told, she'd never seen a forest, a wood, nor even treetops. She'd never been out of London, for that matter. The farthest east she'd ever traveled in her life was to Wapping—where the air held the faintest hint of sea salt, tickling the nose. The farthest west, to Tyburn, to witness Charming Mickey O'Connor being hanged. Except he hadn't been, to the surprise of all that day. He'd disappeared from the gallows and into legend like the wondrous river pirate he was. But wild birds—free birds—were supposed to live in forests and woods and treetops.

And she'd imagined herself a bird as a child on the rooftops, free and flying.

Sometimes, even as a world-weary woman of one and twenty, she still did.

If she were a bird, the roofs were her home, her *place*, where she felt the safest.

Down below was the dark woods, and she knew all about the woods from the fairy tales that her friend Ned had told her when she'd been a wee thing. In the fairy-tale dark woods were witches and ghouls and trolls, all ready to eat you up.

In the woods of St Giles the monsters were far, far worse.

Tonight she'd fought monsters.

She flew over the roofs of St Giles. Her booted feet were swift and sure on the shingles, and the moon was a big guiding lantern above, lighting the way for her patrol as the Ghost of St Giles. She'd been following the Scarlet Throat gang—a nasty bunch of footpads who'd do anything up to and including murder for the right price—and wondering why they were out in such force, when she'd realized they were chasing Kyle.

In her daytime guise as Alf, she had a bad history with the Scarlet Throats. Most recently they'd taken a dislike to her because she refused to either join them or pay them to be "protected." On the whole they left her alone—she stayed out of their way and they pretended not to notice her. But she shuddered to think what they would do if they ever found out her true sex.

Letting a lone boy defy them was one thing. Letting a woman do the same?

There were rumors of girls ending up in the river for less.

But when she'd seen the Scarlet Throats chasing Kyle like a pack of feral dogs, she'd not thought twice about helping him. He'd been running for his life and fighting as he went, never giving up, though he'd been far outnumbered from the start.

The man was stubborn, if nothing else.

And afterward, when their enemies lay at their feet, groaning and beaten, and her heart was thumping so hard with the sheer joy of victory and being *alive*, it'd seemed natural to pull his pretty, pretty lips down to hers and kiss him.

She'd never kissed a man before.

Oh, there'd been some who'd tried to kiss *her*—tried and succeeded—especially when she'd been younger and smaller and not so fast, nor so swift with a kick to the soft bits of a man. Even then no one had gotten much beyond a mash of foul tongue in her mouth. She'd been good at running even when little.

No one had touched her in years. She'd made sure of it.

But the kiss with Kyle hadn't been like that—*she'd* kissed *him*.

She leaped from one roof to another, landing silently on her toes. Kyle's lips had been firm, and he'd tasted sharp, like wine. She'd felt the muscles in his neck and chest and arms get hard and tight as he'd made ready to grab her.

She'd hadn't been *afraid*, though.

She grinned at the moon and the rooftops and the molls walking home in the lane far below.

Kissing Kyle had made her feel wild and free.

Like flying over the roofs of St Giles.

She ran and leaped again, landing this time on a rickety old half-timbered tenement. It was all but fallen down, the top story overhanging the courtyard like an ancient crone bent under a big bundle of used clothes. She thrust her legs over the edge of the roof, slipped her feet blind onto one of the timbers on the face of the building, and climbed down into the attic window.

If St Giles was the dark wood, this was her secret hidey-hole nest: half the attic of this building. The sole door to the room was nailed firmly shut, the only way in by the window.

She was safe here.

No one but she could get in or out.

Alf sighed and stretched her arms over her head before taking off her hat and mask. Muscles she hadn't even realized were tensed began to loosen now that she was home.

Home and safe.

Her nest was one big room—big enough for an entire family to live in, really—but only she lived here. On one wall was a row of wooden pegs, and she hung up her hat and mask there. Across from the window was a brick chimney where she'd left the fire carefully banked. She crossed to it and squatted in front of the tiny hearth—a half moon not much bigger than her head, the brick blackened and crumbling. But this high up it drew well enough, and that was the important thing. She stirred the red eyes of the embers with a broken iron rod and stuck some straw on top, then blew gently until the straw smoked and lit. Then she added five pieces of coal, one at a time. When her little fire was burning nicely, she lit a candle and stood it on the rough shelf above the fireplace.

The half-burned candle gave a happy little glow. Alf touched her fingertip to the candlestick's base and then to the little round mirror next to it. The mirror reflected the tiny candle flame. She tapped her tin cup, a yellow pottery jug she'd found years ago, and her ivory comb. Ned had given her the comb the day before he'd disappeared, and it was perhaps her most precious possession.

Then she picked up a bottle of oil and a rag from the end of the shelf and sat on a three-legged stool by the pile of blankets she used as a bed.

Her long sword was mostly clean. She stroked the oiled

cloth along the blade and then tilted it to the candlelight to check for nicks in the edge. The two swords had cost most of her savings and she made sure to keep them clean and razor sharp, both because they were her pride and because in the dark woods they were her main weapons as the Ghost. The long sword's edge looked good, so she resheathed it and set it aside.

Her short blade was bloodied. That she worked on for a bit with the cloth, humming to herself under her breath. The cloth turned rust red and the sword turned mirror bright.

The sky outside her attic window turned pale pink.

She hung up her swords in their scabbards on the row of pegs. She unbuttoned her padded and quilted tunic, patterned all over in black and red diamonds. Underneath was a plain man's shirt and she took that off as well, hanging them both up as she shivered in the winter-morning air. Her boots she stood underneath the pegs. Her leggings, also covered in black and red diamonds, hung neatly next to the shirt.

Then she was just in her boys' smallclothes and dark stockings and garters. Her shoulder-length hair was clubbed, but she took it down and ran her fingers through it, making it messy. She bound her hair back again with a bit of leather cord and let a few strands hang in her face. She took a length of soft cloth and wound it around her breasts, binding them flat, but not too tightly, because it was hard to draw a deep breath otherwise. Besides, her breasts weren't that big to begin with.

She pulled on a big man's shirt, a stained brown waistcoat, a tattered pair of boys' breeches, and a rusty black coat. She put a dagger in her coat pocket, another in the pocket of her waistcoat, and a tiny blade in a thin leather sheath under her right foot in her shoe. She smashed an old wide-brimmed hat on her head and she was Alf.

A boy.

Because this was what she was.

At night she was the Ghost of St Giles. She protected the people of St Giles—her people, living in the big, dark woods. She ran out the monsters—the murderers and rapists and robbers. And she flew over the roofs of the city by moonlight, free and wild.

During the day she was Alf, a boy. She made her living dealing in information. She listened and learned, and if you wanted to know who was running pickpocket boys and girls in Covent Gardens or which doxies had the clap or even what magistrate could be bought and for how much, she could tell you and would—for a price.

But whether the Ghost or Alf, what she wasn't and would never be, at least not in St Giles, was a woman.

When had the Ghost of St Giles become a woman?

Hugh hissed as one of his former soldiers, Jenkins, drew catgut thread through the cut on his forehead.

Riley winced and silently offered him the bottle of brandy.

Talbot cleared his throat and said, "Begging your pardon, sir, but are you sure the Ghost of St Giles *was* a woman?"

Hugh eyed the big man—he'd once served as a grenadier. "Yes, I'm sure. She had *tits*."

"You searched her, did you, sir?" Riley asked politely in his Irish accent.

Talbot snorted.

Hugh instinctively turned to shoot a reproving glance at Riley—and Jenkins tsked as the thread pulled at his flesh. *Damn* that hurt.

"Best if you hold still, sir," Jenkins quietly chided.

All three men had been under his command at one time or another out in India or on the Continent. When Hugh had received the letter telling him that Katherine, his wife, had died after falling off her horse in Hyde Park, he'd known his exile was at an end, and that he would need to sell his commission in the army and return. He'd offered Riley, Jenkins, and Talbot positions if they elected to return to England with him.

All three had accepted his offer without a second thought.

Now Riley leaned against the door of the big master bedroom in Kyle House, his arms folded and his shoulders hunched, his perpetually sad eyes fixed on the needle. The slight man was brave to a fault, but he hated surgery of any sort. Next to him Talbot was a towering presence, barrel-chested and brawny like most men chosen for the grenadiers.

Jenkins pursed his lips, his one eye intent on the stitch he was placing. A black leather eye patch tied neatly over the man's silver hair covered the other eye. "'Nother two, maybe three stitches, sir."

Hugh grunted and took a drink from the bottle of brandy, careful not to move his head. He was sitting on the edge of his four-poster bed, surrounded by candles so that Jenkins could see to stitch him up.

The former army private could sew a wound closed with better precision than any educated physician. Jenkins was also capable of extracting teeth, letting blood, treating fevers, and, Hugh suspected, amputating limbs, though he'd never actually seen the older man do the last. Jenkins was a man of few words, but his hands were gentle and sure, his lined face calm and intelligent.

Hugh winced at another stitch, his mind back on the woman who had moved so gracefully and yet so efficiently with her swords. "I thought our information was that the Ghost of St Giles was retired?"

Riley shrugged. "That's what we'd heard, sir. There

hasn't been a sighting of the Ghost for at least a year. Course there's been more than one Ghost in the past. Jenkins thinks there were at least two at one point, maybe even three."

A hesitant voice piped up from a corner of the room. "Beggin' your pardon, Mr. Riley, but what's this Ghost you're talking about?"

Bell hadn't spoken since they'd entered the room and Hugh had all but forgotten the lad. He glanced now at Bell, sitting on a stool, his blue eyes alert, though his shoulders had begun to slump with weariness. The lad was only fifteen and the newest of his men, having joined Hugh's service after the death of his father.

Bell flushed as he drew the attention of the older men.

Hugh nodded at the boy to reassure him. "Riley?"

Riley uncrossed his arms and winked at Bell. "The Ghost of St Giles is a sort of legend in London. He dresses like a harlequin clown—motley leggings and tunic and a carved half mask—and is able to climb and dance on the rooftops of London. There are some who say he's nothing but a bogeyman to scare children. Others whisper that the Ghost is a defender of the poor. He goes where soldiers and magistrates dare not and runs out the footpads, rapists, and petty thieves who prey on the most wretched of St Giles."

Bell's brows drew together in confusion. "So...he's not real, sir?"

Hugh grunted, remembering soft flesh. "Oh, he—or rather *she*—is real enough."

"That's just it," Talbot interjected, looking intrigued. "I've spoken to people who have been helped by the Ghost in years past, but the Ghost has never been a woman before. Do you think she could be the wife of one of the former Ghosts, sir?"

Hugh decided not to examine why he didn't like that

particular suggestion. "Whoever she was, she was a damned good swordswoman."

"More importantly," Jenkins said softly as he placed another stitch, "who was behind the attack? Who wanted you dead, sir?"

"Do you think it was the work of the Lords of Chaos?" Riley asked.

"Maybe." Hugh grimaced as Jenkins pulled the catgut. "But before I was ambushed I was at the Habsburg ambassador's house. It was a large dinner party and a long one. I got up to piss at one point. I was coming back along the hall when I happened to overhear a bit of conversation."

"Happened, sir?" Riley said, his face expressionless.

"Old habits die hard," Hugh replied drily. "There were two men, huddled together in a dim corner of the hallway, speaking in French. One I recognized from the Russian embassy. No one official, you understand, but certainly he's part of the Russians' delegation. The other man I didn't know, but he looked like a servant, perhaps a valet. The Russian slipped a piece of paper into the servant's hand and told him to take it quickly to the Prussian."

"The Prussian, sir?" Jenkins asked softly. "No name?"

"No name," Hugh replied.

"Bloody buggering hell." Talbot shook his head almost admiringly. "You have to admit, sir, that the man has bollocks to be passing secrets to the Prussians in the Habsburg ambassador's house."

"If that's what the Russian was doing," Hugh said cautiously, though he had no real doubts himself.

"Did he see you, sir?" Riley asked.

"Oh yes," Hugh said grimly. "One of the other guests bumbled up behind me calling my name. Drunken fool. The Russian couldn't help but know that I'd heard everything."

"Still, there would be very little time to find and hire assassins to target you on your walk home from the dinner," Talbot said.

"Very true," Hugh said. "Which brings us back to the Lords of Chaos."

Jenkins leaned a little closer now, his one brown eye intent, and snipped a thread before sitting back. "Done, sir. Do you want a bandage?"

"No need." The wound had mostly stopped bleeding anyway. "Thank you, Jenkins." Hugh caught Bell trying to smother a yawn. "Best be off to bed, the lot of you. We'll reconvene tomorrow morning after we get some sleep."

"Sir." Riley straightened and came to attention.

Talbot nodded respectfully. "Night, sir."

"Good night, Your Grace," said Bell.

Then all three were out the door.

Hugh picked up a cloth, wet it, and wiped the remaining blood from his face, wincing as the movement reminded him of the bruises up and down his ribs.

Jenkins silently packed his surgical tools into a worn black leather case.

Hugh glanced at the window and saw to his surprise that light was glowing around the cracks of the curtains. Had it been so long since he'd staggered home from St Giles?

He crossed to the window and jerked the curtain open.

The bedroom looked over the back garden, dead now in winter, but it was indeed light outside.

"Anything else, sir?" Jenkins asked behind him.

"No," Hugh said without turning. "That will be all."

"Sir." The door opened and closed.

Outside, a slim figure trotted down the path between the house and the gate that led to the mews. For a moment Hugh stilled before he realized it was the bootblack boy who worked in the kitchens. He felt his upper lip curl at his own folly. The Ghost of St Giles would hardly be haunting his garden, would she?

He let the curtain fall and strode out of his bedroom.

Katherine had named this town house Kyle House. He'd always thought the name pompous, but she'd insisted on it. She'd said it was the name of a great house—a dynastic house. He'd been newly married and still besotted with her when he'd bought the place, so he'd acquiesced, and the name had stood even as their marriage had fallen.

There was a moral there somewhere. Perhaps to not name houses. Or, more probably, to never let passion for a woman sweep away reason, self-preservation, and sense, for that way led to devastation.

Of nearly everything that he'd held dear and that had made him a man.

He passed two maids carrying coal buckets and shovels in the corridor and nodded absently as they curtsied. Made the stairs and took them two at a time to the third floor. It was quiet here. He prowled down the hall past the nursemaids' rooms and opened the door to the bedroom his sons shared.

It was a pretty room. Light and airy. Katherine had been a good mother. He remembered her planning this room. Planning the upper floors when she'd been big with Kit and all had seemed wonderful and new and possible. Before the shouted arguments and her hysterical tears, the disillusionment, and the stunned realization that he'd made a monstrous and permanent mistake.

And that he couldn't trust his own judgment.

Because he'd truly believed himself in love with Katherine. What else could he have called the wild, joyous ecstasy of pursuing her? The complete visceral satisfaction of making her his wife?

Yet barely three years after he'd wed her, all that grand passion had turned to ashes and bitter hatred.

Oh, what a beautiful, fickle thing was love. Rather like Katherine herself, in fact.

Hugh sighed and went into the boys' bedroom.

There were two railed beds, but only one was occupied.

Just turned five years old, Peter was still prone to nightmares. Hugh wasn't sure if his son had experienced them before Katherine's death, but now the boy had them several times a week. He lay curled against his elder brother, red face pressed into his side, blond hair tufted under Kit's arm. Kit was sprawled on his back, openmouthed, his black curly hair flattened sweatily against his temples.

If last night's assassins had succeeded, his boys would be orphans now. He shook off the thought with a shudder, and his mind turned to the Lords of Chaos. They were a terrible secret club that met irregularly to revel in the worst sort of debauchery. Once a man joined he was committed to the Lords for life. Most members didn't know the other members, but if one Lord revealed himself to another, the second Lord was bound to help the first man in any way possible. Hugh had reason to believe that the Lords of Chaos had infiltrated the government, the church, the army, and the navy.

Which was why the King wanted them stopped.

When Hugh had begun his investigation into the Lords, he'd been given four names by the Duke of Montgomery:

William Baines, Baron Chase
David Howell, Viscount Dowling
Sir Aaron Crewe
Daniel Kendrick, the Earl of Exley

Four men who were aristocrats and members of the secret society. In the two months since, he'd quietly looked into the four men, attempting to discover how the Lords were organized, who the leaders were, and when they met and where.

He'd found out none of these things.

None.

Why then would they try to assassinate him? It seemed far more likely that tonight's attack had been the result of political intrigue on the Continent. Wars abroad, rather than a vile secret society that preyed upon the most innocent of victims here in England.

There was no reason at all to link this to the Lords of Chaos.

And yet he could not quite banish the suspicion from his mind.

Hugh grimaced and silently left the bedroom.

In the hall he turned and made for the stairs again, climbing this time to the floor above—the servants' quarters. He walked along the long corridor, lined with doors on either side, passing a startled scullery maid, and then tapped on one of the doors on the left before opening it.

Bell shared a room with two of the younger footmen. Both of the footmen's beds were empty, for they would already be up and about their work at this time of the morning, but Bell's tousled brown head just peeked beneath his blankets.

Hugh winced at the sight, hating to wake the boy so soon after sending him to bed, but this couldn't wait. He touched Bell's shoulder.

The boy woke at once. "Your Grace?"

"I have a job for you," Hugh said. "I want you to find a St Giles informant for me. His name is Alf."

Elizabeth Hoyt is the *New York Times* bestselling author of more than twenty lush historical romances, including the Maiden Lane series. *Publishers Weekly* has called her writing "mesmerizing." She also pens deliciously fun contemporary romances under the name Julia Harper. Elizabeth lives in Minneapolis, Minnesota, with three untrained dogs, a garden in constant need of weeding, and the long-suffering Mr. Hoyt.

The winters in Minnesota have been known to be long and cold and Elizabeth is always thrilled to receive reader mail. You can write to her at PO Box 19495, Minneapolis, MN 55419 or e-mail her at Elizabeth@ElizabethHoyt.com.

You can learn more at:
ElizabethHoyt.com
Twitter @elizabethhoyt
Facebook.com/ElizabethHoytBooks
Goodreads.com/ElizabethHoyt
Instagram.com/elizabethhoytauthor
Pinterest.com/elizabethhoyt

Fall in Love with Forever Romance

SUGARPLUM WAY
By Debbie Mason

The *USA Today* bestselling Harmony Harbor series continues! As a romance author, Julia Landon's job is to create happy-ever-afters. But she can't seem to create one for herself—even after a steamy kiss under the mistletoe with Aiden Gallagher. After a bitter divorce, Aiden has no interest in making another commitment; he just wants to spend quality time with his daughter. But with Christmas right around the corner, both Aiden and Julia may find that Santa is about to grant a little girl's special wish.

Fall in Love with Forever Romance

TOTALLY HIS
By Erin Nicholas

In the newest of *New York Times* bestselling author Erin Nicholas's Opposites Attract series, actress Sophie Birch is used to looking out for herself. When her theater catches fire and a cop scoops her up to save her, she fights him every step of the way...even though his arms feel oh-so-good. Finn Kelly can't help but appreciate how sexy the woman in his arms looks...even if she's currently resisting arrest. But when Sophie finds herself in trouble again, can Finn convince her to lean on him?

Fall in Love with Forever Romance

THE SCOT'S BRIDE
By Paula Quinn

For readers of Karen Hawkins, Monica McCarty, and Hannah Howell. Charlotte Lindsay refuses to abide by Patrick MacGregor, the barbaric highlander assigned to keep her out of trouble. But what's Charlie to do when her biggest temptation is the man charged with keeping her a proper young lass?

Fall in Love with Forever Romance

BACK IN THE GAME
By Erin Kern

Fans of *Friday Night Lights* will love the heartwarming Champion Valley series by bestselling author Erin Kern. Stella Davenport swore she'd never let anything get in the way of her dream—until sexy, broad-shouldered Brandon West walks back into her life. Brandon knows that love only leads to heartbreak, but Stella is a breath of fresh air he didn't even know he'd been missing. When she's offered her dream job in Chicago, will he be willing to put his heart on the line?

LETHAL LIES
By Rebecca Zanetti

Long-buried secrets and deadly forces threaten Anya Best and Heath Jones as they hunt down the infamous Copper Killer. Will they find love only to lose their lives? Fans of Maya Banks and Shannon McKenna will love Rebecca Zanetti's latest sexy suspense!